YESL
THE BALKIEN FROM ANTROBI

ALEX M SHEPHERD

WINKET
BOOKS

Published by
Winket Books
(author's imprint)

Cover design by Harshita Nagaraj
Map and diagrams by Alex M. Shepherd

ISBN 978-0-6487270-1-9 (paperback)
ISBN 978-0-6487270-0-2   (eBook)

SECOND EDITION
November 2019
www.winketbooks.com

CONTENTS

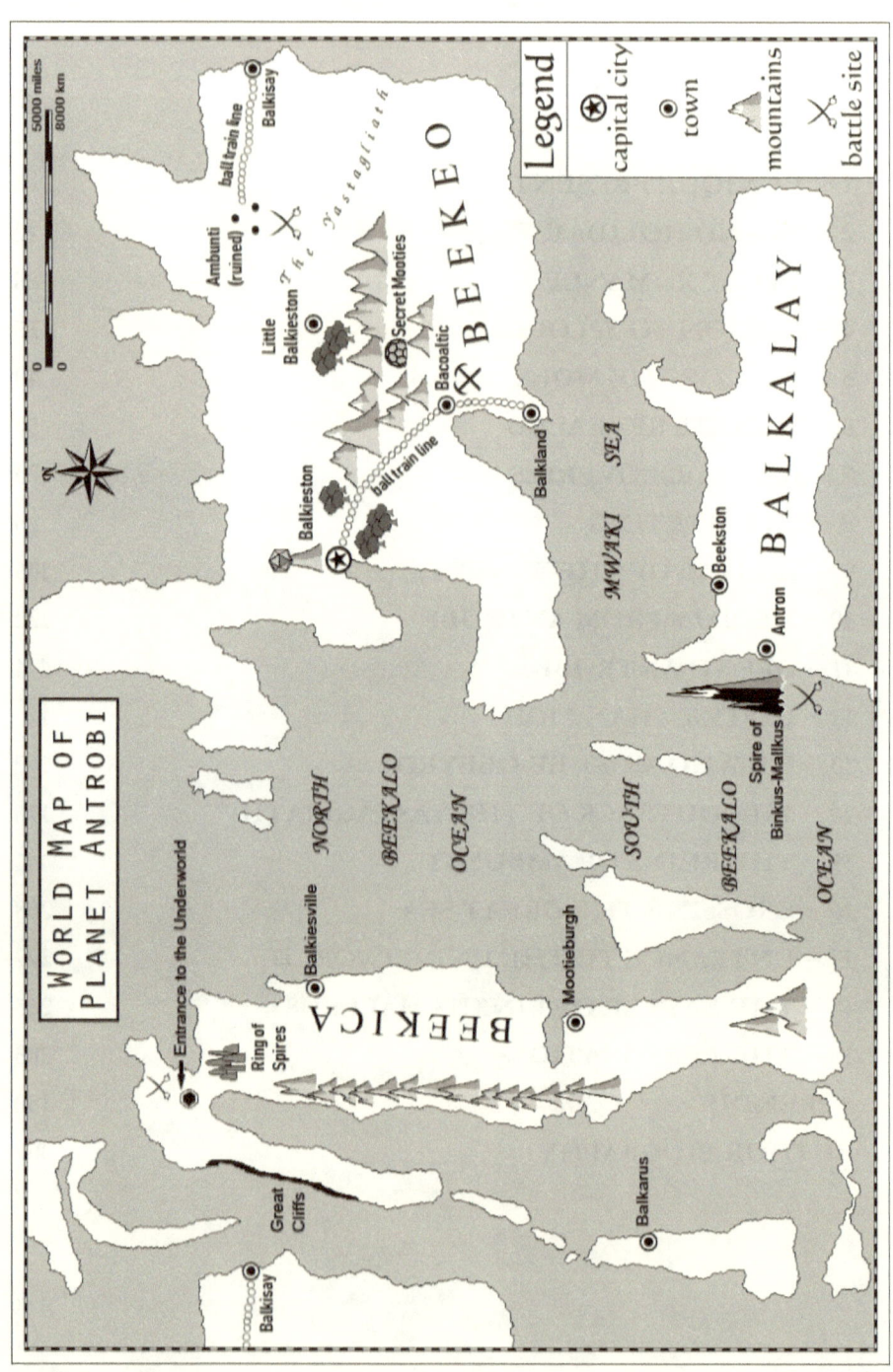

WORLD MAP OF PLANET ANTROBI

Legend

⊛ capital city
⊙ town
⛰ mountains
⚔ battle site

Alex M Shepherd

ACKNOWLEDGMENTS

I extend many thanks to my family and friends, who greatly inspired me in the preparation of this work and for their constructive reviews and input; especially to my parents, Alex & Alice, whose Christmas present during my childhood became known as 'Yes!' from whom the story that follows grew in my mind.

YESL – The Balkien from Antrobi

● ○ ●

PROLOGUE

It was dusk with the last glimmer of dark blue sky signaling the dying embers of a beautiful sunny day. Three children were looking forward to a good night's observing the stars and planets along with fellow members of the Scottish Astronomical Society at the City Observatory.

"We are going to point the telescope to Mars and Jupiter tonight," said the group leader, Jeremy. "We'll look at stars, maybe Vega in the Summer Triangle. We'll start with Jupiter and her majestic moons."

The scope was lined up to view the great gas giant. It was soon Matt's turn to be at the eyepiece while standing atop the old creaky wooden steps. "Wow," he said excitedly, "those equatorial bands and I can see four pinpricks off to either side of it."

"That's the Galilean moons of Jupiter," said Sean, Matt's younger brother. "Ganymede, Calisto, Io, and Europa, the four discovered by—."

The observatory dome walls flickered brightly. "Look!" shouted several in unison.

Matt saw the stark shadow of the telescope race across the wooden paneled wall behind the old oak desk. He looked around through the dome opening. Everyone was almost blinded by the bright flares tearing across the sky to the north-west.

Matt, Kara, his sister, and Sean stared in disbelief as the sky became as blue as daylight again for a few moments. Then the brightest fireball blazed across with several smaller ones alongside and behind it. All eyes were fixated. As quickly as this event started, it was over, save for a few smaller shooting stars heading in the same direction. Just as Matt put his eye to the telescope again there were rumbles like thunder, then an earsplitting BOOM that shook the dome panels and knocked the scope off alignment with Jupiter.

"That meteor must have been very close with a sonic boom like that," said Jeremy.

Mom poured cups of tea after laying out bowls of porridge for breakfast. Matt could not help but look over his father's shoulder at the picture on the front page of the *Scotsman* showing the bright fireball. "Dad, that's how I saw it last night at the observatory."

"It says here that a sonic boom striking the city was so loud that some shop windows were blown in," gasped Matt's father. "They're saying that there were enough sightings up and down the country to be able to locate where any meteorites may have fallen by triangulation. Presently they reckon that it could have landed on or near the islands off the North-West of Scotland, or maybe in the North-Atlantic."

"So, if that's the case, any remains may or may not be found," replied Matt ruefully.

"It's too early to say yet." Dad continued to turn the pages of the newspaper. "They're commenting on the unusual appearance of this fireball. They're surprised at the number of smaller meteoric fragments coming in over a few minutes, much longer than similar events, and that the largest piece did not burn out before going over the horizon as it should have done."

Being a Saturday, Matt was able to wonder at what everyone had witnessed from the observatory. He looked up his astronomy book on the history of meteors and meteorite falls but none of the reports matched what he had seen. That strange green color of several of the meteors was very unusual.

For a few weeks, there were more reports and discussions over the media. Thus, the meteor section of the Scottish Astronomical Society was born. The members, under the leadership of Sean, ran meteor watches on many clear nights watching for and recording their positions. Matt would gaze at the stars while rugged up in his sleeping bag and wonder about the exoplanets that were being discovered orbiting around some of them. The possible presence of life on any of these distant worlds was never far from his mind.

• ◯ •

1 ~ A UNIQUE PRESENT

Little did Matt, a twelve-year-old schoolboy, know as he ate dinner that white Christmas Eve with his loving family that his life was about to change dramatically by the following morning. After he, his sister, Kara, and brother, Sean, said "Good Night" to their parents, it was hard to sleep while in wild anticipation of their surprise gifts but none of them had any inkling of how their lives were to be forever altered from this day they had looked forward to so much.

Matt opened the living room curtains to reveal a snow-covered landscape glistening in the early morning sunshine entering through the window onto a dazzling display of toys around the Christmas tree and was soon joined by Kara and Sean. He was overjoyed at seeing the globe, showing foreign countries where he aspired to travel someday and an illustrated book about the planets of the Solar System among his gifts. There was another globular object catching his attention about the same size as the Earth globe. It was a ball apparently made of wool with stripes of many colors resembling the zones on the planet, Jupiter. He picked it up and cuddled it. It gave a sensation of affectionate softness unlike any he had experienced before from the pets in his extended family. Soon he realized that this wooly ball was his favorite present. There was a tradition at Christmas dinner that each of the children would stand up and say which was their ideal present and why. When it was Matt's turn, he stood up and held up his wooly ball for Sean, Kara, and his parents, Ernest and Olivia Sutherland, and his grandparents. Everyone was hushed as they gazed upon the brightly colored zones on this globe of wool.

His mother quipped, "What about your Earth globe?"

"This is my favorite for now, and I'll have it with me in bed tonight." Matt stroked its fur.

"And Kara," said their mother, to his younger sister. "What is your favorite toy?"

"Oh," said Kara, "The doll's house." She pointed to the beautifully decorated edifice with varnished wooden walls, and a roof painted dark red with ornate gable ends, in the Tudor style.

"And your favorite toy, Sean?" asked Mom.

"My tricycle," replied Sean as he sat on the gleaming machine beside Kara's doll's house.

"Time for bed kids," said Mom after much merriment and the pulling of Christmas crackers.

Matt looked forward to his first night with his woolen pom-pom beside him in bed. After his family visitors trooped out into the cold, snowy countryside to drive home, Matt settled into his warm bed, cherishing the moment with his new pom-pom. As he dozed off, his consciousness drifted into pleasant, vivid, colorful dreams of an alien landscape, unlike on Earth. The nearest example would be the Highlands of Scotland, or the majestic craggy peaks and luscious green valleys of the Swiss Alps, except that the sky was colored purple rather than blue. With a yawn, he was aware of his wooly ball.

On Boxing Day, Kara and Sean were excitedly playing with their new toys. Kara was delicately rearranging the tiny pieces of furniture in her doll's house. When Matt came near, he laid the pom-pom beside the open side of the doll's house.

"Matt," said Kara. "You seem to be taken with that wooly ball. It seems to have every rich color. I'd love to put a carpet of those colors in this little living room."

The order of the colors was arranged in latitudinal zones, beginning with a dark slate grey on the equator, then red zones to the north and south, followed by yellow, light emerald green, violet, and brilliant white on the poles. The whole ball of silk-like wool was a little smaller than a basketball. Almost imperceptibly, Matt and Kara noticed a shimmering on its surface but put it down to the reflected sunlight streaming in through the windows from the gently moving winter tree branches.

"Matt, Kara, Sean, you lot," announced Mom. "I need some help with cleaning the place up. Look at all the present papers everywhere. We need it tidied up for Auntie Ethel's visit today."

The kids let out a sigh.

"You'll find out someday, what it's like to prepare the dinner when you're grown up with your own kids," said Mom. "We need to show Auntie Ethel what a tidy bunch you are."

That afternoon, Auntie Ethel's dark red car rolled up into the driveway. She emerged, wearing her light crimson winter coat carrying her leather handbag worn with long years of use. Her greying dark hair was neatly tied up in a bun with a wide-brimmed hat to match her coat. The kids ran out to greet her.

"Hello," she said from her kind, glowing, smiling face. "And what was in your Christmas stockings this year? I'll come and see."

Auntie Ethel sat down to a warm cup of tea and scones.

"Oh, Matt," she asked. "What's this? What a delightful looking pom-pom." To Matt, this ball almost seemed alive. It was wishful thinking like wishing his old teddy bear were alive when he was a toddler.

"It's my favorite toy this Christmas," said Matt.

"What about your Earth globe you were so enthusiastic about last September?" inquired Auntie Ethel.

"Oh," said Matt, "I'll get it."

Matt was soon showing Auntie Ethel the countries on the globe and describing their geography from the sands of the Sahara Desert to the mountains of the Himalayas.

"Here's Australia," he said with excitement.

"I'm sure that you'll do well at geography as you start middle school," said Auntie Ethel. "But as for your other furry globe, I'm not sure what sorts of land or ocean areas are shown by all those colored stripes; they are so beautiful."

"They could show tropical and polar zones," joked Matt, "or look like those on the planet Jupiter."

"Of course," said Auntie Ethel, "You're a keen astronomer as well. I hope that you'll have many clear skies to look at through your telescope and your new binoculars that I placed under the Christmas tree. What was the last *Sky at Night* TV program about?"

"Oh, yes," answered Matt. "It was about the latest discoveries of extrasolar planets; planets that orbit other stars. I'm excited about the discoveries from the Hubble space telescope and the IRAS infrared satellite, especially the discovery of some accretion matter around the star, Vega, similar to the Asteroid Belt in the Solar System."

"That's news to me," said Auntie Ethel in amazement. "Yet you still seem more fascinated by that ball of fine wool. I wonder if it's made of wool from Australia's finest Merino sheep."

"There are many other planetary discoveries," continued Matt. "Like the discovery of some planets more massive than Jupiter around the star 55-Cancri. I'm sure looking forward to direct observation of these planets when NASA launches the new space telescope in the New Year. Oh, and thanks for these terrific binoculars. I look forward to looking up at the stars and planets from Uncle Herbert's next year.

"Auntie Ethel," Matt said, keeping her interest. "Have you heard about SETI? That is the Search for Extra-Terrestrial Intelligence?"

"Well no," she answered, sounding ignorant. "You mean flying saucers and all that guff. I've seen too many of these movies. Why there's one on almost every Saturday night on TV, I wish they'd put on more murder mysteries. I do so like Agatha Christie's novels."

"I'm not into such earthly matters," said Matt.

"Och well, everyone to his interests," she sighed as she continued sipping her cup of tea.

Mom came in to join them after finishing the dishes.

"Ah, at last," she sighed. "Now, I can have my cuppa."

"I've just been explaining to Auntie Ethel, all about extrasolar planets," Matt said.

"Oh, really," Mom answered, "I do hope that he's not bored you with all this."

"No, not at all," said Auntie Ethel. "I'm sure Matt will grow up to be a professor or a scientist. Won't you?"

The day turned into evening early as the sun set into a pinkish twilight on that cold still day. Auntie Ethel wished everyone a Happy New Year as she donned her thick winter coat and departed. For the second night, as he lay in bed affectionately cuddling this strange wooly ball, he felt a heightened sense of contentment from the day. As Matt drifted off into a peaceful sleep, he started to dream more detailed visions of the strange but beautiful landscape with the tall, jagged peaks that jutted out of the ocean that shimmered in the sunlight, with distinct purple hues that he had dreamed of the night before. Though these crags were mostly bare rock, what vegetation there was had vibrant dark green hues. Around these mighty rock spires, flew many specks which he could only perceive as sea birds like those around the cliffs of the Scottish Islands. Next, he was aware of his ball rolling around his head while looking at this grand vista. He awoke with a start and sat up in bed, while the ball fell off him onto his blankets.

"Where was that?" he whispered faintly, "Oh, just a dream." It was light with the rays of early dawn shining on the forlorn bare winter trees standing on a crisp freshly fallen white blanket of snow.

"Oh, if only that oak tree had leaves with that beautiful rich green," Matt muttered. "Where's my pom-pom?" He jumped up, ripped off the blankets and, rummaged through them. The ball fell out onto the floor, bouncing. It emitted a faint eerie sound as it landed that could be best expressed as 'Wuuug.'

Startled, he picked up the ball and smoothed down its fur. After settling the ball down beside his pillow, it seemed to shimmer a little more brightly than before. As he stroked it, there were momentary shimmers behind his hand on the ball's fur.

"Must be some exceptional wool," Matt whispered as he drifted off to sleep again, the night before going back to school. He once again started to have a vivid dream where he was lying down on a brilliant green meadow. He sensed the ball rolling over his body and around his head, almost like a purring cat rubbing against him.

He awoke as the ball did roll over him and onto the side of the bed, between him and the wall as the morning sun shone more brightly onto the oak tree. Matt was now beginning to be quite startled by the overall presence of this ball, intruding on his sleep.

"What kind of present is this?" he muttered as he rose from his bed with more vigor than usual on a winter's morning.

A high-pitched note emanated from his bed, which sounded like, *"Bweek!"*

Matt turned around and stared at his wooly ball, wobbling back and forth on his bed.

"What the—," he gasped.

"Bweek bweek," was the curt reply from the ball.

"Who are you?" he asked before he realized the full implication of this question.

"Bweek bweek mwaki," said his pom-pom.

"Is this a matter of *whom*?" he asked in a whisper, tailing off with a gasp of fear, awe, and wonder, all at once. Matt's spine started to tingle as he looked out of his bedroom window onto the oak tree.

He couldn't resist his gaze up to the sky where the Moon was still visible in the daylight sky. His heart began pumping more rapidly as he realized that this was no ordinary Christmas present and no usual ball of wool, as it began to waver to and fro on the bed.

"Surely, there had to be some explanation," thought Matt. "Did it have batteries or something?"

The same words sounded shrilly again from this being, *"Mwaki, bweek, bweek, mwaki."* for it was now probable that this could be a living organism after all. The concept of mechanical operation began to seem more unlikely as the ball appeared to be less robotic and had more of a personality.

Without much hesitation, Matt pointed to himself, saying, "Matt, I'm Matt."

"Matt-I'm-Matt," responded the ball nodding just like a human head but with no body, "Beek Yesl."

Pointing to himself again, Matt said, "Matt." He looked at the ball and said, "Beek Yesl."

The ball again nodded, saying just, "Yesl."

It was now apparent this being was intelligent, and these strange words were of a foreign language.

To confirm this supposition, Matt pointed to himself, saying, "Matt," and pointing his finger at the ball, saying, "Yesl."

Yesl nodded to Matt, saying in its shrill voice, "Matt." Yesl then twirled around, saying "Yesl."

It, he or she, is called Yesl, thought Matt, who picked up Yesl from his bed and held the *being* in his arms and looked out of his window. Yesl started to move around, after which Matt began to stroke the wool-like fur. As he gazed upon the meadow and the oak tree, he began to think of things far beyond this present life. Yesl started to emit very soft sounds that were akin to a song sung with a beautiful melody. The only recognizable words were *'boinke'*, maybe a variation of *'bweek'* and *'mwaki.'* Matt was lulled into a dreamlike trance.

There was a knock at the door. "Matt, your breakfast is on the table," said his mother. Matt arose slowly from his state of slumber, tucked in Yesl, got dressed, and went downstairs for his usual helping of porridge and tea. Dad, dressed in his pin-striped suit, was ready for his commute to the office in the city of Edinburgh at the Ministry of Defense local headquarters, engrossed in the *Scotsman* newspaper. Kara and Sean were also dressed in their school uniforms, eating their porridge with a little haste, not wanting to miss the school bus. Matt pondered the full implications of his morning experience, realizing that life would change course if he were to keep Yesl.

"I hope you're sleeping okay and that you have much-needed rest before going back to school," said his Mom.

"I'm doing okay," said Matt as he started to eat his porridge. "Mom, I love the wooly ball that you gave me. Where did you get it?" asked Matt.

"I thought of this surprise for you when we were up at Uncle Herbert's, last August when you lot were building sandcastles on the beach with Dad, I nipped up to a village shop that sold souvenirs, island knitted jerseys and things to see what to get for Grandma and Auntie Ethel. When I got there, I could not help but notice that colorful ball sitting looking rather lonely on the shelf in the darker recesses at the back of the shop with a price tag pinned to it. So, I bought it just for you. I'm delighted you're pleased with it."

This statement was a satisfying answer with which Matt could work on the true origins of Yesl who could not help but think that this was going to be somewhat of a detective mystery; Agatha Christie-style.

The Hebrides of Scotland were involved, and he could not wait to get there. Uncle Herbert and his family had recently moved to live on a small farm on Baraignsay, where there were rugged landscapes covered with peat bogs and heather.

"Where was that shop again?" asked Matt.

"Oh," replied Mom. "It's in the village of Scarivanish, three miles along the road from Uncle Herbert's croft."

Matt knew the shop well. He also knew the shopkeeper, Angus Mackay, a portly man in his sixties. When Matt had been there with Uncle Herbert the previous summer, he remembered Mr. Mackay, who usually wore a green tweed jacket, dark jeans, and fisherman's boots. The shop sold everyday provisions and souvenirs.

Kara asked, "How's your wooly ball? You seemed preoccupied with it this morning."

"Uh - yes," stuttered Matt, as he scrambled for a suitable answer, "I'm very fond of that ball. I've given it a name; Yesl."

"You don't mean that your ball's like a Teddy Bear," added Sean with a giggle.

"I suppose it is like having a kind of Teddy Bear," said Matt, realizing that

8

this line of conversation could be promoted for now as Yesl could be classed in that category.

After Matt had finished his porridge, he ran upstairs to see how Yesl was doing. He went into his bedroom to find that the window was wide open, which seemed odd to him. He looked toward his bed for Yesl. The bed was empty.

Where was Yesl? He thought with a sudden realization of the possible implications.

"Yesl!" he cried momentarily, forgetting about his secrecy. He pulled off the blankets and pillow and looked under the bed. Matt was concerned about where Yesl was, getting worried while looking at the open window. Matt heard a strange soft humming noise coming from outside in the distance. It grew louder, a kind of warbled hum with a regular beat until Yesl flew in through the open window and landed on his pillow beside him.

"Yesl!" exclaimed Matt, "Where have you been?"

Yesl's reply was unintelligible making high pitched humming and warbled sounds that Matt figured was her native language. Matt was so relieved that Yesl had come back to him flying by some vibrations in her fur. The humming sound started up again, and Yesl hovered around the room, out of the window, around the back garden, and landed on his pillow again.

"Yesl," said Matt, "you fly around the garden and land on my bed."

"You fly around the garden and land on my bed," copied Yesl, parrot-like, in her shrill voice in understandable English.

Matt stated what Yesl should say, "I fly around the garden and land on your bed."

Yesl readily copied this sentence. Although Matt was a school student in first-year middle school learning French and Latin, he found himself in the position of English teacher. Yesl was obviously a bright and intelligent being and could pick up new concepts and memorize them quickly.

As Yesl lay on his bed, Matt pointed with his finger saying, "chair." Then he pointed to his bed saying, "bed." He then arose and sat on his chair, saying, "I sit on the chair." Pointing to Yesl, he said, "You sit on the chair."

Yesl hovered up and around the room. Matt got off the chair and gestured with his hand over the seat of the chair. Yesl landed softly on the chair.

"Good. Well done." The apprehensive thought was that of saying good-bye to Yesl for a whole school day when the bus picked him up until he was dropped off at home. Will Yesl go off flying up into the Scottish Highlands, and will she have the right navigational skills to make the return trip?

"Matt, the bus is here!" called Mom in frustration. "Don't miss it."

Matt looked fondly at Yesl, stroked her, saying, "Goodbye Yesl. I'll see you this evening."

He was hoping that Yesl would soon understand the school routine, realizing that he had not prepared Yesl for this day. Matt found himself with

Kara and Sean all in different seats on the bus stopping at many homes picking up their school mates on this first day back at school. Matt's thoughts were still with Yesl, now far away in his bed in his now distant country home. The bus arrived at the gates of their High School in Edinburgh, where the sidewalks were covered in slushy snow. Matt, Kara, and Sean were all back with their schoolmates in the playground, awaiting the bell for classes to start. Matt looked rather dreamy in his first mathematics class of the new term, thinking a lot about Yesl and all that had transpired since Christmas Day.

"Matt. Pay attention! Tell me what X plus Y all squared is?" asked Mr. Hawkins.

Matt stood up nervously, racking his mind for an answer to this equation.

"Ah, X squared plus Y squared," he answered.

The class burst out into laughter.

"Wrong!" Mr. Hawkins shouted. "You're not paying attention! What about the middle part? It is X squared plus two XY plus Y squared. Next time you daydream like that, you'll get a penalty exercise."

After this challenging start to the school term, Matt had to allay all thoughts of Yesl until the end of this long school day.

On the homebound bus run, Matt was hoping that Yesl would be there to greet him. On running upstairs to his room, Matt again noticed the open window, which he had dreaded. As he stood at the window, a grey speck in the sky grew more substantial, which soon became the colors of Yesl. Then the humming warbling sound of Yesl's flying became audible as she approached the window. She drifted in and landed on his pillow. As he stroked Yesl, he felt a spasm of cold run through his fingers.

"Yesl, where have you been?"

"I've been flying," answered Yesl.

"But where?" asked Matt only half expecting any sensible answer.

Yesl replied in broken English, "I was flying very high over mountains."

Matt now had an explanation for the cold fur. He also sensed distinct dampness in her furry body. Yesl's coldness had all but vanished about fifteen minutes after landing, though the moisture took longer to dissipate. Perhaps it was the Scottish Highlands as he supposed earlier, maybe the Grampians or Ben Nevis. Yesl was assumed to have not known about the geography of Scotland or the rest of the Earth. Matt brought down his globe from the high shelf and placed it in front of Yesl.

"Yesl, this is Earth," said Matt hoping that she'd recognize the continents from her travels.

"This is Tombalki," Yesl insisted in her shrill and friendly voice. "That is Tomkil," nodding toward the window through which the Moon shone brightly in the evening twilight. Coincidentally, Matt had just learned the concept of the same place having different names in different languages in French class, having learned that the *United States* was called *Les États-Unis*, having paid more considerable attention in classes after that embarrassing incident with Mr. Hawkins. Matt tumbled to the possibility that these were the names for the Earth and the Moon in Yesl's native language. Matt became curious about learning the names for the stars in Yesl's language and how they would compare with the Greco-Roman names familiar to him. He thought about what the names could be of other planets in the Solar System.

• ◯ •

2 ~ ISLAND HOLIDAY

At the breakfast table, Matt's father bid him a fond farewell before leaving for his work. "Do give Uncle Herbert my kindest regards. I take it that you have that wooly ball in your luggage. Have a safe flight."

"Come on, Matt," said Mom. "Get into the car now, or we'll miss the plane. Have you remembered all your luggage and your tickets? I'm sure Uncle Herbert will be interested in telling you all about the places in the world that he's been to." As she loaded Matt's suitcase and cabin bag into the boot, she thought to herself, *what did I start in my dear boy?*

"Captain Metcalf welcomes you aboard this flight to Altaness. Please ensure that all your cabin baggage is stowed and that you have observed the fasten seat belt sign. We do hope that you will have a pleasant flight." Matt had taken out Yesl and had her at his window seat.

The plane was soon at the end of the runway for take-off. As the engines revved up, Matt felt an adrenalin rush when the turboprop plane shuddered as the runway started racing past his window. Soon the runway slipped away beneath the wings, and the landscape to the west of Edinburgh and the Firth of Forth was in full view. He was on his way to the Isle of his dreams, leaving all schoolwork behind, though missing his parents, Kara and Sean, who had barely arisen from bed to say their good-byes as Matt departed. Kara and Sean looked forward to joining Matt when they were to fly up to Baraignsay in two weeks after their school term finished.

For once, the weather was clear for most of the flight. During the hour-long trip, the plane passed over the Central Highlands as a breathtaking view of rugged mountains stretching into the azure distance. After the morning teas were cleared up by the stewardess, Matt held Yesl next to the window. She quivered with excitement, saying very softly in her shrill voice, "Matt, at last, I'm in an airplane. I've flown over these mountains many times in the last several weeks while you were at school. What's that high peak there?"

Matt thought for a moment as a voice pealed over the loudspeaker. "This is your captain speaking. Over to your right is Ben Nevis, the tallest mountain in Scotland."

After landing at Altaness Airport, Matt slipped Yesl into his bag for disembarkation. As he walked down the steps from the aircraft door to the apron, he saw Uncle Herbert waving to him from the arrival area. "Hello

Matt," greeted Uncle Herbert in his thick Island accent, "great to see you again! How's your Mom and Dad, and how's Kara and Sean? It's been a long time since I last saw them."

Auntie Wendy, who had dark flowing hair and dressed in a warm tweed coat, came to greet Matt, as Kaz, Alison, and Judith came bounding up excitedly to greet their traveling cousin from the big city.

"Hi Matt," said Kaz in his young voice. He had a distinct island accent. His fair tousled hair was blowing about in the wind, while he wore jeans and a colorful *Fair Isle* woolen jersey. Alison had on a blue skirt and matching darker blue jacket, while Judith, with long straight hair, fairer than her sister's, wore blue denim shorts and a blue jacket the same color as Alison's.

"Hi," hollered Matt as they frolicked around the grassy area between the terminal building, with brick walls, metal-framed windows and a corrugated tin roof, and the car park.

"Come on, children," said Uncle Herbert, "We'd better get Matt's luggage." After Matt identified his green tartan canvas suitcase, Uncle Herbert carried it as everyone made their way to their somewhat rusty, but much loved, Morris 1000 Traveler, affectionately known as the *Moggy*, which had traveled many miles in these islands. It was dark green with its characteristic wooden frame on the rear.

After having lunch in MacKenzie's Café in the center of Altaness, a picturesque fishing town, Uncle Herbert began the drive along the winding island roads to the village of Kinrasaig in the south of the island, some thirty miles distant. The scenery was mountainous with heather growing on the hillsides. As the *Moggy* wound its way through small villages of stone-built houses and slate roofs, Matt drew Yesl out from his bag to show to his cousins and to show Yesl herself, the island scenery.

"What a lovely ball of wool," exclaimed Judith.

"That seems an unusually brightly colored pom-pom," said Kaz.

"Can you bring the ball to the front?" Uncle Herbert asked.

Matt showed him Yesl as best as he could, while his uncle kept his eyes on the road.

Uncle Herbert continued, "We'll have to have a better look when we get to Kinrasaig." All the children wanted to hold Yesl and took turns, occasionally grabbing her from each other.

"Wuuug," cried Yesl faintly as Matt took her back.

"I call this pom-pom *Yesl,* and she doesn't like being poked," said Matt.

"Is she really alive?" asked Alison. "It's only a ball of wool."

"Well, sort of; like a teddy bear, I suppose," said Matt, trying not to reveal too much. For the rest of the trip, Matt had Yesl sit on his shoulder next to the window to admire the view.

"You look just like *Long John Silver* with his colorful parrot in *Treasure Island*," remarked Alison.

YESL – The Balkien from Antrobi

As the *Moggy* traveled the last ten miles to Kinrasaig, they passed by a beautiful sandy beach, with Atlantic breakers rolling in. At last, they arrived at their stone-built house with a slate roof. From the back, there was a glorious view stretching across the sea towards the hills to the north of the island, made purple by their distance. The closer hill, covered by heather, was called Tetraval.

As the evening wore on, Matt felt a sense of contentment, on arriving in his Island of dreams. After asking his uncle's permission, he went for a stroll down to the end of the village, with Yesl in his knapsack. He continued walking to a beach on the southern flank of Tetraval, along a farm track over the village's common sheep and cattle pastures. On this beach, Matt sat down on the sand and held Yesl in his arms, away from the human world at last.

"Yesl," commenced Matt, "This is my favorite haunt. We'll be here for a month. You might like to fly around and take a look."

"Oh thanks, Matt," said Yesl. She hovered quite fast up and down the beach and then she whisked, with her warbled hum growing louder, off out over the waves, until she was a speck against the blue sky with the sun dropping to the horizon, before disappearing over the summit of Tetraval.

"I only hope she returns before dark," muttered Matt to himself.

Matt watched the sun turn red and sink into the sea, while a chill appeared in the air.

"Oh, where's Yesl?" By now he was used to these disappearing acts of Yesl. He decided that it was best to start walking back to the house before darkness closed in hoping Yesl would know the way back in what strange surroundings to her maybe. As he walked through the village, there was yet no sign of Yesl. To make it easier for her to find him, he slowed his pace before reaching the central part of the village, as he did not want anyone to see a wooly flying ball racing up the street. Then he heard Yesl's flying sound from behind. She hovered up behind him and alighted on his shoulder.

"That was a great flight. I've seen a lot about my situation."

"About what situation?" asked Matt with concern and curiosity.

"It's a very long story," began Yesl. "I've discovered some things up on that hill, which appear to be bits from our spacecraft. I seemed to have had a memory blackout before I appeared in your house with you at the time you call Christmas."

"Yesl!" exclaimed Matt in a loud whisper as he continued walking up through the village in the advancing dusk, "You've got to be kidding!"

"Matt, you've got to believe me."

"You mean to tell me that you and others have crashed on that hill? We'll need to talk some more about this when I go to bed after tea. I'll have to be with my hosts, especially on our first night. One thing though, my Mom saw you in a shop across the bay and bought you for me as a Christmas present."

It was a cozy first evening by the warm fire. All four children were seated at the main table. Auntie Wendy served up some delicious homemade vegetable soup with rye bread.

"Matt," said Kaz, "did you have a good walk with your Yesl?"

"Yes. I did. Thank you."

"We'd like to have come," said Alison, "Sorry we missed you."

"I'm sure we could all go for a swim tomorrow," said Matt.

"Oh children," said Auntie Wendy. "The water is so cold. It's only June."

"Now children," said Uncle Herbert in his kind voice, "we'd better eat up this food, your Mama has spent a lot of time cooking for us."

The main course consisted of *roast steak* with homegrown potatoes, carrots, and peas. Yesl was perched sedately on top of the upright piano on which, Uncle Herbert would play his favorite piano pieces by Bach and Beethoven.

After dinner, Uncle Herbert asked to see Matt's globe and to talk about some of the places that he'd seen while in the Navy. Everyone gathered around the round coffee table, which had a beautifully carved brass tray with the globe on it. Yesl sat on Matt's lap.

"Now," commenced Uncle Herbert, "We'll have a geography lesson." Turning the globe to Europe, he continued, "There's Great Britain, and there's the Island of Baraignsay. When I was in the Royal Navy, our ship sailed all over the world. One port we went to was Fremantle, near Perth in Western Australia, named after Perth in Scotland."

As the evening drew to a close, Auntie Wendy said that it was bedtime for everyone, including their guest.

Kaz, Alison, and Judith all said, "Good night, Mama and Papa."

"Good night," said Matt as he retired to his bedroom with Yesl.

In the soft light of his bedside lamp, Matt held Yesl asking in almost a whisper, "Now, what did you see on that hill, Tetraval?"

Yesl began softly, "Matt, while flying low over the other side of Tetraval away from the village, I saw something glinting in the light of the setting sun. I went over to look. There, in the heather, half over-grown, lay what looked like one of the evacuation pods from our spaceship on which we'd voyaged for a long time after leaving our home planet, Antrobi. It's all beginning to come back to me. I'm *wugged*. The term to *wug* means to let fall, allow to drop, or to become stranded in some way. We've had a nasty accident with our ship. There were also some other very small pieces scattered over the hillside. There were a lot of us, Balkiens, in our crew. What about our Captain Woozl?"

"Woozl?" inquired Matt. "And you refer to yourselves as Balkiens."

"We are known as Balkiens."

"How many were on your ship, and is there a good chance that they've all survived your space-wreck?"

"There were many more of us on board when we set out from Antrobi. We need to find out what happened to them."

"Wait a minute," interrupted Matt, trying to keep his voice quiet. "You're saying that you were on a spaceship that has crashed into our planet. How did you, Yesl, survive entry into our atmosphere and not burn up like our spacecraft do in an accident?"

"We were ejected in escape pods from our stricken ship. I hope that all of the others made it out like me. What I saw on Tetraval this evening was one of our escape pods, somewhat damaged."

"Yesl, it's late, and we need to be quiet now. We'll keep Kaz, Alison, and Judith awake. I could walk with you to the location and see for myself. This disaster is a lot for me to take in right now, and I know you must be very anxious about your ship-mates."

As he drifted off to sleep with Yesl snuggled up next to his head, as usual, Matt thought about how Yesl came into his possession by Mackay's Shop in Scarivanish, as he drifted off.

While lying awake in the sunny morning, Matt realized that keeping secret that Yesl was an alien from a distant planet was becoming increasingly difficult, requiring courage to tell anyone, not knowing what their reaction would be.

Yesl was often seen seated on a table with a book standing up, open, in front of her. It was a strange sight to observe a wooly ball, occasionally wobbling about with pages flicking by themselves making Yesl appear studious. Her memory retention was superior to that of humans. Her method of vision was still a mystery. How could images of the world be formed in her fur, Matt pondered. Senses of smell, feeling and hearing, must be terrestrial, since, fur or hairs can sense smell like those in the human nose, have nerve endings of some sort to detect hot or cold, vibrate to sound, and send signals to her brain. Yesl's brain composition was yet to be discovered.

His cousins awoke and clattered down the wooden stairs to breakfast.

Matt said to Yesl, "I've not yet told my family here about you. So, you are as yet, just my wooly ball to them, so better stay on the bed for now."

"Matt, I want to get to know the people of your world and find out more from them as well."

"Yesl," replied Matt, "I think that I'll first tell Uncle Herbert, okay."

There was banter at breakfast while eating cereals, and fresh, soft-boiled eggs from his Auntie's chickens that wandered and clucked around the farmyard.

"Herbert, dear," announced Auntie Wendy, "We're out of butter and washing powder. I'll not be able to wash all of the kids' clothes."

"Okay," replied Uncle Herbert with a hint of a gruff. "We'll have to go to Mackay's in Scarivanish. Anyone want to come for a spin in the *Moggy*?"

All four children were excited about this, more so for Matt, as this was an opportunity for the first time to visit the immediate origins of Yesl. As Uncle Herbert started up the Moggy's engine, everyone piled into the back, except for Matt who sat in the front. It was a pleasant ten-minute drive to Scarivanish, along the picturesque single lane road, with Tetraval looking a mixture of mid-green and purple, rising straight from the Machair a mile or so distant. The *Moggy* turned right and pulled into the yard in front of Mackay's shop. The shop was an unassuming corrugated tin shed with double wooden doors, well-worn with use, and still had the flaky remains of brown paint. There were two wooden sash windows, on either side of the door. Everyone clambered out of the car and followed Uncle Herbert into the shop, his wife's grocery list on an envelope in hand.

"Hello Angus," hailed Uncle Herbert.

"Hello," greeted Angus in his thick Hebridean accent. "Welcome, Matt, to Baraignsay. It seems that you have brought the good weather to us. Lately, we've had a lot of rain, and the sheep have had it tough through lambing season with shearing to come soon."

Uncle Herbert continued their natter about daily island life, while Matt took a keen look around the souvenir section of the shop, behind the groceries' shelves. There were woolen jerseys, scarves, and tweed jackets. On a back shelf, there was a felt bowl containing two beautifully colored soft wooly balls, smaller than Yesl. They had price tags; just a Mom had described - £5 each. Matt looked into his small wallet for his pocket money allowance. He had £15. Without hesitation, Matt grabbed the balls and showed them to Angus. After paying £10 for them, Angus put them carefully in a brown paper bag.

"Angus. I'd be interested to know how these balls are made and what kind of wool they have?" asked Matt.

"Och well. I acquire them from time to time, here on the island; bizarre sort of exotic wool."

"I'll say it is. Very soft wool," said Matt.

After buying the listed provisions, Uncle Herbert picked up a copy of the *Altaness Courier*. For the trip home, it was Kaz's turn for the front seat, so Matt took his place with the girls in the back with the brown bag on his lap. On the way up to Kinrasaig, Matt felt and heard a distinct movement with a rustle coming from within the paper bag. He lightly held the open end suspecting that one of the balls was *waking up* and that things could get awkward before reaching the house and Yesl, who would sort it out. He was convinced that these were two of Yesl's crewmates, but which ones? As the Moggy drove up the drive to the front gate, the rustling intensified causing Matt's heart to race, hoping that the Balkiens would not burst out of the bag and fly around in the car.

"Why are you rustling that bag?" asked Alison.

YESL – The Balkien from Antrobi

Floundering for an answer, Matt deliberately collected the shopping and put it all together as Auntie Wendy came and opened the gate. Everyone rushed in, as usual, leaving poor Uncle Herbert to carry in the remaining shopping. Matt rushed through to his bedroom and closed the door and opened the bag. The two wooly balls tumbled out onto his bed as Matt expected to set eyes on Yesl, but alas, Yesl was not home.

Matt sighed, "Yesl must have gone off to Tetraval to look for more bits from their spacecraft." Almost immediately one of the balls took off and started hovering around the room like a crazed bluebottle fly with a higher-pitched warbled sound than that of Yesl. He tried to catch the hovering ball, far harder than catching a fly. There were also some unintelligible utterings.

"Oh, if only Yesl were here," Matt said softly in frustration.

Before he noticed that the lower sash of the window was open, this little Balkien was through it like a shot. It zoomed out towards the hill behind the other side of the village street.

Matt sat down on the bed and cupped his hands over his face. The one that had escaped was about four inches in diameter and had rustic, earthen-colored zones, beginning with crimson at the equator, light brown, post office red, emerald green, and large Polar Regions of a darker red.

The one remaining on his bed, still in a coma, like Yesl, initially was, had bands of slate grey, like Yesl's equatorial or central zone, bright purple, light grey, and white poles, a little larger than the runaway Balkien. Matt had no idea how long Yesl was going to be, so he had no alternative but to vacate the room and go and assist with the preparations for lunch.

Meanwhile, Yesl was soaring over the flanks of Tetraval in a sweeping search pattern, combing for any more fragments of their spacecraft and any signs of other members of the crew. So far, all that was found was her escape pod, partly buried in a peat bog on impact. Yesl hovered around the damaged pod and managed to find some small pieces that had broken off and lay close by. She picked them up by telekinesis and held them to her lower parts like a magnet and began the short flight back to the house. She zoomed over the back crofts on her side of the village keeping away from homes, so as not to be noticed by their residents and flew low up the back hayfield of Uncle Herbert's croft between rows of fir trees and in through the open window into Matt's bedroom. Once through the window, she deposited the pieces by the end of the bed. Yesl warbled up on to the pillow for a relaxing rest. She jumped up in surprise on seeing the other Balkien lying there.

"Boongoo!" she exclaimed. "How did YOU get in here?" she said. She quickly reverted to her Antrobian tongue, trying to arouse the sleeping beauty but to no avail. The door opened, and Matt strode in.

"Yesl, at last," said Matt, "Where were you? A lot has happened today." He explained to Yesl about the two Balkiens purchased from Mackay's shop, describing the colors of the one that awoke and flew off.

"That must be Baingae," announced Yesl finally, "The earthen colors of red, brown, and green describe him perfectly. I'm so sorry I was not here to placate him when you arrived back from the shopping."

"Awful timing," replied Matt."

"I have a good idea where Baingae may have gone," continued Yesl. "Somewhere on Tetraval, where his escape pod is, I think that I've seen it during my sweeps of the area. But it's getting dark now, even for my sight, which you call eyesight, with some sensory perception in the infrared spectrum as you would call it. We'll have to go and look for him tomorrow."

"Agh," gasped Matt in frustration, "I'll not sleep well tonight."

"Oh Matt, I'll soothe you with my *swooth* or fur," Yesl reassured, "Baingae has survived a long space journey ending in a crash. I'm sure we'll find him, or he'll find us more than likely. Don't let this become such a *puchty*, a term which means a problem or issue of some sort. I'm sure that being out there tonight won't be a problem for Baingae. We don't let these things become such a puchty as you do."

There was a knock on the door. "Tea's up," announced Uncle Herbert.

"Okay," said Matt, "Yesl, I'll go through and eat. You'd better stay with Boongoo in case he wakes up."

"I guess so," replied Yesl, "We'll soon have to let your family know about us as living beings from Antrobi. We can't pull the wool over everyone's eyes forever, pretending that we're just a bunch of pom-poms."

"You're right," said Matt as he exited the room.

"We'll have to pick the right moment," said Yesl.

Uncle Herbert chose to sit in his favorite chair by the fire. As he sipped his soup, he held open the *Altaness Courier* reading the middle pages.

"Here's a startling story on page seven," he said looking up at the troupe eating their soup with the clinking of their spoons on their bowls. "They're reporting that scientists from Aldermaston are combing the far side of Tetraval looking for more pieces of wreckage on an unidentified object." Uncle Herbert read out the short article:

UNIDENTIFIED WRECKAGE FOUND ON TETRAVAL

Last week, military scientists based at the British Army Research Headquarters at Aldermaston in Wiltshire, began an investigation on the north-western slopes of Tetraval, near Kinrasaig. They claim to have found many small pieces of wreckage. Some samples were retrieved and taken back to Aldermaston for further analysis. No known aircraft has gone missing in the area recently.

It was suggested that the wreckage might be of a spy plane, flying in British airspace without official CAA approval. The military officer in charge of the investigation, Captain Cammins, said, "So far, the small pieces retrieved from the hillside were made of a metal alloy not known in any manufacturing processes in the industry. Metallurgists have yet to complete their tests on the samples. No further comments can be made at this time while investigations are continuing."

Some of the mystery pieces are also being picked up by the local crofters as souvenirs. It was reiterated that no further parts are to be removed without prior permission from the Department of Military Intelligence.

Matt was taken aback by the discovery by government officials and that the presence of Yesl's spacecraft had been reported in the press.

"An interesting discovery," said Uncle Herbert, as everyone tucked into their second course. "So, we'll have government scientists going over Tetraval disturbing our sheep." Matt's heart pumping, he suggested, "Is it possible that this wreckage could be from an alien spaceship that has crashed here?"

"What makes you think that so quickly?" asked Uncle Herbert as everyone else laughed loudly.

Alison jokingly said, "Maybe the spaceship was full of pom-poms."

Although Uncle Herbert was skeptical at first, everyone started to talk about aliens and teased Matt about his Yesl being captain of the spaceship.

"Do you think that life can exist on the Moon or anywhere else in the universe?" asked Uncle Herbert.

Kaz answered, "Well, I don't think on the Moon since there's no air to breathe."

Judith also answered with a glint of child-like simplicity in her Hebridean accent, "There needs to be water as well as air for that life to drink."

"So, you would all agree that there's no life on the Moon, then," stated Uncle Herbert. What about Mars, which does have air albeit very thin?"

Matt took his turn, "The air on Mars is extremely thin. Although there seems to be very little water on Mars today, there's evidence of water in Mars' past. There are apparently watercourses and, also, evidence that Mars may have had an ocean covering most of its northern hemisphere."

Kaz said, "Well, Mars now seems to be nothing but a cold dead desert."

"I would agree with Kaz there," replied Uncle Herbert, "I would say that Mars is just a heap of dead dust," he added in a deep soft, slow, methodical tone.

Matt then interjected with alacrity to get his word in, "What about the possibility of life on planets that orbit other stars and could be a lot like Earth? I've been reading up on the current activities of SETI; that stands for the Search for Extra-Terrestrial Intelligence and on the latest discoveries of planets orbiting many of our nearby stars."

"Is that so?" asked Uncle Herbert with an air of skepticism. "You do seem sold on the idea that there are civilizations elsewhere, other than on the Earth. What about all the conditions for life on the Earth-like ideal air and water temperatures and pressures, not to mention our protective ozone layer and the Earth's magnetic field?"

Matt was still hesitant to introduce Yesl as a live being.

His heart pumping, Matt said, "Excuse me. I'll be back in a minute." He went through to his bedroom to fetch Yesl. "I want you to introduce you to my family. Fly gracefully and slowly around the room when I give the word, okay."

"This is Yesl," announced Matt on re-entering this family conference. Matt held Yesl in his cupped hands in front of him.

Judith began to laugh, "Oh, we know that!" as the others joined in the now raucous laughter. "What's Yesl, a wooly pom-pom, got to do with extra-terrestrial life?"

Matt was so embarrassed that the only way of saving face was to go through with his declaration.

"This is no ordinary wooly ball!" he declared in a firm voice. "Yesl, introduce yourself in the Queen's English and fly three circuits around the room and land on my right shoulder."

"Hello. I'm Yesl, and I come from the planet, Antrobi," she began in her shrill voice. The laughter stopped immediately. Everyone gasped in utter amazement and surprise. "Matt had cared for me since last Christmas when I was given to him by his mother, your Auntie Olivia," she continued, intending to make sure that this was no hoax with some computer voice box wizardry.

Matt said, "Yesl, fly around the room three times in a clockwise direction and land on my right shoulder." As Yesl began to make her warbled sound, she lifted gently off Matt's hands and hovered around the room, three times as instructed. Her movement was very graceful as she glided over the table and the upright piano in the corner. This motion of Yesl spellbound everyone. On her third circuit, her downdraught disturbed some papers of Uncle Herbert's correspondence from the sideboard and blew them onto the floor.

"Oh, so sorry," said Yesl as she landed on Matt's shoulder." Before anyone said anything, Yesl hovered down towards the papers, which rustled across the floor and were attracted to her body. She flew with them back onto the sideboard and deposited them neatly.

"Thanks, Yesl," commented Matt.

For a few minutes, there was complete silence except for the ticking of the brass carriage clock on the mantelpiece, the gentle crackling of the fire, and everyone's breathing. Alison began to chuckle, "Your pom-pom must have super-duper very long-lasting batteries."

YESL – The Balkien from Antrobi

Matt said in a soft tone, "Yesl is a live being from another world - no batteries inside her, except the energy she derives from the food she eats. Yesl; say something about your home planet and where you're from."

Though overwhelmed, everyone composed themselves and listened to Yesl's story. Kaz seemed the most interested in what Yesl had to tell.

"Antrobi is the fourth planet that orbits the star Qualkambi, which you call Vega. We were on a space mission when our ship crashed into the sea with some of our escape pods landing on your hill called Tetraval."

Auntie Wendy was mesmerized. She slipped her arms around Matt.

"This is incredible," she said with a quiver in her voice. "What can I say? How did you manage to handle all of this? And it was your Mom who gave you Yesl."

"That would certainly explain the wreckage on Tetraval," interjected Uncle Herbert. "Have you seen the papers? There's an article in the Altaness Courier, Yesl. We read it earlier. We'll have to keep this secret from the government scientists who'll be coming through this village, Matt."

Everyone was too excited to sleep that night except for Matt, who slept soundly with Yesl by his head, relieved that his family had accepted that there were visitors from another world after all. There was not going to be any search party the next day as the weather was very wet with a strong cold north wind. Matt was frustrated because he so desperately wanted to go and look for Baingae and beat the government investigators to the spaceship wreckage. The day was spent playing chess. Matt taught Yesl some of the moves, but Yesl found it very difficult to grasp the concept of battle strategies in the game, played by Earth-bound minds. Being from another world with a peaceful, egalitarian existence, Yesl was not able to understand why the beings on the Earth were so frequently fighting. This aspect of humanity was alien to the Balkiens from Antrobi.

Another two frustrating days passed before the wet, windy weather gave way to a glorious, sunny day. Matt finally went for a walk with Kaz, Alison, and Judith towards Tetraval. Yesl hovered along beside them, guiding them to where she thought the spaceship might be, mindful of the presence of the military personnel in the area. There was a whoosh past their heads. The children ducked down, thinking that a skua was diving on them.

"Maybe we are in some nesting grounds," suggested Kaz. There was another whoosh with a very high-pitched whirring noise. They all looked up and could see a tiny black speck moving in the sky from Tetraval. The dot expanded into the form of the furry ball as it approached them slowly. The whirring sound became more audible as it approached.

"Baingae!" exclaimed Yesl as she flew right over to the earthen colored Balkien about one hundred meters ahead of the group over the grassy Machair. Yesl and Baingae joined themselves together in flight in what appeared to be a tight embrace of friendship. The double sphere hovered towards them slowly, with the sounds of the Antrobian or Balkien language being audible above their steady flying sounds.

"Matt," said Yesl, "I've explained to Baingae about you and how we came to know each other. Baingae seems to know where his space evacuation pod is. I'll be his interpreter. He'll take a while to learn your Tombalkien language."

After walking for one-and-a-half hours onto Tetraval, the group came to a sloping expanse of land covered in heather and strewn with granite boulders. Baingae was leading them in a precise direction. As they neared a small knoll, Kaz tripped over something metallic, which moved and made a clanking noise as it hit a boulder. Yesl swooped on it and picked it up with her telekinesis, hovered up with it held onto her swooth like a magnet, and flew over to Matt. As Matt held out his hand, Yesl hovered over, letting the misshapen piece of metal alloy drop into his hand. Matt winced for a moment as he held the shiny object. It seemed quite cold for this warm sunny day.

"Matt," said Yesl. "This is a small part of our spaceship. Pieces like this are scattered all over this hillside and likely in the sea as well."

"We should leave these pieces here because of the government directive we read about in the newspapers," said Matt.

"This is OUR spacecraft," said Yesl. "It belongs to the inhabitants of Antrobi who sent us here, NOT to your government, if you please! We need to gather up as many of our important records as we can find."

"Okay, Yesl," acknowledged Matt, "We'll have to look for your records. How do I recognize them?"

"Our records will be in our escape pods, copied from the main control unit of our spaceship," replied Yesl, "You would call it *back up your data*, to what you people would call a computer. We'll need to access our data records to find out what went wrong. All of the escape pods have what you'd call a *black box* on board to record the last events in the spacecraft before they were ejected, and even after ejection, with radio transmissions to them before the ship finally broke up."

"Let's look for those pods," said Kaz.

"C' mon," said Matt, "Let's get to it."

They continued over the boggy moor with Yesl and Baingae hovering around them. Yesl continued their discussion about the disaster and wondering where Baingae's pod might be. After walking for half an hour, they came down to the rocky shore and, there, lying in amongst the rocks, was the escape pod. It was an ovoid shape made of metal alloy that shone brightly in the sun. It was about three meters long with a diameter of one meter at its widest point. There were a few small dents and scratches on the surface, which seemed minor considering the speed of impact it must have sustained. Yesl and Baingae hovered around it looking for the access hatch.

There was a soft high-pitched buzzing noise as a circle on the surface of the craft about twice the diameter of Yesl depressed into the hull and slid back. Yesl and Baingae disappeared inside.

Yesl reappeared. "You can each come and poke your head inside in turn. Matt took the lead and peered inside the capsule. As his head went through the circular aperture, he beheld a strange but pleasant smell like a rich aroma of lavender. Baingae was hovering about over a panel at the back end of the cabin with small circular screens like the dials in an airplane cockpit and small colored circles looking like buttons set into the panel's surface. Baingae hovered over this in a dance-like fashion, obviously operating the buttons using his telekinesis. There was a whirr-like sound. Another circular door slid open, and a silver sphere popped out onto the padded surrounds in the cabin. It was about the size of an orange. Matt pulled his head out of the opening and let the others take turns to have a look. Yesl and Baingae emerged from the pod carrying the little sphere between them as its door closed smoothly behind them. They hovered over to a flat spot in the heather to lay the sphere down.

"What's in that, Yesl?" asked Matt.

"That ball contains a copy of all of our flight data and images taken on our trip. We'll take it back to the house to look at it."

"So cool," Kaz exclaimed, "Maybe we'll get an insight into where you've come from."

"Now that we've found what we're looking for, shall we head back to Kinrasaig?" asked Matt.

"I guess so," replied Yesl. "Maybe we should try to hide the capsule in case your government scientists pay a visit."

"We could try to move it, all of us," suggested Matt.

Everyone tried to heave the pod out of the rocky hollow and further into a small cavity between the edge of the grassy knoll and the rocks. The object was surprisingly light but still awkward to lift as it was round. Kaz spotted an old fork-lift pallet lying on the stones as driftwood. "Maybe we could take two planks from that pallet and hold them under each end of the capsule."

Everyone managed to lift the pod over to a more concealed location and began to make their way over the heather moorland with Yesl and Baingae hovering a little way behind them carrying the data sphere between them by their telekinesis forming a distinct row of three balls in formation as they flew over the heather. Three human figures appeared as silhouettes on the skyline of the hill ahead of them.

"Uh oh," muttered Matt to the others. The men started to march down the hill towards them. They were all tall of average build, wearing military uniforms.

Matt turned around. "Yesl, Baingae, you'd better hide or immediately fly back to our house at high altitude. This man may take your data sphere."

The men were now only a short distance away. The high ranking one wore a peaked hat and had a ruddy complexion while sporting a thick mustache.

"Who are you?" he asked in an authoritative voice. "I'm Captain Cammins. What are your names, and where do you live?"

"I'm Matt," pointing to himself, "This is Kaz, Alison, and Judith. We're from Kinrasaig."

"Did you not know that this is now a restricted area?" asked Captain Cammins firmly.

"No sir," replied Matt, rather timidly, trying to be sheepish to dispel any thought that he was hiding his knowledge of the article in the *Altaness Courier*.

"Well, you do now," confirmed Captain Cammins, "I strongly recommend that you, all four of you, walk in single file straight back to Kinrasaig. You are now under strict orders not to return here while this investigation continues."

"Uh, what investigation?" asked Kaz, trying to show ignorance of what he had already seen.

"Why, aren't we now allowed on our common grazing?" asked Alison indignantly.

Judith then asked, "Why can't we kids be free to roam on our parents' common land.

"I cannot comment," said Captain Cammins, "as this is an operational matter and is under *the Official Secrets Act*. Anything you may read in the press or see on TV is quite simply speculation and sensationalism. Now move along. We've got a lot to do."

They were worried about the implications of these orders and the presence of military officials on Tetraval. Matt looked around for Yesl and Baingae, hoping that they had not been spotted. The inevitable confiscation of the data sphere would be a severe blow to learning all the secrets of the Balkiens and their mysterious planet, Antrobi. On heading back to their village, they looked back from time to time, hoping that Yesl and Baingae would hover up to join them. All they could see was Captain Cammins, marching along the route from where they had just come. They were afraid that Captain Cammins and his men would find their escape-pod and have it removed from their reach in one of their vehicles. As the place where they left the pod was now out of sight over the brow of a small undulation, they could not see if Captain Cammins had sighted the object.

As they arrived back at the house, somewhat exhausted, Uncle Herbert and Auntie Wendy warmly welcomed them. The warm evening meal gave much-needed nourishment to such a tired crew. As they ate, there were humming noises at the back door. Matt rose from the table and opened the back-kitchen door to reveal the two hovering Balkiens, Yesl and Baingae, who were finding it an effort to stay aloft carrying the data sphere between them. As Matt put out his hand to relieve them of it, it dropped. With a quick reaction, Matt put out his foot to prevent it from hitting the concrete path. It landed on his trainer shoe and rolled up to the base of the dry-stone wall.

"Sorry, Matt," said Yesl, "We're so exhausted!"

Matt picked up the data sphere and carried it inside with the two Balkiens, one on each of Matt's shoulders.

After dinner, the children discussed the day's events with Uncle Herbert at length.

"That was a development," confirmed Uncle Herbert in conclusion, "I've no doubt we'll hear more about this in the news bulletins, though it sounds as if it may all be kept hush-hush, perhaps just as well. I think that all four of you will have to lie low for a few days and keep the data sphere hidden, maybe in the hidden or 'secret' cupboard under the stairs. I'll hang a picture over the top of the paneled door to hide the join in case Captain Cammins should pay us a visit. I think the painting of the North Hills of Baraignsay will fit well."

Everyone said their "Good nights" and retired to bed. As Matt began to doze off, Boongoo started to pulsate a little. Yesl and Baingae immediately joined to Boongoo to keep him from doing something stupid, like flying out into the night. They hummed in their Antrobian language, to reassure him as he began to stir. Boongoo suddenly leaped into the air and hovered around madly, pulling Yesl and Baingae with him. Shortly afterward, there was calm as they settled at the end of the bed.

"Matt," said Yesl, "Boongoo's afraid of you. I've tried to explain to him about our situation. I think we'll sleep on the chair over there tonight."

They hovered onto the comfortable chair in the opposite corner of the room that was dimly lit by the bedside light. By the next morning, Boongoo seemed to have lapsed back into his coma.

"Matt," said Baingae. "I think that his life force has receded a lot during the night, more back to what it was when we found him. Perhaps it was the shock of being in such a strange environment."

"Baingae," said Yesl. "Boongoo's probably finding this a nightmare."

Two days later, the military personnel departed from the area. On the following morning, it was very misty with the hills all but covered in a dense low cloud. Matt and Yesl fetched the data sphere from the 'secret' cupboard and took it into his bedroom where Yesl, Baingae, and a sluggish Boongoo, who was finally beginning to awake, were sitting on the bed. Kaz, Alison, and Judith were sitting or kneeling on the bed. Baingae went up to the sphere and made small oscillating movements as if acting out some choreographed routine.

"He's using telekinesis to input a code to open it," said Yesl.

A line appeared around the sphere's equator, and it opened up into two hemispheres, hinged at one side. On the flat surface of one, there was a myriad of tiny colored circular imprints resembling flat buttons, which could not be pressed in any way by a human finger. The other flat surface had a flat circular grey screen. Baingae hovered and landed on the side with the buttons. He again oscillated over it with another choreographed routine. The screen lit up brightly at first, then became dimmer. After some flickering, an image of an alien landscape appeared in a violet hue. There were gentle hills with tall jagged spires sticking up from among them. The sky was purple, changing to deep blue and then to turquoise close to the horizon. The moving image panned around to what appeared to be a purple colored ocean, again with tall spire-like rock pinnacles jutting from the exotic sea. Into view drifted a myriad of flying Balkiens of many shapes, sizes, and colors. Matt's back began tingling, with the thought that these were real images of a far distant world.

"That's a typical view of our home planet, Antrobi," said Yesl, "You've seen many Balkiens flying there. They are our fellow beings. We do so miss our home planet, and we wonder if we'll ever get back after our accident."

After Baingae moved over the screen, a series of still images appeared. They were mainly of single Balkiens or group photos similar to those taken with human families. Then, one picture of a rather prolate Balkien appeared. This one was an elongated spheroid with a dark blue equatorial band, with greenish mid-latitude bands, culminating in purple, yellow, orange, and crimson spots in the Polar Regions. The slide show stopped there, and Baingae began to explain this image. "That is Winxl. We were very close friends until something terrible happened to her."

With that, the viewscreen went blank, and the sphere closed up as Baingae got out of the way. "Better put this back under the stairs."

● ◯ ●

3 ~ A LOST ROMANCE

Matt lay awake for a while with Yesl, Boongoo, and Baingae huddled up next to his head illuminated by the soft purple glow of his bedside light. Baingae began to emit a strange noise, which was a mixture of humming and singing in a variety of high tones.

Yesl asked in a soft voice, "What's the matter, Baingae? Let us know what it is."

"It's all coming back to me," said Baingae. "It's why I came on this mission, why I joined you and left Antrobi, if only for a season. I so miss my dearly beloved Winxl. Winxl and I were very close to one another before her accident."

"You mean, Winxl was another Balkien with you on the ship, before it crashed," assumed Matt.

"No, it's not like that all," said Baingae. "This happened a long time ago on Antrobi. "I'll tell you about it, but it's a long saga."

"Give me just an intro," whispered Matt.

"Okay," replied Baingae, "It's rather like what you would call a romance; that is a close friendship that I observe between a man and a woman of your people. I mean, we come together and get married just like your Mom and Dad and your Uncle Herbert and Auntie Wendy. You see, on Antrobi, we Balkiens have similar relationships. My dearest Winxl was such a friend to me. Only one day, she had a terrible *wug* into the cold waters of our great North Beekalo Ocean to translate our name into your language."

"You mean you Balkiens are male and female," said Matt.

Yesl hovered onto Matt's chest. "That's correct. I'm female. Boongoo and Baingae are male. Winxl is Baingae's girlfriend."

"Hey," rasped Matt. "I can hear footsteps upstairs. Better keep quiet."

Matt quickly put out the light, turned over, and the company from both worlds fell asleep.

Matt had a more detailed dream with Yesl. He had an uneasy sense that he was falling towards the sea far below him, but there was no upward rushing of wind. There were the purple sky and tall jagged mountains, jutting out of the surreal ocean, reflecting the color of the sky with deep violet hue. The Sun (or was it another star?) reflected off the shimmering waters, whose light was distinctly bluer than the Earth's Sun and noticeably flattened at its poles. He realized that these were scenes from Antrobi resembling those on the

28

spherical viewer. He was floated in a weightless state moving slowly across the purple ocean with the tall mountains gliding past him. In front of him, there were several flying Balkiens; one was recognizable as Baingae.

The others were of similar sizes. They each had a unique range of color zones. One was distinct from the rest and always hovered close to Baingae. This Balkien had an equatorial diameter smaller than Baingae but was shaped a bit like a rugby ball, only more cylindrical with hemispherical ends from pole to pole. Matt surmised that this one was Winxl.

After about ten minutes, he and the Balkiens approached a small clearing, with a variety of dark green mosses from which stood a few rocky spires. This area was on top of a more towering tall rock promontory high above the ocean surface. The Balkiens hovered over this purple-green meadow and landed in its soft moss or short grass. Around the edges of the meadow, there were some unevenly distributed small hemispherical dome-shaped buildings. He could make out that they had hexagon and pentagon panels, like the designs by Buckminster Fuller. The dwellings had windows in place of most of the pentagon panels and had one of the side hexagons missing to form a doorway. Many Balkiens flew out of these roundhouses and greeted the arriving party. They made high-pitched warbles in their Antrobian language.

Baingae and Winxl were hovering around the meadow while in contact with one another at their equators like a dumbbell. It seemed romantically cute. The other Balkiens hovered around each other, like bees around a particular flower. One noticeable absentee was Yesl.

The morning rays of the sun streamed into Matt's bedroom through the slightly open curtains. Beside him were Yesl and Baingae with Boongoo, still looking like only a ball of wool leaning against the wood-paneled wall.

"Yesl, I've just had a most amazing vision of your planet."

"Good. I transmitted those memories to you in your sleep. There's more to come, but we'll leave things at that for now."

Matt sensed a soft nudge from behind him as he started to rise and get dressed.

"Yesl, is that you?"

"What? I'm still as can be." Matt noticed that Boongoo was not where he had been next to Baingae.

"Where's Boongoo?" he asked. A bump appeared on his duvet and moved about the bed. Thoughtfully, he closed the door and then lifted the duvet slowly. Boongoo was rolling about all over the bed like a billiard ball after a quick shot. He tried to grab hold of Boongoo, but he was evasive.

"Matt," said Yesl, "leave him be, he'll be frightened just as Baingae was a week ago. We don't need another episode like that. You'd better go through for breakfast. I'll handle this." As he placed his hand on the door handle,

Boongoo suddenly took off and began hovering around the room like an agitated bee.

"Yesl!" exclaimed Matt. "I can't open the door without Boongoo escaping and scaring my family." Boongoo continued flying about and then started pounding on the window just as flies often do. Matt quickly opened the door and darted out, closing it behind him. He was soon at his usual porridge for breakfast with little discussion about the recent events, especially those of the evening before, except that Kaz was still more interested in learning about the home planet of the Balkiens.

"Baingae's very sad today," Matt began.

"Why?" asked Kaz.

"It's a lost romance," whispered Matt.

"Oh," whispered Kaz with a wry smile. "A romance between two furry balls, a strange thing, indeed."

Overhearing this, Alison started to giggle.

"Alison," said Matt, "Baingae's just remembered that he has lost his closest, well - girlfriend."

Alison couldn't help her soft laughter but realized the sadness of the situation as Matt began to explain all that he knew about it. Matt left the table and went intrepidly through to his room. At his bedroom door, he could still hear some Balkien hovering noises, so he knocked.

"Come in," shrilled Yesl. Matt cautiously opened the door as little as possible, entered, and closed it lightly behind him. There on the bed were Yesl and Baingae with a quivering Boongoo wedged between them. The scene looked affectionate, for all three Balkiens were in a multiple embrace and a triangular formation. They quivered and pulsated and rolled over one another to soothe a distressed Boongoo.

"Matt," commenced Yesl. "This close arrangement of us is known as a *ponkadliath*. It's an Antrobian term of endearment. Boongoo's going to take a lot of convincing about our situation. He had a nasty *wug* when our ship broke up. He didn't make it onto a life-pod. He did manage to hide in a small space near a bulkhead, which broke away and crashed into the sea off Tetraval. He says that the piece of flotsam went down deep into the ocean. He became badly compressed becoming a flattened or oblate spheroid, but managed to float to the surface, and was washed up on Scarivanish Beach, where he was found by a crofter collecting driftwood. The crofter dried him out and gave him to Mr. Mackay at the shop, where you found and bought him and Baingae. Boongoo is now being diagnosed for oblateness by Dr. Baingae."

"How did he know this if he was unconscious?" asked Matt.

"Still a mystery," replied Yesl. "Boongoo may have fallen into a coma on the shelves of Mackay's shop, thinking that he was in some sort of hospital or rehabilitation unit. He'd have gone into what we call a hibernation state to recover from the shock of impact and the resulting oblateness syndrome. He's a little disorientated now that he's no longer in the 'hospital.'"

"Yesl," started Matt. "There's been a write-up in today's *Scotsman* about the events of the last few weeks here in Kinrasaig."

"Everyone from your planet is going to find out about us," answered Yesl.

There was a high shrill sound emanating from the quivering Boongoo before he started to hover around the room erratically and pound on the windowpanes again to escape into the open air. He just managed to squeeze his oblate form under the lower window sash, which was still ajar for the fresh night air and flew outside before Yesl and Baingae could catch him. Matt opened the window a little wider for Yesl and Baingae to follow Boongoo.

That day seemed to drag, while Matt and the others assisted Uncle Herbert around the croft. As Matt reached his bedroom in the early evening, he hoped that all three Balkiens would be lying on his bed, but the bed was empty. His heart sank. He waited patiently and went outside as the sun was setting. During the cacophony of hundreds of starlings, who flocked in dark clouds fluttering in formation over the village, almost indistinct humming noises could be heard. As Matt, Kaz, Alison, and Judith looked on in wonder, there were three larger rounder dots silhouetted against the red evening sky. They grew into dark circles and landed on the nearby stone wall.

"Do not worry about us, *poonketyponks*," said Yesl. "It was a long day. We needed to sort Boongoo out, as he was distressed upon awakening this morning. We had to follow a speeding Boongoo for about five hours into the Scottish Highlands, reminding us of the tall peaks on Antrobi, over on the mainland before he got exhausted and began to *wug* towards some scree slopes on a hill. We had to dive down and catch him before Baingae, and I managed a soft landing in some heather, almost a *wug* for all of us. We had to convince Boongoo that everything was okay. We rested for about an hour, then started flying westward over the mountains to a large town with a railway station. We caught a train from there; I think it was from Fort William to Mallaig. We hid on the luggage racks among passengers' raincoats and umbrellas. We're used to rail travel as we also have railways on Antrobi, only the train carriages are like silver spheres. We then hovered over to and landed on top of one of the lifeboats on the Baraignsay ferry, which docked at Altaness about half an hour ago."

"Very resourceful, Yesl," said Matt.

"You have to be when you go spacefaring," replied Yesl. "All of your seamen like Christopher Columbus and Captain Cook had to be, on their adventures. I've been reading more of your school history books than you have, Matt. Perhaps I could help you with your homework when you go back to school."

"That would sure come in handy," sighed Matt. "And what about Baingae's lost friend, Winxl, I seem to remember?"

"Sorry we didn't get to finish that sad episode with today's shemozzle," said Yesl. "We'll continue in our dreams." With that, they all drifted off to sleep and the Land of the Balkiens.

The vivid dreaming resumed for Matt, where it left off. The scene on the grassy meadow, where Baingae and Winxl were together, began to re-emerge. Baingae and Winxl hovered to one of the small dome-shaped houses in the Antrobian village. They were now alone. Baingae and Winxl leaned on each other, romantically and communicated in their Antrobian language. Winxl parted from Baingae and hovered off, getting smaller until she was only a tiny dot that faded away into the empty steel purple sky. Her warble flying sound also faded off into the whispers of the cool breeze coming up the steep valley from the purple ocean below up into the stark, jagged spires of rock towering into the sky, Baingae was alone and hovered into his little round geodesic house. Inside, there was a single room with pentagonal windows and lined with hexagonal panels in various pastel colors. On some of them were affixed round pictures of various Balkiens. One image was very prominent; it was of Baingae and Winxl with a background of a city with tall rounded skyscrapers and other dome-like edifices.

This scene faded out, and another scene faded in to reveal a dark storm with rain and hail. Matt could feel the cold going through his bones as he began to shiver in his sleep. In the middle of the storm, he could make out poor little Winxl trying to battle through the awful elements while flying to her destination with the updraft sucking her up ever higher. Suddenly there was a violent blustery shower of ice and hail. Matt felt blasted by the cold and cried out in what was now a horrible nightmare. Ice began to accumulate around Winxl's outer swooth, turning her into an ice-ball, which started to fall to the ocean below at ever-increasing speed. The whetted wind battered on his face like stinging bees. Through this, he could make out the colors and some texture of Winxl inside the ice ball. Before pondering this, the waves of a dark ocean rushed up and hit Winxl with a loud bang. Matt fully expected a similar impact to end his short life, except that he just stopped instantly above the roaring tempestuous waves in his vision. Poor Winxl was covered in shattered bits of ice-encrusted onto her swooth. He watched helplessly as the alien sea tossed Winxl up and down. This scene faded as before and another faded in to show a very still, soaked, and bedraggled Winxl lying on a deserted wind-swept stony beach. Fortunately, the storm surge had left her well clear of the waves lapping up on the shore. Matt began to cry as Winxl looked to all intents and purposes to be deceased. A group of about five Balkiens hovered up to the body on the shore and surrounded it in the form of a *ponkadliath* to try to revive Winxl. After about ten minutes, the quintet lifted

Winxl and took her away to their nearby settlement, which also consisted of small rotund, geodesic dwellings.

Another change of scene showed a strange, serene ceremony, taking place in a small cave. Matt appeared to stand at the mouth of the cave. Behind him was a drop down a cliff face on the side of a typical Antrobian tall rock spire dropping to the sea below. It was *Vega-rise* being the star around which the planet Antrobi orbits. The turquoise shafts of *Vega-light* shone into the small cave. In the rounded chamber, there were several circular tiers of Balkiens. In the center of this little arena, there was an elongated spheroid white cocoon still forming itself. Beneath the white layers, Matt could make out the faint colors of Winxl.

Soon the cocoon became more substantial and opaquer. A large burly Balkien appeared to be officiating at the ceremony like a priest. More tears welled up in his eyes as he realized that this was like a funerary ceremony for Winxl. The priest was about the same size as Yesl and had darker colors in his swooth. These were a dark royal blue for his equatorial band, then alternating zones of purple and dark green culminating in black poles. The blue equator and black poles had tiny white spots, looking like stars in the night sky. The colors on this Balkien seemed very appropriate for his religious role. In the audience, there was another Balkien with almost the same color scheme. The entire dialog was in Antrobian warbles in a much lower tone of voice than Matt was used to from Yesl and the others he'd met so far. He wondered what their religion was or if they worshipped some superior Being, like the worship of God on Earth. The scene faded out at the end of the ceremony.

Matt awoke to find that his pillow was wet from weeping and that Yesl was cuddled up beside him, consoling him, "Yesl. What an awful nightmare."

"Matt, I had to tell you what happened that awful night. You see that was Baingae losing his sweetheart, Winxl, albeit temporarily as we perceived at the time. When a Balkien has an injury like that, he or she will go into a sort of hibernating recovery phase. That was a funerary ceremony as you would call it. The priest's name is Wink. His female twin you saw is Mwaki. They are known as the Winkets. They are best friends of Baingae and Winxl. Winxl grew a cocoon around herself to begin a lengthy healing process that we reckoned would take about fifteen to thirty Earth years or so to complete. Baingae's fiancée was not going to be around for a long time with wedding plans on indefinite hold. We marry and give in marriage similar to you, Tombalkiens."

"Poor Baingae, and here he is," continued Yesl as she, Baingae, and Boongoo began to have a *ponkadliath* with Matt in the light of his bedside lamp. "Baingae then joined us as a crew member on our spacecraft, the *Balkieston,* named after the capital city of our planet, Antrobi."

YESL – The Balkien from Antrobi

"You see," said Baingae, "I was now alone and knew as a doctor of Antrobian medicine that Winxl was going to be in recovery hibernation for about four Antrobian years. We Balkiens can live for many of your centuries, unless one has a fatal accident or disease, though in many cases such as Winxl, the Balkien will go into a comatose sleep and grow a cocoon around his or herself as your caterpillars do before changing into a moth or butterfly. However, Winxl will still emerge as Winxl, though her colors and shape may vary a little bit.

"The Winkets in your vision are not only priests in our religion but had trained and mentored Baingae and Winxl on our cultural ways as well as to minister to the Balkien population. I knew that Yesl was planning to train for space travel. So, I decided to join Yesl on her full course to train as an astronaut in Balkieston, where we were to join a crew for a deep space mission. I became the ship's medical officer as you would have ranked him on a space or ocean ship. We'd better get some sleep."

• ◯ •

4 ~ MISSION TO SPLOGITA

There were celebrations amongst the Balkiens graduating from The Balkieston College of Astronautics. The edifice where Boongoo, Yesl and the Winkets trained for half an Antrobian year was a large dome structure, situated in the center of Antrobi's capital city, Balkieston. Next, to the central dome of the College, there was a cone-shaped tower with a shimmering outline of a gleaming sphere mounted over its summit, which almost reflected perfectly the violet sky above the rotund city buildings.

Yesl looked forward with alacrity to her first real space assignment after many short training trips to Antrobi's satellites, and the other member of the double planet system, Antrogi. Dr. Baingae, specializing in the health of Balkiens in extreme conditions, such as temperature and high acceleration spacecraft, accepted the role of a medical doctor on the mission to the planet, Splogita. Due to Splogita's great distance from Antrobi of approximately 60 light-years (Earth years), the mission was set for about three Antrobian years (about 15 Earth years). Captain Woozl was a prolate Balkien; that is taller than his width. He was a little larger than Yesl and had mostly slate grey swooth with bands of white and purple. Mwakus was Woozl's deputy in command. Throughout their years at college, Baingae had become very close to Yesl as his mentor. Boongoo was also a close companion giving Baingae much needed encouragement during his grieving time without Winxl. They reckoned that Splogita had the potential to support life forms similar to the Balkiens. There was something very distinct about the spectral signature from Splogita, which was very intriguing to many Balkien scientists, attracting them to go and explore this little-known world so far away.

On the day of launch, large assemblies of Balkiens spread out in many rows or were in ponkadliaths. On a round dais, Woozl, Mwakus, Yesl, Boongoo, and Baingae were ready to depart on the small scout ship, shaped like an ovoid, for the mother ship, *Balkieston*. To say farewell, to them were the leading representatives of their clan, the Winkets. The Winkets were Wink, who had officiated at Winxl's interment ceremony for her recovery hibernation and Mwaki, his twin sister. During the celebrations, there were emotional hugs between the Winkets and other Balkiens on the *Balkieston's* crew. There was much humming and buzzing, which were the Antrobian form of singing and music. The crew flew the short distance across the apron of the spaceport toward their craft, which stood on its three legs with the skyline of the city of Balkieston with its exotic Antrobian art-deco buildings of cylindrical, rounded or crystalline skyscrapers, topped by large bubble-like spheres. The sky above the city was a bright pale violet hue, which changed to deep purple higher up. Now distant specks, the spacefarers flew in through a small round door of the ship. The dark aperture shrank until it was no longer visible as the round door slid shut into place. After about five minutes, the craft started to hum and lift gracefully shrinking as it sped away into the distance until it was a tiny glinting speck and vanished into the wild purple yonder. Wink looked up to realize that they had gone out of sight, bringing on an air of sadness for the Winkets as they had now bidden farewell most of their closest mates. Back on the terraces where the Balkiens had gathered there was some more buzzing and warbled noises as they began to disperse, flying off in all directions.

Meanwhile, on board the scout ship, Captain Woozl, Mwakus, Boongoo, Baingae, and Yesl were seated around the round window that looked out of the lower surface of the ship. They were sitting in semi-circular cup-like seats, known as *bocklasses*, arranged around the circular window. As the ship ascended, the round apron of the spaceport shrank. The buildings of Balkieston soon came into view, spread out before them, with many of the buildings having great full spheres or hemispherical domes, like marbles scattered over a dark emerald green carpet. The light from Antrobi's purple daylight began to illuminate the crew in its incandescent glow. As the ship accelerated ever faster from the ground, the coastlines of the continent of *Beekeo* came into view in the large porthole. The vibrant green of the forests contrasted with the purple sheen of the *North Beekalo Ocean*.

Yesl and Baingae turned their gaze from the purple continents below up toward the black cosmos studded with a tapestry of bright pinpricks of light. One star became rapidly brighter. Its single point of light divided into a tight cluster of stars, multiplying like microscopic cells dividing under a microscope. In the next few minutes, these stars grew into small silver spheres joined by silver struts becoming larger until Yesl and the others could see gargantuan geodesic spherical structures joined by wide metallic tubes with lines of portholes. The great ship soon filled the lower window of the scout ship as it turned away from Antrobi to rendezvous with the *Balkieston*. One of the pentagonal panels in one of the three front side spheres just behind the head sphere, which was the ship's bridge and crew quarters split into its five triangular panels and opened out like the petals of a flower. The scout ship was soon docked inside the most gigantic leviathan ever assembled by the Balkien race.

Soon their home world, appearing like a glistening purple marble with dark green areas and many white fluffs of cloud, began to shrink visibly as the

Balkieston departed Antrobi bound for distant Splogita. The ship accelerated past Antrobi's sister planet, Antrogi in the double planet system. The spacecraft continued accelerating towards the gas giant, Spalminkatrix, and passed by at high speed. For such a mission to be possible in a reasonable lifetime, even by Antrobian standards, space travel at speeds much faster than the speed of light had been mastered, though some unknown physical phenomena were yet to be understood. The ship was fitted with engines that could generate anti-gravity waves around it to counteract the effects of the extreme accelerations. To produce the thrust needed for such a voyage the engines operated using a complex system of gyroscopes or wheels turning within wheels.

About half an Antrobian year later (two and a half Earth years) the *Balkieston* arrived in the star system, Yastagil, not knowing what to expect. As the ship decelerated on approach to their objective, it was possible to observe the planets in orbit around Yastagil. The system had three gas-giant planets and seven small rocky worlds orbiting the second gas-giant planet, named Spoonkathtil. This Jupiter-like world was visibly oblate on account of its fast-rotational speed making one rotation in only about three hours. Splogita was the outermost of seven satellites. On closer approach, Splogita was discovered to have an oxygenated atmosphere similar to that on Antrobi. There the similarity to Vegan worlds ended dramatically. It soon became apparent that the water thought to have been present in abundance as oceans were noticeable by its absence. Splogita appeared barren with nothing but searing desert. When the *Balkieston* assumed parking orbit, all the Balkiens could see, was a vast dry sandy colored plain, pockmarked with craters, very similar to Mars, except for the thicker atmosphere. The excited buzzes and warbles of the crew became much quieter as each of the round bodies of swooth lay silently on their cup seats around the circular viewing window of the ship's bridge.

"That's exploration, you win some, you lose some," said Yesl, philosophically.

As the ship orbited around the planet's night side and into the rising Yastagil, its greenish-yellow rays shone through a part of the atmosphere distinctly bluer than the rest, which had a pinkish hue due to wind-blown dust particles from the vast deserts. Into view came a more enormous crater, filled with a beautiful deep blue lagoon of liquid with light shimmering waves. In the center of this lake was a sizeable emerald-colored island with small clouds that formed circular ring patterns around the island's central mountain colored with deep emerald greens at the base, turning to dark green hues merging into purples and mauves, culminating in a white snow-capped peak. Above the snowline, there was stark light grey rock jutting up into space itself. The disappointments turned to ecstatic awe and wonder with fascination all rolled into one. With every orbit, more studies were done on this lake and the island, as preparations were made to descend to the surface and explore further. On each successive orbit, more spectral analyses were carried out on the expanse of the deep sapphire blue lake. The results showed it to consist of pure, clean water, which was uncannily fresh without any dissolved salts. Boongoo, the scientist on the crew, was baffled by this state of perfection. The conversation amongst all the crew members in Antrobian shrills and buzzes went something like this in English.

"Captain Woozl," reported Boongoo. "The water in that lake is too perfect in composition for it to be natural. It could only be kept that pure artificially. The rest of the planet looks a little too harsh for us down there."

"Boongoo," replied Woozl. "We haven't come all the way out here cooped up like cramped oblate Balkiens in a pongball or tin-can just to act like wimps, turn around and go home without landing."

"But," Yesl butted in, "Boongoo's got a point. If we go down there and that intelligent life is unable to assist us if our ship is damaged, we'll be *wugged* forever with no hope of ever going home again. I'm not sure about living in that desert with hot, dry winds and that terrible dust impregnated into all of our swooth."

"The spectral analyses we did on this planet from Antrobi looks very intriguing though," said Boongoo. "I've called up the spectrographic results on the view-screen and am comparing them with the current readings we're taking of the lagoon."

All the crew members hovered around the large circular monitor screen on which the two spectral graphs were displayed; the rather noisy one processed from the data received on Antrobi and that of the current observations. Their resemblance was astonishingly stronger than they had expected.

"Considering the long time, it takes light to travel from here back to Antrobi, this is remarkable," said Boongoo. "It was almost as if the inhabitants, if any, were sending out a message about their presence by creating this almost perfect environment which shone out with a distinct spectral signature to any intelligent life forms which might be looking out for such phenomena."

On looking out of the spaceship's windows, all the Balkiens could see was that the rough, dusty desert sand quickly gave way to a beautiful white sandy beach that surrounded the whole lake in the ancient crater. On another orbital pass, the Balkiens began to notice shimmering speckles or a myriad of tiny flashes of light emanating from a small area on the tall peak just below the ice cap on its summit. It sparkled on and off with regular intervals of about two minutes, occurring over the next three orbits. On the fourth pass, it was by now sunset (Yastagil set) over the lake and the island casting a long shadow across the water with the peak's shadow reaching onto the wild and now almost pitch-dark desert. In this shadow side of the island, there were tiny green glowing patches of reflected light that was nearly circular, with some elongated ones along the island's shoreline. The isle was by now measured to be approximately one hundred and sixty kilometers in diameter, looking small in such a vast inland sea. The central peak appeared to be about one hundred and twenty kilometers high. The planet's atmosphere was extra thick to be able to have an ice cap at that altitude.

The crew was not sure what the glowing patches of light were, but speculation about habitation could not be ruled out. The sparkly flashes seen on earlier orbits might have been a signal meaning that their craft was detected, which to the potential Splogitans would have appeared like a moving star in their night sky as Yastagil was setting. There was no knowledge of what sort of eyesight these beings would have, how intelligent they were, or how sophisticated was their detection equipment. Only further exploration of the planet would reveal answers.

• ○ •

5 ~ CALL OF THE MOLKTRONS

Captain Woozl called a meeting of the crew and decided on a landing party of three Balkiens, Yesl, Boongoo, and Baingae, who would descend to the surface in one of the ovoid landing craft, identical to the one found close to Mt Tetraval. Boongoo was the craft's pilot, while Yesl had the responsibility of introducing the Great Balkien Civilization to any locals that they might encounter. The trio boarded their shuttlecraft. Their decent was like being still in the same orbital motion above the deserts of Splogita, while the majestic *Balkieston* raced away from them until it was a speck in space barely distinguishable from the myriad of other stars. The gyro engine on board was revved up to full speed to slow their capsule to a descent trajectory directly toward the center of Splogita's Great Lake, as named in the Antrobian Language. Soon the craft slowed down enough to begin its descent into the Splogitan atmosphere. As it did so, small wings and tail fins extended out to guide its descent glide path. The three Balkiens sensed the distinction of *up* and *down* as the sky turned from jet black to deep purple and to blue. Soon the ship was gliding over the featureless deserts at a much-reduced speed and an altitude of only around one hundred meters. While Boongoo was piloting the craft, Yesl and Baingae discussed how they were going to explore the island. They were apprehensive about any inhabitants.

The ship flew low across the great lake, almost skimming the waves. Looking towards the sea horizon ahead of them through the cockpit windscreen, all they could see were the small shimmering waves and the thick hazy sky. Over about ten seconds the haziness cleared and there in front of them was the tall mountain peak of the island towering majestically above them. It was far higher than anything on Antrobi. Boongoo had to engage the gyro engine into reverse thrust before they came too close to the coastline. The ship settled on the water and bobbed about on the waves which, while appearing small in flight, were now appreciably larger. The shoreline had long sandy strands with deep turquoise water in the bays and inlets. The foreshore had lush deep green vegetation. As Yesl gazed up the slopes, the dark green merged into what looked like vegetation in many bright colors and becoming a deep purple hue before the ice cap on the summit.

Yesl, Boongoo, and Baingae decided that they would now continue underwater as a mini-sub for the final approach. Underwater, the lakebed was now clearly visible in the surprising crystal-clear water.

As they slowly came into the shallow bay close to the shore, they noticed many flashes of light in front of them. It seemed that the lake was teeming with tiny fish-like creatures. The ship came to a halt floating under the water a short distance from the beach. The little flecks now looked like little silvery circular-shaped creatures swimming in the lake.

The ship surfaced and with one last whine of the engine levitated out of the water and hovered toward a small secluded clearing under a clump of large tree-like plants. They were emerald green with rotund trunks and sausage-shaped offshoots, like cactus, covered in little grey spots giving them an aged look. A small woodland of these plants receded from the shoreline to the island's hinterland. The ship finally landed, and the engine turned off so as not to attract attention. Yesl called Woozl on the *Balkieston* through its communication and locator satellites deployed on arrival, to report their safe landing and position. The Balkiens ran tests on the atmosphere outside in case it was not suitable for their swooth and bodily functions. The results on the ship's atmosphere analysis equipment were returned as okay though the oxygen content was a little lower by Antrobi and Earth standards.

Each of them, Yesl, Boongoo, and Baingae wore a headset with metal bands around their equatorial swooth and two going over their upper poles crossing over at right angles to one another. There was a small antenna on the top to give their position to the mother ship. These gave the Balkiens the appearance of the orb in the British Crown Jewels. They began to fly over the emerald woodlands and meadows. As they continued to fly higher and higher up in front of the cliff faces of the vast mountain, Boongoo began to feel heavy and started to drop away or *wug* from the rest of the group towards the forest below by now much thicker. Boongoo hollered in his high-pitched sound to the others about his predicament. He suddenly *wugged* down into the dense forest before the others became aware of the problem. Yesl and Baingae continued up the cliff face when they too began to feel giddy. They turned around only to realize that Boongoo was not with them. As they began to *wug*, Yesl turned on her distress beacon before impacting on the solid surface of one of the rounded dark green tree-like plants. They were now exhausted, lying on the forest floor while Boongoo was nowhere to be seen. Yesl had hoped that the homing beacons would attract the attention of the *Balkieston*.

Trying to fly was an enormous effort. Yesl and Baingae wondered if she had missed something on the atmosphere test and whether there was some gaseous ingredient that was sapping their strength or worse still, slowly poisoning them. Yesl still had her positioning gear o, but Baingae's gear had come off as he hit the trees during his fall. Boongoo had dropped out of sight some ten minutes earlier, creating an extensive search area, with no strength to take off, let alone commence such an arduous task. Hours passed while Yesl and Baingae lay on the forest floor, with fragrant moss-like plants, mainly colored green and purple, studded with tiny flecks of many colors, which were grouped to create an almost hypnotic mottled effect. Dr. Baingae began to wonder if it was this beautiful smell that was inducing the sleepiness. However, their condition was now stable as darkness fell. A deep blackness enveloped the Balkiens. Yesl and Baingae were genuinely concerned for Boongoo.

As if in a dream-like state, they perceived a myriad of tiny lights moving over the mosses towards them. As the lights came closer, they appeared to be little glowing pearls that shimmered with a silvery essence. These glow-worm-like creatures started to surround both Yesl and Baingae and undermine them as they lay in their sleepy state. Soon there were enough of the pearl-like beings under them to lift Yesl and Baingae. Yesl and Baingae could do nothing to get away from the glowing pearls. They noticed strings of them moving beside them as they rolled along the slightly sloping ground. Fortunately, Yesl still had her positioning gear and summoned up enough strength to turn on the camera on her device, which relayed images of this scene to Captain Woozl on the *Balkieston*. A string of the lustrous pearls looked like a necklace fit for a princess. Yesl and Baingae could see themselves reflected in the collective glow of these tiny beads that were roughly the size of glass marbles. They sensed themselves floating along the moss carpet, not knowing where they would end up. Baingae said that perhaps they were being taken to a hive or lair. There was a passage through an entrance tunnel or deep cavern whose walls were illuminated by the light of the glowing pearls.

Soon, they emerged in a more enormous cavern, which may have been inside something like a termite mound. All the rocky surfaces were covered in a myriad of the glowing pearly creatures, giving a significant light to the scene. In the middle of the floor was a much larger spherical pearl-like creature looking like the queen bee figure in a beehive on Earth. The significant being was the same size as Yesl, but a giant to all of her subjects. She emitted a pearly glow, which seemed very smooth except for faintly shimmering vibrations of light from within. There was a continual buzzing drone of the sound of the voices of these beings communicating with one another. Occasionally, Yesl could pick out rapid rhythms, which may have been forms of music or singing. Yesl had forgotten all about Boongoo until Baingae pointed him out, clearly visible across to one side of the 'Queen Pearl.' Yesl immediately tried to fly or levitate over towards Boongoo to ponkadliath with him but could not move as she had no strength.

Baingae uttered a name to call them, the '*Molktrons.*' Strangely, these little creatures remind me of the Mallkets, which are another type of spherical being that we have on Antrobi. So, we called them the 'Molktrons.'"

Countless millions of them inhabited the island in hundreds of cave systems, like the one where they were. It seemed like one colossal *termite* mound protruding from the large lake. Soon they were surrounded by hundreds of Molktrons all over their swooth as if in their style of ponkadliath. Baingae tried to communicate with them in his Antrobian hums and buzzes, not thinking that the Molktrons could understand him or the others. To their extreme surprise, the Molktrons, especially the Queen, could comprehend the Balkiens easily. Soon their buzzes became like Antrobian in a thick accent. The Queen briefly explained that she and all the Molktron communities were slaves to some hidden master whom she figured lived deep within the island rock or deeper within the planet.

The Queen said in their language, "The little worker Molktrons rubbed hard over the mosses on the forest floor to cause a gas to seep up into the air that would asphyxiate your swooth causing you to lose your strength and *wug* into the trees and be taken in by us. We, the Molktrons, wanted to stop you Balkiens from continuing to fly up to the summit of that great peak. We sensed that you were strangers that could help us and worried that you would go into the lair of this evil master being high up in that very tall mountain."

"It certainly is an Enigma to all of us," said Matt.

"We Balkiens," continued Yesl, "had a minimal concept of evil intent until we encountered this terrible being on Splogita. It seems that the '*Enigma*' is an appropriate name for it. We were taken aback to observe all the evil that occurs on your planet, Earth."

"It would be wonderful if our society here on Earth was like yours on Antrobi." He gave out a longing sigh. "I get bullied at school."

"Oh, Matt," said Yesl. "You'd love to come to Antrobi to a better world."

"But how?" he asked. "It's a very long way, even on your ships and your means of return is wrecked."

"Yes," said Yesl. "We're finally stranded and lost in space. We wonder if they'll ever miss us on Antrobi. According to our calculations, we're not due back from Splogita for another six of your years."

Baingae started to make some rather sad, warbled sounds.

"Baingae is expressing his sadness that he may never see his beloved Winxl again," said Yesl. "He's regretting coming on such a risky venture and wishes he had waited on Antrobi while Winxl was in hibernation. But Baingae, you've been a precious member of our crew. If it wasn't for you, we might all have still been stuck on Splogita as helpless prisoners under the evil Enigmatic Master there."

Matt suggested, "Maybe you were taken to see the Queen Molktron."

"How did you guess?" asked Yesl. "That was very close to what it was. It's amazing how these life forms seem to have an uncanny resemblance to us no matter what planet they're on, though there were some differences as we'll explain."

YESL – The Balkien from Antrobi

The pearly Queen Molktron, who started to glow more brightly, filled the cavern with light. She had five darker circles on her upper surface that may have been eyes. There were five lower circular patches inside her glowing skin of an orange hue. The Queen managed to relate how they once had a beautiful, idyllic existence on this world before the Enigma came.

"It seemed to be some ethereal entity that just appeared from the sky," began the Queen, "possibly from the nearest galaxy, which you Balkiens call the Binkalthtic Galaxy; that is the Andromeda Galaxy. Many centuries ago, this *thing* appeared overhead and caused a terrible heat to come onto the planet. Many of us fried to death. Much of our oceans evaporated, and our climate changed. Only this lake and this island survived. This evil presence, which seemed to be looking for a *body* to manifest itself in, tried to take over some of our Queens and their worker Molktrons as well. It succeeded in some cases by possessing the minds of the Queens, bringing terrible wars and conflicts, which eventually wiped out about ninety percent of our population. It still possesses one of our Queens and her whole family community of Molktrons. We'll let you three have your strength back, but you must try to leave this planet you call Splogita at once before the Enigma tries to destroy you or your ship."

The farewell ceremony with the Molktrons was an emotional one involving the Queen, the three Balkiens, and the rest of the Molktrons forming a somewhat familiar form of ponkadliath. They all hugged and touched one another. While the Molktrons glowed in various alternating colors, the Balkiens warbled in concert with the Molktrons, which sounded very musical. The three Balkiens regained their strength sufficiently to fly up through the Molktron tunnel to the surface, which was only about twenty meters long and about thirty centimeters to a meter wide.

As they hovered towards the cave opening, the morning daylight streaming through the entrance blinded them. The three paused before emerging behind a rock outcrop only to witness some terrible blinding flashes of various colors flickering all over the cave walls. Yesl managed to contact the *Balkieston* with her radio set, which was still by the cave mouth, left there when taken in by the Molktrons. Radio communication was hard with the static generated in unison with the flashes. Captain Woozl was very glad to hear from them as they had missed two scheduled remote communication calls while with the Molktrons. Woozl reported that bright flashes were emanating from the Splogitan Peak, which was almost blinding the crew of the *Balkieston*. There were also faint sounds of thunder, which seemed strange considering the brightness of the flashes. Baingae said that as the flashes emanated from the top of the mountain, they came into a thin atmosphere at that altitude; hence, the sound was faint. As soon as the three had agreed on this reasoning, there was a sudden BOOM and roar of thunder that echoed all around the area. The flash that went with it was also blindingly bright. The three were immediately *wugged* back into the cave by the shock wave.

"It looks like we'll not be able to leave here with this storm or whatever it is going on," said Yesl, who was shaken. "We'll have to seek refuge with the Molktrons until it stops."

All three started spinning and vibrating to shake off the dust they had been thrown onto and hovered back down the tunnel, with the bright flashes beginning to dim down as they descended back to the Molktron cave. After a while, the flashes became a useful torch in what would have otherwise been poor infrared vision, for the Balkiens were able to see more into the infrared spectrum than humans. When near darkness finally enveloped them, they were relieved by the collective glow of the Molktrons with their high-pitched humming. The three Balkiens made contact anew with the Queen.

"You are back so soon," said the Queen. "You need to get away before the Enigma catches you."

"But there were terrible flashes when we got to the cave mouth. The searing brightness would have blinded us," replied Yesl. "Did you hear that boom of thunder?"

"We did," replied the Queen. "It sounds as if the Enigma is very suspicious and angry at your trespassing on this planet. He has deemed that you're not welcome here with your ship detected in orbit. Just as well, we stopped you going right up into his lair and probably being zapped out of existence or arrested and kept as his slaves. We're all slaves to the Enigma, here. You must try to leave stealthily as soon as the lightning ceases. The Enigma will run out of energy and stop this awful action at dusk. That is when you must try to go out through the forest to your ship, NOT above it."

"We'll do that," replied all three Balkiens in unison.

"We're so sorry about your position," said Yesl. "We've never come across anything that could be so cruel to others. This evil has never happened on Antrobi, where we're from, though there are ancient legends of evil encounters."

Yesl explained further about their mission to Splogita and how they had seen a unique light spectrum from this star system. Before attempting to leave for a second time, the Molktrons appealed to the Balkiens to be rescued from their suffering and enslavement one day. Yesl reassured the Queen that they'd try to do something, but that it would be many years before they could return, due to the vastness of space. After a repeat farewell ponkadliath, which was more emotional than the first, Boongoo and Baingae, led by Yesl hovered quietly up the cave to the entrance, dimly lit now in the very peaceful twilight. As they emerged from the cave, they levitated by telekinesis, just above the forest floor. They went past many incandescent little Molktrons, doing what looked like menial tasks of cleaning up unwanted weeds and plant debris off the ground, trying to make it tidy and opulent. Yesl figured that this must have been the work that they had to do as slaves. All three kept as quiet as possible moving through the deep forest of succulent, giant cactus-like plants. Their tops coalesced to form an almost sealed forest canopy, making the forest very dark in many areas. If it were not for the glow of the pearly Molktrons, darkness would have been so deep that they would have become lost. While on their way, Yesl used the locator beacon on her communication unit strapped to her body to successfully find the other two communication units belonging to Baingae and Boongoo so as not to leave any clues of their presence behind.

The night sky studded with stars had unfamiliar constellations from this position in the galaxy. It was by the starlight that Boongoo opened the door of the scout ship. Yesl, Baingae, and Boongoo took one last look around the serene Splogitan landscape, littered with groups of glowing Molktrons at the edge of the forest they had left. They entered the ship and closed the round sliding door.

"We'll take off and immediately enter the water," suggested Boongoo.

Boongoo levitated over the pilot's control panels. Dials and lights flickered as the hum of the gyro engine started up. Soon the ship lurched out of its parking position and hovered towards the water's edge, still dimly lit by starlight with a faint glow on the horizon as dusk faded into the foreboding night. No headlights were turned on to avoid being noticed by the Enigma. Suddenly there was another blinding flash, heralding the start of another outburst of the Enigma's short temper. This flash just warned Boongoo in time as it lit up a rock promontory that the ship was about to hit. Boongoo managed to avert a nasty crash, while only sustaining a minor dent on the port side. More flashes allowed Boongoo to steer clear of the rocks and lower the ship into the deep dark waters. It had been planned to put their craft down on the seabed until dawn. However, the continual flashes penetrated deep into the lake, making for excellent navigable visibility. The ship's crew was amused at the idea that the Enigma's flashings were now assisting in their departure by lighting the dark waters of the lake. They dived to about one kilometer in depth. Even at this depth, strange rounded rock formations could be seen on the lakebed while the flashes were going on. The lakebed was undulating and strewn with rounded, almost spherical boulders, where some were rougher than others, and some broken. There was also what seemed like broken bits of flat stones lying on the seabed. As they sped through the water to the far shore, the flashes grew dimmer. Boongoo reckoned that it would be safer to move up to just under the surface in case the flashing stopped thus plunging them into total darkness and danger of a seabed collision.

The flashes became less frequent then stopped suddenly. Boongoo eased the ship onto the lake's surface, above which the stars, including Vega, were visible.

Dawn broke over the tall mountain of the Enigma and the Molktrons, which was only a small black spire of rock set starkly against the brightening dawn sky. Boongoo looked ahead and began to turn the ship on the lake's surface towards the shore, avoiding the need to fly until necessary.

"This is Boongoo calling *Balkieston*." Boongoo repeatedly called three times, but to their surprise, there was no answer. Just static, louder than usual, suggesting a communication problem. Boongoo took off from the lake and began to fly just above the barren sandy desert plains. The yellowish light of Splogita's sun, Yastagil, rose to one side of the distant mountain of the Enigma. As they flew on westward away from the star's light, the mountain began to sink below the desert horizon. They hoped to remain hidden from the Enigma over the planet's horizon. As soon as Boongoo keyed in for a satellite navigational fix on their position, a significant malfunction came to light. There were no navigational readings at all. Hovering around to get a better location for signal reception was only going to waste fuel for the hoped-for return trip. Yesl was becoming concerned about these problems, especially the lack of signals, which were critical for successful navigation to the *Balkieston*.

"This is Boongoo calling *Balkieston*."

"What's happened to the satellite navigation?" asked Yesl.

"Don't know," answered Boongoo. "Perhaps our receiver antenna was damaged while we were under the water or parked on the beach. Anyone of the Enigma's lightning flashes could have knocked it out. We'll find a hiding spot to land and investigate."

Boongoo continued their flight over the desert dunes to a rocky area near a meteor crater. As the craft hovered over the edge, they noticed jagged piles of debris littering the crater floor to one side. They landed close to this debris that looked suspiciously like the wreckage of some structures, windblown and covered literally by the sands of time.

Boongoo left the craft to look at the navigational antenna on the ship's roof and found no damage, except for a small bit of something like seaweed on the antenna dish. He straightened the receiver dish by Balkien telekinesis and emergency tools; all connections checked and tested and found to be in working order. After these minor adjustments, the three Balkiens took turns to fly over the debris field, always leaving one in charge of the ship in case of any mishap. As they examined the mysterious ruins close to their craft, it became apparent that these were the scarred and tragic remains of a city that once stood here. Yesl remembered the Queen Molktron mentioning that much of the planet's civilization was cruelly destroyed when the Enigma arrived.

"This is our first encounter with anything abhorrently evil and destructive," said Yesl.

YESL – The Balkien from Antrobi

Yesl, Boongoo, and Baingae re-entered their ship and closed the airlock hatch and again tried to contact the *Balkieston* and Captain Woozl.

"This is Boongoo calling Balkieston." There was yet more static for a moment, then:

"*Balkieston* here, Woozl speaking," came over, but very crackly. "Where have you been? We've been calling you repeatedly."

"We've also been calling you, but our system had failed. We've just fixed it," replied Boongoo. "We landed in a crater just over the western shore of the lake."

"I didn't quite get all of that Boongoo. Could you repeat the—?" were Woozl's very last crackly words before total static returned. Frantic efforts to regain contact with the *Balkieston* were futile. They sat inside the cabin for the duration of one complete orbit of the *Balkieston* and tried again. There was nothing.

"Look on the brighter side," suggested Baingae.

"What brighter side?" asked Boongoo, rather gloomily, while his swooth heaved about and vibrated in his frustration.

"At least we finally made some contact with Woozl," answered Yesl, trying to calm the situation.

"It seems likely that Woozl did not pick up all of our info about our location before we were cut off," said Baingae. "Remember, he said, 'I didn't quite get all of that Boongoo. Could you repeat the—.' We could not repeat it. If Woozl missed the last bit about being west of the island, there's a large search area to look in, not to mention running the gauntlet of the Enigma."

Taking charge, Boongoo announced firmly, "I'm pilot of this ship. We fly up into the orbit of the *Balkieston*. I've calculated the *Balkieston's* orbit from the time of last communications contact, assuming that the *Balkieston* was overhead at that time."

"Your assumption is correct, we hope," argued Baingae. "Our survival is at stake here."

"This is all we have to go on," said Yesl supporting Boongoo. "We go with Boongoo or lie in this junk heap and dissolve into utter oblateness, while the *Balkieston* gets blown up by the Enigma's fireworks while searching for us."

"I guess you're right," said Baingae with some humility. Boongoo maneuvered himself over the ship's controls to start the motor for their ascent. It was disappointing to cut this two-Antrobian-year mission so short due to the terrible animosity of the planet's chief ruler, who would think nothing of blowing them and their ship into a million pieces. However, they were all so touched by their heartfelt encounter with the Molktrons and were very saddened to have to leave them in their terrible state of enslavement. It was in their best interests to depart from Splogita in one piece and let the universe know of this tyrannical regime rather than to risk annihilation leaving no warning.

With the engine running, the ship levitated slowly at first and soon picked up speed as it raced away from the crater, where they had landed, which soon became small in comparison to a myriad of others littering the planet's surface. As they had calculated, their departure was timed to coincide with the Balkieston's last known orbital position, which took them over the beautiful lake and the island, hoping that there would be no lightning flashes.

"Boongoo to Balkieston," called Boongoo on the remote communication once again. There was no reply. Boongoo repeated this call about four or five times without response. The ship flew into a matching orbit with the Balkieston's last known orbital position. The satellite navigation tracking was enabled, but no signal could be picked up. By now the small craft was critically short of fuel for this unexpected difficulty in making rendezvous with the mother ship. Also, without remote communication contact, the three Balkiens were beginning to contemplate the worst possible scenario in which they might be marooned in a decaying orbit around a strange planet.

"Where oh where is the *Balkieston*," asked Yesl, as she began to be very sad. All the Balkiens sank into their cup seats as oblateness overcame them to some degree. As they were discussing their fate, the ship once again came into orbit over the lake. From the island mount, the flashes suddenly erupted from the Enigma and came dangerously close to the ship.

As Boongoo started up the engine to take evasive action, a bolt of lightning came streaking up towards them, then BANG! There was a massive jolt, which threw anything loose, all over the cockpit. The Balkiens, strapped into their cup seats or bocklasses, were not thrown around. The lights started wavering. Warning lights lit up. Alarms wailed and beeped, and the ship began to spin violently out of control. From the windows, the planet turned around them ever faster. Boongoo's emergency training that he had practiced many times before going on the mission kicked in. First, the gyro engine was disengaged from forward-drive to slow the spinning of the ship. The gyroscope flywheels were put into reverse to counter the uncontrollable spin. Although the spinning stopped, the landing craft was now in orbital decay as it entered the planet's atmosphere.

"Boongoo," shrilled Yesl. "Can you start the engine to slow us down before we burn up on re-entry? Apart from the ship burning up, the Enigma will spot our burn trail and attack again."

"I'll try the backup engine, but fuel is low," answered Boongoo. The engine was engaged and began to spin up while the ship was turned into a reverse position so that the motor acted as a brake. While considerable speed was lost, the power and fuel were low. There was still a lot of heat generated by the friction of the air outside as the craft hurtled towards the lake. Boongoo thought to try to land at the spot from which they had taken off, reasoning that they could find refuge with the Molktrons. Boongoo attempted to guide the beleaguered craft towards the shore but was rapidly losing altitude. The waters of the lake rushed up towards them, then THUD! The ship hit the water very hard, causing considerable damage to the hull. The ovoid ship bounced and skimmed across the lake, rolling over and over as it went. The three Balkiens were dazed and very dizzy. The craft rolled up onto the beach and smashed into some rocks then crashed through the trees where it was parked before their departure. It finally bashed nose-first into a tree trunk, breaking the front cockpit before finally coming to rest. All was suddenly quiet, except for steam that was hissing off the hot hull. Yesl and Baingae immediately freed Boongoo from the wreckage, being trapped between his bocklass or cupped seat and the broken glass and debris from the final impact. The three of them sat on the mosses near their wreck, as Yastagil began to set.

"Looks like this will be our new home," said Yesl with resignation. "Our only means of escape is in smithereens, and the *Balkieston* seems to have disappeared altogether."

"I sure hope that our mother ship is okay," said Baingae with more than a little concern. "I'm sure that Captain Woozl will come looking for us. At least we managed to crash land close to a previously known position."

As the Yastagil-set gave way to twilight, they could see a faint glow appearing in the forest. It was from the Molktrons. As before, the three let themselves be carried into the woods by the little rolling pearly beings. They were too battered and shaken to fly unaided or to find their way back to the Queen Molktron's cave. All three Balkiens passed through the now-familiar cave entrance. It was as if they'd just gone for a sortie and coming back after a day's adventure. It was hard to believe that when they left the previous night that they'd begun their long voyage back to Antrobi. They hoped that a rescue craft would be dispatched to look for them, as all remote communication had stopped.

As they were carried down the cave passage into the warm glow of the cavern illuminated by the Queen Molktron in all her colors, she began to sing her greetings in her musical high warble notes. Amid the happy greetings, there were two dimly illuminated apparitions on the other side of the Queen being attended to by many worker Molktrons. Yesl had to focus a little to be sure, but it was indeed Woozl. It was also hard to mistake the *Balkieston's* acting communications officer, Moonzl. Moonzl was about the same size as Yesl and had very soft swooth in shades of green and dark red, with a slate grey equator and white poles, like Yesl. The Molktrons were also tending Smalkle and Smoonkshie.

Smoonkshie was larger than Boongoo but smaller than Yesl and was a little prolate; taller and slimmer. He had a royal blue equator with almost rainbow color banding, culminating in deep purple at the poles. Smalkle was similar in appearance, but was just a little smaller than Smoonkshie, with a rainbow-like range of color bands, except that his equatorial band was indigo.

"Yesl, Baingae and Boongoo!" piped up both Woozl and Smalkle. "We've been looking all over for you since our remote communications went down. You have done the sensible thing to return to your last known position in this event of separation. Is your ship parked back in the same spot as before?"

Yesl's swooth kind of fell flat to indicate the reality of the situation as she said with resignation, "Yes we are in the same spot, but we've crashed. The scout ship's wrecked. We were shot down by the Enigma with a long bolt of lightning while looking for the *Balkieston* in orbit over here. We couldn't find you. We tried to take evasive action when the lightning started up, but as we were low on fuel, we were in extreme danger."

"So that was the awful bang we heard, thinking it was a loud peal of thunder," said Woozl.

"We'll have to stay here for now," announced Woozl calmly. "The Enigma's going to know all about us after that smash which I'm sure would have shaken the whole island. Our rescue ship is on the other side of the lake. We landed in your other landing spot by the ruined city, where your last remote communication was made. Pity we missed you, but we don't know by how long. The reason for our loss of contact has been that the Enigma's lightning attacks have destroyed at least two of our four navigation and communication satellites. The other two seemed to have been struck and thrown into useless highly elliptical orbits. The Balkieston is now in orbit around the main planet, Spoonkathtil, well away from any potential attacks. Smoonkshie and Smalkle are in charge of the rescue scout ship. We'll need to recover as much data and supplies as we can from the wreck. I realize that carrying a lot of valuable equipment across the lake by ourselves is not going to be easy. We're not going back to Antrobi, without our valuable images, data, and evidence of what's going on here."

"Woozl," suggested Baingae. "Why don't the two of you fly back to your ship and come back in the ship, underwater, as we did and surface on the beach near the wreck, to pick up our supplies and equipment?"

"Good idea, but maybe too risky," replied Woozl. "On the other hand, all of us flying across the lake with our bits and pieces aren't a great idea either." After some debate in the cave, in Antrobian warble high notes, the decision to go underwater in the rescue ship was made.

All seven of the Balkiens remained in the Molktron cave for about seven Splogitan days, before Woozl and Moonzl flew back across the lake to their ship. Boongoo, Smoonkshie, Smalkle, and Baingae went back to the wreck to salvage their data spheres and equipment. Yesl remained with the Molktrons and kept in regular remote contact with Boongoo and Woozl in case of any mishap. As before the rescue ship traveled deep down in the lake and surfaced on the beach near the wreck where Boongoo and Baingae waited with the salvaged items. While this was being quickly loaded aboard for their final departure, all seven of the Balkiens, Yesl, Woozl, Moonzl, Boongoo, Baingae, Smoonkshie, and Smalkle, had one last farewell ponkadliath with the Queen Molktron and the many worker Molktrons. There was again strong emotion in this ponkadliath. Woozl sensed that the Molktrons were desperate to be released from the onerous tyranny of the evil one inside the mountain. In their singing languages, the Queen exchanged a lot with Woozl, Yesl, and the others. One of the data spheres was brought into the cave to record these conversations about what was inside the mountain and the history of the planet, including its recent tragedies.

The appointed worker Molktrons carried the seven back to their ship at night to avoid the gaze of the Enigma. All boarded the ship, closed the door, started their engine, and taxied slowly down the beach and slipped into the water by the light of the nearby Jupiter-like planet, Spoonkathtil, in the western sky, which was now in opposition to Yastagil. Splogita was the largest of seven moons of this planet. The light from Spoonkathtil was much brighter than Moonlight on Earth. The Molktrons, including the Queen, who rarely ventured outside her cave, looked on with great hope of liberation, from the edge of the forest.

Once the Balkien ship was gone, they looked over the wreck of the Balkiens' first ship, where they left some workers to guard it and rolled through the woods back to their cave. The Queen illuminated the succulent cactus-like trees of the forest with her slowly varying bright colors, singing soprano tunes all the way.

The rescue ship traveled in darkness underwater and surfaced on the other side and taxied over the hardened wilderness on its undercarriage. Their craft took off into the night and straight across to Spoonkathtil without even one orbit of Splogita, which would have been a good farewell gesture to the Molktrons but was considered too risky. Retrieval of the two remaining navigation satellites was abandoned for the same reasons, leaving them with insufficient navigation equipment for future exploration, except to go straight home. The scout ship finally entered the *Balkieston's* cargo bay and was securely fastened. There was another emotional ponkadliath among all the crew, who were very thankful that all had returned and were only minus one scout ship and the four navigation satellites, with no lives lost. Their association with the Molktrons enriched their lives.

They started up the main engines to begin on their long voyage back to Antrobi. As the Balkieston picked up speed, it was not long before the planet Spoonkathtil slipped away beneath them, relative to the generated artificial gravity. Splogita was now only a speck next to Spoonkathtil. Some of the Balkien crew saw rapid variations in brightness on Splogita. They surmised that these were more bolts of lightning emanating from the Enigma. After a few days, the star Yastagil grew fainter with the three gas-giant planets appearing only as dots. Soon, Splogita was no longer visible to the Balkiens without the aid of a telescope. Yastagil's red dwarf companion star could be seen through the port-hole windows in the starboard side of the ship as they sped off into the deep cosmos.

"Run a check on our course, Boongoo," ordered Captain Woozl. "Those images on the view screen don't look right. The star we are heading towards seems a little on the yellow side for Vega and is too round."

"The calculated course seems to be correct," replied Boongoo.

"Did you double-check our universal heading after departure from Planet Splogita?" asked Baingae.

"Yes, I did," replied Boongoo. "Here are the calculations on the screen."

After a pause, while perusing the sizeable circular viewing monitor screen, filled with Antrobian symbols for numbers, Woozl hovered over to the pentagonal front window of the ship's bridge. The Balkieston had now slowed to interplanetary speed and was on her final approach to her destination.

"Oh, we're so looking forward to being back in our homely mooties in Balkieston," said Yesl.

"And I sure hope that Winxl's awoken out of her long recovery sleep," sighed Baingae.

"Have a closer look at the filtered image of our star Qualkambi (Vega) on the view-screen," said Woozl.

"The image on the screen seems a lot rounder and yellower than Qualkambi," said Yesl.

"Then how are you so sure about your navigation coordinates, Boongoo?" asked Woozl.

"I can support Boongoo's work," said Baingae. "I triple-checked these figures on the ship's computer and ran several simulations of our trajectory after we got out of range of the Enigma's lightning bolts that were striking our ship."

"I've run a spectral analysis on the star we're heading for," said Smalkle.

"You mean Qualkambi," said Smoonkshie.

"The results of the analysis will amaze you," said Smalkle. "Have a look at these two spectrograms side by side on the screen."

All the Balkiens hovered from their various posts around the bridge, which was a large hexagonal room full of blinking lights and rounded screens displaying images of stars in space and navigation trajectories.

"The image on the left is that of Segunthtil (Sun) from our records from Antrobi," said Smalkle. "The one on the right has just been taken of the star in front of us; remarkably similar! We have also taken spectral analyses of Segunthtil's planets that are now plain to view. The planets that we assume to be Antrobi and Antrogi that we head towards on our present course look a lot like Tombalki (Earth) and Tomkil (Moon) from their spectra and different sizes too. What we thought was Spalminkatrix behind us is Boonkle-Mallkis (Jupiter). The spectrogram of this gas giant is a little different from the library spectrogram measured from Antrobi on our long-range spectroscopes. That reddening may be due to that great ovoid spot among the colored bands on that gas planet's surface. Have a look."

There was silence as all the Balkien crew gazed at the findings and then out of the pentagonal window toward the still distant bright yellowish star. To the left, there were two distinct bright points of light. Very close to the bright bluish one was a fainter point.

Just then a massive slowly turning rock came rushing toward the ship and raced past on the starboard side; then another to the port. Then three smaller tumbling boulders whooshed past.

"Asteroids!" exclaimed Captain Woozl. "Everyone to your positions. Take evasive action!"

Several smaller rocks whizzed past.

"WE'RE SURE TO BE HIT BY ONE OF THESE!" exclaimed Boongoo.

BANG!

There was then another crunch and the sound of screeching metal and breaking glass.

"PREPARE THE LIFE PODS!" shouted Woozl as he wavered over the colored controls to begin copying all the ship's latest data into the data spheres on the life pods.

There was a frenzied scramble of Balkiens flying to and fro and off the bridge into the small rounded rooms to the side. Then an enormous asteroid the size of a large city whizzed past bashing off the spheres to the starboard. The whole ship started to revolve at about one turn every fifteen seconds.

"OUR ENGINES ARE HIT!" shouted Boongoo.

"ABANDON SHIP!" ordered Woozl. "WE'LL NOT SLOW DOWN ENOUGH! We'll hit Tombalki with enormous speed and burn up."

The Balkiens raced into the life pods. There were yet more crashes and bangs as rocks hit the struts of the ship. One hit one of the engine spheres. It exploded with a blinding flash and a deafening bang. Pieces punctured the struts holding the spherical modules together. The emergency airlock doors leading onto the bridge and those of the life pods slammed shut with tremendous force trapping any Balkiens who may not have evacuated in time. For them, it was now too late.

More rocks pounded the stricken vessel. With each hit, more pieces got broken off. The ship began to break up completely.

Almost as suddenly as the meteoric rocks appeared, they stopped, and space was clear again, but the damage was done. The *Balkieston* was a wreck.

The small round doors of two of the escape pods containing Captain Woozl, Smoonkshie, and Smalkle in one and Yesl, Boongoo, and Baingae in the other slid open again. They came back onto the bridge, which was still pressurized, though a lot of air was lost before the access doors closed to seal in what remained of this once mighty ship. All six of these Balkiens hovered around the controls and ran tests on what could still operate. Looking out of the pentagonal window in front of them, they could see thousands of bits of their shattered ship floating around in space. There were individual hexagonal and pentagonal panels, which were barely recognizable from their jagged edges along with a myriad of tiny floating fragments like dust glinting in the light from Segunthtil.

The Balkiens floated around aimlessly in a state of shock around the only pressurized section of the ship, being the bridge.

"The rest of the crew should all remain in their escape pods and be ready to separate when ordered to do so," commanded Woozl. "I presume that all engine units are out."

"All interstellar ones are," replied Boongoo.

"Then our return to Antrobi is not possible," said Woozl.

"What about our life support systems?" asked Yesl.

"Other than what is on the bridge - none," answered Spoonxl.

"Then we have no alternative but to end this mission on Tombalki ahead of us," said Woozl. "We have to make landfall there if we're to survive as a crew and hope that a Balkien rescue ship will look for us. At this speed, it will take about two hundred and fifty days to reach Tombalki. Our life support systems can only last about twenty."

"Woozl," asked Spoonxl, "what about the small gyro engines in this bridge section, used to lift it off from Antrobi for attachment to the rest of the ship? We can use them to quicken our speed toward Tombalki."

"Then we must do so," said Woozl.

"How much of the ship is left?" asked Yesl.

"This bridge sphere and the three spheres attached immediately behind us, which are badly damaged," said Woozl. "There are bits of the struts remaining on these, but the rest of the ship is in fragments."

The emergency engines were revved up using power backup from the remaining spheres, still attached. What remained of the Balkieston started to accelerate towards Tombalki and Tomkil hoping that these worlds would be suitable for their settlement or to await a rescue mission from Antrobi. Out of one of the side portholes, which only had a few scratches from the meteoric impacts, the Balkiens could see a thin gossamer-like line stretching right across space seeming to cut the gas planet, Boonkle-Mallkis (Jupiter) in half along its equator.

"What we may be seeing is a huge ring of tiny asteroids orbiting right around Segunthtil (the sun)," said Woozl. "Similar to the rings around this system's smaller gas planet, Seluncus (Saturn), further out than Boonkle-Mallkis. There are no such asteroids between the orbits of Antrobi and Spalminkatrix; hence, this accident."

"What happened to our navigation?" asked Baingae with alarm. Both Boongoo and I had double-checked the figures, and they were correct."

"What about that last bolt of lightning that just struck our rearmost spheres as we were accelerating away from Splogita towards Spoonkathtil, when we lost contact with Boongoo on the scout ship before it crashed?" suggested Smalkle. "There was quite a loud thud and a deep rumble coming from the back, and the whole ship jolted quite badly. Then there were quite a few smaller flashes that distracted us."

"And we never ran checks on all our systems at the time," said Yesl.

A week later Tombalki and Tomkil were much closer as the last remaining vestige of the *Balkieston* was decelerating on her auxiliary engines to place the ship in a parking orbit of Tombalki. Captain Woozl steered the stricken vessel towards this planet with continents, oceans, and cloud formations appearing to be a lot bluer than the purple hues of Antrobi. He knew that this was not Antrobi as the other body of this double planet, Antrogi, had shrunk drastically and had the appearance of a dead airless moon similar to, but appearing larger than Antrobi's outermost moon, Boonkpolm.

Suddenly there was a big bang followed by a horrible screeching noise from one of the engine compartments. Smoke started billowing through the doors of this chamber at the rear of the bridge. Due to this malfunction, the remaining three engines were no longer balanced, and the disk of Tombalki started to revolve around the ship at increasing speed. "We must abandon ship NOW!" shouted Woozl. "EVERYONE TO THEIR PODS, HURRY!"

More grindings and groaning came from the back of the bridge. As all the crew raced into their assigned life pods, the doors of these slammed shut. The blackness of space started to turn orange, followed by a tremendous roar. There were explosions outside as the remaining struts holding the three other spheres broke away and began to burn up with the intense heat of atmospheric re-entry.

"Pull the pod release mechanism!" hollered Yesl. "We're burning up."

"I can't!" said Boongoo with fear in his voice. "WE'RE ALL GOING TO BURN UP. THE RELEASE MECHANISM'S JAMMED."

As the bridge section roared through the Earth's atmosphere, it heated up, causing the release bolts for the life pods to weld to the life pod davits. Though the bridge sphere was getting very hot, it had been built to withstand this sort of re-entry, but some of the systems onboard started to emit thick smoke and blow up in small explosions and blue flashes.

The pod that Yesl was in came right across the ocean, which raced up towards it. Then there was blackness.

• ◯ •

6 ~ SECRETS REVEALED

Kara and Sean looked out of the window of their plane as it was landing over the water at the end of the runway at Altaness Aerodrome. There was a warm reception committee led by Uncle Herbert, Matt, and Kaz next to the apron on that pleasant sunny if breezy afternoon. Auntie Wendy, Alison, and young Judith stayed at home in Kinrasaig as there was not enough room for everyone in the old Moggy. The drive to Kinrasaig past the island's beautiful sandy beach was welcoming to Kara and Sean as they were very excited about going to Mt Tetraval to look for more remains of the Balkieston. At dinner, Auntie Wendy served a delicious roast steak. Uncle Herbert started the conversation with all six of the children with the Balkiens sitting on various perches around the room, including the piano.

"I'm sure that both of you had a great flight up here," said Uncle Herbert in his natural extrovert and pleasant tone. "Also, it is great to see you all from so far away in our galaxy. A warm welcome to you, Yesl, Baingae, and who is this one?" Uncle Herbert continued as he pointed to Boongoo, who was rolling along the piano keys with sufficient pressure to play some music akin to playing the scale.

"That's Boongoo," answered Matt. "He was still in his coma last week. We certainly had some dramas with him when he woke up and flew all the way back over to the mainland before Yesl and Baingae caught up with him."

Boongoo started to roll along the piano keys in a more organized sequence and played a meaningful tune.

"Balkien music!" exclaimed Alison. "We'll have to have a jamming session later."

"Welcome, also, for their first visit, Kara and Sean," said Uncle Herbert. "I'm sure you're all eager to get down to Tetraval and look for more of your spaceship. Though the military presence is all but gone, they still have a watchman camped on the Machair in a dark green tent with his Land Rover parked outside. He'll have a radio and a mobile phone to summon patrols if he observes anything suspicious. It may be best to let Yesl and Boongoo go by themselves for now. There was a great deal of military activity around here. There was a lot of resentment from us crofters as we could not get access to our sheep due to the restrictions on our common grazing. We wrote letters to the papers and our MP. The strange thing is that some of our sheep seemed to have circular gaps in their fleeces as if the wool had been cut out. We'll see what happens at the sheep shearing gathering next week. That'll be your opportunity to look over the hill without arousing any suspicion."

"I guess that's a great idea," answered Matt, "but I still can't wait to resume the search."

"I don't suppose that anyone's caught on to the possibility that the main wreck of the *Balkieston* will be somewhere out there in the depths of the North Atlantic," said Yesl.

"You mean a sunken space wreck way out to sea," remarked Kaz in excitement.

"Kaz," said Uncle Herbert. "You've got to remember that there's often a great human tragedy involved in such disasters. Look at the 1500 people or so who drowned in a ghastly cold North Atlantic when the Titanic sank in 1912. So, what about the Balkieston, all the way from its home planet crashing so violently into the same ocean as the Titanic? Here's Yesl, Boongoo, and Baingae who may be the only survivors, who may have lost the rest of their crew, including Captain Woozl."

"I know that Baingae has been mourning the total separation from his beloved Winxl, asleep in hibernation on Antrobi with his means of ever seeing her again lying probably two or three miles down in the darkness of the deep," commented Matt, "and maybe shattered to pieces on hitting the ocean."

Auntie Wendy brought out her exceptional home-made broth with slices of freshly baked bread. The compelling discussion faded into the sounds of the clinking of spoons on the soup bowls. In the background, Boongoo and Baingae were beginning to compose a duet on the piano. Their style of playing was out of this world.

Kaz, meanwhile, thought about his father's words about the shipwrecks, wondering if any other Balkiens had survived. Perhaps they were lying on beaches or on the moors waiting to be found and revived.

"There's only one way to find out," suggested Yesl as she nodded while sitting on the top of the piano. "We'll have to go and explore the area to see if there are any others around."

"Perhaps there are more of them *for sale* at MacKay's shop," suggested Matt wistfully.

"Every week since you told me to look out for more of these balls, Matt," said Uncle Herbert, "I've gone to MacKay's to get the groceries and seen no other *pom-poms* on his shelves, except for one. Knowing you were coming up, Kara and Sean, I *bought* it at the shop on the way to meet you at the airport today."

"I'd like to see this one," said Matt excitedly.

Just before dessert, Matt went upstairs to his assigned room with Yesl, Baingae, and Boongoo on his shoulders in ponkadliath. He came to his bed and was startled on the sight of an apparition on his bed, which at first looked like a human figure lying asleep. On closer inspection, Matt recognized his jeans, white socks, sneakers, and his Fair Isle patterned woolen jersey. The *head* was, in fact, the newly acquired Balkien on his pillow. The room, partly built into the roof space of the house with sloping walls, covered with light blue wallpaper with flowery patterns and a small dormer window, which looked out on the front grassy area of the landholding. It was now dusk, and the hill in the distance, silhouetted against the darker clear evening sky with Venus shining brightly.

"Moonzl," called Yesl, first in Antrobian, then in English. All three hovered to huddle up to their fourth known survivor, who had descended to Splogita in the rescue ship and was there to greet them in the cave of the Molktrons.

"So, what's with the *manikin* on my bed?" inquired Matt with an air of surprise. "It must have been Auntie Wendy's idea."

"Dessert's up," called Auntie Wendy from downstairs.

"You go to your strawberries-and-cream pudding, Matt," said Yesl. "We'll look after Moonzl until he awakes. He was on a different pod from that of Boongoo and Baingae."

Moonzl had a somewhat different appearance to the other Balkiens. Like Yesl, he had a slate grey equatorial band and white-polar regions. Moonzl's mid-latitudinal swooth consisted of varying shades of green and dark red. His unusual feature was that his swooth was fluffier than that of the others. The closest resemblance was Mohair wool.

The next morning, Matt awoke to a clear blue sky with the low sunlight streaming through the window, between the curtains onto the far wall. His familiar Balkiens were rolling about the bedclothes, but Moonzl was as still as ever. As Matt stroked him, he noticed a more distinct shimmering effervescence on his swooth. On seeing this, Yesl came over to hold onto Moonzl.

"Moonzl is of a different race of Balkiens in our planetary system from any of us," explained Yesl. "He is from our closest satellite, Angapooka. He was resourceful in locating us on Splogita when the Enigma knocked out our navigation satellites."

Moonzl started pulsating on the bed. Yesl began to communicate with him in his singing language. Moonzl bounced up about two feet into the air and started flying around the room. Unlike the previous occasions, Moonzl landed gracefully beside Boongoo, now perched on a corner of an oak chest of drawers with a dressing mirror on top and settled there. All four of the Balkiens sang and warbled to Moonzl for about ten minutes.

"Moonzl is explaining that he last remembered slamming into a cliff face near the summit of a hill in the thick mist before waking up just now," said Yesl. "Maybe that was somewhere on Tetraval. He was caught up in the mists while on his way back to their cave on the other side of Tetraval. There are another two crew members of the *Balkieston* hiding out there. He is very concerned about what they will be doing in searching for her, as she will have been deemed missing for over two weeks now. We guess that Moonzl was found in his comatose state on the hill pastures and brought to Mackay's shop for his pom-pom souvenir stock. He needs to return right away over to the sea cave on Rhannaig Point to make contact with the others. We're saying that Moonzl is not yet fit to fly by himself nor should we carry him and try to look for this cave. We've no idea where this is."

"Wait a minute," suggested Matt with confidence. "I think I know of this cave. I've seen it on a previous walk. Uncle Herbert was there on his last sheep roundup for the shearing last year. He missed the lamming season roundup as the result of Captain Cammins' edicts. Maybe we could walk over there and carry you all in our knapsacks to avoid any suspicion of the Army watchman."

Perhaps it was just as well that the next two days were miserable and wet, though this was very frustrating for all six children, who were excited about going walking to Rhannaig Point to return Moonzl to the cave. Their first day was spent playing Monopoly downstairs, while all the Balkiens remained on Matt's bed upstairs attending to Moonzl's recovery. Dr. Baingae was able to massage his swooth to coax his healing telekinetically.

Matt was not faring well on the Monopoly board. He had just landed on Piccadilly with a hotel on it, owned by Alison, and dropped out of the game two moves later. After paying out his last monies to the bank and Alison and turning in his battleship token, Matt went upstairs to the more critical matters, regarding Moonzl. He saw on the dark blue bed cover a ponkadliath in progress with Moonzl surrounded by Yesl, Boongoo, and Baingae.

"Come and join us," said Yesl. "Moonzl would like to meet with you more."

"And why not?" asked Matt with a smile on his relaxed face.

"You cheated," Judith could be heard shouting from downstairs. "The dice would have rolled to a four if it hadn't landed on the edge of the board, not a six!"

"It would have been a four!" shouted Alison.

"Now kids," shouted Uncle Herbert sternly, "if you don't stop that fighting immediately, I shall take that game back to the shop. I know its bucketing rain today. I'm sure that the weather will be better tomorrow, so don't set a bad example for our Antrobian guests."

Moonzl seemed a lot more colorful and in a strange way, radiant. He seemed to have a faint glow about him in the dimly lit room on this dismally wet day, with drizzle and a misty leaden sky. Matt began to stroke the other Balkiens and passed his boyish hand over Moonzl. As he did so, he could sense a very gentle tingling emanating from Moonzl's swooth onto the palm of his hand. It was charming and gave him a sense of wellbeing.

"Moonzl's giving me a little tingle just now," he said.

"That must be his beginning to release his pent-up energy as he is beginning to heal," commented Dr. Baingae as his swooth moved over his spherical surface, to make the Antrobian equivalent of facial expression.

"Hello, Matt," was Moonzl's first words in English.

"Hello, Moonzl," greeted Matt gladly. Moonzl continued some conversation in Antrobian with the others.

Two days later, Matt finally awoke to a bright sunny morning. At last, it was going to be possible to walk to the cave and deliver Moonzl although he was much better now. After a hearty breakfast with Auntie Wendy's home laid boiled eggs, everyone went down to the back of the croft behind the cowshed with the Balkiens. Moonzl was set down upon a stone wall. He started to hover rather unsteadily at first, raising himself off the stones. Boongoo and Baingae flanked on either side of him in case he *wugged*. He managed to fly over to the other side of the field and then lost strength and landed, narrowly missing a puddle of water. Boongoo and Baingae brought her up to rest.

"Moonzl is not yet up to his old self yet," said Matt firmly.

"Guess we'll have to walk there ourselves," said Kaz in agreement. "We can take the southern route, avoiding the watchman's tent. If we encounter him, we could let the Balkiens out of our knapsacks to hide."

All six of them set off with packed lunches, with the Balkiens distributed amongst them in their knapsacks. They walked along the dirt road and then onto narrow tracks made by the sheep and then along the steep southern slopes of Mt Tetraval. The afternoon was bright and sunny, with small fluffy clouds scurrying in the oncoming sea breeze. The scents of the Highland heather filled their nostrils, as they progressed along the purple and green pastures. On getting closer to the cave, Alison and Judith said they would stop for their sandwiches. As they found a suitable spot and settled down to eat, some sheep came up to them with curious looks on their faces.

"Matt," said Judith, "do you see something strange about that sheep's fleece?"

"Yes, I do," answered Matt with curiosity.

"I do too," said Kaz. "It looks like a neat circle cut from its back."

"Look, there's another one," said Alison. "That one's got one large circle and some smaller ones around it."

"Looks awfully like those strange crop circles in the cornfields of Southern England, a few years ago. Don't they?" suggested Matt. "Very odd, I'm sure that's a new form of identifying the sheep. We'll ask Uncle Herbert tonight about it."

Sean, who had Boongoo in his knapsack and Kara who had Baingae in hers, looked in their packs for their drinks of juice and to check that all was okay with their charges. Boongoo and Baingae flew on ahead a little to see if the hillside was safer for them. They came back to say that they could see the cave, but that they were on ended at an almost vertical cliff face, which would necessitate ascending right up the hill to avoid it safely.

After finishing their lunch, they continued climbing up the hill before walking along the steeper higher slopes towards Rhannaig Point and the cave, which was hardly the safest route to take, but it was expedient to avoid undue attention from the watchman. Suddenly Judith slipped and began to roll down the heathery slope towards the steep drop below. Screaming for help, she broke her fall by grabbing onto some heather stems.

"I can't hold on much longer," she shouted.

All members of the party threw off their knapsacks. As they did so, all four Balkiens squeezed out of them. Yesl, Baingae, Boongoo, and Moonzl flew down to Judith's aid and held onto her by telekinesis.

"Judith!" shouted Yesl in her high-pitched voice, "try to climb up, and holding onto the heather. We'll hold onto you." All four Balkiens started to emit much louder hovering sounds while holding to a terrified Judith as she slowly climbed up the steep slope to safety. After about five minutes of this, Judith finally reached close enough for Matt to take hold of her hand, just as the Balkiens' strength was giving out.

"Judith," asked Matt with great concern, "are you okay? That was a frighteningly close call! What happened?"

"I think I just slipped on some loose stones," replied Judith with a very shaky voice, almost crying.

"Maybe we'd better go straight back to the house and come another day," suggested Matt, taking charge. "That was a very serious near miss! Well done, Balkiens for your rescue!"

"We've dealt with worse than this before on Splogita," replied Yesl. "Still it was just as well it was Judith, your youngest member. Any other one of you may have been too heavy for us Balkiens to handle."

"So, do we proceed or turn back?" asked Sean. "We dare not risk being out too far from home late at night. We'll have every helicopter in the Baraignsay area out looking for us, and it'll be all over the papers."

"Listen," said Matt, "it is half-past two. It's early July with sundown at around ten o'clock. If we're brisk, we'll be back by seven. It will be best if we climb up until we get to gentler slopes, then head westward down to Rhannaig Point. We're now well past our friend in the green tent. I'm sure he won't be tromping all over this hill every day. We're now risking our lives excessively in trying to avoid being discovered."

Moonzl spoke out for the first time in English, "We must not have our camp in the cave discovered by your authorities."

"Still," continued Matt, "we can't risk a life-threatening incident like that occurring again."

The party continued to climb to a safer slope and then descended via a safer route to the cave. As they came over a ridge, there it was, a large darkened sea cave set in a craggy sea cliff with the waves of the sea breaking and crashing on the rocks below. It looked as if there was no way that everyone was going to descend into it and be home by seven in time for tea. They all sat down in the heather and looked out across the rocky inlet to the cliff on the other side. Presently, two tiny dots could be seen flying towards the cave out of the clear blue sky over towards Scarivanish village. By now, all four Balkiens were sitting on the heather beside the six children.

"Those are Smoonkthil and Bonkatu presumably out looking for me," said Moonzl.

Moonzl lifted off the heather, hovering more confidently than he did back at the house and began to fly across the chasm, separating them and the cave.

"Moonzl," called Yesl in Antrobian, "don't *wug* into the sea!"

With that, Yesl and Boongoo followed after Moonzl to see to her safe passage across to the cave. Baingae stayed with everyone on the bank. They all waited for ages for Yesl and Boongoo to come back, but alas there was no sign of them until a quarter to five.

"We'll need to head back," said Kaz, "before it is too late."

"Yesl and Boongoo have not returned yet," said Matt. "However, you're right. Baingae, could you go over there and tell the others that we have to head back to Kinrasaig now?"

"Okay," said Baingae in his unique Balkien tone. "I'll fly over to tell them of your departure and come back to join you."

"I've got a better idea," suggested Kaz in his confident way, "a much better idea. Why don't you wait there with Yesl and Boongoo and come back later? You know where Kinrasaig is. We could go back by the easier northern route that passes closer to the green tent. Best not to have any Balkiens on us in case we're stopped and searched. We've now delivered Moonzl."

"Okay Baingae," said Matt, "we'll see you all later with your news about Smoonkthil and Bonkatu. I expect you have a lot to discuss. Maybe see you all tomorrow if not tonight."

With that, Baingae took off across the chasm. Matt fetched his binoculars and focused on the interior of the cave. He could see Baingae as a tiny greenish-brown orb moving towards the cave entrance. As Baingae slowed down to land on the cave floor, he could make out Yesl, Moonzl, and Boongoo. There were also another two slightly larger Balkiens next to them. Their colors were a combination of crimson and light orange, which he presumed were Smoonkthil and Bonkatu. Everyone arose and set off on the long trek back to Kinrasaig. They took one last look at the cave as they passed over a ridge and trudged on through the thick heather across the often-boggy moorland. After an hour, the sunset and dusk descended looking darker over to the east where everyone could see the village lights of Kinrasaig.

"Ah well, not so long now," said Matt with relief. Within about one hundred paces of the gate that opens out onto the Machair, the six were accosted by the watchman while on his return to his tent.

"Good evening," he greeted. "What might you kids be doing out here as late as this? You should be at home by the fireside with your folks watching TV or something."

"We've just been out for a walk," answered Matt confidently.

"We sure had a good day out after all that rain," added Kaz.

"Is that so?" asked the watchman inquisitively, "and I suppose that's ALL you were doing - just plain old walking - not chasing any sheep or cutting any more *wool circles* on their backs like those crop circles in Wiltshire. I believe they're human-made. Haven't you seen the sheep yet?"

"Ah, yes we have," replied Matt. The others began to giggle with a little innocence. "We saw one or two with the circles thinking that they were a new method of identification."

"Identifying them? You do have some inventive imagination," exclaimed the watchman. "One of my jobs has been to track down any perpetrators of this insidious menace. The other is to patrol this area to check that there is no illegal trespassing as this has been a restricted area until recently. I'll have to search you all and your luggage to prove that you have no possible equipment with which to cut these wool circles into the sheep's fleeces. So. Off with your bags! Nice and easy now."

Everyone complied. Each bag was opened and rigorously searched. It was like being at airport security screening in the middle of the sandy Machair with not a plane in sight. Knapsacks and lunch boxes were turned out and opened. They also had to submit to frisk searches before being allowed to repack their bags and continue home.

"It seems that you were 'just' walking. I'm Lieutenant Evans receiving orders from Captain Cammins back at Aldermaston. Who might you be?"

"I'm Matt; these are Kara and Sean, my sister and brother and cousins, Kaz, Alison, and Judith who live here in the village."

"Well, hurry off home now," ordered Lieutenant Evans. "Your Uncle Herbert will be looking for you by now. It's nearly dark."

"That certainly was a close call," said Matt as they walked up through the village street.

"Obviously," began Kaz, "Lieutenant Evans knows we're at Uncle Herbert's. I'm sure he'll report back to Captain Cammins, and they'll put two and two together."

"I know," said Matt. "It's an encounter we could have avoided. Only we couldn't risk passage over near that precipice at such a late hour after the incident with Judith. You know I don't think she would still be here if it weren't for the help of Yesl, Boongoo, and Baingae together. We all owe our lives to those humble little *pom-poms*. Judith began to shed some tears, realizing what a near-miss it was. Matt put his arms around her to reassure her.

"I sure would love to have the Balkiens with me in bed tonight," she sobbed as they walked up to the house at last in the dusk. As they approached the back-kitchen door, they could smell Auntie Wendy's cooking. There were also three distinct Balkien flying sounds coming up over the roof of the cowshed. They alighted on their shoulders as they entered the house.

"You're home so late?" inquired Uncle Herbert. "We were beginning to worry about you. I hate to say it, but I was about to call up Lieutenant Evans to go and look for you."

"Actually," replied Matt, "we were stopped by him at the Machair gate. He kept us for over half-an-hour, searching our bags and asking numerous questions about our walk and markings on many of the sheep. We saw some of the sheep on the hill with what resembled *crop circles* on their wool. I had assumed that they were for identifying the sheep."

"Oh, nothing of the sort," said Uncle Herbert. "I've heard a little about these, but we still use only combinations of blue and red dye to mark our sheep; no cutting out of circles or anything like that."

"And we were searched because under suspicion of being guilty of cutting such circles in the sheep's fleece."

"You'd all better have your dinner before it gets cold," said Auntie Wendy.

"So, tomorrow is the sheep shearing gathering," said Uncle Herbert. "We will soon find out about these strange fleece circles. I'm sure that there must be some pranksters about."

That night the Balkiens went to cuddle up to Judith for a ponkadliath with her in bed as promised. They soothed her to sleep with their fine swooth. She had the most remarkable dreams about Antrobi.

After breakfast the next day, everyone set out with Uncle Herbert leading the way with his sheepdog towards Mt Tetraval. It was great to see the sun shining over the countryside, which had a wet sheen after the recent rain. The villagers were also making their way to the day's sheep gathering.

"Hello, Angus," greeted Uncle Herbert. "It sure is a fine day for the shearing."

"Och ay, it certainly is," replied Angus in his Hebridean accent, which was not dissimilar to an Irish accent. "It'll be a great day for shearing. I'm sure that we'll harvest some good wool for the Baraignsay weavers today."

"I hope that not too many of the sheep will have these small wool circles cut out of their wool. My nephew Matt and all the kids here said that they saw some of the animals with these circles on their fleece."

"Is that so? Och well, I'm sure it won't be too much of a problem by the time the fleece is washed and spun into yarn for the weavers. I've heard some reports about the wool circles, and hello to all of you young fellas. Are you having a great holiday away from the mainland?"

Uncle Herbert and Angus and all the children came walking past Lieutenant Evans who was at the gate leading onto the Machair, watching everyone walking towards the sheep pens followed by their two black sheep collie dogs. By now, there was quite a procession of the village folk, mostly the men and their sons wearing their old rugged clothing with well-worn dark jackets and cloth caps, carrying shears and old sacks for the wool. They walked along the sandy dirt road, which wound its way through the short green grass, with beautifully colored wildflowers. Though it was sunny with a clear blue sky, the wind was getting up a little. As yet, no one had told Angus Mackay about the true identity of the *pom-poms* in his shop.

"I'm sorry that there have been no other wooly balls for sale in my shop lately," he said. "I just sold you my last one last week. I did, however, sell three of them in the middle of May to a couple and their three children. Och ay, I think they were from somewhere in America. Oh, let me see, I think it was Arizona. Ah yes, I remember them talking about being from Tucson or somewhere like that."

Matt suddenly felt dismayed at the thought of three of the *Balkieston's* crew being taken away to a distant land in an unconscious state, thinking that he should tell Yesl and the others.

"Could you tell me what they looked like?" Matt asked Angus.

"I don't remember," replied Angus. "I seem to recollect that they had a few pinkish bands mixed with some shades of light green. One had mostly a few shades of blue. Oh, the three children were delighted with them. I remember the eldest daughter was taken with the bluish one about the same size as the first one your mother bought for you, Matt. The name Erin rings in my mind. Och yes lovely Erin. She was such a lovely little girl. She liked being in the islands. So, did her two little brothers. I saw the three of them out running holding their new wooly balls as they ran down to the beach with their mother and father from my shop that day."

"Have you seen them since, or did they leave any address?" inquired Matt anxiously.

"Och no, Matt, they just came into the shop to buy some food for their lunch and the newspaper, I expect that they would have gone home back to America by now."

Matt's heart was not racing so much now as it sank in how disappointed he was at the thought of what would become of the three missing Balkiens. They continued to walk along the grassy Machair up to the lowest slopes of Mt Tetraval. Before everyone began to fan out to round up all the sheep, Angus spoke up again.

"I do remember that this American family did go to stay at a Bed & Breakfast in Inverainort over near Altaness. They didn't say which one. But there's only one guest house run by a Mrs. Mackinnon over that way."

"We're close to the sheep pens now," announced Uncle Herbert. "It's time for us all to go up across Tetraval to round up the sheep."

"I wonder if we'll see a lot of wool circles," chuckled Alison in her Island accent.

"Better not mention the circles too liberally," warned Matt.

"Oh spoilsport," uttered Kara. "It's a good laugh."

"Look," said Kaz sternly. "It was no laughing matter, being stopped by our dear friend in the green tent. Had we had any otherworldly evidence with us, you'd be banned from here and on your way back to Edinburgh!"

"Now kids, what's all the fuss about?" asked Uncle Herbert.

"Oh, nothing really," said Matt trying to play down this little tiff. "It's just that Lieutenant Evans suspected us of being involved with the wool circles."

"We'll soon see the extent of the problem when we start shearing," said Uncle Herbert. "Now we'd better get going."

About an hour or so later, all six of the children fanned out across the far side of Tetraval over the thick heather telling Uncle Herbert and Angus that they would round up the sheep from Rhannaig Point.

"That's okay," said Uncle Herbert. But don't take unnecessary risks near those cliffs around the cave over there."

Once on their own, all six of them made their way to the grassy knoll where they had been the previous day. There, Yesl was waiting for them.

"What kept you so long?" she asked. "I've been sitting here for ages getting my lower swooth all damp after the recent rain."

"Sorry about the delay," answered Matt. "I've important news for you, Yesl. We all had a long chat with Angus Mackay, the shopkeeper, from whom our Mom bought you last year. He told us that he'd sold three other members of your crew as *pom-poms* to an American family in May."

"Oh Matt," gasped Yesl, "did he describe their colors and their sizes?"

"Yes, he did. One was about your size and had many shades of blue."

"Oh, that must be Monku. He is what you may call our flight engineer or technician who maintained all the ship's navigation equipment. It was Monku who first mentioned that something was amiss in our positioning after leaving Splogita. I was hoping that he'd be here to shed some light on what happened. What about the other two?"

"I think he said that the others were similar in colors and a bit smaller than you, Yesl, like Baingae or slightly larger. They had shades of pink and light green swooth."

"Must have been Mwakus and Bwinkus, they're twins. Oh, I'll miss them. I wonder how they'll wake up in America."

"They were with a family with an elder daughter and two young boys."

"Oh, I hope they'll treat them well. We'll have to try to find those Balkiens someday."

Yesl started hovering over the heather, as she led all six of them around the cliff top, not too close to the edge, around to the entrance to the cave where Moonzl and the others were waiting. The descent down to the cave entrance was tricky, as they had to clamber down a steep gully that was slippery in places towards the little stony beach below the cave entrance. They walked across the pebbles, which grated under their feet as they approached the cave with Yesl hovering just above their heads. Moonzl flew out of the cave to meet them, followed by Baingae.

"Hi, everyone," greeted Moonzl.

"Come and see our little base," said Baingae.

Everyone climbed up the grassy verge that led to the cave entrance. The cave had a smoothed-out floor of small pebbles. To one side, there lay the space evacuation pod, which Matt had seen on the northern side of Tetraval if it was the same one. Sitting on top of it and around the cave floor of grey and pinkish pebbles were about ten or so more Balkiens all humming and warbling away in fluent Antrobian.

"They're all greeting you in their way," said Baingae. "They've been here for about six weeks, having discovered this cave as a good hideout from Captain Cammins and his patrols. They all awoke one by one over a few days after one sunny morning to find themselves covered by messy seaweed down on the lower beach. They said that they bathed in the ocean to clean their swooth before drying out in the sun. They flew out over to the north and discovered this space pod. They managed to start it up and fly it around here. They hid it here just before Captain Cammins' helicopters would have spotted it on the other side of the hill."

"We always wondered what happened to the pod we left behind earlier," said Matt.

"They also wondered what happened to the missing data sphere that we took," said Baingae, "until, I told them in Antrobian that we had it."

The children sat cross-legged on the pebbles while the full contingent of Balkiens of various colors, shapes, and sizes began to cuddle up to them in ponkadliath, which was the Balkien form of greeting.

"I've some bad news about Monku, Mwakus, and Bwinkus," said Yesl as she relayed what Matt had told her earlier. There were Antrobian utterings between them as they sat facing the silvery elongated ovoid craft with its round door open and folded back onto the hull. Everyone could see themselves reflected on the shiny mirror-like surface.

"Monku," began Yesl, "is a great member of our crew, who was one of the first of us to consider coming on this mission. He always dreamed of going exploring into deep space and signed up for the initial training for it. I'm sure that he will wake up okay from his comatose state."

"It seems that most of us have suffered unconsciousness after impact in this accident," said Dr. Baingae. "In my medical career, I've seen all too often that we Balkiens are knocked unconscious during any high-speed impact, which would kill most of you humans outright. Depending on the speed of the hit, it can take many months or years to wake up. Winxl is a case in point. She must have hit the ocean in her ice tomb at an incredible speed; hence her long-term recovery on Antrobi."

"The three Balkiens bought by Erin's family were in a different pod to ours," continued Yesl. "Boongoo, Baingae, Moonzl, and I were in this one here. Monku, Mwakus, and Bwinkus had gone to another pod as the *Balkieston* was breaking up while the ship burned through the Earth's atmosphere. It was terrifying to think we'd never see them again. It's great that we found them. Only we so wish that they were not taken off to Arizona."

Yesl was subdued in her demeanor as the facts of this encounter began to sink in.

"Oh Yesl, I'm sure that we'll meet up again someday," said Matt. "Maybe I'll get to go to a youth camp or even to a university over there when I grow up."

Boongoo suddenly buzzed out from inside the space pod excitedly. "This pod happens to be the one in which Woozl came down to rescue us from Splogita when our other one crashed. The data spheres from it have a lot more info about our undersea voyage as we left that island on Splogita than on the data sphere that you've got. Come and see."

Every Balkien flew inside the small capsule. Judith and Alison clambered inside while the others poked their heads in through the doorway to look at the circular view screen at the far end. As Boongoo started to replay some video footage recorded on Splogita, the first scene showed a dimly lit beach, punctuated by bright flashes, with Boongoo explaining that they were those of the Enigma. There was a lull in the lightning when the exposure began to adapt to the twilight scene from that other world so far away. The film zoomed-in to one of the gaps between the thick trunks of the large tree-like plants in the forest. There were many tiny glowing lights, slowly moving around the forest clearing.

"The Molktrons," said Yesl in awe.

"Wow!" whispered Alison.

"What a lovely scene," said Judith.

"Amazing to see alien glow worms," said Kaz.

"Glow-worms?" questioned Kara.

"They look more like glowing eggs," said Sean.

The next few scenes showed all the Balkiens re-boarding the vessel and the Molktrons, including a much larger one, in the forest clearing, awaiting their departure.

"The Queen," gasped Yesl. "I thought that she rarely emerged from the cave for fear of being harmed by the lightning. It's the first time I've seen the Queen Molktron away from her lair. What if the lightning strikes?"

The next scene was of them lifting off and heading for the water. Just before diving in, there was a total screen white-out, which even flashed brightly in the cabin, dazzling everyone like a camera flash in a darkened room.

"That was WAY TOO bright for the Molktrons!" exclaimed Baingae.

"Oh, I hope that the Queen's okay," said Yesl. "If only we'd noticed that the Molktrons were all exposed as we took off. We might have gone back to investigate after that flash. It seems that only the camera recorded it. We had our window visors down, so didn't notice it as we entered the water."

The next few scenes were of the lakebed as the ship proceeded underwater to the far shore. There were single bright frames of the seabed during flashes, which Boongoo had edited into a surreal slide show. Matt took photos of these. More video of their departure from Splogita showed the desert planet with the emerald isle in the middle of the deep blue lake. The next images showed Splogita in a crescent form next to the larger crescent shape of Spoonkathtil, the gas-giant planet which, Splogita orbits around as one of its seven moons.

"Coming out of there is a bit like emerging from a cinema after a blockbuster movie," said Matt. "We'd better be getting back to the sheep shearing like we're supposed to be doing.

"All six of you, better get going back to Uncle Herbert," said Yesl. "We'll fly back later after we've been here a while longer."

The climb back up onto the heathery moorland from the cave was a bit tricky, especially for Judith and Alison. The Balkiens assisted them until they were all on safe ground. The walk back to the sheep pens was uneventful until they caught up with all the herded sheep, led by the villagers and their dogs to the shearing pens.

"Hello children," said Angus Mackay, as they joined the procession. There was a loud cacophony of bleating and baying of the sheep.

"Lots of wool circles!" he announced. Matt and the others looked with astonishment at the circular holes in the fleeces.

"It's so strange," said Kaz. "Like the crop circles in southern England a few years ago."

"Looks like there'll be a police hunt for the pranksters involved in this," said Sean.

Many of the animals had crisp freshly cut circles on their backs, while others had ring marks where the wool had partially regrown. They all arrived at the sheep pens. There were not only the sounds of the bleating of the sheep and the barking of the dogs but much consternation at the state of a lot of the fleeces due to the wool circles. Lieutenant Evans was there among the sheep, and everyone took photographs and statements from the villagers. All the children came up to Uncle Herbert to assist with operations.

"Can we help in any way," asked Matt.

"You can help put all those fleeces or what's left of them, into those sacks and take the filled ones over to our truck," said Uncle Herbert. "We've only just started shearing proper. Angus was asking about where you had been. I know all about your reasons for being away from us for a bit, however, better watch out about your movements, especially with all this business about the wool circles. There are a lot of suspicions. I never expected there to be so many of them. We'll still be able to make yarn but as for selling many complete fleeces, forget it."

"Look at our crop of wool," complained one crofter. "It's all but ruined! We'll get the pranksters who perpetrated this even if we have to search the whole island. It's an absolute disgrace. No one seems to be able to bring up their kids these days. They're left to run riot and wreck everything."

"I don't know what the world's coming to," agreed another man in his fifties, wearing a cloth cap, black boots, jeans, and an old tweed jacket. "I've seen vandalism on the Mainland, but out here in the Islands? It is sheer madness and a lot of damage and loss to our livelihood."

"It's bizarre that vandals could manage to catch most of the sheep and do this without hurting them in any way by cutting their skin in the process," said Kaz in an inquiring tone.

"As a matter of fact," interrupted Lieutenant Evans as he briskly strode up. "I've noted the lack of any such wounds and the nature of these circles. I've actually taken some complete samples of the circles incised meticulously; both fresh ones and older ones to be sent back to our labs at Aldermaston for extensive forensic analysis. We'll do DNA testing and the whole nine yards to track these hooligans. We'll have this reported in the papers all right. As a matter of fact, where have all of you been? We've not seen much of you helping to round up many of the sheep; gone for a nice little jaunt over this controlled area? I'd like to see that camera of yours."

Matt hesitated, asking, "What camera?"

"That one in your pocket. I'd like to see what photos you've got. You shouldn't be taking any in this restricted military area where photography and filming are banned."

Trying to hide his nervousness, Matt handed up his camera for examination. Lieutenant Evans took it, switched it on, and started viewing the photos beginning with the most recent. Matt was tense, realizing that all the shots he'd taken at the Balkiens' hideout would be confiscated or deleted at best and that the Balkiens would their secrecy. He flicked through them one by one on the camera's viewer. "You're really into photographing wool circles, aren't you? Better by far than the ones I'm getting. I'm sure that the papers will give you good money for these. This story's going be a real scoop;

not just for your local rag; the Altaness Courier is it? But the Times, the Guardian, and dare I say it, the Scotsman."

Just as he was about to look at more photos, Angus came up and said, "Come and look at this one."

"Okay, I've seen enough photos of wool circles. Here's your camera, you can take photos all you like here but don't let me catch you with a camera here in the future." He handed the digital camera back to Matt, much to his relief. They followed Angus to what he was pointing out. There was a sheep about to be sheared that had three wool circles, which coalesced in a triangular pattern. Matt quickly aimed his camera and took some shots of them. Lieutenant Evans did likewise. Matt also took photos of Uncle Herbert with the sheep and of the other kids passing the camera around each other for poses at this newsworthy scene.

As the last fifteen sheep went into the pens, Kaz pointed out the third in line and noticed a Balkien with rainbow colors on its swooth clinging to the back of the sheep.

"Look," Angus said. "And there's another pom-pom for my shop."

"Matt," whispered Kaz. "There's a Balkien on that sheep."

"What's that on my sheep?" asked a Kenny Mackenzie with astonishment.

Matt quickly pulled out his camera to photograph the spectacle before the shearing of that sheep. A general commotion began.

"So!" shouted Lieutenant Evans. "There's the cause of these wool circles."

Matt managed to take about three photos before his screen went blank as the batteries ran out.

"Argh!" he hissed. Just then the Balkien suddenly took off without warning as the shearers were beginning to snip at the fleece and Angus was about to remove the ball for his shop as it was his sheep. It let out a loud hovering sound as it raced into the sky and disappeared up over the hill.

"That's our culprit. Now you've all seen one of these aliens in the flesh. After shearing that fleece, it is a Government requirement that I take the crop circle part for analysis Angus. You will, of course, be compensated."

"At least we now know who's been eating our sheep's wool," said Kenny. "Let's calm down and finish off the last few animals before calling it a day."

Everyone dispersed, bewildered, discussing all that had transpired that day and all about the wreckage discovered over the last few months.

• ◯ •

7 ~ **MANY DISCOVERIES**

Everyone welcomed Auntie Wendy's piping hot soup that evening.
"Lieutenant Evans is certainly going to have a field day now," said Matt with an expression of foreboding in his eyes.

"Just think," said Kaz. "Most of the village may be talking about the Balkiens and that they made the wool circles in the sheep. I wonder why they'd do that."

"Maybe they eat wool for food," said Alison with an innocent smile.

"Very plausible," said Kara.

"Perhaps wool is the closest approximation to their swooth," said Sean. "I mean they must need nourishment after being in space for so long and then wrecked on our coast."

"That rainbow-colored Balkien that suddenly took off from Angus's sheep stirred it up," said Matt.

Uncle Herbert came in after his shower and joined everyone at the table.

"Delicious soup," he said. "I must admit, I was beginning to put two and two together about the wool circles. It was just too much of a coincidence that these circles only appeared after finding the space wreckage this year."

"Remember Angus telling us about the Balkiens, bought by that American family," said Matt. "How will we ever track them down?"

"Angus mentioned that they stayed over at Inverainort in a Bed &Breakfast," said Kaz.

"There's only one that I know of in Inverainort," said Uncle Herbert. "And that's Mr. & Mrs. MacKinnon's."

"Why don't we visit them?" asked Matt.

"Well, we might," said Uncle Herbert. "We could go up there tomorrow. It would get us away from the village after today's hullabaloo. I'd love to have a cup of coffee with them and maybe a wee dram or two of Scotch. I'm sure that's where they would have stayed in May." Just then, Auntie Wendy opened the kitchen door to let in the cat. Before she could close the door, the trio of Balkiens, Yesl, Boongoo, and Baingae hovered in a line into the living room and alighted on the piano.

"I'm worried about Lieutenant Evans, ACTUALLY spotting a Balkien, ACTUALLY in the flesh and flying," said Matt.

"There will no doubt be some searching going on," replied Uncle Herbert.

"What if Lieutenant Evans calls in reinforcements," said Kaz, "and searches the hill and discovers the hideout at Rhannaig Point."

Yesl hovered over to the dinner table. "Matt. Let's see the photos you took of that Balkien on the sheep." Matt fetched his camera, inserted the spare battery, and turned it on to show Yesl the last three shots. The last one was the best, clearly showing the rainbow-colored swooth on the sheep's back.

"That's Smalkle," said Yesl, "one of the two who arrived in the rescue scout ship on Splogita. We didn't see him at Rhannaig Point, maybe because he was gorging himself on that sheep and was asleep there."

"Maybe those at Rhannaig Point should be warned of this incident, in case Smalkle was not part of that contingent," said Matt.

The car traveled along the single-lane road through the heathery moorland to the village of Inverainort, comprising a few stone cottages with slate roofs and peat smoke billowing from the chimneys. After parking the car on the gravel parking area in front of the guesthouse, Matt knocked on Mrs. MacKinnon's thick wooden door, which had a well-weathered brass door knocker in the shape of a fish, and a brass octagonal door handle. The door creaked open slowly.

"Oh, hello Herbert, do come in," greeted Mrs. MacKinnon in a warm Hebridean accent. "Would you require rooms for these fine boys?"

"Ah no, not, for now, we thought we'd just come for a visit on our way to the shops in Altaness," replied Uncle Herbert. "I've brought a wee dram to share." Uncle Herbert and the boys trooped in and were invited to sit on the settee in the main guest room. Matt deposited his knapsack next to him on a small side table, Yesl, Boongoo, and Baingae inside.

"Would you like a cup of tea?" asked Mrs. MacKinnon.

"It sure has been fine weather these last few days," said Uncle Herbert. "The sheep shearing went well yesterday, except for the wool circles on many of the fleeces." Uncle Herbert and Mrs. MacKinnon then shared some Scotch.

"Oh, I've heard rumors about these," said Mrs. MacKinnon. "Some say that hooligans are cutting these circles out for a prank. There's little to keep them out of mischief."

"There are many more circles than first thought," said Uncle Herbert. "Then there's all this business of strange wreckage on Tetraval, maybe from outer space?"

Matt started drinking tea and brought Yesl out.

"Oh, another of these lovely woolen balls from Mackay's shop," said Mrs. MacKinnon. "Aren't they wonderful? I don't know where he gets them. I had an American family staying here a few weeks ago, who had bought three of them. They were as large as that one with beautiful purple colors. Their three kids were delighted with them. They almost glistened when they cuddled them."

After a scintillating afternoon of island gossip, Matt asked, "Could we sign your visitor's book as guests of your wonderful island?"

"Oh, of course, you may," replied Mrs. Mackinnon, still thinking it an odd request from a young schoolboy. Matt went to the sideboard to look at the book. He turned back through a couple of pages and there in front of him was the vital information he was looking for:

Mr. & Mrs. Dan & Helen Fredrickson, Erin, Dan & Nick
2601, North Orchard Blvd, Tucson, AZ 85743, USA
A warm welcome — love to come back for more wooly balls!

Matt quickly copied down the address on a piece of wrapping paper.

As they drove down the village street, Matt noticed that there was an Army jeep parked in their driveway.

"What on Earth is this?" gasped Uncle Herbert.

"Better drive on," said Matt. "It might be Lieutenant Evans on an inspection visit. We'll go on and collect driftwood for lighting the fire and drop off our alien passengers to lie low in case we're searched."

Uncle Herbert parked his car along the verge of the track leading to the beach. Everyone got out and started walking briskly across the sand and sat on some rocks looking out to sea, as the waves came in washing foam spray over the lower rocks covered in brown seaweed. Matt opened his knapsack by a rock pool and told Yesl, Boongoo, and Baingae that the coast was not clear at the house. "We'll fly over to Rhannaig Point for the night," said Yesl, "and see you in the morning."

"I don't like the look of this," said Kaz.

"Me neither," said Matt. "We may have to cut our holiday short or go off touring."

"Oh kids, I'm sure all this about the wool circles will blow over provided we keep all of the Balkiens well-hidden for now and that they do not eat any more wool off the sheep," reassured Uncle Herbert. "We'd hate to see you all go home and not finish your holiday."

Matt looked back toward their car in the distance. Right behind it was the jeep with three military-clad figures hovering around inspecting their vehicle.

"Better go Balkiens," said Matt. They hovered off low over the rocks and flew into the distance towards Rhannaig Point, keeping as close as possible to the wave crests and mingling with a flock of seagulls, without scaring them with their alien presence. Matt then immediately picked up a piece of driftwood. The others gradually picked up more pieces as they walked back towards their car. The Army personnel were on the sands now, walking briskly towards them.

"Captain Cammins," said Matt in a hushed tone.

"Well, well, well, if it isn't Matt and his friends having a jolly good walk on the beach, eh? Collecting driftwood? I've heard all about yesterday's shenanigans. We saw you coming down the village and expected you to turn in for home."

"We've come back from Altaness and came to get much-needed driftwood for lighting the fires," said Matt, who was dressed only in shorts and a T-shirt, like the others.

"Bit warm to be lighting fires today, isn't it?"

"We also cook on a peat burning stove."

"I see. We'd better inspect your bags, nonetheless."

Everyone put down their driftwood and Matt's knapsack for inspection. Captain Cammins and his men went through their bags in great detail, finding only the remains of Aunty Wendy's packed lunches. He let out a frustrated grunt and a sigh at finding nothing.

"All right be off with you lot," said Cammins.

"Will we be able to go onto the Machair to look for driftwood or help with the sheep?" asked Matt.

"I'm afraid that won't be possible!" replied Cammins with authority. "Next time you go looking for driftwood don't go beyond the western end of the sandy part of this beach, okay. The area beyond is now out of bounds as of this morning."

Matt repacked his bag and placed it and the driftwood in the car. As they came up the drive towards the gate, Auntie Wendy came running out to greet them.

"I hope you had a good drive. We've just had a visit from Captain Cammins himself, looking for you and asking some awkward questions about our alien visitors. They went on a search of the bedrooms but did not find anything. It was so stressful, with you not being here. I don't know if I can take much more of this. It's those wool circles that have started this. The Machair is now completely out of bounds again. We've had the press and TV crews from the Altaness Courier and the mainland."

"Calm down," said Uncle Herbert. "We've already seen Cammins and his men down at the beach, checking us out."

Alison, Kara, and Judith were now helping them put the driftwood on the peat stack next to the garage.

"Did they find Yesl?" asked a concerned Alison.

"No," replied Matt. "We let them go to Rhannaig Point before we were searched."

"Searched again?" asked Kara.

"This driftwood was a smokescreen for Captain Cammins as he and his buddies came towards us at the beach. He certainly seemed very suss about our presence there," said Matt as he went through his bag to dispose of the lunch leftovers. "Where's my camera? I hope Captain Cammins didn't take it."

Kaz fumbled around the back of his jacket and pulled it out and handed it to Matt. "Why you took it without asking perm—" said Matt, breaking off this accusation, realizing that it may have saved the day.

"I wanted to take some photos of those sheep on the way back from Mrs. MacKinnon's. They had what looked like more wool circles. I put it back in my pocket and not your knapsack, so as not to disturb the Balkiens in it. The pocket had a large hole, so it slid inside my jacket lining."

"Not to worry, Kaz. That saved Cammins from finding it during the searches. I'd forgotten all about it when we let the Balkiens go. More wool circles! Those guys must have a voracious appetite for wool, being like their swooth, I suppose."

"Dinner's up!" announced Auntie Wendy. "Thanks, awfully for the driftwood, even if it was only for your smokescreen."

Yesl, Baingae, and Boongoo continued flying low across the waves. After passing the cliffs on Tetraval's southern coast, they went higher as they rounded the last rock outcrop into view of their secret cave, which was gloomy in the fading light as the golden sunset over the ocean grew redder. The three Balkiens approached the cave entrance, deep in the small cove, expecting to see the shiny polished silver hull of their scout ship. As they came in to alight on the floor of pebbles, all they could see were the pebbles.

"What's happened?" cried Yesl.

"Why have they gone?" asked Baingae, "and where?"

"They were spooked," said Boongoo.

"Better have a quick look around and beat it," said Yesl. "Maybe they had to leave in a hurry."

The three Balkiens could find nothing around the cave to indicate any reason for the sudden disappearance of their craft. They were about to fly back to Kinrasaig when Boongoo noticed a golf-ball sized steel ball lying half-hidden in the long grass by the stony beach. As they flew over it, Yesl telekinetically attracted it towards her swooth. This ball and three more like it rose from the grass. Boongoo and Baingae hovered around the area and found four more spheres. After a five-minute check, they only saw one other bigger silver ball. They attracted all eight of them to their swooth and flew back to Uncle Herbert's home under cover of dusk via the south side of the hill, this time at high altitude until they saw the village's streetlights.

Everyone was sitting in the TV room, having cups of tea, watching the beginning of a spy thriller. Just as the plot began to thicken, Kaz called out, "Look out the window! There are Yesl and co."

"So it is," said Matt. "I was not expecting them back tonight. I'd better go out and see. Tell me what happens next. I'd hate to miss the plot."

Matt took his torch around to the front of the house. There were three subdued Balkiens with their clutch of eight silvery balls. "I'll take these, and we'll go inside." The silver spheres were placed on a plate on the kitchen table, much to the relief of Yesl, Boongoo, and Baingae.

"Matt," said Yesl. "The ship has gone completely from the cave, and all there was were these balls."

"Oh, Yesl, whatever next? Now the plot thickens," said Matt with consternation as he quickly lost all interest in the spy film at this turn of events. "What are these balls?"

"I think they're small data spheres," said Baingae, "like your computer memory cards, but they can only be read on our ship's equipment."

"Then why were they left behind?" asked Yesl.

"We think they may have departed quickly before being spotted by Captain Cammins," said Boongoo.

Matt fetched some biscuits and placed them on the plate by the silver balls and carried it through to the TV room with the Balkiens on his shoulder.

"What strange silvery biscuits," said Judith with a giggle.

"The Balkiens brought back these silver spheres from the cave," said Matt. "Their ship's gone. I'll tell you later." The plate was passed around for all to select biscuits and view the silver data balls, which interested everyone more, while passively watching the movie.

"He must have gone with the others as he was a member of that crew," replied Matt. "I was so looking forward to getting to know Moonzl better, but I suppose he is valuable to the group."

"It's bedtime for you kids," said Uncle Herbert. "It looks like the party may well be over on Tetraval, as it's likely, all of the Balkiens have taken flight."

The next morning, it was still sunny but a little windy signaling that a change in the weather was on the way. "What'll we do on our remaining week here?" asked Kara at breakfast.

"Certainly, no more walks on Tetraval," replied Matt. "I'm not sure if we can keep Yesl, Boongoo, and Baingae here anymore." They were sitting on top of the upright piano, with Boongoo hovering over the keys practicing a distinctly Antrobian sounding melody. A definite tune was being composed, or was it a known Antrobian anthem, performed on a terrestrial instrument? It was a beautiful calming piece that Kara tried to practice herself.

Uncle Herbert came in at that point asking, "Who's playing that lovely music?" before noticing Kara on the piano stool and Boongoo hovering silently over the keys playing them by telekinesis.

"That's one of our favorite tunes from Antrobi," said Yesl as she began to sing the lyrics in Antrobian. When they finished the song, Yesl told that it was about their yearning for adventure and about their space voyages and Splogita. "We wrote it and composed the music on our way back from Splogita. Here, we play one of our first recitals."

Everyone clapped and hollered for an encore. It was such a sweet song, even though no human could understand a word of it. "We'll have to do an English version soon," said Yesl." The words begin like this:

To our purple planet, we said farewell
To soar far and wide to exotic worlds
To go to yonder star for many a year
But so missed our homely mooties

From these foreign skies past our ship
We looked up to the stars in heaven
One of which was our own Antrobi
And longed to be on her heaths again

These words much inspired everyone. As breakfast was underway, Matt said, "What if Captain Cammins pays us another visit?"

"Certainly, a serious thought," started Uncle Herbert, looking out the window. Captain Cammins' jeep was making its way slowly up their driveway.

"Matt, he's coming here. Hide the Balkiens, do something!" exclaimed Uncle Herbert. Matt quickly ran upstairs with Yesl, Boongoo, and Baingae hovering close behind him. He quickly looked for a suitable place to hide them. He eyed the fireplace.

"All of you," said Matt. "Quickly hide in this plastic bag and fly up into the chimney. The bag is to protect you from soot.

"Stay in there until I come back," he said and went downstairs. "Hello Matt," said Captain Cammins with a wry smile through his long mustache, while removing his cap. "Where are they?" he asked with piercing eyes.

"Where are who?" asked Matt, trying to play ignorance.

"Your wooly friends, of course!"

"You mean our sheep and the wool circles?" replied Matt.

"I mean those creatures that ate the wool circles," rasped Captain Cammins.

"Excuse me," said Uncle Herbert in a firm voice. "Do you have a search warrant?"

"Shortly this whole area will be in lockdown. Men, search this house."

Captain Cammins then barged through the living room door to go upstairs and search for the Balkiens. Matt, Kaz, Sean, and Uncle Herbert followed Cammins upstairs as he began the extensive search of Matt's bedroom, turning out all of his drawers in frustration. After about fifteen minutes of exasperating searching, he had all but given up when he wandered pensively over to the fireplace, bent down low, looked around the ashes in the grate, and then looked up the chimney. Matt gasped in horror at what he thought was about to happen. Some soot fell on Cammins' face. He reached his left arm up into the chimney and pulled down the plastic shopping bag. He looked into it and found it full of soot.

"What may I ask is this?" he asked.

"I don't know how the soot got there," replied Matt in all truthfulness.

"Perhaps this was some little gift left by the chimney sweep or Santa Claus," said Cammins rhetorically as he left the room, more frustrated than ever. "There's something fishy going on."

After Captain Cammins departed, everyone looked at each other in disbelief at the invasion of their privacy.

Kaz was the first to break the silence. "Things are hotting up," he said. "Captain Cammins won't give up easily. He'll come and search this place stone by stone if he has to."

Poor old Auntie Wendy was in tears saying, "What'll we do? These lovely beings from space haven't done anything except to have an accident in this hostile world. Why does everyone have to be so suspicious these days," she continued sobbing.

"That settles it," said Uncle Herbert decisively. "The current living arrangements can't continue. Matt and all of you will probably have to move out for now, though we can't send you back to Edinburgh prematurely as that'll arouse even more suspicion with your parents."

"What about Mrs. MacKinnon's?" asked Matt.

"Excellent idea," replied Uncle Herbert. "I'll call her now to see if she still has the rooms she suggested. I'm sure she'd love to have you, Matt, Kara, and Sean, stay there for a while. We can come and visit, albeit discreetly."

Matt nipped upstairs to see if he could find the Balkiens, wondering why they had not flown around to the back door. They were on the floor, bedraggled, all covered in soot from the chimney, with more soot flaking off their swooth, as they rolled about, onto the blue Persian carpet making a blackened mess everywhere. "Oh, Yesl," said Matt. "Look at you! How did you not manage to fly out the top of the chimney?"

"We had a feeling that we were not safe in the chimney," said Yesl. "So, we tried to fly out, Boongoo first, then I got stuck in the top, and Baingae nudged into me, and I couldn't budge. I was beginning to get oblated as well as covered in soot. Then Baingae saw a hand reach up and grabbed the bag into which the soot I dislodged fell. Boongoo came back to the chimney pot and beat me back down, and we all fell in a heap on the ashes. Now, look at us."

"At least you weren't caught or discovered," said Matt. "We'll all have to have a bath. I'm sooty too. And I'll get the vacuum cleaner for the carpet."

"How did Captain Cammins not discover the eight silver balls during his search?" asked Sean. "They'd been left on the plate along with the biscuits the night before in the TV room."

"I put them into a small bag and put them into the secret cupboard," said Matt. "Yesl, remind me to pack them up later before we depart."

After their hot bath, Matt and the Balkiens were all washed, leaving their swooth wet but very clean. Matt laid the three Balkiens onto the black roof of the cowshed to dry in the sun. In the evening, Matt, Kara, and Sean placed their bags in the car under the darkness to leave in the morning.

After some tearful farewells with hugs, Uncle Herbert drove Matt, Kara, and Sean up to Mrs. MacKinnon's. There was a routine road check at Scarivanish, close to Mackay's shop. After the roadblock, Uncle Herbert pulled into the shop to buy the Altaness Courier. Matt walked to the back of the shop, where the Balkiens were normally stocked to see if any were for sale. Matt fully expected this niche market to end after the events during the last week. To his surprise, another two cuddly Balkiens were lying asleep on the shelf amongst the tartan scarves and woolen beanies. One had rainbow-like colors on his swooth and was slightly smaller than the other, who had a fascinating range of dark to light bluish and turquoise hues on his swooth. Each of the two Balkiens was wearing a beanie. Matt, without further thought, took out almost the last of his pocket money to buy these two balls.

When he presented them for payment, Angus said, "Matt, I'll make you a special deal. I know that these are the last two that I'll ever stock now that I know who they are, where they're from, and with all of the publicity. I'll sell you the beanies for £10 and throw in the balls for free."

He handed over the money and received the goods in a colorful red and green tartan cloth bag.

"Thanks, Angus," said Matt. "I'll take good care of these ones. They'll go to be with their mates, and I'll see that they get home safely someday."

"Och well. I do hope that you manage to find those three that went to America."

"I'm sure that I will. I already have the family's address. We're leaving for home now, so I'd better say goodbye."

"Och well then, we'll miss you, but I'm sure that it's all for the best. We bid you farewell and wish you all well on your adventures."

Everyone left the shop as Matt glanced out toward Mt Tetraval, where there were two jeeps. Uncle Herbert made a hasty departure from the shop and drove to Inverainort without stopping, fearing that their precious new 'cargo' might be discovered. Yesl, Boongoo, and Baingae hovered over the tufts of purple heather about fifty meters from the road as their presence in the car were too risky in case of roadblocks.

The car finally pulled up to the small gravel driveway with thick grass all around it except for the narrow path leading up to Mrs. MacKinnon's front door. As Uncle Herbert led Matt, Kara, and Sean into the cozy front living room of the stone-built cottage, Yesl, Boongoo, and Baingae hovered in through the door to join them.

"Yesl," said Matt. "I've just acquired two new crewmates of yours at MacKay's, likely to be the last ones he'll ever stock."

"Let's see who they are," said Yesl as all three Balkiens hovered over Matt's knapsack on the settee beside him. Matt opened the bag and gently pulled out the two new additions to their expanding collection.

"Smoonkshie and Moonxl," said Yesl in amazement. "Smoonkshie was one member of the crew on the scout ship that rescued us from Splogita after our accident. Smalkle was the other, recognizable from the photo of him leaping up from the sheep."

"No accident," said Baingae. "Remember that we were struck by the Enigma's lightning bolt that damaged our navigation systems and two of the navigation satellites that we set up in Splogitan orbit.

The two Balkiens in the beanies had predominantly purple and blue swooth on their equators, while Moonxl had almost all the colors of the rainbow on the rest of his swooth, and Smoonkshie had shades of blue. Both were about six inches in diameter and were slightly prolate across their poles.

By now, Mrs. MacKinnon was well informed about the truth of the Balkiens arrival on Earth. Yesl started to converse with Moonxl in Antrobian. Occasionally, Moonxl would join in the cacophony. Baingae began to translate for everyone saying, "Moonxl is saying that all he remembers is the *Balkieston* being hit by rocks bashing into the ship's hull and of a sudden decompression which was very painful. Next, he remembers that he was thrown into a life pod, maybe by Smalkle. There was a loud bang, and suddenly, the pod was full of water. Maybe the door was not sealed properly. Then all we can remember in a comatose dreamlike state was being on the shelves with these hats on us, with what looked like small baby Balkiens affixed to them."

"Ah, the little *pom-poms* on the beanies," said Matt. Everyone laughed. The beanies were removed from the two newcomers. Dr. Baingae conversed with them and hugged them in their Antrobian way.

"I'm just thanking Smoonkshie, for rescuing us from the Enigma on Splogita, at great risk to himself and Smalkle," said Baingae.

"Moonxl says that he is happy to hear that Smalkle is alive and well."

"Maybe Smalkle flew back to the cave hideout after leaving the sheep and called for their departure before being discovered," said Matt.

The telephone started ringing on the sideboard. Mrs. MacKinnon arose from her lounge chair, putting her cup of tea down to answer it.

"Hello, Inverainort Bed & Breakfast. Can I be of assistance?" she asked. "Oh, hello, Herbert. What can I do for you? Matt, Kara, Sean, and I are all having a nice relaxing cup of tea." There was a pause.

"Oh, yes, Darjeeling tea."

"You'd like to have a word with Matt. He's right here, cuddling his newly acquired rainbow-colored soft wooly balls." Matt got up from his chair and took the handset.

"Hi, Uncle Herbert. Good to hear from you. You got back okay. I hope there weren't any roadblocks."

"Good."

"What?"

"What's Dad saying about the alien on Tetraval?"

"In the Scotsman?"

"On the front page; the whole country will know about this."

Mrs. MacKinnon left the room momentarily and came back with the day's papers still wrapped in their cellophane sleeve.

"Do I need to call my Mom and Dad tonight?"

"Okay, I'll do that. Is Dad all right about what he read in the papers?"

"On the TV news as well?"

"Thanks for calling us. I'd better hang up and call home. Bye for now."

"I'll call back afterward."

Matt put the phone down and gasped as he saw the front-page spread in 'The Scotsman.' There was a full front-page leading article on the events that had occurred at the sheep-shearing meet. The headline read:

ALIEN BEING SIGHTED AT SHEEP SHEARING MEET

Beneath the headline was a color photo of a sheep with a wool circle and a sharp image of a Balkien taking off hurriedly from the scene, recognizable as Smalkle.

Matt, with some trepidation, picked up the phone and called his parents in Edinburgh.

"Hello, Mom, good to hear from you. I hope that all is okay." There was a long pause.

"So, Dad's read the Scotsman as well; we also have it here."

"Oh, don't worry," said Matt reassuringly.

"Look, Mom. Don't worry about his job at the Ministry."

"We'll be back home safely on Tuesday's flight. I'll say goodnight and see you, then."

"Schoolwork? That'll be okay Mom."

"Good night, sweet dreams."

Matt placed the phone down gently, letting out a sigh of relief.

"What's asking, Matt?" asked Kara.

"She's worried that we're involved up to the hilt with the aliens as reported here" replied Matt. "Looks like Dad's worried about a possible threat to his job if his employers find out that we, his children, are involved in all of this."

● ○ ●

8 ~ THE MEETING

Matt, Kara, and Sean were all seated as Mrs. MacKinnon served up their three dishes of bacon and egg on toast. Mrs. MacKinnon glanced out of the sunny window as she brought in the teapot and laid it on the table.

"There's your Uncle Herbert in his car," she announced. "I'm sure you'll have time for a cuppa before heading off to the airport."

"Now Matt, Kara and Sean." began Uncle Herbert as their Morris proceeded across the bleak peat moorland toward the township of Altaness. "We must keep all this about the Balkiens and the spaceship wreckage on Tetraval a secret for now. Your father, being in the Defense Ministry, may not be able to keep this from his bosses, which could open an enormous can of worms."

"I'd love to tell my parents though," replied Matt.

"Not wise," said Uncle Herbert, "I have my doubts that it was wise to show Yesl and Baingae even to us. What if all the other kids at Kinrasaig School should get wind of this? What with Captain Cammins and his troops and the media publicity, we have to be careful."

"It seemed to be very exciting while I was with you in Kinrasaig. Now, as I fly back home and to school, it all seems very different."

"Matt," reassured Uncle Herbert as he turned onto the airport road past Altaness. "You managed to keep Yesl a secret very well until you came here. Just keep it up. I know that you have spoken a lot about astronomy and extraterrestrial life to your Auntie Ethel. Just be careful, however, not to say too much to her at this stage. We're at the terminal. I'll park here, and we'll check your bags in for Edinburgh."

With encouraging farewells, Uncle Herbert saw all three of them pass through airport security and onto the two-engine turboprop aircraft. Matt had Yesl on his lap for part of the flight. The sun reflected off the glistening waters of the sea lochs of the Western Scottish Highlands.

Mom warmly greeted Matt, Kara, and Sean as they emerged from the baggage carousel area at Edinburgh Airport.

"I wonder what you've got in those bags," said Mom. "You'll have to learn to travel much lighter next time if there's to be a next time. I tell you that your father was thrown for a loop after your call two days ago. He knows much more than you realize about the Balkiens. It's been the leading story on the BBC news for about five days now. He's going to have some words of warning tonight, and we've had some discussions over all of this."

"Mom," asked Matt. "Why is Dad against us having anything to do with the Balkiens? Their only problem was to have an unfortunate accident."

"Your father is in the Ministry of Defense and has to follow orders from the Government, or he'll likely lose his job. Then how will we ever pay the bills and our mortgage? Never mind sending you all on expensive airplane trips to the Hebrides to get more deeply involved with these aliens. Now let's find our car."

It was a sunny but blustery day as all three trooped with their mother to the multi-story car park with their luggage trolley. Matt was uneasy about this homecoming.

As Matt looked out of the window, he saw Dad's car arriving home from work. He left all his spherical friends quivering in ponkadliath on the bed and went downstairs with his brother and sister hoping for a cordial greeting. The door opened, and Dad walked in, wearing his business suit.

"Hi, Dad," they said in unison.

"Hi to you all," said Dad. "I do hope you had a great time in Baraignsay. We've certainly had a blow-by-blow account of your activities."

Picking up yesterday's Scotsman, he opened it to the page with the full report on the sheep-shearing story.

"We read it for ourselves up there," said Matt looking for a better answer.

"It's obvious you know all about it. There's your mug shot on page two and no doubt your wooly friends gorging themselves on the sheep. Captain Cammins and I have had lengthy conversations over this at the Ministry." Dad started to whistle a jazz tune, possibly a number by Glenn Miller. "I must say that I would rather that the wreckage was from beyond our atmosphere than of an enemy spy plane, but we cannot be too sure, hence all of this secrecy."

"Yes," said Matt with an air of relief, "it seems like the former is true."

"Maybe so," replied Dad, "but we must go through due process."

"Your breakfast is on the table," announced Mom as she entered his bedroom. "Matt. You are still really fond of those wooly balls. THOSE wooly balls!" she exclaimed softly. "Where did you get those other five? In Baraignsay?"

"Yes," answered Matt as he quickly recalled *buying* Boongoo, Baingae, Smoonkshie, Moonxl, and Moonzl at Mackay's shop. "Uncle Herbert took us to buy the groceries. I couldn't resist having these five soft wooly balls as a company for Yesl when I saw them for sale."

"Matt. You must have spent a fortune on them. Wool is expensive these days, what with the sheep farmers having a hard time last winter. Did Uncle Herbert help you with the cost?"

"Well, yes, but only a little."

"Now Matt," said Mom. "I'm sure that you all had a great holiday. You'll have to hunker down to your schoolwork, you know."

"Yes, I know. I'll try to do my best."

"You'll not try; you will, and don't let these soft balls take over too much of your time. I don't know what's going on up at Uncle Herbert's. Have you seen the papers? Look on page two of today's *Scotsman* where there's another article. There's a report about some strange goings-on over on the hill near his cottage. They say that they have discovered some remains of a UFO."

"And there's a picture of Kinrasaig," Mom continued. "You read it after school, okay? I'm sure you must have been aware of some of this. Now it's time to get ready. Dad will soon be off to the office. I'm apprehensive that he will find out that you may be mixed up in all of this, which could jeopardize his job."

After the routine morning school bus run, Matt could not help but think about his associations with the Balkiens during History class.

"Who was the king of Scotland who also became king of England, Matt?" asked Mr. MacMillan, the history teacher, "Matt! Are you paying attention, boy?"

He was suddenly ejected out of his dream-like state to deal with this impromptu situation. "Antrobi," he blurted out, automatically.

"Wrong, boy!" Mr. MacMillan exclaimed as the rest of the class burst into spontaneous laughter. "And what or who, may I ask is Antrobi?"

"Could you repeat the original question, Sir?" asked Matt, hoping that his *faux pas* would go amiss.

"Who was the king of Scotland who also became king of England?"

"Ah, Jimmy the Sixth," answered Matt, rather cheekily, to try to divert the conversation away from things Antrobian.

"That's better, boy!" exclaimed Mr. MacMillan. "Ah, yes…. Jimmy the Sixth, a wild monarch of this fair kingdom; the Scottish King James VI, who became James I of England; a significant period in Scottish history my boy. I'd like all of you to write an essay for homework on James VI and I for this class next week."

"Phew!" sighed Matt, having evaded the query over Antrobi for now.

It was soon time to start his maths homework, the only set assignment from his first day back at school. His Dad had now returned from work at the Ministry and was engrossed in reading the Scotsman.

"Now children, have you seen the UFO article?" he asked inquiringly. You must have been aware of the UFO controversy in Kinrasaig?" Matt had to think of a satisfactory reply hurriedly.

"Yes, I was," replied Matt. "I was going to get around to talking about it today."

"Have a look at this?" he continued as he showed the Scotsman to Matt open to the lead headline article on page two. He took the paper and began to read the controversial article:

REMAINS OF UNIDENTIFIED CRAFT FOUND ON HEBRIDEAN PEAT MOOR
By our West Highlands correspondent

Last week, there was a flurry of activity on the Scottish Island of Baraignsay. The Army has been called in to investigate local claims that strange wreckage of an unidentified craft discovered on moorland may be of a UFO. The Army personnel involved in the search under Captain Cammins first thought that the debris was of an unidentified spy plane.

Local villagers, including six children from the village of Kinrasaig, were asked by Captain Cammins to stay clear of the cordoned-off area. Investigations are continuing amid local protests by the crofters in Kinrasaig who complain that they are unable to herd their sheep on the common grazing pastures.

"Dad, I've finished reading it," said Matt.

"I take it that you lot and the Kinrasaig lot are those six children," Dad surmised.

"Captain Cammins," Dad announced, "is a well-known colleague of mine with whom I've had meetings and shared in seminars in London and at Aldermaston. I'll have discussions with him about Baraignsay. I know of all your conversations with Auntie Ethel about extra-terrestrials. I don't want to lose you as you go on some wild ride in a flying saucer. You need to be sensible about this. I'm also worried about your involvement; concerning my job."

Matt went upstairs hoping that Yesl would at least be present, but to his dismay, his bed was empty. The red curtains fluttered aimlessly in the light evening breeze coming in through the open window, left that way for Yesl and company to return. Doing his little bit of homework was very tedious during this worrying time. After finishing his assignment, Mom came in with his usual cup of cocoa.

"Matt," she said. "You look so worried. Is there something troubling you at school?"

"I am troubled," he replied, somewhat evasively.

"I could not help but overhear your conversation with Dad over all of the shenanigans in Baraignsay." Mom continued. "Oh, where's Yesl?" she asked, looking around at the empty bed.

Just at that moment, the familiar warbling sounds of more than one Balkien were heard in the distance, getting rapidly louder and closer to the open window in Mom's presence. Before Matt could do anything to hide his secret, Yesl, Baingae, Boongoo, Smalkle, Moonxl, and Moonzl arrived through the open window as if making a Royal Entrance by the red curtains. To Matt's surprise, albeit pleasant, Mom greeted the party of spherical beings warmly, "Hello to you all. We were worried about you this evening."

"I'd meant to tell you, Matt, that Mom found out about us yesterday evening but did not get a moment with all that was going on," said Yesl.

"I was surprised you managed to keep Yesl a secret from us since Christmas," said Mom. "I'd never have guessed the true nature of what I bought at Mackay's shop last summer, *secretly* of course for your Christmas present. We all have secrets, don't we? I'd better say, 'Good Night' to the *seven* of you."

"Good Night," said Matt and the Balkiens in unison.

It was a sunny afternoon in early September when Matt was picked up from school and taken by his mother along with Kara and Sean to Auntie Ethel's large house set in beautiful well-manicured gardens up in the Braids on the south side of Edinburgh. Yesl, Baingae, and Boongoo flew over.

As Mom drove into the driveway and stopped the car, everyone leaped out of the car and ran to greet Auntie Ethel, who was her usual jolly self. The roses were in full bloom with aromas wafting on the breeze.

"Time for tea," announced Auntie Ethel. "I'm sure that you're all looking forward to your Darjeeling brew and cakes."

As Matt wandered past the old wooden garden shed, he could see Yesl, Boongoo, and Baingae sitting inside looking out of the window. With Auntie Ethel's permission, he opened the shed door and fetched the Balkiens, and brought them to tea on the garden patio and seated them on the end of the table.

"Oh look," continued Auntie Ethel, "Matt, you still have that wonderfully colored pom-pom, and two others as well."

"My dear Auntie Ethel, we have an important announcement to make," said Matt, with a nervous look on his face. "See Yesl here. You'll be wondering why I'm so fond of *her*. Remember all of our conversations about SETI and the presence of civilizations on other planets."

"Ah yes," assured Auntie Ethel with a nod of acknowledgment.

"Yesl," continued Matt. "Yesl is a genuine alien being and a great friend too."

Matt gestured to Yesl, who started to make her warble hovering noise and lifted herself into the air. Boongoo and Baingae followed Yesl. All three hovered around the rose flowers like giant bumblebees. Auntie Ethel looked on in amazement. They flew out over the city for about ten minutes and came in over the hedge in a 'V' formation and hovered over to the tea table and landed softly in their original positions, causing some of the napkins to be blown off with their downdraught.

YESL – The Balkien from Antrobi

"Incredible!" exclaimed Auntie Ethel in disbelief.

"Hello, I'm Yesl, and I come from the planet, Antrobi."

"Well I never," whispered Auntie Ethel as she stared in wonderment. "I always knew and sensed that there was something odd about that ball, ever since last Christmas. So, I'm not that surprised at all. I've always wished that there was life in other worlds. I guess that wish has come true."

"You see," said Yesl as she showed off shimmering colors on her swooth. "We kept this secret only between ourselves and Matt until we went up to Uncle Herbert's. When it was time to leave Auntie Ethel's after such an exciting and strange afternoon, they bade farewell to the Balkiens as they departed to fly back home on their own.

Yesl was perched on Matt's shoulder while he was busy with his homework, helping him with his physics assignment about gravity and orbital motions of the Moon and planets for which Yesl could render assistance. Having Yesl there each night had a pleasant soothing effect on his soul.

The bedroom door opened. It was Dad standing with his arms folded, still dressed in his business suit, having just arrived home from work. The sun was still intense before the onset of dusk.

"Matt," he began. "Who is this perched on your shoulder?"

Matt was startled.

"I thought I heard that ball talking in plain English; all about orbits and planets."

"Dad, that is my physics homework tonight," replied Matt showing him the textbook for the exercise.

Dad began to whistle one of his jazz tunes as he was in the habit of doing, while he was thinking. "Oh, I see. I sure hope to see you with much-improved grades in your schoolwork. I'll be going down to London with my colleague Captain Cammins to an important meeting regarding the search program on Baraignsay this Thursday to Saturday. Your Mom's arranging for you to go and stay at the Marlston Country Hotel from Friday evening to Saturday and for you all to go for a walk up to the reservoir. You all need some exercise. I'm sure you'll enjoy it."

"Oh, we'd love that," replied Matt.

"And as for those wooly balls," said Dad in a worried tone, "I'm not too sure about having them in this house at all."

"Oh, don't be a spoilsport. Yesl will help me with my homework."

"We'll have to see about that. I'd rather that these balls were not in this house when I get back. Good night."

Dad closed the door softly. He could be heard descending the stairs, whistling another jazz tune.

It was a quarter to nine as Ernest Sutherland, Matt's Dad, and Captain Cammins, walked briskly along Whitehall towards the Ministry of Defense Headquarters after emerging from Westminster Underground Station into a breezy, sunny morning. Like most people walking to their places of work, they were dressed in dark suits, carrying their briefcases. Captain Cammins had his laptop case.

"I'm sure that this meeting will just simply be a formality to secure the continued funding for our research at Kinrasaig," said Captain Cammins. "It's fascinating. My men have just discovered more pieces of a strange metal alloy scattered among rocks at Rhannaig Point."

"Have you brought samples with you to the meeting?" asked Mr. Sutherland.

"They're in my briefcase; two large pieces."

"I have got one of the silver spheres found by my son on Mt Tetraval."

"You haven't," replied Cammins with glee. "That impetuous boy and his little cousins."

"Wait a minute. You're talking about my eldest son. I know he's got his agenda over this, but he has assisted us greatly."

They walked up the steps leading to the double doors of the main offices for the Ministry of Defense. The imposing building with large sandstone blocks and massive round pillars all along its façade topped with two ornate rounded bell towers at each end. After taking the lift to the third floor, they found themselves seated with about fifteen other delegates.

"I thank you all for coming to attend this presentation by Captain Cammins on the research into the strange wreckage found up in the north of Scotland," said the chairman. "I especially welcome Mr. David Easter, Head of Treasury and Professor Holzapfel, Head of the Department of Metallurgy at Cologne University in Germany. I now hand over the proceedings to Captain Cammins."

Captain Cammins walked up to the lectern to give his slide presentation from his laptop. With pointer in hand, he began his discourse. The first few slides set the scene with maps of Baraignsay showing the location of the wreckage found. Slides showing scattered remains of the *Balkieston* followed.

"Now we come to some interesting images of who we think were the crew on this space cruiser," announced Captain Cammins as he showed the photo of Smalkle just taking off from a sheep after leaving a wool circle.

David Easter interrupted, "That photo is blurry. Have you any better shots?"

"That's the best I could take as that pom-pom, call it what you like, took off very quickly," replied Captain Cammins in his posh English accent, albeit a little nervously.

"This seems to be an auspicious project involving a bunch of wooly pom-poms," said David Easter. "Don't you all agree?"

He continued to the conclusion with a proposal to extend the research into the ocean off Baraignsay by sending down submersibles. He then sat down.

The chairman stood up from his place at the front end of the long, varnished oak table.

"I now invite professor Holzapfel to take the stand."

"Thank you, gentlemen, for inviting me to oversee this exciting research on the analysis of these metals found on the island of Baraignsay." The Professor, who sported a greying beard, wore dark-framed glasses and was balding from his forehead, began his presentation. He was dressed in a light blue suit and a crimson tie, which had the Cologne University shield on it.

He continued in his distinct German accent, "I now present the results of our analysis of the main metal alloys found in this wreckage."

The first few slides were of more images of the bits of metal. The next few showed graphs of the statistical results of the spectral and chemical tests.

"I beg to interrupt sir," began David Easter. "I've yet to see any striking contrasts between your analyses on this strange alloy and those results on known alloys of terrestrial origin."

The Professor continued. "It has been challenging to find suitable acids to dissolve this material and analyze the constituent elements."

He concluded his presentation with a proposal for further spectral analysis building on that carried out at Aldermaston.

The window blinds were raised to let in the rays of the morning sun. The dull drone of traffic could be heard outside in the street.

"I now invite questions from the floor," said the chairman.

David Easter arose first. "Gentlemen, I have seen interesting presentations on what should have been an exciting program of research, but I fail to see where all of this is going. I would have liked to see much more information and clearer pictures of the beings who were supposed to have flown this ship. All I saw this morning were two or three very fuzzy images of pom-poms; the kind I might make for my little kids; and as for the results of the chemical analysis."

Professor Holzapfel began, "This research is only the beginning. There is more planned."

"Then, I would like to see a definite proposal made for this further work before I allocate precious funds to continue this project."

"Might I add, Mr. Easter, that we could find many more interesting things in the ocean if we go diving for them," said Captain Cammins, who pulled the two samples out of his briefcase and passed them around.

"That may all be very well," said David Easter looking at the bent and partially melted nuggets, "but we have to remember that we'll have to search an extensive area of the sandy ocean bottom. If this spacecraft broke up into tiny pieces like those samples here, there may well not be anything other than more of these small pieces. These seem to be difficult to chemically analyze, as shown by the results presented here this morning."

Captain Cammins sat down and let out a sigh of frustration.

Ernest Sutherland opened his briefcase and pulled out the silver sphere that he had. "I'd like to pass this around everyone. It was found in one of the caves near Rhannaig point."

Everyone was hushed as the object was passed around for everyone to look at before being handed back to Matt's father.

"Very intriguing," said Captain Cammins.

"Looks just like a large ball bearing," said David Easter. "Could any metallurgy be carried out on this? Maybe with similarly inconclusive results?"

"Any more questions before I close this meeting?" asked the chairman.

"One more," said Captain Cammins. "Maybe we could find more pom-poms on Mt Tetraval."

"More wooly pom-poms, hah," said David Easter. "A few weeks ago, you allegedly saw one of them on the back of a sheep. Did you see any others yourself?"

"Well no actually," said Captain Cammins with the beginnings of a stutter.

"That's just it," said David Easter, "an expensive pursuit in my eyes."

"Any more questions," asked the chairman.

There was an awkward silence with gasps of frustration among the delegates.

"Then, I declare this meeting closed."

Everyone collected their laptops and papers and left the conference room.

Mom, Matt, Kara, and Sean drove around the final bend on a country road on that overcast and breezy Friday evening into the village of Marlston on the county border. In the center of a cluster of stone-built houses, there was the Country Hotel. Accordion music was playing in the pub. There were peals of laughter from inside as everyone was merrymaking over a few beers and some Scottish country dancing. Mom and the three children entered in by the stylish front glass-paneled doors and walked across the reddish patterned carpet up to the wooden reception desk. A young lady, with long straight brown hair, wearing a white blouse, asked courteously in her local Scottish accent, "And what can we do for you?"

"Have you got our reservations for tonight?" asked Mom in reply. "Booked under the name, Sutherland?"

"Certainly," replied the young receptionist. "Let me see." She pressed a few keys on the computer. "Ah, yes. We do have your two rooms. One with a double bed and the other with a double and a single, and we can put up a camp bed if needs be."

"That would be great," replied Mom. "Thanks."

After the formalities of the booking, everyone went upstairs and settled into the two well-apportioned rooms, which had high ceilings with ornately decorated cornices and oak-paneled doors. Mom and the three children sat on the big bed in the larger room.

"So, what now?" asked Mom. "You've no idea what your Dad and I went through after, that story about the wool circles on the Ten O'clock News last week."

Matt let out a sigh, "I'd no idea that you and Dad had argued over the visitors from Antrobi."

"Matt," said Mom. "It's not your fault. In a way, I'm glad this has happened."

"Oh, what'll we do?" asked Kara. "Surely, you and Dad can sort this out."

"Let's not worry about that now," said Mom with a sigh that revealed her exhaustion. "We came here to have a good weekend and enjoy some country walks up the glen to the reservoir. The Balkiens will love it here. Let's go downstairs for dinner."

As it got later, after their meal, the noise of laughter and the accordion music ebbed away as people retired. After going back to their rooms, Mom was soon asleep. Matt was alone on the king-sized bed, huddled up with his company of six Balkiens, Yesl, Boongoo, Baingae, Smoonksie, Moonxl, and Moonzl. One of the curtains remained open over the tall wooden sash window. The stars were bright in the night sky. Matt crept out of bed on the creaky carpeted wooden floor and walked to the bay window without disturbing Kara or Sean. All six of the Balkiens huddled around Matt's head in ponkadliath. He went between the curtain and the window and looked up to the constellation of Lyre and Vega. They all gazed up in wonder at Vega. Matt had goosebumps as he imagined the planets Antrobi and Antrogi in orbit around Vega and imagined the massive tall rock mountains protruding from the purple oceans. He also remembered Yesl's descriptions of their surreal cities. He tucked up in the large bed with his company and fell into a peaceful sleep full of dreams about Antrobi and the Balkiens. There was a particularly poignant scene in these visions, in which there were several geodesic roundhouses or *mooties* and other beehive-like stone dwellings set in a small hamlet amidst a beautiful dark olive green meadow in the bright bluish sunlight of Vega, known as *Vegalight*. Around one of these mooties was a large group of Balkiens, one of whom looked remarkably similar to Yesl. Some of the others also looked familiar. In the vision, Yesl hovered up to him and introduced her parents. Her mother looked like her, except her father was a larger burly Balkien colored dark grey with bright bands of purple and white.

"Meet Mama Yesl and Papa Woozl, who was related to Captain Woozl," said Yesl. "This is Baingae as you know and Winxl, his fiancée. Here are the Winkets, Wink, and Mwaki."

"Oh, the priests at Winxl's internment ceremony," said Matt.

Matt tried to turn his head around in awe and caught a glimpse of what looked like a massive full Moon in purple hues, but about ten times the Moon's size. It filled about a quarter of the sky. His head met resistance that turned out to be the large double pillows on the bed. He awoke with a start and then noticed the Earth's full Moon shining onto him and all six of the Balkiens.

"Yesl," he whispered. "That was a wonderful sight. I wish we could go there. Only your ship's wrecked, and I guess we're all stuck on this old Earth."

"That was a family reunion we had before Winxl's accident," said Yesl. "It was not long after this reunion that things started to fall apart."

It was a dull wet morning, and it felt to Mom, Sean, Kara, and Matt as if they were on holiday as they sat down to breakfast in the hotel dining room.

"It's Dad's infernal job," began Mom. "Things just came to a head while you were all on Baraignsay. I think that he's been very stressed about his boss finding out about the aliens being in our house."

"I'm sorry that my association with Yesl had caused this stress," said Matt.

"Remember it was I who acquired Yesl in the first place. So, don't you feel guilty at all. It's my problem. I'll have to deal with it."

"A problem?" inquired Matt. "It's great having Yesl and co. I wouldn't give up this experience for the entire world. Though I admit that this has changed my life, and I get teased at school over my perceived strange behavior, and I admit my grades are below par."

"Matt, I know that you've been through a lot. You do want to go to University, don't you?" asked Mom. "You'll have to hunker down and earn a place there."

"I'd love to go and study in America, Mom."

"America?"

"Maybe somewhere on the West Coast; maybe ASU, that is Arizona State University."

"America's a huge country. You'd be a bit lost there, far from the bosom of your family."

"I'm sure I'd meet some cool dudes, there."

"Cool dudes - of the round fluffy kind maybe?"

"Can't completely deny that possibility."

"Matt. What'll you study?

"I'd like to do Astronomy or Astrophysics."

"Pity that we had to cancel our walk today," said Kara.

"Look. It's simply just too wet," said Mom. "We could get lost in that low mist up the glen. There'll be another time; maybe with Auntie Ethel. We certainly enjoyed the food and the county dancing."

"I thought that I could see the Balkiens doing their versions of eights and reels over the ceiling rafters" Kara chuckled.

"It may be that everyone was too merry to notice floating wooly balls," remarked Matt.

"I bet most people thought that it was part of the act by the band," said Sean, "a great show!"

After the car pulled into the driveway, Matt grabbed his bag with the Balkiens in it and rushed upstairs to his room.

"Matt," said Yesl from the open bag. She flew out and hovered around the room with papers and clothes everywhere. "I hope that your Dad hasn't gotten hold of any of the things we brought back from Baraignsay.

"As far as I know, I don't think so," replied Matt. "My suitcase from Baraignsay is still in the car, where it was left when we got back from the airport before all this happened. Still, I am a bit uneasy about anything that may have been left here last night."

All six Balkiens emerged from the carrier bag and hovered around the house and the garden for what they all thought might be the last time in a long while, if not forever. Tears welled up in Matt's blue eyes.

"I'm going to miss you all," he sobbed while hugging Yesl. The others formed an instantaneous ponkadliath around him. "I'll miss your wonderful assistance with my maths and physics, especially you, Baingae and Boongoo. How will I keep up and improve my grades for entry to an American University?"

"I'm going to get my bike and cycle up to Corstorphine Hill, where there is thick woodland. We may find a hiding place or secluded spot to build you a small mootie until we can get something fixed up, maybe at Auntie Ethel's." With his knapsack on his back, he cycled up to the entrance gate, which led up a narrow path that went through two grassy fields, where sheep and a few cows were still grazing.

Not more wool circles, thought Matt, picturing images of these in a future edition of the evening paper. He cycled up the cinder path to the edge of the wood and ventured into its dark shade. He laid down his bike and opened his knapsack, to let Yesl, Boongoo, Baingae, Smoonkshie, Moonxl, and Moonzl out into flight.

"What a thick forest; reminds me a little bit of Splogita," remarked Yesl, half expecting to see the Molktrons rolling out from below the undergrowth.

"There are a great many denser forests than this here on Earth," said Matt, "and much darker and just as hazardous. We'll have to find you a home here. I know. There's an old stone tower on the top of the hill. I'm sure that you've seen it from my bedroom window."

"Yes, I have," said Yesl. "I've flown over it a few times."

"I won't be able to get in as the iron-gate is always locked. I'm sure that you'll be able to fly up to the top and in through a slit window and find shelter," said Matt.

"We'll miss being with you at night," said Yesl.

"It'll be an empty bed, that's for sure. I'd better head back now before Dad gets home, or I'll have an awful lot of explaining to do."

"Dinner's up," called Mom. Little was discussed at the table, while Matt thought about writing to the Fredricksons in Arizona, and what to say to them without sounding stupid.

Dear Dan & Helen, Erin, Dan & Nick,

I have visited Kinrasaig in the Isle of Baraignsay where you all traveled and stayed at Mrs. MacKinnon's in Inverainort. I'm sure that you had a wonderful trip as we did in July, visiting there also.

I enclose a newspaper cutting from the 'Altaness Courier,' published on the island, and in the Scotsman about the recent encounter with the Balkiens, who are beings from another planet, space-wrecked on Earth in the North Atlantic.

I don't wish to alarm you, but I believe that you purchased three soft-wooly balls from Angus Mackay's souvenir shop in Scarivanish in mid-May when you were over. They may soon wake up from their comatose state as the ones that we bought did (see enclosed photos). Check the websites for the 'Altaness Courier,' the 'Scotsman' newspapers, and the UK BBC TV for confirmation of these stories. Be careful to take care of your three balls and be in touch about them.

Yours sincerely
Mathew

Matt sealed the letter, wrote the address he had copied from Mrs. MacKinnon's visitors' book, and mailed it in the letterbox at the end of the lane, hoping for a positive reply someday.

Helen fetched the mail from the mailbox, which was full of the usual, bills and junk mail. It was a warm morning in the desert air, promising to be a hot day. As she sorted it out, she picked out an airmail letter from the United Kingdom. "Oh, this is interesting." On reading it, her eyes began to bulge like saucers. "Dan, you'd better see this," Helen passed the letter with enclosed newspaper cuttings and photos to her husband.

"Yes, dear, I'll look at it after work."

"You'd better read it now. It may concern those soft-wooly balls we bought for the kids on Baraignsay."

"Mom. What about them?"

"Erin. Someone called Matthew, who was staying at our guesthouse in Baraignsay, has written to say that those balls are in fact aliens from outer space! I must admit they do look rather *spacey*".

"They have had an iridescent look about them lately," remarked Erin. "Oh, my ball is so warm and cuddly in my bed. I've given him a name. He's called Monku. Oh, Mom, I've had incredibly vivid dreams lately."

"Oh, my dear little Erin, not nightmares, I hope."

"Oh no, quite the contrary, beautiful dreams. I wonder if it's Heaven or somewhere. There are this incredibly beautiful emerald green meadow and a purple sky. In the distance, there are odd rounded buildings, and behind them, there are the tall Rocky Mountains. Oh, the place is so wonderful," said Erin. "I'd love to go there, but the place seems to be so out of this world."

Little Dan Jr and Nick brought their light green and pink pom-poms downstairs and laid them on the breakfast table. Dan Jr announced that his pom-pom was called Mwakus and Nick had named his, Bwinkus.

"Strange names for them," remarked their Dad, Dan Sr. Monku was beginning to look very radiant with all the shades of blue in his swooth.

"How did you all think of those unusual names?" asked Dan.

"Oh, these names just came into our heads quite unexpectedly about a week or so ago," said Erin.

At that moment, everyone could hear a faint warbling hovering sound from upstairs, which grew louder. Monku entered through the kitchen door, flying about five feet from the floor. The bluish Balkien settled down beside the other pom-poms. Everyone was startled, though not overly so, thinking that Monku was some battery-operated flying toy. Erin went to pick up Monku, but Monku quickly flew up and buzzed around the kitchen, before flying out of the window and off over the trees and rooftops of the houses in their suburban street.

"Oh, my lovely Monku has flown away from us," cried little Erin with tears welling up in her eyes.

"We've got something weird going on here," said Helen with some anxiety. "Maybe we'd better call those people in Scotland."

"Did they give a number?" asked Dad.

"Yes," replied Mom.

Helen called the number, and it was Matt's Mom, who answered the phone.

"Hello, this is Helen Fredrickson calling from Arizona. Is Matthew home?"

"He's doing his homework," said Mom. "What's it about?"

"It's about those fluffy pom-poms we bought in Baraignsay. Matthew wrote us a letter about them."

"I'll put him on."

"Is that you, Helen?"

"Hi Matthew," said Helen in her distinct Arizona accent. "We just received your letter about the pom-poms. One just flew away! Our little girl, Erin, is distraught at losing her cuddly Monku. Thanks so much for writing to us about this. We just got your letter today, and Erin's still crying about losing her dear Monku."

"Monku," replied Matt excitedly. "We know him well. As I wrote, these are no ordinary balls of wool. They're alien beings from another planet, but they're very friendly, once you get to know them and they accept you. Just be patient. I've got about seven of them staying here. I have one called Yesl, who speaks English very well. I may send her out to meet you. She can stow away on a plane to New York or Los Angeles and then fly cross-country to your house."

"That would be awesome. Erin wants to speak to you."

"Hi Matthew," came the little girl's voice on the phone.

"Hi, Erin," said Matt.

"Can you get me back my Monku? Please!"

"You'll get Monku back soon. I'm going to send my pom-pom called Yesl to you. She may take about seven days to get to you. It's a long way from Scotland to Arizona. She's colored with most of the colors of the rainbow and is a little bigger than Monku. They were space-wrecked while trying to get back to their home planet, Antrobi."

"Wow," said Erin. "They are aliens from space. I'm a little scared having had Monku as a pom-pom."

"Don't worry Erin," said Matt reassuringly. "Yesl now speaks excellent English. I was very spooked when Yesl first woke up after my Mom gave her to me for Christmas last year. She bought her at Mackay's shop in Baraignsay last summer."

"That's where we bought our pom-poms," said Erin. I look forward to seeing Yesl. Will she look for Monku?"

"Yes, she will," said Matt.

"Hello, Matthew," Helen, Erin's Mom, interjected. "We're so glad you contacted us, or we'd have been more shocked than we were."

"I'm planning to send you my pom-pom, Yesl, to sort this out. Meantime keep an eye on the other two you have, like Monku, they'll fly off when they wake up and try to look for their other crew members."

"Matthew, I'd better say cheers for now."

"Bye-bye." Matt hung up the phone and went to bed.

On Saturday morning, Matt cycled over to the woods to meet up with Yesl and the other Balkiens at the old stone tower where they were hiding out.

YESL – The Balkien from Antrobi

Leaning his bike against the stone wall, he called out, "Antrobi," the password they had all established for meeting up in these new circumstances. Yesl and Baingae came hovering down from the small slit window in the little turret on top of the Corstorphine Tower, which had been built in 1871 to commemorate the centenary of the birth of the famous novelist, Sir Walter Scott. The usually locked thick oak door with intricately decorative wrought iron hinges started clicking and clanking and then slowly creaked to open. The other Balkiens had manipulated the lock by their telekinesis to let Matt inside and up the narrow stone stairs to the top parapet where their hideout was, overlooking the city of Edinburgh.

"Hi, all," greeted Matt.

"Hi Matt," greeted Boongoo, who was seated with Smoonkshie and Moonxl.

"I've got the news," continued Matt. "I had a call from that family in America, who had bought the three including Monku from MacKay's shop in Baraignsay. Their little girl, Erin much loved Monku. He awoke suddenly and flew off in fright as most of you did."

"Matt," said Yesl. "Monku will speak no English and will have got lost somewhere in the deserts of Arizona. What about the others, Mwakus and Bwinkus?"

"As far as I know, still asleep," replied Matt as he entered the little stone round room in the top lookout turret on top of the central square tower. The Balkiens had four of the silver spheres, plus the larger one laid out on a small rug on the stone floor.

"We only have four of these now," said Yesl. "Where are the other three?"

"I'm sure that they were in our bags," replied Matt. "Oh, I hope Dad hasn't found them and passed them onto Captain Cammins."

"I thought I had them all, but I can only find these five," said Yesl. "Our secrets may be exposed."

"What are they anyhow?"

"They contain data; a bit like your thumb drives in your computers. Only they can be read while near a reading device such as those in our scout craft."

"I'll try to find the others when I get back," said Matt. "What about Monku? I suggested to the Fredrickson's that I send you, Yesl, over to Arizona to look for Monku."

"How shall I get there?" asked Yesl.

Matt noticed a movement under the red tartan rug spread on the stone floor. The corner of the carpet moved to reveal Moonzl.

"Hi, Moonzl," greeted Matt. "I only had you for a short time in Baraignsay before you went to Tetraval from our house."

"Moonzl has not learned a lot of English yet," said Yesl. He went over to our Rhannaig Point hideout meaning to come back to us that evening, but with all the drama with Cammins and his cohorts and the discovery of

Smalkle and the wool circles, they had to flee in a great hurry in their scout ship."

"We went over to the cave to find that you'd gone, figuring that to be the reason," said Matt. "Then we found these seven data spheres, four of them here."

"So that's what happened to them. Two of these spheres contain our navigation data, without which it is hard to navigate our ship. After they'd taken off, they got lost over the Atlantic Ocean and managed to come back trying to find Baraignsay to look for the spheres. They landed the ship somewhere on the west coast of where you call Ireland." Moonzl drew a rough sketch map of Ireland on a piece of paper with the pencil moving under telekinesis apparently by itself. "The dot shows the position of our ship," said Yesl.

"That's in County Galway on the West Coast," said Matt. "Hopefully, two of these spheres are the ones you need."

"Well, just take them back to our ship and try them," said Yesl. "Then, hopefully, we could fly over to Arizona to look for Monku. It'll be a distance to Galway to locate our ship.

"Matt. We may not be able to hide here much longer, and given all that has happened, it may be best if we all depart for North America in our ship and meet up with Monku, Bwinkus, and Mwakus."

"Oh, will you be gone long?"

"Probably."

"I'll miss you a lot," said Matt with a tear in his eye.

"It's for the best," said Yesl. "It's untenable to stay in your presence any longer under these circumstances. Your parents are right. You need to study hard to enter University, and we don't want to make it difficult for your Mom and Dad. We had to train hard at Space Academy in Balkieston before going on the mission to Splogita."

"I'd like to go to University in Arizona," said Matt. "Then I could be with you all again in a few years. It'll be a long time."

All the Balkiens in that little turret cuddled Matt in one last ponkadliath. Matt shed some tears as he remembered all the times that they had together since that Christmas Day about six months before.

"We can be in touch on the internet," said Yesl. "I'm sure that we will be in regular contact at the Fredrickson's. Only better watch out not to let your parents know too much about this. We'll take these balls over to Galway to our ship and come back for the rest of us."

"You could stow away on a flight to Belfast and fly the rest of the way over those luscious Irish green fields, said Matt. We will tell you when to come over to see if those balls worked."

Matt reluctantly walked down the stairs to the old oak door and went outside into the thick woods. As he mounted his bike to cycle home, the door slowly shut firmly. Yesl flew over the parapet and hovered alongside Matt until he reached the main road.

"Bye-bye, Matt," she called.

"*Au revoir La Voise*," having a French name for Yesl, as he cycled down the road from the foot of the path leading from the woods. Yesl flew off back to the tower.

At home, Matt looked in vain for the remaining three silver balls, suspecting that his Dad had found them in his bag and taken them on the night that they had all stayed in the hotel. Matt had been in his room for about ten minutes when there was a soft knocking on the window. It was Baingae. He opened it, and Baingae hovered in.

"Baingae," he said. "It's so good to see you here."

"Matt," said Baingae. "We've come to say 'goodbye.' The spheres you brought did work, and our ship is now fully operational. It's presently hidden in the hills south of Edinburgh."

"The Pentlands," said Matt.

"We'd like you to see us off at the Old Tower. Be there tomorrow morning," said Baingae as he flew off over the trees. That evening as the family ate dinner; Mom suggested a visit to Auntie Ethel the next day. Usually, Matt would only be too excited but realized that he would not be able to see his friends off.

"Mom, I'd love to come up to visit, but I'm seeing some friends off to America," said Matt.

"Oh, are you going to the station or the airport?" asked Mom. "I could pick you up there."

"No, it'll be okay. I'll catch the bus to see my friends and then get another one to Auntie Ethel's and see you there in the afternoon."

"Well if that's okay. You'll take ages, Matt, with the infrequent Saturday services. Auntie Ethel has to go out at four o'clock to meet her sister, Agnes, at the Waverley Station. She's coming up from London for a few days."

A tired Matt had to leave early the next day to walk to the Old Tower as he said that he was catching a bus and not cycling. He arrived at the Tower only to find that nothing happened when he called out "Antrobi" several times. He waited and waited and waited. There was still no sign of Baingae or any of the others.

"Perhaps I was meant to go to the Pentlands," he thought as his frustration grew as he looked at the locked door of the Tower. At nine o'clock, a man in a dark blue uniform with a peaked hat walked up with a bunch of keys and opened the door of the Tower. "Been waiting' long to see Walter Scott's Centenary monument?" he said. "It's £5 for admission."

Pulling out the money reserved for his bus fare to Aunty Ethel's, he paid the admission fee and received a leaflet about the history of the Tower. He climbed up the stone stairs and went into the turret room. The floor was bare except for the tartan rug now folded up and placed on a wooden chair. Everything else, including the silver spheres, was moved out. Matt was crestfallen as he looked out over the city and the woods on the crisp, sunny morning. He then saw a black speck in the western sky. It grew larger and rounder, coming slowly but steadily towards the Tower. Matt heard the familiar sound of Baingae hovering just below the parapet and had to head off down the stairs. As Matt walked out along the path, Baingae joined him and hovered alongside.

"Our ship is over there in that clump of trees," said Baingae.

Matt came to a small clearing in the thicker woods where there were thick piles of rotting leaves from the previous fall and cinders within small circles of stones from old campfires. There was the gleaming silver ovoid-shaped scout ship, with Yesl and the others inside the open circular door.

"This is goodbye," said Yesl from the opening. She looked more commanding and in charge of operations. It was now hard to imagine her as just the cuddly pom-pom.

"I guess it is," said Matt.

"We're off to America. This ship now has plenty of power for the short trip; to us that is. Hope you manage to bear up okay, Matt."

"I will," he replied with another tear welling up. "You took ages, and now I am late to visit Auntie Ethel, and I have no bus fare as I had to pay to get into the Old Tower to look for you."

"Matt," said Yesl. "We'll give you a lift to Aunty Ethel's in the ship."

"That'd be so cool!" exclaimed Matt letting the excitement of a ride on an Antrobian spaceship overtake his sad emotions of their parting. "But I'm sure that I'm too heavy."

"You'd be too heavy for the trip to America," said Yesl, "but we're sure that for a short hop, it will be okay, climb in."

Matt clambered in through the small round aperture and lay on the floor of the cabin with his eyes positioned next to one of the small windows in the craft. Boongoo, who was the pilot, started moving over the array of rounded buttons and monitor screens. Matt began to hum that beautiful Antrobian melody again, feeling much happier about the turn of events.

A light humming sound started up as the ship lifted slowly off the ground and up through the dense tree canopy. Soon the trees dropped away below. The Old Tower was now just a small square shape in the lush green canopy.

Matt felt the acceleration as the ship raced towards an impressive view of Edinburgh Castle with the mount of Arthur's Seat beyond with a bright yellowish-green hue in the evening sunlight. In a matter of minutes, they were already over towards the Braids where Auntie Ethel lived. It was so graceful a flight. Soon the grounds of the nearby golf course rushed up to meet the ship as it came to a gentle clearing in some more trees. The Balkiens were in one last ponkadliath with Matt.

"Matt," said Yesl, "Did you enjoy the ride?"

"It was so cool. I only wish that we were not parting in this way."

"Matt. We'll meet up again. Just work hard at your physics and maths. We feel that you will be riding a lot in our Antrobian ships one day."

"Really," Matt excitedly said as he climbed out through the door back onto *terra firma*. "Sure was a great 'bus trip'."

At the door of the ship, they all had one last ponkadliath before they boarded the silvery vessel.

"Bye, Balkiens," called Matt.

"Bye, Matt," said Yesl. "You've been so good to us for being a friend that we know so well."

The door swung softly shut. Yesl and Baingae were at the porthole window. The ship hardly made a sound as it glided deftly through the trees. Matt ran out into the open, close to the 18th hole of the golf course where a few casual golfers were too busy concentrating on their final putts to see what was happening. The silver craft, reflecting the soft sunlight of the late afternoon, grew ever smaller as it receded into the steel azure sky. He looked longingly at the tiny spec of reflective sunlight. In a moment, it was gone.

Matt thought, "Gone out of my sight for now," as he gazed up into a now-empty sky. He thought of the Balkiens on board looking out over the expanse of Western Scotland, with Boongoo at the controls. Matt walked down the hill towards Auntie Ethel's house for his family visit, now being only fifteen minutes late. He knocked at the front door. "Oh, hello my dearest Matt," greeted Auntie Ethel. "Do come in. I've been waiting to hear all of your news. Can I get you a cup of tea?"

Matt sat down with his aunt at the little breakfast table in the drawing-room.

"Matt, have you seen the article on page three of today's 'Evening News'? It's about cuts to the funding for the search for the space debris on Baraignsay."

Sipping his tea from the red rose cup, Matt held up the paper to read the article:

FUNDING FOR SPACE-WRECK RESEARCH AXED BY TREASURER

Following a critical government meeting at the Ministry of Defense HQ in London last Friday, a decision was made to ax all further funding for Project Space-Wreck. At the meeting were, Mr. David Easter, head of the Government Treasury, with delegates including Captain Cammins, commanding officer-in-charge of the operations on the Isle of Baraignsay,

Earnest Sutherland, working for the Ministry of Defense in Edinburgh and guest speaker Professor Ludwig Holzapfel, head of the Department of Metallurgy at the University of Cologne in Germany.

The results of the analysis of the metal alloys in the parts of the wreckage of the alien spacecraft recovered from the crash site were inconclusive. Samples sent to Cologne for examination by the team headed by Professor Holzapfel were extensively analyzed using advanced chemical and spectroscopic techniques. He said, "This metal is impossible to analyze."

David Easter weighed up both sides of the debate and decided to terminate the program on Monday, based on the impossible nature of the analysis, both at Aldermaston and Cologne.

He added, "It's time we stopped this quest; looking for bits of strange metal and wooly pom-pom like beings, said to be from this supposed spacecraft."

It was also stated that as the wreckage was not from any known type of spy plane or other aircraft, funding was misappropriated. Army operations are now being wound up with all personnel returning to their barracks.

"Auntie Ethel," began Matt excitedly. "We could breathe a sigh of relief. Perhaps I'll have a much more normal life now and concentrate on those studies. I'll miss Yesl's help with the physics, though."

Matt lowered his head a little with tears streaming from his sad eyes. Auntie Ethel placed an arm around his shoulders.

● 〇 ●

9 ~ ARRIVAL OF THE WINKETS

Matt had corresponded with the Fredricksons as he grew up, who were a great encouragement in his studies and with Yesl and the rest who were now involved with their growing children, especially Erin.

"Ladies and gentlemen," announced the stewardess at the gate. "We would like to begin boarding this flight to New York. Please switch off your mobile phones and have your boarding cards ready."

Matt made his way to his assigned window seat for the long trip to America to begin his University Degree in Astrophysics. He was looking forward to finally meeting The Fredricksons and especially Yesl. Before the aircraft pushed back, he could see what looked like the Altaness plane situated a few gates away. Less than an hour into the flight, Matt gazed out of the starboard window and saw, spread out below, the coastline of Baraignsay. The village of Kinrasaig was a clump of small scattered houses. Mt Tetraval soon came into view from under the wing. Beyond lay the endless North Atlantic with gentle rolling swells. He thought of the possibility that somewhere beneath those waves lay the remains of the *Balkieston*.

Crossing to the West from New York over the Prairies on the second flight, there was an endless flat patchwork of square fields, which gave way to an infinite expanse of desert.

"The captain has turned on the *Fasten Seat Belt* sign. Please put your seatbacks in the upright position in preparation for landing."

Matt was looking out of the window across the vast expanse of sandy desert.

"In a short while, we shall be arriving at Tucson International Airport," intoned the captain. Matt had spent all his high school years, finding out more about the Balkiens and space flight, aspiring to be an astronaut. In many ways, he felt that he was following in the footsteps (or the swooth) of Yesl and Baingae.

Matt emerged from the gate into the arrivals area after clearing customs and immigration. He was amazed by the bright steel blue sky and the desert hills in the distance across the airfield. He turned around, and there was a couple with their two blond mid-teenage boys, both in shorts and T-shirts and a girl in her late teens dressed in denim shorts and a T-shirt with a colorful flower pattern. He wandered over toward them with his knapsack in which he used to carry Yesl and the other Balkiens on Baraignsay.

"Hi, I'm Dan," said the father as he reached out his hand to Matt. "You look lost. You must be Matthew."

"Yes, I sure am," said Matt with alacrity.

"So good to finally meet you," greeted Dan.

All of the Fredricksons hugged Matt in turn. After his embrace with Erin now in her late teens, Matt noticed something, or someone, in her small shoulder bag on the airport seat nearby. Erin led him over.

"Have a seat," she said.

As everyone sat down, Erin opened the bag, and there was a Balkien with swooth in many shades ranging from green through turquoise to blue.

"That's Monku," said Erin softly.

"Oh Monku," said Matt excitedly. "I haven't seen any Balkiens since Yesl had to leave us. I got to know Yesl so well that it was hard to see her go when they took off from that golf course near my Auntie Ethel's so long ago."

Erin reached into her bag and brought Yesl out discreetly.

"Yesl!" gasped Matt. "Oh, Yesl, it's been so long."

Matt hugged Yesl for a minute or two, "Oh Matt. You're so much taller. I've missed you!"

"C' mon, you guys," said Dan. "We've got food waiting for us at home. We'd better get along the road."

After they arrived at the Fredricksons' spacious bungalow in Tucson suburbia, they went out into the back yard, planted with exotic desert flowers and succulent cactus plants. To one side, two rounded cacti looked like a pair of Balkiens in a twosome ponkadliath. Matt chuckled as Erin showed him these.

As everyone sat down at the garden table, Helen poured glasses of lemonade. By now everyone was dressed in T-shirts and shorts, enjoying the fresh warm desert air. Erin had brought out a large basket. Two Balkiens hovered alongside her head as she placed the basket on the table. There was a beautiful ponkadliath of Balkiens inside it.

"Balkiens," called Erin as they started to quiver in the basket. They began to hover around the table like bees near some flowers.

Matt was ebullient to see Mwakus and Smalkle alight onto the table close to his place setting. "Oh, there's Yesl, Boongoo, Baingae, Moonzl, Monku, Bwinkus, and Smoonkshie. Not to mention Mwakus and Smalkle."

Yesl hovered up onto Matt's shoulders. "It must have been a long time for you, Matt. We flew straight over here via Iceland and Greenland after we left you. We nearly didn't make it. We had a forced landing in Greenland due to a computer malfunction on our ship, and we nearly froze inside a glacier following an avalanche, which severely damaged our craft. We had to continue on manual-pilot on half power as one of our gyro engines became jammed on impact with the ice. It took us about two months to get here.

Meanwhile, Monku went missing up in the Grand Canyon. Mwakus and Bwinkus also woke up and flew off as you warned us. So, there were no Balkiens here for about nine months until the following spring. Our ship has been in that shed over there for about five years as we needed one of the three silver spheres that went missing on leaving Baraignsay."

"The ship's now only something in which we played at being astronauts when we were kids," said Erin. "All of our school mates thought that it was just a space toy built for us out of junk by our Dad. I often sat in it and read books about the stars. I read about SETI and aliens during the time that all you Balkiens were missing, having given up on ever seeing any of you again, thinking that would be just a wonderful memory for us. Yesl finally showed up here and explained what had happened. Their ship was lying in some woods in Minnesota. So, we flew up to Minneapolis St Paul and rented a truck. Then we drove to the forest plantation and put the ship in the back and drove it back here in about four days. What a long drive! We put it in the shed when we were too busy with studies to play in it anymore."

Matt got up from his chair and ran inside. A few moments later, he came out with two of the three missing spheres.

"I honestly thought that our Dad had taken them when I couldn't find them. These turned up behind my wardrobe about four years later when I moved it out for redecorating my room. They must have fallen out of my bag when I was unpacking. There is still one missing that I could not find."

"Good for you," said Monku as he telekinetically picked up the spheres and flew over to the shed. Matt and Erin walked over and opened the door for Monku, and there was a not-so-gleaming ovoid space scout ship, full of dents from the forced landing in Greenland, sitting in that old wooden shed covered in years of dust, like an old vintage car that had not seen the highway for a decade or more. Monku wavered over the door, and it whirred open slowly. He hovered inside with the silver spheres slowly orbiting him like silvery moons around a bluish planet. A round panel opened, revealing the other four spheres and the larger one set in little cups for reading data on them. The two silver balls settled from Monku into two of the three vacant openings. Almost immediately there were whirrs and buzzes as if the ship was waking up and rebooting itself like some advanced computer system.

A round screen began to display colored video footage. Matt recognized himself with Uncle Herbert at the sheep shearing meet along with Kaz, Alison, Judith, Kara, and Sean.

"That's us on Baraignsay when we wondered about the wool circles on the sheep."

"Oh, what were they?" asked Erin inquisitively.

"They turned out to be holes eaten by our Balkien friends for nourishment," replied Matt.

"Yeah," said Erin. "Years ago, Mom couldn't figure out why Dan's winter woollies all had huge holes in them until we caught Monku eating the wool. It cost us about $300 to replace those garments." Erin chuckled. "Mom said that either Monku had to find other food or he had to go. Monku apologized once he learned English and now nibbles on the local cacti when he needs to. The cactus plants are the closest resemblance to the succulent tree type vegetation we have on Antrobi."

As Matt and Erin viewed the video of the sheep shearing event and everyone there, Captain Cammins suddenly approached the camera, and the view rocketed off up into the air, leaving everyone far below. Soon the jerky image revealed most of Mt Tetraval far below.

"That was Smalkle filming while he was eating the wool being caught by Captain Cammins as we fled," said Monku. "Smalkle explained all about it after they arrived on this ship at that time. They had to flee the island as the situation became untenable for us there. We must have left those data globes behind at our hideout as we fled."

"One's still missing," said Matt. "I could not find it at all. I can only guess that Dad got it while we spent the night out at that hotel. He probably gave it to the British Intelligence to investigate. Mind you, all the funding for the investigations on Baraignsay was suddenly and surreptitiously cut following a review meeting that my Dad had to attend in London."

"Ah, Matt," said Erin softly. "We'd never have met if we hadn't stopped at MacKay's shop as kids and bought Monku, Bwinkus, and Mwakus."

"I guess I'd never have looked for your address in the Mackinnon's guest book at Inverainort if Angus hadn't told me that you'd bought these wonderful balls."

Erin and Matt leaned towards one another while the video played out to the last scene showing the Balkiens packing everything up to leave the hideout; leaving the data globe abandoned. Monku then moved over the ship's control panel, and a detailed chart of the Earth appeared on the screen.

"Looks like we now have full navigation again," said Monku. The image quickly switched to Mars, then to Jupiter and other Solar System planets, mapped on their arrival. Erin gazed upon the round monitor with Monku perched on her right shoulder with her long flowing blond slightly curly hair draped over Monku's silhouetted form as viewed from behind. She was still wearing her denim shorts and a blue University of Arizona T-shirt to match the colors of Monku.

"Matt," said Erin. "I think the romantic story of Dr. Baingae and Winxl on Antrobi was so fascinating and wonderful; so sad that Winxl's not here now." Matt could observe some tears on Erin's face. "You know. I was always fascinated by astronomy and the possibility of aliens from space before we went to Europe and found these. We have been interested a lot in SETI."

"I was too," said Matt, "even before meeting Yesl."

"Incredible," said Erin. She lay in Matt's arms as they sat on the opening of the little scout ship with Monku in that old wooden shed. I'm so glad that you came to us and not just for a short holiday, but to study at Arizona State in astrophysics. I've news for you. I'll be one of your classmates in your Astronomy 101 class."

"Oh, that's so cool," said Matt. "I'll get to know you much better. No more short-long distance phone calls from Scotland."

"I'll tell you a lot more about Monku and the other two, here. We've often looked up at Vega with our backyard telescope. It's in that observatory dome over there. Come. I'll show you."

Together with Monku, Matt and Erin went into the telescope dome which Dan had built for the family not long after they got to know the Balkiens. Yesl came hovering over to them.

"This dome has hexagon and pentagonal panels that remind us of the modules on our spacecraft and our buildings on Antrobi," said Yesl.

"In our latest July issue of the SETI magazine, there's a report about possible strange radio signals that are just audible above the static noise recorded at the Kitt Peak Observatory," said Erin as she opened up the dome and showed the workings of their ten-inch reflector telescope. The sun had just set, and soon it would be time for some stargazing. Erin booted up the computer to replay a recording of this signal downloaded from the internet. To everyone's astonishment, Monku and Yesl became very alert and pulsated with excitement as they listened.

"That's almost certainly a signal from Antrobi," said Yesl as they listened further to this recording. There was a lot of noisy static in which very faint tones and beeps were just audible, which sounded a bit like Morse code and yet different in that it was faster.

"We'll try to process it on our ship's systems," said Monku.

As night fell, everyone, both human and Balkien alike looked at Vega through the telescope, wishing that they could resolve their home planet, Antrobi. Afterward, they all went over to the shed in the light of the rising Moon to process the signal recording on the ship's systems.

"The signal is sent from Balkieston trying to make contact with us," said Yesl.

Yesl and Monku worked at the ship's computer to filter out the radio static and managed to produce a much clearer coded transmission.

We've tried to decipher this message according to all the codes we've got," said Yesl. "None fit."

"Is it in some secret code?" asked Matt.

"Could be," said Yesl. "The signal is transmitted to base 20, but none of our decoding algorithms make any sense of it."

Matt and Erin looked at the pattern of Morse like dots and dashes on the view screen on the ship's console.

"We are unable to decode this," said Yesl.

"Maybe the message had to be sent in a secret code for some reason," said Erin.

"But, why?" asked Yesl.

"Ever had the unexpected?" asked Matt.

Monku hovered up to the screen and paused to look at the displayed pattern. "Those first few words talk about our geodesic dwellings," said Monku.

"But why send a message across the cosmos about a house?" asked Erin. "Surely they're not trying to sell us real estate."

"I agree," said Matt.

"Then the undecipherable code begins," said Yesl.

"Come on, everyone," said Helen in a friendly tone, "Time for bed. Y'all have University enrolment and orientation tomorrow."

"We'll have to sleep on this," said Matt.

Orientation week was an exciting time for Matt and Erin. On the day they both signed up for the Astronomy 101 class they walked along the main thoroughfare of the campus, which had turned into a carnival atmosphere in the bright desert sun. There were many stalls displaying activities of the clubs and societies that were keen to sign up first-year students. Matt and Erin came to the Arizona University Astronomical Society (AUAS) stall.

"Hi," greeted one of the two students running it. "Interested in astronomy?" He was quite a bit taller than the average height, had mid-brown hair down to his shoulders, and sported a thin beard. He wore a mid-blue AUAS T-shirt with khaki shorts with large side pockets on the outer legs.

"Dead keen," answered Matt.

"We've signed up to Astronomy 101," said Erin. "I'm local. Matt here comes from Scotland."

"Good to meet you both. I'm David Larsen. I'm starting my final year in Astrophysics this semester."

"I'm Erin. We would both like to join up."

"Okay. Here are the membership forms for you to fill in. Matt, you must have heard all about the wrecked spaceship over there. I've followed it a lot while studying here."

"Yes, we know a lot about that space wreckage in Scotland."

On a Saturday evening in October, Matt and Erin met up with David Larsen, at a club star party in Sabino Canyon, northeast of Tucson.

YESL – The Balkien from Antrobi

"Your spectral images for your term paper intrigue me," said David as he peered into the eyepiece of a six-inch refracting telescope.

"I certainly did not expect to see almost identical spectra from both Vega and Upsilon Andromeda," remarked Matt, who stood with Yesl sitting on his shoulder.

"We've taken many images on several nights, especially stacking the thirty or so we took on Tuesday the sixth," commented Erin who stood there rugged up in her dark blue anorak. Her dangling hood hid Monku, Baingae, Bwinkus, and Mwakus.

"We certainly have a very multicultural membership in this Astronomy Club," chuckled David as he stroked the swooth of Yesl and Monku.

"We're suspicious of these results concerning our home planet, Antrobi, with identical spectra as that from Splogita, the planet of Upsilon Andromeda," said Yesl.

Matt graciously let Erin have the next view in the telescope.

"Look, Matt, come and see what I see. Something is winking on and off near Vega."

Yesl hovered to the eyepiece. "Matt. Get your camera into video mode. Just record the winking light in the telescope. It might be a coded message."

Matt managed to record about five minutes of the winking signal. After the star party, Matt and Erin stayed up late to write up their results and conclusions. After these findings, Yesl had an uneasy feeling about her home planet. She feared that her compatriots on Antrobi could be in similar difficulties to the Molktrons.

Matt was invited to have Sunday roast at the Fredricksons'. After the meal, Matt and Erin went into the shed, with Monku, Mwakus, and Bwinkus. Yesl, Boongoo, and Baingae were also visiting Matt.

"In the light of your term paper results," began Monku, "we want to revisit those signals we could not decipher before the semester began. Any suggestions?"

Matt thought for a moment as he laid his hand on Erin's shoulder.

"What about the first mention of the geodesic house?" asked Erin.

"A complete geodesic polyhedron or a truncated icosahedron, as we have here, has twenty hexagons and twelve pentagons," said Matt. "Maybe each segment of code consists of five or six series of pulses. Try rearranging the sets of six and five pulses."

These were easy to separate by the more extended spaces between them.

"You know how a mootie has a single pentagon on top then five hexagons, five pentagons, and so on," said Matt. "Pull out all six pulse and five pulse groups in the original, then place the five pulse and six pulse sets in the order of the truncated icosahedron, beginning with the top pentagon."

All the Balkiens copied the code onto a strip of paper for each segment, starting with the first five-set and five six-sets of pulses, imagining that the icosahedron peeled like an apple from the top pentagon.

"This is now making some sense," said Yesl. "Good for you, Matt and Erin."

They poured over the strips of paper on the bench near the little space pod in the shed as the sunset.

"I'll translate," said Yesl. "*Antrobi, calling the Balkieston, where are you? You're six years overdue. If you hear this message after decoding it, be careful about coming home to Antrobi. A terrible thing has happened to us. Watch out. Be——.* Only twenty-five of the thirty-two faces on the truncated icosahedron are represented here. The message has been cut off. We've tried to pull more data from the static, but nothing."

Matt and Erin looked at each other with anxious eyes. "Matt, you look worried." They had matching facial expressions indicating a sense of foreboding. Yesl hovered onto his lap as they both gently stroked her swooth.

"I'm so glad that we know now and that we successfully decoded the warning about returning to Antrobi," said Erin at last.

"It's the first thing we've heard from Antrobi since we left for Splogita," said Yesl. "It's that there was an identical spectral signature from Vega to the one we detected on Splogita, for which we set off on our mission. Are you thinking what I'm thinking?"

"The Enigma?" asked Matt.

"Yes," said Baingae, "and what about Winxl?"

"We've yet to look at the winking signals I recorded at the star party recently," said Matt.

Matt drove back to the campus that night with a heavy heart with Yesl, Boongoo, and Baingae perched on the front dashboard of his blue Chevrolet Cobalt.

"Flagstaff eighteen miles," announced Erin.

Matt and Erin were heading north along the Black Canyon Interstate, I17, for their Christmas break. Some of their Balkien friends were with them, being Yesl, Boongoo, Baingae, and Monku on this trip. Matt and Erin had tuned in to their favorite country, western station, which played guitar twanging country songs about rural life and farming. The desert countryside rolled by with majestic mountain peaks and sandstone mesas with a constant stream of cars vans and trucks resplendent with chrome finishing.

"Won't be long now until we taste Grandma's delicious soup," said Erin. "Matt, you'll simply love it up here, meeting more of my family."

"Ay. It is going to be a great time for us up here. I've great plans for this trip, Erin. I think there's going to be some excitement."

"What you mean by that, Matt?"

"You'll soon see."

"Boodibah," intoned Baingae as he began to pulsate at this conversation.

"We'll soon know all about it," said Yesl quizzically.

The sun was now low in the western sky as they turned onto the interstate, I40, going east for several miles until they reached the turn-off to the little village east of Flagstaff, where Erin's maternal grandparents lived. As they pulled into the driveway, they were standing at the door to meet them. Their front yard had exotic cacti of various species growing out of sandy desert soil and shingle. Matt and Erin emerged from their vehicle. Their four round companions hovered over to meet their host.

"Welcome to you both," said Grandma, and to all these otherworldly friends as well.

"This is my boyfriend, Matt, from Scotland, who was in my Astronomy 101 class last semester.

"Hi. Welcome to our home," said Grandpa.

Looking at their still-hovering Balkiens, "These are Yesl, Boongoo, and Baingae under Matt's care and Monku undermine," said Erin pointing at each of them in turn.

"It's one thing to hear all about these visitors from Vega from your parents but another altogether to see them in the flesh, err swooth," said Grandma in her warm western drawl. "Come on in for a glass of iced tea."

It was a quiet and relaxing evening sitting on the back deck as the sun set behind the nearby hills.

"What plans do you have for tomorrow?" asked Grandma. "I know that in three days, your Mom and Dad will arrive for Christmas with Dan and Nick to open all of their presents."

"We plan to drive over to the Meteor Crater tomorrow and explore a bit and have lunch at the visitor center there," said Matt.

"That will be great for you, Matt," said Grandpa. "Part of a University assignment?"

"Partly," replied Matt. "I need to take photos and collect rock samples for my term paper on astrogeology next semester and spend time with Erin. The Balkiens are also very excited about going there."

Yesl began to pulsate. "I'm picking up strong telepathic feelings that seem to induce uncanny memories of the Winkets."

Boongoo and Baingae also began to pulsate on Matt's pillow. Baingae thought more strongly about Winxl. Matt was late in falling asleep with his excited little friends while Erin experienced similar pulsations from Monku, who slept in the next room.

The dawn drive on I40 east was relaxing. After about an hour Matt, Erin, Yesl, Boongoo, Baingae, and Monku arrived at the visitor center on the southern edge of the Barringer Meteor Crater where Matt parked their car on the far side of the as yet sparsely occupied parking lot at that early time in the morning.

"Sure, worth it to get here for sunrise and for us to walk to the other side of the crater before all the tour buses arrive," said Erin.

Their breath was visible as the sun was rising over the flat eastern horizon casting its long shadows. Matt and Erin began to walk off the parking lot onto the light sandy ground with their boots crunching on the gravel. The Balkiens hovered alongside them for about an hour as their shadows toward the eastern rim of the crater grew shorter. They then walked gingerly up to the edge of the crater holding each other's hands. As it became warmer, they took off their jackets and tied them around their waists.

They sat down on a large boulder a short distance from the crater's edge. The Balkiens landed in a ponkadliath on a rock close by, and they all enjoyed the peace of the moment. The silence was pierced only by distant bird calls and the odd breath of wind.

"Erin," began Matt. "This is so wonderful here; you and I alone together, as far as Tombalkiens are concerned; only the Balkiens here."

The Balkiens quivered a little.

"Matt, you've been so good to me over these past years," said Erin placing her arm around him affectionately. "Thanks for getting in touch with my family over those pom-poms we bought from Mackay's shop. What would we have done without you? You have been very brave taking on the responsibility for these poor beings coming to grief on their space voyage."

"I'm sure it was my destiny, Erin."

"But you must have thought about your change in circumstances."

"Yes, I have to confess that there were times when my Dad was very concerned about the Balkiens being at our house though things got a lot easier after the Treasury Minister, David Easter, canned the whole project over budgetary constraints. We hardly heard from Captain Cammins after that, as Dad transferred to a new position."

"That's good. It's never a good idea to be alienated from your parents."

Matt and Erin sat arm-in-arm gazing across that vast crater in the strengthening sunlight for about fifteen minutes.

"Erin," said Matt with a quiver in his voice as he withdrew his arm and fumbled in his waist pouch in which he kept his cell phone and his camera. He pulled out a little round purple velvet box with curved edges and knelt in front of Erin with one knee on the desert ground.

"I'm not sure how to say this," he said falteringly. "I saw this in that jeweler's shop just after I sat my maths exam. It's for you." Matt opened the little case to reveal a beautiful golden ring studded with a small sapphire, a ruby, and an emerald."

"Oh, it's beautiful!" said Erin beaming.

"Erin, I love you very dearly. Will you marry me?"

YESL – The Balkien from Antrobi

Erin laughed, hardly surprised by this proposal after sighting the ring box coming out of Matt's pouch. They stood up and embraced one another. The Balkiens all hovered up over to them and surrounded them in a composite ponkadliath.

"Of course, Matt," she said as their eyes became misty.

Monku with her light blue hues started to pulsate and detached himself from the ponkadliath for a moment.

He could hear a more distant Balkien flying noise above them, which seemed familiar to her. This Balkien descended towards the group from the sky above the rim of the crater. It was flying with a deeper tone of warble. This Balkien was slightly larger than Yesl and had a dark blue equator with alternate bands of purple and dark green culminating in very dark grey polar regions. White spots speckled the blue equator and near black poles that almost looked like stars in the sky. The Balkiens hovered right up in front of the group and began speaking in Antrobian with the now-familiar lower-pitched squeaks and buzzing sounds. Yesl flew over to this visitor.

"It's Wink of the Winkets!" she exclaimed before lapsing into Antrobian herself to explain more about their predicament.

Wink hovered over to a small ridge near the crater's lip. Everyone followed by either walking or flying after Wink. There before them was Mwaki, who looked almost identical to Wink. Another rather prolate but smaller Balkien hovered up from the crater below. This one had a blue equator, lighter than that of the Winkets, with bands ranging from a lighter blue through green to yellow with brown and crimson regions on its poles. Baingae suddenly let out a high-pitched whoop, pulsated a lot, and went flying in a zigzag fashion around all present.

"Boodibah! Winxl," he said in English. Then he lapsed into speaking excitedly in Antrobian. Baingae could not believe it at first, overcome with joy. Baingae hovered towards the Winkets and Winxl who were now seated on a large flat ledge of rock, just below the edge of the crater. Baingae glided onto the rock ledge to make a slow embracing contact with Winxl. Tears welled up in both Matt's and Erin's eyes as they held each other's hands.

Baingae and Winxl had the greatest ponkadliath of all time. Soon Boongoo and Monku joined in with the Winkets. Mwakus and Bwinkus also appeared as they hovered up over the lip of the crater. Matt and Erin could not help but melt into one another's arms and hugged each other intensely while smiling at the reunion between Baingae and Winxl. Soon Matt and Erin were also in the ponkadliath with all the Balkiens. An ovoid scout ship was parked on the edge of the flat bottom of the crater. Its shiny surface reflected the surrounding cliffs between its small round windows, arranged in a row along its length.

"We are the Winkets, Wink, and Mwaki of the Splinkatrix, our mother ship we have traveled in from Antrobi," said Wink with Yesl translating. "We were sent out to look for you on the missing *Balkieston* after you failed to return to Antrobi by the due date. How did you end up here?"

"We had a major problem on Splogita," said Yesl in Antrobian, with Baingae translating into English. "We encountered a terrible force, some evil ruler. We've called it the *Enigma*. It fired out bolts of lightning at our ship, which struck our navigation systems as we tried to escape its grip. With our ship unknowingly damaged, we went badly off course and hit the Asteroid Belt in this planetary system. Most of the *Balkieston* was pulverized by the small rocks hitting us, except for the bridge section, the only part we could steer through those deadly boulders. We tried to make an emergency landing here on Tombalki, but one of our emergency gyro engines malfunctioned so we could not slow down. We all abandoned ship in the space pods as the *Balkieston* burned up on re-entry. We believe that the main wreckage lies in what these guys call the North Atlantic Ocean, near an island called Baraignsay."

"The Splinkatrix mothership is presently in a parking orbit around the Moon," began Wink. "Winxl had just been rejuvenated after waking from her hibernation of just over one of our Antrobian years. We happened to be present one day when Winxl's now thick white cocoon began to pulsate as the Vega-shine started streaming into the hibernation chamber she had been in since before the *Balkieston* took off."

"I remember looking forward to my meeting with Baingae," interjected Winxl while her swooth wavered slowly back and forth.

Wink continued to narrate the event of Winxl awakening:

A gap appeared in the cocoon, and a colorful Winxl could be seen moving around inside. She had created a space for herself by pushing the walls of the cocoon outwards. We, the priests, Wink and Mwaki, hovered up close to be by her side."

"Winxl," said Mwaki. "Great to see you wake up."

"Where am I?" asked Winxl.

"Winxl," said Wink. "You were in a serious accident in the North Beekalo Ocean."

"Where's Baingae? I've got to see him," said Winxl anxiously.

"You were sucked up into a terrible thunderstorm, where you froze and, with that weight, fell hard into the sea," said Mwaki softly. "You were very cold, wet and oblate; found washed up on a northern shingle beach by Captain Woozl, while he was on leave in his village. You were unconscious and had to be taken to *Balkieston's* main medical center and treated for your oblation and *wugging*."

"Oh yes," said Winxl. "I now remember leaving Baingae to fly back to Balkieston. Oh, I do wish that I had heeded Baingae's warning not to fly such a northerly course alone, but I had to get back to Balkieston for that primary audience with King Zozl, my great uncle."

The Winkets pulled the cocoon apart at the tear, and Winxl rolled out onto the rock-hewn niche where she'd lain.

"But where's my beloved Baingae?"

"All of this happened about one Antrobian year ago," said Wink.

"One year! That's about eighteen hundred days. I'd love to be taken to see Baingae."

"Ah Baingae," said Wink in a sober and quiet tone as his swooth shimmered slowly. "I'm sorry to say that Baingae went away on a space mission and he hasn't yet returned. Things have also changed in the South Beekalo Ocean, off the West Coast of Balkalay. Something terrible is going on down there. On one of the islands, there's a bright presence with many lightning flashes emanating from there."

"I'm feeling fine now," said Winxl as she hovered slowly from her niche leaving the remains of her cocoon that had confined and healed her, over to the opening of the cave to be with the Winkets in the warm, bright Vega-shine.

"Who are you?" she asked.

"We are the Winkets," said Wink.

"We're priests of the first holy order, dedicated to the Great One, creator of all that is; this whole universe. We were appointed to oversee your re-introduction into Antrobian society when you awoke from your long sleep. We're so sorry about Baingae. He wanted to achieve something in your absence. He had planned to be back, about three Angapooka orbits ago. We're very concerned about what may have happened to the *Balkieston* on the planet Splogita. I think that the lightning I mentioned may have something to do with it. You see, it has the same spectral signature as that observed on Splogita at mission launch."

We took off on the Splinkatrix for Splogita and found the crashed scout ship on the beach on the island on that planet. We found the wreckage tarnished over time. We discovered that two of the remaining navigation satellites were in decaying orbits, which were both retrieved.

"We have never encountered a being that tried to destroy us and our ship before," continued Wink. "We were so delighted to meet those meek little pearly beings called Molktrons. We were also so sad to see them cruelly treated by the bad one."

"You mean, the Enigma," said Yesl.

"Yes," said Wink "We had lightning bolts come at us, but we managed to escape unscathed. The Splinkatrix followed the flight path of the *Balkieston* at very high speed, as we had to use maximum power to evade the Enigma. We followed the trajectory of some wreckage we found that presumably came from your ship, which concerned us greatly. We thus actually plotted a course in the same direction that these pieces were traveling before retrieving as many as we could to verify identification. We followed that course for many of your months, leading us here to Tombalki, which was very close to our direction of travel. We found some evidence of wreckage on the island you call Baraignsay. We, first of all, headed for a hidden cave on that island. We homed in on signal beacons emitted by these balls. Mwaki had two of the one-inch silver balls on top of her swooth."

"We found eight of these at the cave when we were last there," said Matt, with Yesl translating for the new arrivals. "We had some trouble with the British authorities for a while."

"That's how we homed in on you over here," said Mwaki, the other Winket twin, with translations by Yesl.

"And the rest is history," said Wink. "As priests, we were commissioned to look after Winxl's spiritual development and tend to her emotional needs. How could we not ignore her pining for Baingae?"

"We had to campaign repeatedly for funds from the Balkarus Credit Union," said Mwaki. "We needed to build the Splinkatrix and develop the new engines and navigation technology for this mission."

"I guess that I thought these were the only data spheres," said Yesl.

"But you have one missing, don't you?" asked Wink.

"Our newly invented search sensors were designed to pick up any signals emanating from these types of spheres, known to be on your ship so we could find you all," said Mwaki. "You know of Washington DC and the Pentagon."

"Yes," said Matt. "The Pentagon is the top military headquarters for the United States, the country, or land we're in."

"Matt," said Mwaki. "The missing sphere has been traced to the Pentagon."

"That only means that my Dad must have got a hold of it and sent it to Aldermaston or something," said Matt with some realization of the implications of this. "How did you find us?"

"You must have the other spheres with you in the town close by," said Wink. "We landed in the crater here for concealment, being closest to the spheres we detected."

"Just as well we brought them with us on this trip," said Erin, "We nearly left them in Tucson. Here they are." Matt pulled all seven of the spheres out of his now rather battered knapsack.

"We did follow your road vehicle a little way up, but decided to wait for a good meeting opportunity," said Wink.

At this point, Matt and Erin embraced and kissed one another. It all started with a Winket. The ponkadliath lasted for a while before the whole group hovered or clambered down to the scout ship, which was some climb down over rocky terrain at the crater's rim. The Balkiens flew into the cabin of the silver ovoid module standing on its landing legs on the sandy desert floor. It was much more comfortable for Matt and Erin to clamber aboard with them. Wink placed one of the data spheres in a little cup on the control panel. Images flashed up on the round monitor screen in front of them. Matt and Erin held hands, while Baingae and Winxl sat joined to one another on Matt and Erin's shoulders as they leaned on each other.

The screen showed rapid sequences of shaky video images. First, there were rocks in space, flying past, and towards the camera.

"The Asteroids?" asked Matt.

Then fragments of what looked like the main spacecraft breaking up flashed across the screen, followed by a lot of yellow and orange flames for about five minutes. The screen went blank. Wink inserted another sphere. The images were now mainly sky blue, with short flashes of what looked like the blue sea and green grass with rocky coastlines in between.

"That looks like Rhannaig Point and the cliffs where we found these spheres," said Matt.

They viewed all the other spheres in like manner showing many scenes since the *Balkieston's* launch with one notable exception.

"It seems that any scenes of the *Balkieston's* final impact into the ocean are missing," said Yesl with dismay.

"Maybe that sequence is on the missing sphere," said Matt.

"The one in the Pentagon," said Erin.

"It'll, therefore, be harder for us to locate the main wreck of the *Balkieston*," said Yesl. "Not only are images recorded on these spheres. There are valuable positioning data as well, which would have helped us locate that wreckage, mainly the ship's bridge and crew quarters somewhere in the North Atlantic."

It was late evening when Matt and Erin finally arrived at Erin's parents' house. The Balkiens were in the back seat, except for the two Winkets, who had to remain with their scout ship. Erin picked up the roll of newspapers wrapped in cellophane, which had been flung onto the patio by the newsboy from his bike. As she unrolled them in the large kitchen, there was the headline:

IMAGES FROM UNKNOWN ALIEN SPHERE

On the front page, there was a picture of the ocean with some small rocky islands and an inset of a data sphere like the ones they had just been viewing earlier that day. Matt held up *The Arizona Star*, for them to read.

"Those islands in the photo," began Matt, "seem a lot like the islands around Sgeir Mor."

"Where's Sgeir Mor?" asked Erin.

"Sgeir Mor lies west of Baraignsay," said Matt. "It says here, 'The scientists at the Ames Research Centre in California took more than five years to decode the data that were emitted by the silver sphere when activated by an alternating magnetic field. These images were a terrific breakthrough in tracing the origins of the spheres found on a remote Scottish island about six years ago by the British Army. It is unknown if the image, pictured left, is of a terrestrial island or possibly that on an alien world or extra-solar planet.'"

Erin smiled into Matt's eyes. He grinned at her in affirmation.

"I'm sure that it's only a matter of time before someone else reading this recognizes that it's Sgeir Mor," he said. "I'd love to get a hold of the translation code for reading those spheres."

"Where there's a will, there's a way," said Dr. Baingae.

The TV was burbling away in the background until Matt pricked up his ears. "And, coming up, more on that story about the images from that alien silver sphere, found on a Scottish Island," intoned the newsreader.

"Now we have an exclusive report on those stunning images downloaded from that mystery silver ball found on a Scottish island, six years ago. We now go over to our London studio for this report."

The news correspondent began, "This silver sphere was found on a Scottish island six years ago by a schoolboy, who was assisting his uncle in herding sheep that July."

"The islands we see in this alien image have been determined to be those of Sgeir Mor, west of the Isle of Baraignsay, where strange wreckage was found, believed to be from an unidentified craft. The metal alloys are of unknown origin."

A video showed orange flames around the edges as the camera passed over Sgeir Mor and plunged towards the ocean, and then it suddenly went blank.

"It is believed that the wreckage of the main ship is somewhere to the east of Sgeir Mor. Plans are being drawn up to search for this wreck. This report comes to you live from London."

More commercials came on.

"But funding for this project was suddenly cut three months after the discovery of the wreckage," said Matt. "The UK government thought it a waste of funds when they could not analyze the metal alloys the pieces were made of."

"Maybe the missing sphere and the results were sent to Washington just before or after the cuts were enacted," said Erin.

● ◯ ●

10 ~ SIGNALS FROM ANTROBI

Matt went to the mailbox to collect his mail and opened a letter from the Department of Finance of the State University of Arizona. Matt held the letter in his hand, his eyes opening wider. He gasped with astonishment at what he was reading. He put down the letter and summoned Yesl, who hovered through from his bedroom.

"Yesl," he said. "We have a problem."

"What's the puchty?" asked Yesl.

"This is no little puchty!"

"What is it?"

"$35,570 and 65 cents!"

Matt picked up the letter and showed it to Yesl. "How am I going to finish my degree with this hanging over me like a sword of Damocles?"

"You're so near finishing your thesis."

"Yesl," shouted Matt as he thumped the table, causing the breakfast dishes to shake. "I haven't got $35,000 to pay this stinking rotten account right now. If I don't pay this by Monday of next week, they'll cancel my enrolment, and not let me sit my final exams in three weeks! Yesl, it'll be all over for me, and I'll have wasted three years of my life on this degree."

"Matt," said Yesl calmly. "Try to be calm. Don't get into a puchty over this."

There was a knock at the kitchen back door. Yesl opened it by telekinetically turning the handle.

"Erin, you're a sight for sore eyes!"

"Matt. What's the matter? Why are you so upset? Has another Balkien had a serious wug or something?

"This is the wug," said Matt as he picked up the bill, crushing it slightly and thrusting it in front of Erin. "I haven't got $35,000 to pay this. I thought that my scholarship had covered it."

"You need a hug," said Erin as she embraced him. "What about using a credit card for now until we can sort it out?"

"Except for about $3,000, it's maxed out, mostly for tuition fees and rent for this place."

The Winkets hovered in through the open door. They alighted on Matt and Erin, one on one shoulder of each of them.

"Wink and Mwaki," said Yesl. "Matt has a very serious puchty. He's just received a bill for $35,570 for the last two year's tuition fees, which he thought were covered by his scholarship, granted for only the first two of his four-year-program."

"Matt," said Wink. "We have an idea. Why don't we sell some of our technology to the US government to cover your debt?"

"Are you serious?" asked Matt. "Are you sure that this is for the best?"

"I don't know that it'll make any difference to us," said Wink. "They're already talking about raising the *Balkieston's* main bridge section and are going over it with a fine-toothed comb using mini-subs deep in the ocean. They can't determine how they made the metal alloy. They want to recreate this metal so that they can build a similar ship for NASA to use on interplanetary missions. Matt, we are still detecting those signals from Antrobi like those on Splogita. We should think about going back to our home planet on the Splinkatrix to investigate."

"Wink," said Erin. "We'll miss you all here on Earth."

"Wink's right," said Matt. "Antrobi may be in serious trouble like Splogita was. Think of all your millions of fellow Balkiens in distress."

Yesl quivered and warbled. "Our relatives and ancestors," she said softly. Matt picked Yesl up and held her close to his bosom. Erin also embraced them.

"Oh, you poor Balkiens," she said softly.

"If we all go back to Antrobi to convince them that the Enigma is truly evil," said Mwaki, "how will they believe us? Maybe they'll listen to you Tombalkiens."

"What, Us?" asked Matt.

"Could you come with us to Antrobi?" asked Yesl.

"That's a huge step to contemplate," said Matt. "And we humans are not well adapted to long-distance space travel. We've only been to the Moon, so far."

"But that's in your slow rockets that need lots of heavy fuel to propel you for only a short distance. Winket technology has developed a ship that'll manage to transport you all that way in a short time."

"It's twenty-five light-years to Vega. I'll be an old man by the time we get there."

"Oh no," said Mwaki in a poetic tone. "It'll take no time at all, just a little short transit. You'll hardly know it."

Matt leaned against the kitchen cabinet, folding his arms. "It's an awful lot to think about."

Yesl hovered over onto Erin's shoulder "Maybe consider this your first assignment after graduation, Matt. What about you, Erin?"

"As Matt says, this is a lifelong commitment," she said.

YESL – The Balkien from Antrobi

For the rest of that day, while Matt and Erin attended their last lectures on stellar and planetary formation, they thought about this awesome mission they were being called to go on.

Matt drove north along Orchard Boulevard on his way home with Erin at his side. Her long hair was flowing in the draught coming in through the open windows. The sun was now sinking into the blue western sky and casting its light onto the golden desert landscape. Wink, Mwaki, Yesl, Boongoo, and Winxl appeared from the blue and flew alongside the car by Erin's open passenger window.

"Hi, Winkets," said Erin.

"Hi," said Wink.

"You'd better fly into the back seat before we get to the traffic lights ahead," said Matt as they hovered onto the back seat.

"We want you to take the next right at the lights," said Yesl. "We need to show you something and suggest a plan."

"Yesl," said Erin. "We promised that we'd be home for Mom's dinner."

"It'll not take long," said Yesl.

"Okay," said Matt as he pulled over into the right lane. "Erin, you'd better call your Mom to say that we might be a bit late."

"Okay," said Erin as she reached for her mobile phone. After driving up the road out of town, the car turned into a clearing bounded by small bushes and some taller *Eucalyptus* trees. Matt parked the car next to a somewhat larger Antrobian scout ship than the one in which the Winkets and Baingae had arrived. Matt and Erin gasped in unison.

Everyone got out and admired the ship, which had a silver sheen with a touch of cobalt blue. It was the size of a tour bus and had a row of round porthole windows. Matt got a folding picnic chair from the car's boot and placed it at the round open doorway.

"Welcome aboard," said Wink.

Matt and Erin climbed onto the chair and walked into the most spacious cabin they'd ever seen on a Balkien craft. Balkiens of various sizes and colors occupied half the velvet-covered cup seats.

Wink first spoke in Antrobian, then in English.

"These are our friends, Matt and Erin, from Tombalki, who befriended Yesl after their accident in the *Balkieston*. They may be able to help us with our problems on our home planet, but presently the male companion, Matt, has much need of assistance in the form of our money, sgegas. We do have a financial system of exchange on Antrobi."

Erin took in a slow deep breath as she climbed into the cabin. "Oh, this beautiful fragrance reminds me of my school trip to Switzerland and our time among those fresh Alpine forests."

Wink and Mwaki hovered to the back of the cabin and retrieved a light metal ingot, about the size of a small hexagonal paver.

"This is one of many spare tiles that we use to repair our mother ship, the Splinkatrix, should there be a need. We know that your space agency, NASA, would love to acquire this material, to assist with their research. As many of the original crew of the *Balkieston* have intermarried and had many baby Balkiens or Poonketies in the last few years, they will remain here on Tombalki, to oversee how your people will use this technology to build their spacecraft or rebuild the *Balkieston*. The plan is for you to sell this for a price that will repay your college debt."

"Oh, Yesl…" started Matt.

"Show this to your director of studies, Professor Rudniki, tonight. Smoonkshie, here, told him about your issues and he has contacted NASA and made a deal for $500,000 to be deposited into your account. We'll send a DVD with the program to read the data spheres on Tombalkien computers. Make sure you install it and back it up. Here are instructions on how to build a standard ship on these three data spheres to go with this ingot of the metal alloy and instructions on how to reproduce it and build our type of spaceship, whether it is a scout ship or the main ship including the propulsion systems. Have a good evening."

"But my debt is a lot smaller."

"You'll need the rest of this money for your part in our mission to Antrobi. Now run along. We must take off from here before others come up and spot us."

As Matt drove out onto the road, the ship's round door slid shut. It rose quietly and rapidly into the air and whizzed off towards the setting sun. Yesl and the Winkets had the ingot in a shoebox and the three data spheres in an old egg carton.

"Matt you will be indebted in Antrobian Sgegas to the *Balkarus Credit Union* of Antrobi for this deal which is conditional upon a Winket's agreement that some form of payment is made in future," said Yesl.

"What does that entail?" asked Matt.

"We'll worry about that later. Have you thought about you and some of your family coming to Antrobi?" asked Yesl. "Smoonkshie and Moonzl have been talking to Sean, Kara, and your cousins in Scotland about this as well. Naturally, your parents are very concerned. There'll be a great reward in store for you all."

Matt entered the driveway of the Fredrickson house and parked in the front yard next to the rounded bushes.

"Hi, Matt and Erin," greeted Dan.

Matt and Erin went with the Balkiens into the shed in the back yard to store the shoebox in the old scout ship within. The Winkets and Yesl, sitting in the scout ship, were exchanging stories in Antrobian about their adventures in space. There was an audible Balkien hovering sound from outside followed by a soft thud on the wooden door. Erin got up to open it and there hovering into the shed were Smoonkshie and Moonxl.

"How are you both doing?" asked Smoonkshie.

"Heard you will both graduate from university soon," said Moonxl.

"That's right," said Erin.

"Yesl suggested that we have a celebration," said Smoonkshie.

"How do you Balkiens dance?" asked Matt.

"We do something like this," said Smoonkshie.

Smoonkshie and Moonxl started to hover and orbit around each other. They then advanced towards one another until they touched and retreated, repeating this movement in a rhythm, before once circling one another. Yesl and the Winkets joined in, creating a well-choreographed, sequence of maneuvers.

"Erin quickly put on a CD of some classic rock music.

Soon Matt and Erin were jiving; surrounded by all Balkiens present doing twirls and bouncing off one another in the air.

"We should have a dance party and invite everyone, both Terrestrial and Antrobian," suggested Erin.

"What a wonderful idea," said Matt. "I'd love to see how you Winkets will adapt to our music."

"We've seen you going to disco dances," said Yesl. "We have our form of dancing to our music on Antrobi. We'd love to try it out on your songs."

"How about we organize a barn dance," said Matt.

"We could have it in the big barn on my Uncle's farm up the road," said Erin. "We could have a gathering thereafter your graduation ceremonies. We could invite everyone in the Astronomy Club."

The sun was setting behind the trees on a balmy evening with the noise of the evening crickets reaching a crescendo. Many cars were drawing up and being guided into the field next to the great barn by parking attendants. Matt, arm in arm with Erin, was showing, Kaz, Sean, Kara, Alison and Judith inside. Kaz had emigrated to Australia to live in Perth. Erin's brothers Dan and Nick were also present. They were now freshmen at the same university where Matt and Erin studied.

"Hi!" greeted Uncle Herbert. "It's sure been a long time since you left Scotland and it's great to see you again, and you have a fine lass here. When's the big day?"

"Not sure," said Erin. There were greetings and hugs from Matt's parents. His father had by now become accustomed to his son's involvement with the Balkiens, which had been made much more relaxed after David Easter's cuts to the project on Baraignsay.

"Yesl tells me that there may be trouble on Planet Antrobi," said Matt.

"And you all may still be going off on that space jaunt, I suppose," said Dad with an air of suspicion. "If you do, make sure you call home regularly." He started whistling some Glen Miller number as he always did. It was the first time that Matt's and Erin's parents had met at this time of merging their families.

About ten Balkiens hovered in and around the rafters pulling party streamers as both humans and Balkiens arrived, to the sounds of music from the 70s to the 90s.

As the live band came on to play, the lead singer made his introductory speech.

"Thank you for coming to be with us to celebrate Matt and Erin's graduations from Arizona State University being a unique and auspicious occasion for we have invited the Balkiens from planet Antrobi to join us. So, without further ado, let's take to the floor!"

With much clapping and cheering, the band blasted out covers of great oldies hits.

As everyone danced, the Balkiens flew out above the crowd and started formation-flying to the music, forming rows, which moved in and out toward one another. They then formed lines of balls as they snaked in and around the rafters to the beat.

"We're sure raising the roof tonight with our extra-terrestrial guests," announced the lead singer. After a few more numbers, Matt and Erin sat down at a table in the corner with their beers. The gyrating Balkiens continued to put on a great display of formation flying and twirling. Smalkle twirled around the rafters a few times during a rock 'n' roll number but broke off suddenly and flew towards the romantic couple and Yesl.

"Yesl, Matt, Erin," said Smalkle as he alighted on the table in front of them. "I've just had some disturbing news about Antrobi."

"Oh, Smalkle," said Matt.

"We've seen a strange signal coming from the direction of our planet. It's a sort of 'wink, wink, wink' light signal like the one we saw through the telescope at the observatory. It's like what you guys would call Morse code. It's not good news. Remember the term-paper you did on the spectral analysis."

"Yes, we do," said Erin.

"Remember that you said that there was now an identical pattern emanating from Antrobi," said Smalkle.

"Yes."

"The secret message transmitted on a repeated signal loop is that the population of Antrobi is in grave trouble. Their minds are being oppressed by something terrible, enslaving many of our Balkiens, in the power of a tyrannical invader."

"The Enigma," gasped Matt as he clasped Erin's hand. The festive atmosphere seemed to fade into the background as this realization began to sink in.

Baingae and Winxl were still whirling around the room, gyrating over every table along with the Winkets. Moonxl hovered up to the microphone and started to speak in Antrobian, then in English; "The moment you've all been waiting for. We would also like to announce that Matt and Erin are recently engaged!"

"I'd like everyone to raise their glasses," said Dan as he stood up from his table. Everyone raised their champagne glasses. "I propose a toast to Matt and Erin."

There were a deep resounding drum roll and a clinking of glasses. There were cheers and clapping. The drum roll started like many others, then became a strange otherworldly warble drone. Matt half expected to hear the Scottish bagpipes. But instead, there was a rapid beat with a longer harmonic. Beautiful tones were sounding like wind chimes and Antrobian singing from a trio of Balkiens levitating around the lead singer's mike. They were Moonxl, Smoonkshie, and Monku.

"This is cool and groovy!" exclaimed Matt as he and Erin dashed onto the dance floor and jived to the unique sound. They forgot about their troubles during these festivities. All the Balkiens were in synchronous moves above them. As every person jived, the Balkiens flew over, under and between them. Five numbers were performed by the three Balkiens who coined the name *Moonkalettes* for their band. The last performance was by a Scottish bagpiper who played *Amazing Grace* and *Auld Lang Syne*. Everyone enjoyed it including Matt's parents, Uncle Herbert and Auntie Wendy, whom Matt had not seen in many years, since his departure from Scotland.

As the evening drew to a close, everyone had begun to disperse, starting up their cars and driving off into the night.

"We had a fine graduation dance," said Uncle Bob to his wife, Angela.

Matt looked down the long line of headlights on the road leading from the barn. The hovering Balkiens landed either on seats or the parcel shelf. Matt turned on the engine and rolled down the window. It was almost pitch dark in the desert air, except for a thin crescent moon and some isolated stars peeping through the *Eucalyptus* trees. Summer crickets could be heard above the chatter of everyone saying their 'farewells.'

"Before we head back to Scotland, we'd love to go to Disneyland in Los Angeles and ride in Space Mountain," suggested Sean.

"Me too," said Alison.

"Now all of you," began Helen, Erin's Mom. "We'd have to fly to LA and check into a hotel there and spend a whole day at the theme park. You've all only got a week before you fly back to Scotland; not to mention the long lines or queues and we have to fit in a visit to your Grandpa and Grandma's in Flagstaff."

There were some groans of disappointment. The Winkets listened.

"I have a great idea," said Wink as he quivered on the sideboard of the main living room the next morning.

"What?" asked Yesl.

"Another trip up to the meteor crater," implied Kaz.

"Maybe or to the Grand Canyon and much more," said Wink. "We now have two scout ships parked up there in a remote part of the Canyon for some privacy. We could take you for a space ride around Tombalki.

"Coooool!" crooned Matt. "What a great way to experience space after all our hard work.

"Yesl's arranging for two scout craft from the Splinkatrix to pick us up at night in two days from a location just within the Grand Canyon to take us in an orbital flight," said Wink.

"The Splinkatrix is presently in an orbital position beyond the Moon," said Moonxl.

Everyone, both human and Balkien, had driven from Flagstaff and parked in a remote part of a parking lot near the edge of the Grand Canyon. They hovered or walked around a rock promontory hidden from the view from that parking lot. The sun set behind the distant hills to the west on that beautiful balmy evening. Then there was a distant humming sound with a low-frequency resonance. Two silvery shapes appeared from below in the canyon and landed on the flat desert soil just in front of everyone present. Matt, Sean, Kara, Erin, Yesl, Boongoo, and Baingae would ride in the smaller of the craft. Kaz, Alison, Judith, and Erin's brothers, Dan and Nick, in their late teens, would ride in the larger craft accompanied by Monku, Bwinkus, and Mwakus. They all clambered aboard their own silver craft and settled in the cabins. Matt and Erin were huddled together, looking onto the sand at the edge of the crater.

The door slid shut. Wink, as the pilot, and Moonxl, as co-pilot, started the gyro engines and the craft lifted slowly at first, then more rapidly into the sky. Soon Matt and Erin could see the landscape far below with the outline of the meteor crater, then the ribbon of headlights on the Interstate, I40. The spacecraft rose rapidly towards outer space itself. The sun rose again as they headed higher and towards the west. Matt and Erin were amazed to see the Earth's curvature. "We're going to take you on a short space ride and go once around the Earth," said Moonxl.

As Matt held Erin's shoulder, they began to sense that the ship was falling as they began to float about the cabin. "Weightlessness," said Moonxl.

"Hey," said Erin. "We're actually in space. There's the Moon."

"That's California," said Matt as the Earth's curvature became more pronounced. "You Balkiens have wonderful spaceships."

The other ship piloted by Mwaki and Smoonkshie was alongside to port as a distant speck of sunlight reflected off its shiny hull. "There are Kaz and the others," said Erin.

"They're about fifteen miles away," said Moonxl.

"Wow. We are on the threshold of the Universe," said Erin softly.

"This is only the start of what could be a very long voyage," said Yesl.

After ascending to a height of about six hundred miles, both ships passed over the deep blue Pacific Ocean. From such an altitude, the sea seemed very smooth like a hammered metallic finish. There were long curved lines of little storm clouds rising from this sheen. Soon this smooth surface was peppered with tiny black specs.

"We're passing over many Pacific islands," said Matt.

"Hawaii," added Erin as they both pressed their faces as close to the porthole window as possible in their weightless state, with Sean, Kara, Yesl, Boongoo, and Baingae all floating about. This orbital glide continued for another fifteen minutes over the bright blue ocean, with the bright, fierce sun shining in through the starboard windows, contrasted against the blackness of space. To the port side, everyone could see the inky black sky studded with apparently far more stars above the Earth's soft azure curvature, than they could see from the ground. Below, more extensive landmasses came into view, which was a pale bluish-green, where they were visible below the clouds.

"Papua New Guinea," announced Matt.

"Wink hovered to join them leaving Moonxl in charge of the flight.

"Down there is a place called Ambunti," said Wink, "I'll tell you about our history there and in Australia. This visit is not our first to the planet, Tombalki. I've heard about a Balkien mission to this planet many thousands of your years ago."

Matt was astonished, "Really."

"Your mention of that name, Ambunti, jogs my memory of that event," said Wink. "Those Balkiens came in a much more primitive ship, which took many of your years to get here. That mission returned to Antrobi with many tales to tell. That crew met up with tribes of your humans living in mooties built out of parts of their trees and covered with dried grass."

"We would call that a thatched roof," interjected Erin.

"That may explain some of those people's ancient legends," said Sean as everyone was now listening to Wink's account.

"We're passing over Australia now," said Kara. "That's the Northern Territory."

"Matt got out his binoculars to look closely at the Outback.

"This is my first sighting of the Land Down Under," said Matt. "I'm planning to go and visit Kaz, who has recently migrated to Perth in Western Australia."

There was a flicker as the view screen at the back of the cabin lit up, showing a close-up view of the deserts they were passing over. The arid landscape depicted was covered with what looked like small rough-hewn pinkish-brown marbles scattered around.

"These rocky spheres may look small from up here," said Wink who was floating in front of the screen. "They're huge rounded boulders about the size of this ship we're on. I believe that somewhere down there is the actual landing site of that ancient mission and that going to Ambunti was part of their outward exploration."

"How interesting, Wink. Maybe when I visit Kaz, we'll have to make a trip up there from Perth," said Matt. "As we speak, we're passing over that city now. I can see the beaches, the Swan estuary and the port of Fremantle."

"My turn for the binoculars?" inquired Kaz.

As they were orbiting westbound, the sun soon set in the east behind them as they drifted back into the night side of the globe.

Onward and over the Middle East and Europe, many lights of distant cities were visible. Soon they approached the lights of Tucson. The gyro engines whirred into life, slowly at first after everyone had fastened the Balkien version of seat belts for slow down and descent. There was no need for heat shields as the ship slowed down in orbit and descended vertically to land by just running the engines to counteract the earth's gravity enough to allow a rapid descent and slowing down before softly landing back at the secluded spot and disembarked. The Moon was now high, providing light so they could walk back to the parking lot.

"Thanks a lot, Wink and Moonxl," said Matt.

"That flight was terrific," said Sean.

Matt and Erin entered the lounge with Moonxl on Erin's shoulder. The Balkiens were on the settee in a ponkadliath, with the rest of Erin's family sitting in front of the TV.

"We're so pleased to see you," greeted Dan as he shook hands with Matt and hugged his daughter, Erin.

"We had a great time up at Grandpa and Grandma's, and our trip was out of this world," said Kaz excitedly.

"Our view of Australia was magnificent," said Alison.

Matt's Mom and Dad entered the room, bringing a tray with cups and a teapot for everyone.

"So, you got to go on your jaunt in a flying saucer after all Matt," he said and continued his whistling of more jazz tunes. On the tray on the table, alongside the cups and saucers, there was a plate with Helen's best homemade cookies. There were cookies arranged around a gleaming silver sphere. Everyone let out a gasp in unison. Yesl and Baingae hovered over the silver sphere, and it gently ascended from among the cookies to be attached telekinetically to Yesl.

"Matt, my son, congratulations on graduation from ASU! I thought for a while that you'd let those pom-poms take over your life, but I now see that they needed some assistance. I, therefore, feel it my duty to let all of you go on a much longer trip on that 'flying saucer.' I have to admit that things ground to a halt after our finance officer, the erstwhile David Easter canned the much-needed funding for the continuing search for more evidence on Baraignsay. I kept this sphere in the back of our wardrobe for many years until I went on a business trip to Washington earlier this year. I took it down to the Goddard Space Centre in Maryland to have it examined. They indeed came up with some weird and exciting, if scary, findings.

"I then explained that I had a son graduating from ASU. So, after tests, they gave this back to me to bring down to the Astrophysics department here. The metal alloys were of special interest to NASA for possible use in spacecraft building."

"That's the sphere we have been looking for all of these years," said Yesl. "We can load it into our systems on the space pod out in the back shed."

"By the way," continued Ernest Sutherland, Matt's Dad, "Captain Cammins tendered his resignation from the MOD not long after David Easter pulled the pin on the project funding. He and that Professor pal of his from Cologne were reported missing about a year later. Both British and German police forces were involved in a Europe-wide search for them. Neither they nor their bodies were found; only Captain Cammins' car, abandoned in the Black Forest in Germany. There was evidence of his traveling on the Eurostar train to Paris, and that was it. Mind you; there were unusual marks on the ground not far from the hidden vehicle."

"After the official graduation ceremony," said Matt, "I presented a shoebox with three data spheres along with PC software to read them plus ingots of the Antrobian metal to Professor Rudnicki for forwarding to NASA as per an agreement from the Winkets."

Erin started pouring cups of coffee and tea for everyone.

"Why don't we take these cups of coffee and the cookies to the back shed," said Uncle Herbert.

"We'll load up that long-lost sphere," said Baingae. "Boodibah!"

After trooping to the old weathered, wooden shed and stepping inside, everyone stood around the space pod under the single fluorescent strip light.

"This pod could do with a good dusting," said Erin. "I'll get a bucket of soapy water to clean it in the morning."

Wink hovered inside the pod's cabin and placed the last sphere in the computer system's cup support. Wink hovered around the colored circular imitation buttons. Images flickered onto the round screen. The yellow flame quickly faded to reveal the blue ocean.

"There's Sgeir Mor flashing past," said Kaz.

The ocean rushed up to meet the viewer. Then all went blank for a few minutes. As Wink moved to turn the system off, the screen brightened. Water droplets ran off the lens, revealing the surface of the sea bobbing up and down. On the horizon, the rocks of Sgeir Mor were still visible.

"Here's your mail," Dan said, handing Erin a few letters.

"Oh, the usual credit card bills and junk mail," said Erin as she placed the envelopes on the table. One caught her eye, as she reached for a knife to open it. She read the letter from the Jet Propulsion Laboratory. "Dad, Mom, Matt, I've been offered that job I interviewed for at JPL in Pasadena! I'm so excited."

"Congratulations," Matt said hesitantly. There was a moment's silence. "I guess that I'll have to go without you."

"Oh Matt, I'd love to come to Australia with you, but this is an important start to my astrophysics career. I'm sure that we can keep in touch on the internet." Matt and Erin hugged each other for a few minutes. Yesl, The Winkets, Baingae, and Winxl joined in on their shoulders. Matt and Erin walked out into the moonlit back yard. They embraced one another for a while and were in ponkadliath with the Balkiens.

"Matt," said Erin at last. "Not only is this job important to me, but it involves my role in working out what is happening on Antrobi."

"That's right," said Moonxl, who had just hovered out into the moonlit back yard to join them.

"Erin," said Matt with a heavy heart. "I love you, and I'm going to find this separation hard."

"Me too," replied Erin. "Still, spare a thought for what Baingae and Winxl went through, and here they are together again."

"You'll get to learn a lot about planetary missions on that job," said Wink as he rolled around Erin's head. Matt agreed.

There were fond farewells at the airport as Matt's parents, Kara, Sean, Uncle Herbert, Auntie Wendy, Alison, and Judith left for Scotland. Matt and Kaz were booked to fly to Perth, Australia, two days later, where Matt was to take up a contract position at the Perth Observatory leading to the development of the Square Kilometer Array in Western Australia. It was that evening that Matt and Erin sat with Yesl and the Winkets in the shed next to their ovoid ship.

"You know," began Wink, "We could get this thing going again with that sphere."

"So, we could," said Yesl. "Let's try it out."

With the last sphere now in place, Wink turned on the systems, which flickered into life. Mwaki wavered over some buttons on the right. At first, there was a grinding noise, which turned into a quiet hum. The ship then lifted off from the floor momentarily and heaved about the shed knocking over a few empty boxes.

"Matt," said Erin as she laid her hand on his. "I'd love to visit you and Kaz in Australia this Christmas before you all head off to Antrobi on the Splinkatrix."

"Oh, that would be terrific," replied Matt. He reached into his pouch and pulled out a small red box.

Matt opened the little box. He pulled out two chains. On each was the half of a golden heart symbol. He gave one to Erin to hold. Matt held the other half up to joining with the half that Erin was holding. The two halves fitted neatly together to form a whole, golden heart shape. The serrated join was hardly noticeable. Tears welled up in each other's eyes as they held each other. Baingae and Winxl hovered onto their shoulders.

"Oh Matt," she wept, "this is going to be so hard. Now I know what you went through, Winxl."

Erin grasped Winxl's swooth firmly and held her up to her cheeks with tears settling onto her swooth.

"As I wear this broken half heart on the voyage to the purple planet, I'll always think of you across the cosmos."

"This will only be temporary," Erin sobbed. "We'll rebuild the *Balkieston* and join you like Baingae to Winxl; we'll be together again."

Yesl hovered onto Matt's shoulder.

"I never would have thought of this great adventure and meeting this wonderful lady, Erin, on that Christmas morning when I found you, Yesl, in my Christmas sack."

Matt and Kaz emerged from the ocean after an invigorating swim in the calmer waters on Cottesloe Beach, Perth, Australia on a sunny spring afternoon. The small waves lapped gently on the shore. Matt and Kaz dried themselves and sat down on their towels. The Winkets, Yesl, Baingae, and Winxl huddled up against Matt's bare chest as they lay in the late afternoon sun. There was a warble tinkle emanating from Matt's bag. He reached for his mobile phone. It was a text message from Erin:

"Hi, Matt, Missing you lots. These weeks have been hard without you. The job is going great. I'm currently doing work on observations of Vega. Tell the Balkiens there are some more winking signals that natural phenomena can't explain. Love ya, Erin xxx"

"Kaz. I don't normally let anyone else read my love letters, but you'd better see this," said Matt.

"We'd better be at tonight's observing meet," said Matt.

Kaz and Matt arrived at Perth Observatory with their Balkiens. Matt and Kaz had joined as members of the Astronomical Society of Western Australia. In the central telescope dome used by astronomy club members, Matt asked if he could point the telescope at Vega.

"Certainly," said the club president. "But it'll be low in the north near those trees. Ah, there it is - just." Vega was shining brightly but shimmering in the low sky. Matt had a look through the telescope. There was a winking star close by that winked on and off just like a torch. It was much fainter than Vega itself. He quickly placed his digital camera on the eyepiece and began recording in video mode for about two minutes, until the winking stopped.

"Sorry to keep everyone waiting," he said to the group, "but wanted to get pictures of a strange winking light close to Vega. See for yourselves."

Matt descended the ladder to let others get their turn at viewing. One teenage girl gasped as she viewed the image of Vega, "That is so strange. What's that winking to the right of the star?"

Back at Kaz's single-story detached 1950s home, in the suburb of Palmyra, Matt replayed the shaky video to the Winkets through the TV.

The translated message read:

"Enigma — trouble — we are in desperate terror — Molktrons in distress — can you see us Yesl — Winkets — be warned — be prepared."

"The video ends there, Matt," said Wink.

"The signals stopped before I turned it off," said Matt.

"Mwaki, Yesl," continued Wink. "We have a problem."

"Looks like Antrobi and all of you at home are in some strife," said Matt. "I'll check my email."

Matt turned on Kaz's computer and clicked on an email from Erin:

"Hi my sweet Darling, Matt,

It was so good to talk on Skype last night. I only wish that it did not have to be this way. I so miss our times together and your smiling face as you relax in my arms! Now to astronomical matters, we have collected new spectral analyses of Vega last night and attach jpg images of these. There is also a MPEG movie of the winking light seen around Vega, which we cannot explain. Show it to the Winkets.

Love Erin xxx"

Matt, Kaz, and the Balkiens went to bed. Wink and Mwaki cuddled up to Matt as he drifted off to sleep.

YESL – The Balkien from Antrobi

In the dreams induced by Wink, Matt perceived himself to be in a meadow, with vibrant dark green mosses and a carpet of tiny richly colored beads sprouting from the green moss fibers. Wink and Mwaki were hovering in front of him with Winxl sitting on the green, mossy turf beneath them. He looked up to an enormous thin crescent moon forming a wide arc across the sky. On the inside of the crescent, he could see bright flashes of lightning, flickering on the night side of that large moon. Wink and Mwaki flew up to each side of his head and cuddled up to him. They started pulsating vigorously on him until he awoke.

"Wink, Mwaki," said Matt. "Were those your thoughts transferring to me?"

"Yes," confirmed Wink. "You saw strange flashes on our sister planet, Antrogi."

"You mean the giant crescent moon," said Matt.

"Larger by far than your Moon, just a little smaller than Antrobi," said Mwaki.

"We observed this message in the telescope and what Erin has sent confirms our worst suspicions," said Yesl.

"It looks like the Enigma has invaded Antrobi and the minds of almost all of the Balkiens there," said Wink.

Matt groaned as he bent over, hugging the Winkets and Yesl. "Oh, Antrobi! I have been dreaming of a beautiful planet and a perfect Utopian society in which we'd see no tears or suffering."

"The message mentioned the Molktrons," said Baingae. "Look at the jpg images on Erin's email attachments. These spectrograms look identical to those we saw from Splogita before we left for that planet."

"You mean the presence of the Enigma," said Yesl.

"It looks that way," said Baingae.

Everyone in the room was crestfallen.

"We had been planning to return to Antrobi soon, but what'll we do now?" said Wink. "Stay on, Tombalki?"

"Our Balkiens need our help," said Yesl. "It's our home, our whole heritage, civilization, and our destiny that's at stake." Yesl hovered over to Matt's shoulder. "Remember how miserable the Molktrons were when we visited them," she continued. "Those poor little ones were in abject slavery. Now the same has happened to the Balkiens, OUR HOME! This thing, whatever it is, has exerted its evil influence on our planet already. Maybe it is influencing things here on Tombalki as well."

"Yesl," said Matt calmly. "We'll do what we can to help you, but this is a major challenge for us all."

"Matt," said Yesl. "We Balkiens may need all the help we can get from you people of Tombalki. You understand what evil intent is and will know how to resist its insidious temptations better."

"This entity," began Wink, "this Enigma has a mind of its own and has a will to exist and wishes to bring unhappiness and oppression to all civilizations it encounters on its movements through the cosmos."

"Okay," said Matt. "If it can reach Antrobi from Splogita, what can stop it from coming to Earth as well? Things are bad enough as they are. If the Enigma came here, we'd probably have a world war."

"Like those on Splogita," said Baingae.

"We saw the remains of a once-vibrant Molktronic civilization," said Yesl. "When our ship fell back after being hit by a bolt of lightning, we ended up close to the remains of what must have been a ghastly holocaust."

"How do we suppose that had come about?" asked Winxl. "The Enigma must have destroyed it all."

"Much worse than that, oh much worse," said Wink. "Matt, have you still got those four smaller data spheres that Baingae and Yesl picked up from the cave hideout on Baraignsay?"

"Yes," he replied, "I'll get them from my bag in the bedroom."

Matt returned with the four that he had. Wink had meanwhile got his data-viewer, which was a spherical device that could open up into two halves hinged together. When opened, one half had a round screen with small colored circles that looked like inset buttons around it, while the other half had a rounded hollow indent.

"Place one of the spheres into that cup and touch the green circle," said Wink as Matt did so. The images shown were jerky but showed what looked like massive explosions and smoke rising from burning cities on a desert plain. There were myriads of tiny blackened spheres rolling away from these scenes of chaos.

"These four additional spheres were given to us by the Queen Molktron at our second attempt leaving Splogita. If the Enigma knew that they were on board, it would have wiped us out if it could," said Yesl.

"You've heard of *Divide and Conquer*," suggested Matt.

"On the button," said Yesl. "Now, we see some clear understanding. This entity came to Splogita to poison the minds of the Molktrons, Sploonkothteros, and the Gongothera, who were undersea creatures in the lake so that they fought one another destroying their planet. I suspect the Molktrons themselves, being simpletons, are immune to this evil and see it for what it is."

"What we're saying," said Wink, "is that Antrobi is under serious threat of destruction and somehow we have to stop it. If not, our home will be in danger, and Tombalki could be next."

Wink and Mwaki hovered up onto Matt and Kaz. "We're suggesting that all six of you come to Antrobi on the Splinkatrix and somehow convince the Balkiens not to listen to the mesmerizing powers of the Enigma."

"We'd love to help, but it would be risky to travel all that way without enough food. We certainly enjoyed our orbit above the Earth, but I reckon our bodies are too frail to make such a long voyage," said Matt. "I'm sure that you Balkiens can convince your country Balkiens to see wisdom."

"I'm afraid it's not that simple," said Mwaki. "The Enigma will control our minds. If the Molktrons had let us fly up to the summit of that tall mountain in the center of the lake on Splogita, we'd have been finished. We felt our minds being influenced by evil thoughts. We thought of harming the Molktrons in their cave but had to resist intensely. You people are the perfect candidates for this mission because you can resist this influence far better. Your forebears had to fight in two world wars. If we don't stop this now, I tell you that you may have a very destructive World War III caused by the Enigma's arrival on Earth."

There was silence, except for crickets chirping. Matt and Kaz sighed for a moment.

"This is heavy stuff," said Kaz.

"That's it," said Matt. "Count me in."

"And me too," said Kaz. "Kara, Alison, Judith, and Sean are coming to Australia for Christmas to join us on our mission to Antrobi."

"Just one thing," said Wink, "We'd love to take you to see what you call the Devil's Marbles in the NT."

"That would be cool," said Kaz.

"We'll go in our scout ship tomorrow," said Mwaki. "As we mentioned on our orbital flight around Tombalki, we think that it may be the site of the previous visit by Balkiens to Tombalki. There are many records of this visit in the annals of ancient Antrobian legends. We need to take pictures and any information back with us in case the Enigma destroys these historical records."

Matt and Kaz gazed out of the scout ship's round window as they flew over the vast Australian outback.

"Look down there," said Yesl. "See these stone marbles in the rocks?"

"These are the same ones we saw from space on our orbital flight," said Kaz. "There's that larger rounded one you pointed out to us, Wink."

"Land in that clearing in front of it," said Yesl.

Soon the ship landed softly amongst the enormous rounded granite boulders in the desert landscape of the Devil's Marbles National Park. Matt and Kaz clambered out as Yesl, Baingae, Winxl, and the Winkets flew out. Matt gazed up at the boulder closest to their landing site. "These look to all intents like stone carved Balkiens."

"We have reason to believe that this is the location for that ancient visit," said Yesl.

Matt and Kaz wandered over to look at a strange marking on the stone marble, partially buried close to the ship. Wink looked at it intently and took some photos with his spherical camera. Matt and Kaz did the same.

"Could this be some ancient symbol?" asked Matt.

"It certainly is," said Baingae excitedly. "I remember seeing images of this in the museum in Balkieston. Beneath this symbol, which is now very faded, is something left behind by those intrepid explorers. Get that spade, Kaz."

Matt and Kaz dug down through the red dirt next to the granite boulder until Matt struck something metallic. After some more digging Matt and Kaz, they finally lifted out a tarnished metallic sphere.

"Let's take this back to Antrobi," said Yesl. "It may contain valuable information about the history of this planet."

This larger sphere was laid in the only data reading cup on board.

"I'm not sure that we shall be able to read this sphere as the data will be in a much older format," said Matt.

"Matt," said Yesl. "We don't keep changing our data formats; we only improve them. We should be able to read it. Switch the computer on."

Buzzing noises emanated from behind the round monitor screen. The screen flickered, and then an image appeared of the same scene where they sat, which was remarkably crisp and clear. The moving pictures showed the craft in which the ancient crew had landed. Unlike the sleek rounded silver vessel, they had landed in now, this one had many triangular facets and was more spherical but with a flattened bottom section from which the three landing legs protruded.

"There's a familiar Balkien hovering towards the camera," said Mwaki.

"If I'm not mistaken, that's Boonkihara," gasped Yesl. "Boonkihara is a well-known wise old sage who has lived far longer than most of us."

Boonkihara appeared about twice the size of Yesl or either of the Winkets.

"Oh, his colors on his swooth look so vibrant," said Yesl. "Last time I saw him speak at a large gathering, his swooth was more faded than that. Ssh! He's speaking in Antrobian."

Yesl translated: "Greetings from Tombalki! Here is where we landed on our historic mission into space to visit the planet from where we have seen an odd and colorful spectral signal. We are recording this message on this sphere which will be buried right here in case we never make it back to Antrobi. We have to say that something terrible has happened elsewhere on this planet over on its largest landmass far north of here."

The speech ended as two other blue and red Balkiens flew past the camera. The scene wobbled as the camera was lifted and pointed towards the round boulder showing the very hole, which they had just dug. Above it was a clear image of the same symbol on the rock.

"That faded marking is a star map," said Matt. "Those dots form the constellation of Cygnus. The one representing Vega has a circle around it. See the larger circular inset beneath."

"Those dots show the planets in the Vegan System," said Wink. "See the ringed double dot. That's pointing to our home planet.

"It's going to be odd, having Christmas Day on the beach," said Erin. Kara, Alison, Judith, and Sean had arrived in Perth for Christmas, a week after Matt and Erin's romantic reunion.

"That was a long flight," commented Alison as everyone sat around the wooden outside table in the cool of the evening in Kaz's backyard near Fremantle.

"If that's long, think about our long space flight to Antrobi," said Yesl.

"Oh, it was a very emotional farewell to our families when we left London," said Alison.

"I go to Antrobi with excitement but also with a great deal of apprehension of the troubles we're going to encounter there," commented Matt.

"I have just had a message from Captain Wink on the Splinkatrix that all of the conversions for your human needs, such as bathroom facilities and human-sized beds have been carried out," said Yesl.

"We certainly don't want you to get backache while trying to sleep in our cup-shaped beds," said Dr. Baingae.

"As we depart sometime in mid-January," began Yesl, "many of us have to remain on the Earth to assist NASA in the rebuilding of the *Balkieston*. We have left two scout ships and instructions to rebuild the *Balkieston* with them. I wish that you could have come, Erin, but your services at JPL along with those of Monku and Moonxl will be precious."

Matt nodded with a tear in his eye.

● ○ ●

11 ~ OFF TO ANTROBI

As Matt, Kaz, Alison, Judith, Kara, Sean, Yesl, the Winkets, Baingae, Winxl set off along Great Eastern Highway from Perth; it was hard to believe that this journey was to be twenty-five light-years long. They drove to Balladonia Roadhouse where there was a small museum, housing remains of the NASA Skylab, which crashed there in 1979.

The next morning, they drove along a dirt road to the rendezvous point and bush-bashed off the track to a place the Winkets showed them. Among the bushes, there was an extra-large ovoid-shaped three-legged shuttlecraft, gleaming in silvery-blue. A ramp led into a round doorway on the side. Other Balkiens were hovering around it like bees at the entrance to their hive pulling large spherical containers up the ramp using a cable-like device. These were containers for all the food and supplies needed for the trip. The transfer was among the last of many, between the Earth and the mother ship, the Splinkatrix. Kaz parked the car under a dense bush and handed Erin the keys.

"I'll miss you, Erin. I'll miss your text messages when we're well out of mobile range," said Matt.

Baingae hovered onto Matt's shoulder as he and Erin embraced for several minutes. Winxl joined Baingae from Erin's shoulder.

"Look at the four romantic ones," said Wink. "Two Tombalkiens and two Balkiens in love! Oh, I only wish it was not this way."

"One small step for Kaz, one giant leap to Antrobi," he said as everyone started walking up the gangway and entered through the door in the side into the large cabin.

All was serene on board. Everyone sat around a large round porthole window. It looked directly onto the ground beneath the ship. All around were neatly arranged hemispherical cups, made of a velvet-like material. Each contained a Balkien. The two burly Winkets were seated in their pilot seats. Matt, Sean, Kara, Kaz, Alison, and Judith each sat in the more spacious cup seats available.

"So, this is finally the start of our long journey to Antrobi," said Yesl. There was a hum as the gangway was slowly retracted into the hold beneath. The door slowly slid across the entrance, closing off their last contact with their world. It was also Matt's final contact with Erin as they blew one another kisses.

YESL – The Balkien from Antrobi

The Winkets moved about the ship's controls. A low humming sound started, and the desert ground seemed to drop away from them. Matt waved frantically to Erin as she grew smaller. Soon Erin disappeared into the more distant scattering of bushes while the ship ascended into the Earth's upper atmosphere showing the Australian Outback stretching out before them. It was not long before all of them could make out the coastline of Western Australia.

The Earth's outline came into view, beginning with one side of the porthole window becoming dark. Soon the whole Earth filled the large porthole. Beautiful bluish light filled the cabin, which grew fainter as the Earth slipped away beneath them.

"There's Tomkil," said Baingae, observing the Moon as the accelerating spacecraft passed.

The Earth appeared to shrink until it looked like a little blue marble. After about two hours, the Earth and Moon were just tiny pinpricks of light not far from the glare of a smaller sun. Some hours later, the cabin became lighter again. The edge of Jupiter slid into view from one side of the porthole.

"Welcome to Boonkle-Mallkis," announced Captain Wink. Matt looked through his binoculars at the two tiny crescent shapes. The Earth and Moon were hardly visible amongst the many stars in the field of view. He thought of Erin, his parents, Uncle Herbert and Auntie Wendy on Baraignsay all contained on that faint speckle of light.

Everyone gasped. Boonkle-Maulkis loomed large, almost filling the porthole. The giant gas planet almost looked like a very smooth gigantic Balkien. There were many bands of swirling clouds, in sharp detail, better than any images transmitted to Earth from the Galileo and other missions. The Great Red Spot had swirling clouds on its edges. As they all gazed at Jupiter's countenance, a bright speck appeared. As it grew in size, the single silvery dot split into four separate ones. Each enlarged to become spheres made up of many triangular facets. A few minutes later, everyone could make out four metallic spheres arranged at the points of a tetrahedron connected by tubes.

"The *Splinkatrix*," said Yesl. "I remember designing of this deep space exploration ship before we left Antrobi on the *Balkieston*."

As the craft lost speed about the *Splinkatrix*, everyone on board became weightless and floated around the cabin.

One of the four spheres was gigantic, about twice the diameter as the length of one of the largest ocean cruise liners on Earth. Five triangular sections opened from the center outwards like the petals of a flower. A purple light emanated from the opening as it widened and took on the shape of a five-pointed star. Once fully opened, a large docking bay with regular geometrically arranged chambers appeared. In each, there was a scout ship identical to the one they had left Earth in. Their craft slowly glided into the opening and maneuvered towards a vacant bay. A porthole opened in the side of the docking bay, and a tube came out toward the door of the craft and docked with a clunk.

"Welcome aboard the Splinkatrix," announced Wink as he and Mwaki hovered toward the exit. "We will remain weightless as we float to our main quarters. Once settled in the ship will generate low artificial gravity by accelerating at a constant rate until we reach halfway using our gyro engines. Then we turn around to face backward and decelerate pointing. That way, we soon reach incredible velocities in mid-flight."

"How long will the voyage take?" asked Kaz.

"It depends on how much fuel we use," replied Wink, "and what the rate of acceleration is. It also depends on how long we shut down the main engines in mid-flight before we brake. Mwaki recited her little verse:

> *Off to Antrobi, we shall hurtle*
> *Where the skies are hazy purple*
> *Where the hills are pointed high*
> *And the cities are incredibly nigh*
> *C'mon, little Winkets!*

Wink and the other Balkiens were hovering off the scout ship in a single file into a long tubular corridor. The Balkiens were in a long line, like marbles in a marble-runner. The six humans floated along with them in their weightlessness. Yesl pulled Matt as he held onto her swooth, while Boongoo towed Kaz. Alison had Baingae as her motor, while Kara had Mwaki, Sean to Wink and Judith to Winxl. The flight through the corridors seemed to take forever.

There were many round doors of different colors in the labyrinth of tubular passages. The party was ushered in through a bright green door at the end of the corridor. The door swished open to reveal a cavernous round room with control panels full of round monitors displaying images and data, shown in an exotic script with rounded characters, presumed to be Antrobian writing. Everyone was relieved to be out of narrow pipe-like passages. The control room had a massive pentagon-shaped window divided up into five triangles. There was a majestic view of Jupiter's cloud belts. Jupiter lit up the room with a reassuring glow, which reflected off the faces of the humans and Balkiens alike.

"This is the main bridge, as you'd call it on a sea ship," announced Yesl, "from where all commands come. Now that we're all aboard and all the scout ships safely stowed in the docking bay, we're ready for our trans-Antrobian trajectory."

"First," Yesl continued, "we'll have to welcome the Tombalkiens on board. I see that many of you have not yet met Tombalkiens."

YESL – The Balkien from Antrobi

As Yesl continued in her fluent English, Baingae translated the crew briefing into Antrobian for the Splinkatrix's crew.

Captain Wink emerged from the group of Balkiens and started to speak in Antrobian. Now it was Yesl's turn to interpret for the guests from Earth:

"We have now completed our final pre-flight checks and accounted for all of the Balkiens making the return trip to Antrobi on this flight."

"Like our program, the human race had embarked on an extensive search for extra-terrestrial life. The eldest of our members, Matt, was enthusiastic about this quest. As a child, he found Yesl. He befriended Yesl on Tombalki after the *Balkieston*, broke up in the Asteroid Belt, and we were *wugged* down into the Tombalkien northern sea in our evacuation pods.

"We have had to make modifications to some quarters on this ship for their use during the voyage. We are beginning to wean them off Tombalkien food to help them get used to our Antrobian nourishment."

"Please welcome our Tombalkiens, Matt, Kara, Sean, Kaz, Alison, and Judith aboard."

At this announcement, many of the Balkiens made an orchestrated series of hums, shrills, and high-pitched squeaks. "That is our style of singing and music," said Yesl. "This is our welcome aboard song. Do come to Antrobi in peace and we'll look after you. We know that you've had to leave your family and loved ones behind to help us on our mission to restore our home planet to its former state."

The humans were ushered along a short passage to their cabins by Yesl and other Balkiens. Each cabin had a small porthole that looked out of the top sphere of the tetrahedron-shaped ship. These cabins looked aft through the triangular structure forming the stern. The other three spherical pods contained the main engines. Matt looked at a diagram on a circular card that Captain Wink had given him, showing the basic principle of the flight plan to Antrobi, affectionately known as the *Purple Planet*.

After some warbling Antrobian announcements, Yesl, who was seated in one of the cabins with Matt and the others, fastened their specially fitted seatbelts in their semi-spherical seats.

"Please observe the fasten seatbelt sign." quipped Yesl. "Your period of weightlessness will soon be over as 'engine start' is requested by the Captain."

The now polar view of Jupiter or Boonkle-Mallkis was magnificent in all of its cloudy detail. The ship was in a near-polar orbit around the planet. The brightly colored curved horizon filled half the view from the bridge. Contrasted against the inky blackness of space were myriads of seemingly tiny anvil-shaped thundercloud tops that spread across the entire edge of Jupiter's disk. There was a lurch, and every floating thing fell towards the side of the cabin on which the portholes faced towards Jupiter's North Pole. A throbbing hum pervaded the ship, which slowly increased in pitch. The throb abated as the engines increased in speed. Gravity returned. Matt and the others sat upon their cup seats and looked down through the porthole windows towards Jupiter's cloud tops now. At first, there was no perceptible movement of the ship at all. After about another half an hour, Matt had to strain to see those fascinating cloud tops on the planet's edge, which had become more indistinct as the clouds grew smaller. Another hour or so later, it was much harder to perceive that brilliant cloud detail. Jupiter looked more like images photographed by telescopes. Everyone gazed in awe for another two hours.

"Matt," said Yesl, "doesn't that look very similar to the top swooth of a gargantuan Balkien?"

The polar clouds in many hues of browns, brick reds, and pale greys were in ever-increasing concentric semi-circles on the daylight side of the planet. As time passed, Jupiter was now like a smoothed half Balkien in the inky blackness. The sun's light peered into the cabin.

"Yesl," asked Alison, "why is the sun's light so red?"

Yesl replied, "That's because we continue to accelerate to ever-increasing velocities. The light from stars behind us will become noticeably redshifted."

"Oh, the Doppler shift," said Matt.

After another three hours, Jupiter became a bright, slightly redder star. Artificial cabin lighting was now on, as the sun's glow grew dimmer and noticeably redder.

"We're on our way to Antrobi," announced Yesl. "We are going home at last, but for you, a whole new adventure has just begun."

Matt continued to gaze at the vast universe through the porthole just before he went to bed under normal gravity conditions. His relationship with Yesl had changed as she was now involved in carrying out her other Balkienian duties with the rest of the ship's crew. There were several dull thuds at the circular door that sounded distinctly like the welcoming thud of soft swooth on his bedroom door on Earth. He rose from his bunk and by waving his hand over the sensor by the door, he made it swish open.

It was dear ol' Yesl. "Matt, I'll keep you company tonight, if indeed it is 'night' out here in space. We'll now refer to sleep periods and wake periods."

Yesl turned off the lights. The stars in space shone with uncanny brightness. Matt and Yesl gazed out at the thousands of stars. The Milky Way was so bright and distinct. The sun, or Sol, was now just a very bright star as the ship was about twice the distance of the planet Neptune. Somehow Matt felt a surreal connection with space and a strange relationship to the Balkiens, particular to Yesl amid the familiar constellations. He half expected to see Earth roll into view, then realized that his home-world was almost invisible to the naked eye. Matt fetched his binoculars and, taking care not to look directly at the sun in case it may be still bright enough to harm his eyes, just managed to pick out his home planet. Yesl had assisted him in locating Tombalki and Tomkil. In the binocular view, he could make out the distinct crescent shapes of Earth and the Moon. Matt felt goosebumps, realizing that the world he'd known was now a speck of light. His eyes began to water as he thought of his beloved Erin. Yesl cuddled up to him for her comfort as much as his. They settled in the bunk with the sound coming only from the very distant throb of the ship's anti-gravity engines that were propelling them ever so quickly into an endless vast void. Matt remembered the early NASA probes Voyager 1 and Voyager 2 which had taken three decades to venture out to only about half the distance that the *Splinkatrix* had by now traveled.

● ○ ●

12 ~ FASTER THAN LIGHT

Matt awoke to find that Yesl had already arisen to tend to her astronautical duties. He looked down at the stars through the porthole situated on the bottom of the accommodation sphere past the three long tubes that linked this sphere to the three other spherical modules. The sun was now distinctly dimmer than it had been before he went to bed. It was hard to distinguish the surfaces of the ship and space itself except for the internal lights dotted along the tubes and around the faceted spheres. Any chance of looking directly back at the Earth-Moon system was rapidly fading. He fetched his binoculars and again looked towards the distant stars visible between the rear sections of the ship. It took Matt five frustrating minutes to locate Jupiter and Saturn, now appearing very close to the sun, which was now only a little brighter than an average star. Matt managed to pick out two specks of light, one dimmer than the other close to the sun. His eyes watered. The round door swished open and in flew the Winkets, Baingae and Winxl.

"Matt," said Baingae. "You're gazing aft towards Sol. Are you're homesick?"

"I'm thinking of my parents and other relatives, particularly Aunt Ethel, who is getting on in years, back on Tombalki and of my beloved Erin and her folks. It will be sobering not to be able to see Tombalki and Tomkil anymore."

"Oh, Matt," said Wink. "Don't keep looking back. You want to come up to the bridge and look forward to our destination."

"Oh, it's so good to be going home at last," said Winxl, "with my beloved Baingae."

"Winxl," said Baingae. "You traveled the cosmos to find me. I should have waited for you to awake. I was so impatient and left you to go on a voyage, wrecked on Tombalki. But you came for me."

"Baingae," said Winxl. "We found you. It all worked together for good. If it was not for my persistence in negotiating with the Antrobian Astronautics Corps and that of the Winkets, we might never have launched this mission. How was the Balkieston crew to get home in a wrecked ship beneath a deep ocean on a planet without technology for interstellar travel?"

"And we have six Tombalkiens with us," said Mwaki, "to help rescue our planet Antrobi from who knows what. What if we hadn't come away? We might well have fallen under the evil spell of the Enigma, and it would have been all over."

"So, don't feel guilty, Baingae," said Winxl reassuringly.

Baingae and Winxl landed on the window beneath them and looked out on the Milky Way Galaxy significantly red-shifted. They lay there with their equatorial swooth beginning to coalesce in an embracing ponkadliath, known as a *binkety*.

Three weeks later, as the Splinkatrix continued to accelerate the view of the stars from behind the ship began to appear redder as the higher light frequencies became more red-shifted. As everyone awoke after another sleep period and looked out of the aft hexagonal porthole, they saw a dark starless hole in the fainter red star-field right where the sun should be, which grew in size as the hours passed. Yesl, Baingae, Winxl, and the Winkets were present. Matt shed a tear, as he thought of his beloved Erin far behind this inky blackness. Wink hovered up to lay on his shoulder. "I only wish that my dearest Erin was with us on this voyage," said Matt. "I wish we could have waited for her."

"I know," said Wink. "We couldn't wait as the situation on Antrobi may close in on us. And she couldn't relinquish her job at JPL as she was working on the Enigmatic spectrum issue."

"Yesl," asked Kaz. "Why's there now a dark hole in the starfield behind us?"

"We've accelerated past the speed of light," replied Yesl. "The light from directly behind us can no longer catch up with the ship. When we go up to the bridge, we will observe this light coming towards us from Earth; shine backward onto us at the front as we overtake it. It'll be like this for another three of your Lunar months until we slow down enough on approach Antrobi."

On the bridge, where Captain Wink was on duty, the view of the stars ahead of the ship had become brighter and blue-shifted.

Upon the bridge, there was now a weird sight consisting of blue stars intermingled with red ones. The Winkets passed around circular blue and red light filters. Matt held up the red filter screen to block out the blue stars ahead.

"Mwaki, Smoonkshie," said Matt. "I can now see our sun in the constellation of Columba as seen from Earth in this part of the sky directly opposite from Vega."

Matt passed the filter to Alison. "It's now so faint."

Kara was next to hold up the filter to look at the reversed view of the stars from behind their direction of travel.

Wink had a look through the filter. "These stars are part of the constellation of Spoomankis, our constellations from our legends similar to yours."

Matt got hold of Yesl and cuddled her. He had a rather sad expression on his face. "Will I ever see Erin again?"

Yesl rolled around his head. "Of course, you will. Look at Baingae. Remember how he was all alone without Winxl and space-wrecked too."

"Will you travel to Earth to bring her out here?" asked Matt.

"We'll have traffic between Antrobi and Tombalki," replied Captain Wink.

"I now realize the absolute vastness of space," said Alison. "Our lives and history are now on an invisible speck next to a dull red dot in this viewing filter."

"Space is indeed very vast but is all in our stride. C'mon little Winkets," said Kaz, trying to make up a rhyme. He was working on lyrics for some songs that he would put to Antrobian music. He was also beginning to say simple words in Antrobian such as "Good Morning" and "How are you?"

"All these singing tones are hard to get our head around," said Judith.

"Not to mention all of those rounded characters," said Sean. "The safety signs around the ship help, though."

The starlight from the forward window was now very bright, almost daylight, which bathed the control center in a shadowless illumination. An image of Vega's spectrum displayed on the ship's view screen. The doors swished open.

Baingae flew in to watch. "Captain Wink, I can see a familiar pattern in that image."

"This spectrum is almost identical to that, which we saw as we approached Splogita," said Boongoo.

"You're right," said Yesl. "This could be the Enigma's signature all over again."

"Like with the Molktrons?" asked Wink.

"Yes," said Smoonkshie.

"Just as Erin found out in our University research," said Matt.

Everyone looked at one another in silence with only the hum and clicking of the equipment.

"Looks like our mission's got a lot more challenging," said Matt.

"I expect that many of the Balkiens will now be slaves to the Enigma just like the Molktrons," said Wink, with dismay.

"I sincerely hope that is all it'll be," said Baingae. "This thing can influence and warp the minds of our population."

"How do you mean?" asked Kaz.

"How did all those cities on Splogita get wrecked?" asked Mwaki, somewhat rhetorically. "Don't you all see? There was war! The beings that once lived there, who were very much higher in intelligence than those poor, humble, little Molktrons were influenced to fight one another. You know one group against another."

"You mean just like all the wars we have on Earth?" asked Kara.

"Yeh, sort of," said Yesl. "But it's probably a bit more subtle than that."

"We don't know what's exactly behind it," said Wink. "When we visited Splogita, we flew over quite a few of the ruins to investigate them until we saw bolts of lightning suddenly emanating from the mountain peak on the island coming straight for our scout ship. We dived into the lake and proceeded underwater towards the island to evade the attack. We surfaced on the island and discovered the wreckage of the scout ship in which you had your accident, after being shot down by the lightning."

"And that's when we met those lovely glowing little Molktrons," said Winxl. "They took us to their cave by rolling under us through the dark forest until we reached the Queen in her cave of Molktrons. She explained all about your encounters with the Enigma. Her worker Molktrons told us that a bolt of lightning streaked up into the sky with a thunderous roar. They saw a bright flash, far distant at the end of the lightning streak. We figured that that was when your ship's navigation equipment was badly damaged, resulting in your space wreck on Tombalki."

"And the rest is history," said Sean.

"And here we are on our way to Antrobi to who knows what," said Judith.

Everyone gazed at one another with expressions of amazement and in trepidation.

It was another wake period but no routine day of continued acceleration while gazing at the bright starfield now more violet in hue.

"The time has come," said Captain Wink.

"For what?" Matt asked.

"For we have neared the midpoint on our journey," said Wink. "We turn off the engines for about two of your weeks and coast at a constant speed and gradually turn the ship around to face back towards Tombalki, and we shall be weightless. When we turn on the engines again, they will apply reverse thrust to brake and slow us down towards Vega. It'll take as long to brake as it has to accelerate thus far.

"We have now plenty of time on our hands," said Captain Wink. We will assemble in the viewing studio in one hour. There are important issues to discuss what we discovered on Splogita."

Everyone was seated in the viewing studio in front of the large round screen. Being seated was a case of floating in a fixed position in the room.

"Ladies and Gentlemen, both Tombalkien and Antrobian," began Yesl. "As all of you know, we did not come directly to Tombalki on this vessel. We journeyed to Splogita, the original destination of the ill-fated *Balkieston* mission, on which some of us on this voyage, including myself, were crew members. The Winkets here along with Winxl and a support crew were commissioned by the supreme King Zozl of Antrobi to go to Splogita and look for the lost ship. There was such a reluctance ever to go and look for the *Balkieston,* and if it wasn't for poor Winxl here pining for her beloved Baingae, we might never have departed. I will now introduce Mwaki for her presentation."

The screen lit up, and the Splinkatrix logo was displayed, consisting of a circular decal with the two planets, Antrobi, and Antrogi with a dark purple starry background. To the right of the two worlds was a drawing of the Splinkatrix. Above were images of both the Winkets and yellow Antrobian rounded lettering. Wink moved over some things that resembled buttons on a round desk, and a picture of a planet in space appeared.

"This is Splogita on our final approach after many months in space. This ship is much faster than the *Balkieston*, the pioneer of interstellar space travel.

"Our first view of that huge mount on the lake looks beautiful. Until —."

The next image showed a massive streak of lightning streaking up toward the ship.

"We had to take evasive action to avoid extensive damage. We applied reverse thrust. The lightning stopped. We continued in orbit around to the side of the planet away from the lake and assumed a geostationary orbit there, from where we deployed our exploration scout craft.

"This image is one of the most disturbing; ruined buildings and twisted wreckage."

Matt and the others let out a sigh.

"We found that most of the planet was like this," continued Mwaki. "We were so disturbed by what had happened."

There were more images showing scenes of devastation upon the desiccated deserts of this devastated world, even though the sky and its star hung most beautiful, along with the vast vista of the gas planet around which Splogita orbited.

"These were the humble Molktrons, with which we made immediate friends."

There was an image of the lake, where the glowing Molktrons crowded the beach in the evening twilight.

"That's where we landed and later had our accident," said Yesl.

Mwaki continued, "This next image shows the now tarnished wreckage of that scout ship. If it weren't for the Molktrons telling us about your subsequent rescue and successful departure, our mission would have ended there, assuming that the *Balkieston* was lost with all Balkiens. Oh, I'm so sad for those poor little beings, under such tyranny. We managed to salvage all of the remaining equipment from that wreck, but we fear that some of it was missing and that the Enigma may have got hold of info relating to where we had come from."

"ID theft," said Matt.

"Sort of," said Wink. "Maybe that's how the Enigma found its way to Antrobi."

"We thought that we'd retrieved all of our data from the wreck before our rescue and departure," said Boongoo.

"Well, you might have," said Mwaki. "The thing is that the Molktrons told us that there were five rather bashed data spheres lying in the undergrowth a little away from the main wreckage that must have been thrown clear on impact. The Molktrons only managed to carry three of them to their cave. When they rolled back for the other two, they had vanished."

Smalkle flew into the room with five spheres. "These data spheres have library information about the history and culture of the Balkiens. Two of these are copies of spheres one and three that went missing, which contain enough information for an enemy to determine our whereabouts."

"So, we left our calling card at the scene of the crime," said Baingae.

"Unfortunately, yes," said Yesl curtly. "An obvious security breach in hindsight, but then we had not encountered evil of this sort and so never took precautions about data security."

"To continue," said Wink. "We must go back to the story of how the Molktrons became enslaved and how the Enigma influenced the minds of the other beings, *Gongothera* and the *Sploonkothteros* on Splogita to fight amongst each other that led to their destruction and ruination of their cities we explored for possible wreckage of the *Balkieston*. The Molktrons explained that the beings that lived in those cities developed changed personalities. They stopped having regard for their fellow creatures and became only concerned for themselves. These two species of beings were larger than the Molktrons. They were spherical but were different from us. Rather than swooth, the Gongothera had smooth skin and had a face with many eyes and could hover like us. The Sploonkothteros had a surface that resembled fish scales and could live underwater in the lake."

"That'd explain the underwater ruins you told us about while we were on Earth," commented Matt.

"They coexisted well," continued Mwaki, "until the Enigma appeared from space, appearing like some grotesque apparition in the sky one night and hovered around the great Mountain of Light revered by the Gongothera who were spread all over the planet and lived in compact cities. There were several lakes all around that world, with beautiful green forests and meadows, but many had dried up after the Great War, fought between them and the undersea creatures, the Sploonkothteros. The Sploonkothteros, under the influence of the Enigma, rose from the depths and began throwing rocks onto the Gongothera's dwellings, hurting them. There was a hideous war that resulted in total obliteration using destructive weapons that they developed, or perhaps almost total, of these races. Most of their Molktron helpers also perished in the holocaust that so ravaged the planet that there was irreversible climate change causing all the lakes, except this one, to dry up. The ones we met have held dear to their legends and sagas, which happened many of your centuries ago."

"The Molktrons are enslaved to the Enigma and are only allowed to survive on condition that they maintain the greenery of the forest floor, which can only be cultivated and propagated by their presence. It was because of the Molktrons' demise elsewhere on the planet that all of the lakes dried up and the vegetation withered away."

The familiar Splogitan spectral signature was monitored as they traveled on towards Antrobi. The view from Matt's cabin window was now beginning to look like a typical night sky studded with bright stars, which were still blue-shifted as his window now faced forward towards Vega after the ship had turned around in mid-flight.

From the bridge, which now faced back towards Earth, the hole in the sky surrounded by red-shifted stars shrank. Quite suddenly the hole filled in with dark red stars as the ship had decelerated to sub-light speed. There was a strange change in the general ambiance aboard the Splinkatrix as this occurred. Looking ahead from the other bridge aft, Vega was now becoming very bright. Matt and Kaz could make out tiny starlets extending out in most directions from Vega.

"What a beautiful sight," said Kaz. "Do we see Vega's planets?"

"Vega has thirty-six known planets and many other planetoids or minor planets," said Yesl, "far more than in your Solar System. The Antrobi/Antrogi system orbits Vega as the fourth planet and only a little bit further in than the equivalent orbit of your Jupiter. Our equivalent of Jupiter is the gas giant known as Spalminkatrix."

The room was now lit brightly with the bluish-white light of Vega. It was no longer possible to view Vega through any telescope or binoculars, without risk of eye injury to the humans or harm to the visual swooth of the Balkiens. To the naked eye, now through dark film, it was possible to observe that Vega, with its intense bluish light, was flattened or oblate, due to its high rotation speed. Matt, looked through his binoculars at the planets, avoiding a direct view of Vega. These two planets were now also displayed on the viewscreen.

"There they are!" he exclaimed. "The two distinct points of light must be Antrobi and Antrogi. Have a look, Kaz."

"Antrobi and Antrogi," said Yesl, "our first sight of home for many years."

As time passed, the two planets became visible to the unaided eye as two crescent shapes, like two moons. The other three smaller crescent-shaped moons were now visible.

"Angapooka, Balkle, and Boonkpolm," said Wink. Soon the crescent planets grew larger so that with binoculars, it was possible to make out the shapes of the purple-colored oceans and dark green continents. Many of the Balkiens were buzzing around with excitement on their homecoming after the five Lunar month voyage. The stellar constellations were distinctly Antrobian. The familiar stars such as Rigel, Betelgeuse, Aldebaran, and Sirius were familiar, but the constellations were different.

"We shall assume a standard geostationary orbit around Antrobi," said Captain Wink.

Antrobi and Antrogi filled the view from the main bridge with the Splinkatrix now in a forward orientation after braking.

"It does look like an Earth-type planet," said Kaz. "I just knew they existed."

There were familiar cloud patterns and weather systems across the oceans and the continents. The striking difference was that the color of the seas was violet. The continents were mostly dark green.

"So exciting," said Kara in amazement amid everyone's gasps of wonder.

"Looks a bit different to how I remember my last look on our home planet as we departed for Splogita," said Yesl. "What about those light green and sandy brown areas? All the continents were darker green than this."

"You're right," said Wink. "Look at that light brown area to the northeast on the Yastagliath."

"Antrobi," called Yesl. "I never thought that I'd be returning to our home planet speaking an alien language and with aliens aboard with us on a different ship."

Antrobi loomed more massive as the Splinkatrix descended into a parking orbit.

"The bay of Balkieston," said Yesl as everyone looked down upon the violet inlet surrounded by what looked like beautiful dark green forests on either coast. Matt took up his binoculars to look down at the head of the bay upon the City of Balkieston.

"Yesl," said Baingae. "The city seems much larger than it was when we left. There must have been an awful lot of building."

Captain Wink was trying to make contact in Antrobian with Balkieston's Antrobian Astronautics Corps HQ, the Centre of the Balkien Scout Service.

"We can't make contact with anyone on Antrobi at all," he said in English.

"We will now have to invoke the *no contact* landing procedure. That is, we send down a single landing craft to somewhere east of Balkieston and land in a remote area. We cannot land at the spaceport without permission. That breaks every safety rule in the book!"

"Strange that we have not been detected and contacted on our arrival," said Wink. "We are only about sixty days late on our planned mission."

"Come and look at something," said Kaz as he pointed to a different view of the planet below. "Do you see what I see?"

"It's the same terrible flashing lights as we saw on Splogita," said Yesl in a chilling hushed tone.

Everyone had packed their bags and transferred to the shuttlecraft to take them to Balkieston. The craft was in the hangar within one of the aft spheres of the mother ship. As the triangular panels of the pentagonal doorway began to open out, the brightness of the Antrobian surface shone in to transform the darkened hangar into a brightly lit display of all the other shuttlecraft. The craft eased out, slowly at first, into space outside. There was a quick transition from almost weightlessness to being thrust into the cup-like seats in which they and the Balkien crew were seated as the craft began its descent towards Antrobi. Yesl, Baingae, Winxl, and the Winkets were on board, leaving Smoonkshie in charge of operations on the Splinkatrix.

The ship began to shrink slowly at first then very rapidly became a small silhouette of four black dots against the large bright half-disk of the planet Antrogi, the other half of the Antrobian double planet system. Soon the black sky became a deep purple, which grew lighter as the craft descended towards a region northeast of Balkieston City on the continent of Beekeo.

"We can't land at the spaceport without permission from space traffic control," said Captain Wink. "We'll put down in the forests well to the east of Balkieston."

To the port side, they could see a large, gleaming city of shining metallic buildings. There were silver domes, both spherical and geodesic. The sky was still purple.

"Much of the familiar skyline of Balkieston of my memory has changed beyond recognition," said Yesl.

"It seems so much larger, even to us Winkets," said Wink. The ship flew on past a group of tall rock pinnacles, like vast cathedral spires. The forests were of dark green vegetation.

"Such odd trees," said Kaz.

"We are on an alien planet," said Judith. "What do you expect to see, Christmas trees?"

"The nearest resemblance is broccoli," said Matt.

"You're right," said Sean, "huge broccoli-trees. Maybe we can eat from them."

"We'll have to test you on some of these foods," said Dr. Baingae with authority. "We have successfully adapted your diets what is available on Antrobi during the voyage. You've all done very well."

The craft came over a grassy clearing between the broccoli-trees and touched down softly on its tripod legs. Everyone clapped and cheered exuberantly.

"Here we are on Antrobi at last," said Matt."

"Well now," said Wink. "We have to double-check the environment before disembarking. We didn't expect to have to land in secrecy."

"Very similar to how we started from Perth on Earth," said Alison. How do we get to Balkieston?"

"There's the train," said Yesl.

"A train?" asked Matt in astonishment.

"We have similar rail travel to you," said Yesl. "Except that the rail cars look like silver balls that move along rails."

"Air pressure is okay," said Yesl. "Oxygen level is 22%."

"That's good," said Matt, as the side door slid open. There was a gust of wind that was a strange combination of warmth and chill at the same time.

Kaz took in a breath of the fresh Antrobian air. "Sure, was a l-o-n-g flight."

"Slip slap slop with your Vega screen," said Baingae. "We don't yet know how the rays of Vega will affect your skin yet, though we have a thick ozone layer here. Also, both planets have a strong combined magnetic field, necessary for protecting our delicate swooth."

The humans walked down the ramp, the same one they stepped up when leaving the Australian bush, out into the open clearing. Above the rounded outlines of the broccoli-trees, there were tall rock spires in the distant purple haze. The shadows were distinctly sharper than on earth as Vega appeared smaller than the sun on Antrobi.

"Oh," said Alison as she screwed up her eyes. "That sun, err, Vega's so bright."

"We're almost as far out from Vega as your Jupiter is from the sun," said Yesl. "Our seasons are a lot longer, with an Antrobian year being about five that of Tombalki."

"Your habitable zone," remarked Matt.

"That's right," said Baingae. "We have our second planet, Klatis, at the equivalent orbit of your Tombalki. There, it is a scorching roiling desert, with frequently erupting volcanoes. Its day is about two thirds as long as its year, so the night side can still get pretty cold. A few planetary missions have been flown there, where an underground base was set up for the shelter of hardy Balkien crews doing scientific research. We've had cases of Balkiens evacuated with heat-related oblateness."

As Vega set, the luminance of Antrogi grew brighter.

"That's incredible," said Sean. "Antrogi's phases are becoming fuller so much more quickly than those of our Moon or Tomkil."

"And it's so much bigger and brighter," said Kara.

"I think the explanation is simple," said Matt. "This is a double planet system. Let's form a circle. Now let the Winkets demonstrate the motion of these two planets. Wink, you represent Antrobi, where we are and you, Mwaki, represent Antrogi."

Wink and Mwaki started hovering into positions in the middle of the circle of Tombalkiens and Balkiens. The light of the real Antrogi now represented the light from Vega shining on the 'daylight' sides of the Winkets who each revolved around a common center. Wink was about four Winket diameters from Mwaki.

"So, we see here," continued Matt, "that these two Balkien planets orbit one another such that each always has the same face towards the other as our Moon faces to the Earth. Due to their closeness, they are thus tidally locked. If this were not so, there would be extreme ocean tides far greater than of Earth, and probably many terrible earthquakes, or should I say antrobiquakes. There would also be a lot of atmosphere-polluting volcanoes."

"You will notice how we have the night and day from Vega," said Boongoo. Now that Vega has set relative to us, it is now shining brightly on to the face of Antrogi towards us."

"Our day is about twenty-six of your hours," said Yesl.

Everyone had unique watches made that divided the Antrobian day into twenty parts based on Antrobi's twenty-hour clock. Each hour is divided into twenty intervals; you might call minutes, while each of these is divided into twenty smaller periods.

Kaz pulled out a sheet of paper and unfolded it. "I've worked out that and Antrobian hour is about seventy-eight of our minutes, An Antrobian minute is nearly four of ours and your second is nearly twelve of ours."

An Antrobian hour later, the light from Antrogi was more magnificent. One could see while Antrogi was bright.

"We'll have to settle here for the night," said Yesl. "I'll look after you here. The Winkets will soon fly off towards Balkieston to investigate the situation there. Oh, it's so good to be back on Antrobi. My swooth's already beginning to rejuvenate."

"Must be the higher level of oxygen," said Matt. "I've never felt better."

"We'd better stay on board the ship tonight," said Yesl.

"Did you hear that?" asked Monku.

"No, what?" asked Matt.

"I thought I heard a Balkien flying in the trees," said Wink.

Just then, there was a high-pitched warble emanating from the woods to the side of the clearing, bathed in the glow of Antrogi-light. Under the canopy of the broccoli-trees, it was almost pitch black. The source of that noise emerged from that dark abyss and flew all around the ship haphazardly.

"It is a little Balkien," said Yesl, who immediately flew after in hot pursuit of the little creature. They virtually played tag around the clearing and the ship and dared Yesl to go into the darkness of the forest. Wink took off and followed to assist Yesl who managed to telekinetically attach the little Balkien onto them-selves whom they brought to the entrance of the ship. They exchanged some dialog in Antrobian.

"Who is this first Balkien contact since our landing?" asked Kaz.

"We're having some trouble understanding this one," said Yesl. "Her name is Quinket. She is anxious about us holding her captive. She seems rather, mischievous."

Quinket had thin light multi-colored bands on her swooth. Three other Balkiens hovered in from the woods and called in Antrobian.

"Who are you?" asked the larger Balkien in the group.

"I'm Yesl. These are Wink and Mwaki."

"Where are you from?"

"We have just returned from our search and rescue mission to Splogita."

"What's this craft doing here? Why are you arresting Quinket, on what charge?"

"Questions," said Wink. "We're only holding onto your Quinket because she looked as if she was going to hurt herself on the ship. You must control her more."

"You Balkiens of the Empire," said the large Balkien, who had bands in blue shades on his swooth. "We don't trust you."

"What Empire?" asked Yesl. "What is this? We've been away for years out to Splogita and Tombalki."

"Splogita! That says it. You're spies of the Emperor!"

The large Balkien let out a loud shrill holler. Many other Balkiens appeared from the woods and menacingly surrounded the ship and guarded the door and hovered closer.

"And who or what are these six tall standing things with appendages?" asked the large Balkien, who looked to be in the role of a tribal chief. "Spies of the Emperor, no doubt?"

"These beings are from the planet Tombalki," replied Yesl.

"What were you doing on, Tombalki?" asked the chief. "That'll be another planet of the Empire. Listen. We have nothing to do with Splogita. That's a swear word around here. Got it! Now let our Quinket go."

Wink and Yesl released their hold on the little one. She flew to be with the chief, who was presumed to be her father.

"Please hear us out," said Yesl. "We mean no harm. We've come from the Splinkatrix and landed here, as we could not get clearance to land at Balkieston Spaceport."

"The Splinkatrix," said the chief. "Now I'm beginning to understand. What exactly was your mission, and when did you leave Antrobi?"

"We launched this mission to look for the *Balkieston* that did not come back," said Wink. "We had to go and look for Dr. Baingae for poor little Winxl here. Mwaki and I, as priests of the Great One, swore an oath to look after Winxl's spiritual and emotional needs when she awoke out of her hibernation in Beekaria.

"Winxl, Baingae," said the chief. "We've heard a lot about you. Welcome back! Sorry about the inquisition. Well, I never! You left here many years ago. We've read stories and legends about you. You sure have been gone for a long time. I'm the chief of the tribe here and Quinket's father. My name is Kloonket. These are all our extended family. Tell me about your alien guests."

"These six are from Tombalki," said Wink. "They've come back with us as they greatly assisted our recovery on Tombalki. They had some issues with their kind, for helping us after we crashed."

"The *Balkieston* managed to leave Splogita," said Yesl, "We met up with a terrible evil force on Splogita. As we tried to get away, it sent up a long bolt of lightning that struck the rear part of the ship and destroyed our navigation equipment, causing us to go off course, and wreck on Tombalki. Most of the *Balkieston* now lies in the deep ocean on Tombalki."

"Do you mean the Emperor?" asked Kloonket. "A terrible evil has befallen us here. We are hiding out here in the forests, away from civilization. It might have been better if you'd not returned. Antrobi, today, is no longer the wonderful planet you left."

"Quite the contrary," said Yesl. "That's precisely why we brought the Tombalkiens. We saw that the Splogitan spectral signature had started emanating from Antrobi and figured that something was wrong."

Kloonket had picked up a bit of English by telepathic thought transfer from Yesl and the Winkets. "Where's the Splinkatrix?" asked Kloonket.

"In standard Antrobian Orbit," replied Mwaki.

"Then you'd better call her captain immediately and get her to go into hiding," said Kloonket, "Go into orbit around another planet or something."

Mwaki hovered into the scout ship to contact the Splinkatrix. Everyone turned in for the night.

The tall spires of rock were bright in the dawn Vega light in the deep purple sky. The Tombalkiens were eating fruit, picked from the broccoli-trees. Matt passed a dark green fruit to Kara.

"It tastes like broccoli," he said. "Delicious. It looks like we'll have a staple diet while we're here."

"I'd love to see good ol' Balkieston Town again," said Yesl.

"We could take the train," said Kloonket. "We'll find a way to get the Tombalkiens into a freight car."

"You mean those ball trains," said Alison.

"Yes, the ball trains," said Kloonket. "A line runs close to here. There is a collection point for trains going into Balkieston Central Station.

"Do these ball cars roll along?" asked Judith. We'll get dizzy."

"Not these," said Yesl. "They have smaller wheels or rims that roll around the spheres, leaving them stationery as they are linked up, just like your trains on Earth."

It was a twenty-minute walk through the thick broccoli forest for the Tombalkiens, with the Winkets, Yesl, Baingae, and Winxl, led by Kloonket. The tree trunks were a mid-green, with their roots sprawling out across the moss-covered forest floor. The tree canopies almost joined up, letting through only a small amount of Vega light. They came to a clearing and there before them, were several rows of large silver spheres standing on rails. Some had round windows on three levels. Kloonket led the party to the second ball from the back of the train. All hovered or clambered aboard.

"Don't we need tickets or something," asked Sean.

"Ssh," said Kloonket. "We're stowaways. We've no sgegas, and anyway, the guards would not let you Tombalkiens on without a lot of security questions."

There were a jolt and a clanking sound, and then a low rumble as the ball car started to move. Everyone could see the broccoli trees passing the windows, and in the distance, great tall rocks could be seen rising high above the dark green forest canopy, scraping the purple sky.

"I never thought that we'd be completing our space journey to Balkieston to the sounds of clickety-clack on a train," said Matt. "Just like a London commute."

The ball car lurched a bit as the train trundled through the Antrobian countryside. On the bends, one could see all the ball cars ahead snaked out like a silvery necklace on the track. Soon, the outskirts of Balkieston came into view. There were rows of mooties or dome-shaped dwellings. There were tall buildings in rounded and sausage-shaped forms in the downtown areas. The train slowly ground to a halt in a siding, overgrown with what on Earth would be typical railway weeds. These had beautiful multi-colored flowers.

"This is our stop," said Kloonket.

Everyone got off and made their way to a well-cultivated flower garden and park area. There was a citadel with many glass spires with the tallest pyramid-shaped spire in the center. There were the hum and drone of millions of Balkiens flying to and fro, like being near a vast beehive. Thousands of moving black dots filled the purple sky. Each one represented an individual Balkien being with a lifetime of memories.

"This skyline is unfamiliar to me," said Yesl.

"To me as well," said Wink. "Yonder temple over there is all I know." Wink and Yesl both nodded to draw attention to a structure of spheres and tubes that stood tall with one ball at its apex. It looked dull, lacking the gleam of the other buildings and dwarfed by the present-day city. Everyone walked or hovered through the meadows over to the abandoned monument. Yesl huddled up to be in Matt's arms. He cuddled her up to his face. "What's wrong, Yesl?"

"This is our place of worship. The Winkets were the priests here. They dedicated this temple to the Great One, creator of all that is in the universe. These spheres once glowed and shimmered."

The party ambled past the temple structure and into an area where there were mounds covered by more exotic flowers. Some stones were lying around.

Yesl was quivering with sadness. "This was our city square. It's all that's left. Surely, we've not been gone that long. Most of the city we knew as poonketies or children, and before we left for Splogita is gone or rebuilt."

"Oh, Yesl," said Matt. "I'm so sorry. I remember our visit to Rome on Earth with our parents on vacation. There was a modern city with cars, buses and church buildings. But then there were the ruins of Ancient Rome at the Forum and the Coliseum."

"A terrible thought," began Matt, "The theory of relativity. Maybe our devices for counteracting this were damaged on both the Balkieston and the Splinkatrix on departure from Splogita, maybe by the Enigma or by some force on Splogita?"

● ○ ●

13 ~ HE WHO MUST BE OBEYED

The party sat on a knoll amidst the ruins not far from the forlorn temple. Yesl's swooth oscillated slowly.

Yesl," said Matt, "You seem to be so down."

"Matt," she said. "This is so disturbing. Here is where I met with all my family and friends. Where are they now? This thing, this Enigma or whatever it is, has changed our planet."

"One very powerful Antrogian now rules this planet," said Kloonket. "You have been away so long that you've missed this change. He is the veritable Emperor Zinkel-Mallkis, who must be addressed as *Your Sphericity*, meaning a perfect sphere. He is a very large Antrogian, about the size of a mootie or a house on the Earth and is multi-colored. We refer to him as *He Who Must be Obeyed*. Emperor Zinkel-Mallkis has definitely been influenced by and is under The Enigma."

"We did see some lightning emanating from the south of this planet," said Yesl.

"That's right," continued Kloonket. "The Emperor stays up in that Citadel most of the time, but he has another headquarters down in the great mount of Binkus-Mallkus. This tall peak is so high that it reaches into space, far above the snowline."

"That's far higher than your Mt Everest on Tombalki," commented Yesl.

"We have dared not go near that region for about two years or ten Tombalkien years," Kloonket continued. "This was not long after your departure to Splogita about seven Antrobian years after the *Balkieston* left."

"Thus, our concerns about the spectral signatures we detected are confirmed," said Matt. "Are we now becoming fugitives like the Molktrons?"

Acting Captain Smalkle was on the bridge of the Splinkatrix, overlooking the magnificent view of Antrobi with Antrogi in crescent forms straight ahead. The intercom sounded.

"Smalkle here,"

"It's Mwaki. I'm speaking only in English so as not to be overheard by this planet's new ruler. We have landed safely, but things are not good down here. You must take the Splinkatrix away. Go to orbit around Spalminkatrix. We need to keep our ship from being captured by this evil ruler known as Emperor Zinkle-Mallkis."

"Will do."

Captain Smalkle started up the engines, and the ship sped away from the Antrobian System, heading for Spalminkatrix. After only twenty-seven Earth hours, there was Spalminkatrix, shining brightly through the main window of the bridge. The gaseous giant planet about two and a half times the size of Jupiter was like a great Balkien with many thin bands of brightly colored swooth. There was a thin gossamer line piercing right through its equator.

"That's the thin rings of Spalminkatrix as we see them edge-on," said Moonxl. It was a ring like that of Saturn, which extended beyond the orbit of Spalminkatrix's outermost moons.

"Smalkle," said Moonxl. "That strange colorful spot on Spalminkatrix was never there before."

"What spot?"

"There's a large circular pattern on the planet at about thirty degrees, north. It's a lot more colorful. It looks so round."

"Sure, it's not one of the moons."

"Never seen any of Spalminkatrix's moons look like that. Run a scan over it."

As the ship moved into orbit, the apparition did not move relative to the planet.

"It looks like the image of a very colorful Balkien," said Smalkle.

"There is a Tele-message from Wink," said Smalkle.

"Display it," said Moonxl, who read it out.

'Our planet has been taken over by a capricious ruler who is only out for himself. I write using Matt's reconfigured mobile Earth phone to stop our messages from being intercepted and decoded. The emperor is called Zinkle-Mallkis, from Antrogi, Wink.'

"I remember Zinkle-Mallkis on Antrogi," said Smalkle. "He was mayor of the town of Zagarthia." Moonxl looked towards the spot on Spalminkatrix. "It looks suspiciously like Zinkle-Mallkis as I remember him - very colorful."

The planet's surface was emitting green lightning flashes. One flash came leaping up toward and dangerously close to the ship, which then lurched with a dull thud.

"We must pull out of here," shouted Smalkle. "Engines full reverse!"

Moonxl and Smalkle wugged onto the window of the bridge as down suddenly became upon gravity reversal resulting from Smalkle's command. They hovered over to the control consul, which had turned to face the other way.

"The whole planet bears the Emperor's color banding with his image also inset on the spot," said Smalkle. "As I look closely, I see that the whole planet now also looks like Zinkle-Mallkis, certainly a big statement."

More green lightning flashes kept coming up toward the ship, as they pulled away. There was a sudden bang as a lightning bolt hit one of the rear struts, then another. The Splinkatrix continued to pull away until it was out of range of the flashes.

"Damage assessment, Moonxl," said Smalkle as loud metallic creeks and deep groans were emanating from the rear of the ship. Smalkle quivered as he observed bent and tangled metal through the rear porthole from the bridge where two of the rear struts holding the rear engine spheres in place had once been.

"We've taken two bad hits on two of the three rear struts," replied Moonxl. "It is recommended to reduce the engine acceleration factor to one-fifth of the Antrobian gravity. Anymore and these struts could collapse and cause the engine pods to fall into one another and explode, resulting in total loss of the ship." The side struts began to creak alarmingly.

"SLOW DOWN!" shouted Moonxl. If these struts break, we'll have a sudden decompression.

"That bad?" asked Smalkle.

"This will mean no interstellar travel until these struts are rebuilt."

"Continue at this speed to Roonkle, the outermost planet, and we'll orbit there. At this rate, it'll take two Angapookan months to get there. This ship could normally do it in ten days. We hope not to be discovered there. We'll not be able to outrun any enemy action in this crippled state. Better send a message to Matt and Wink."

"Wink," said Matt. "I have a message from Smalkle. It says, "Bolts of lightning have attacked us from Spalminkatrix, which have badly damaged our ship. We can only travel at interplanetary speeds. We're going to the outermost planet; we'll call Pluto."

"Pluto," said Matt. "Smalkle just said that they couldn't go at interstellar speeds."

"Maybe that's a coded reference to your outermost planet," said Kaz.

"You mean to Roonkle," said Yesl, her voice quivering in shock.

"Our great ship nearly wrecked," said Matt sounding crestfallen.

"We'll have to catch the last train back to our hideout," said Kloonket.

The railway trip back was uneventful, except that the ball train they were hiding on missed their stop leaving the weary party with a two-kilometer walk through the darkening forest back to the scout ship. Other Balkien members of the resistance group had cut down bits of the broccoli-trees to camouflage the craft and to prepare a meal for the travelers.

"Wouldn't it be great to have a campfire and cook this lovely food on," said Judith.

"What about being spotted?" asked Kaz. "Any smoke rising might attract unwanted intrusion."

"That's right," said Yesl.

"I guess it's still warm," said Alison. As the night temperature began to drop, the Balkiens formed a warm cuddly ponkadliath around the Tombalkiens. They gazed up at the clear sight of Antrogi, becoming brighter as Vega set behind the trees. The vegetables from the broccoli-trees picked that day by the Balkiens at the camp were delicious. These looked like a smooth version of cocoanuts, but with softer and thinner skins. The light blue insides were a cross between coconut and watermelon and had a sweet, creamy taste.

"I find this food gives me a lot of energy and must be very nourishing," said Matt. "Wouldn't you all agree?"

"It's great," said Sean.

"Me too," said Kara.

"I wish we had this back on Earth," said Alison.

Kloonket, meanwhile, was having a crash course on English through telepathic communication from Yesl and Baingae. Quinket was making a nuisance of herself by hovering mischievously all over the campsite. She flew into and out of the forest a few times, risking getting lost in the dark forest canopy, a labyrinth of thick green succulent trunks and roots intermingled with thick knurled branches. These trunks had a silky velvet-texture which often shimmered if one rubbed one's hands on it.

"That little Quinket's buzzing around like a blowfly," said Sean.

Kloonket called out in Antrobian as if to say "Quinket. Will you stop that racket and simmer down. Be a good girl and ponkadliath with the others."

Quinket did one last orbital flight around the ship and settled on top of Wink next to Baingae who were in ponkadliath with Matt.

"You know, Quinket could so easily get herself lost in those woods at night," said Matt.

"Of course, she could," said Kloonket in almost perfect English, repeating this statement in Antrobian. "Quinket has always been a bit of a *Puchty Balkle*. That is a nuisance Balkien-ball."

Yesl gently hovered up above the top of the trees. "I can see the city lights of Balkieston in the distance."

"We could open the upper canopy on the ship and see from there," said Wink, who flew into the craft. There was a whirr from the top of the ship as the transparent canopy opened. Wink emerged, saying, "Come on up, everyone to see this magnificent view."

Everyone clambered or hovered up to the top chamber, which had the canopy dome on it, like an astronomical observatory. Matt and everyone could see the magnificence of the city lights over the dark green forest, bathed in the light of Antrogi beneath the deep purple sky.

"That may seem beautiful," said Kloonket in a harsh tone of voice.

YESL – The Balkien from Antrobi

"Matt, have you got your binoculars?" asked Yesl. Matt went down and brought them up. Through them, he could see many buildings of different rounded shapes. Many had glistening lights, some of which flashed and moved. "Have a look, everyone. There's a tall building with a large sphere on top of it, looking like a huge golf ball on a giant golf tee. The ball's very colorful and has a kaleidoscope of moving color zones. If I'm not mistaken, it looks like the image of a giant Balkien."

"Precisely," said Kloonket. "That's what I want to tell you. That huge dazzling image is in fact of a very important Balkien - actually an Antrogian. This very large Antrogian is almost the size of this ship. He has been King and Emperor of both of these planets for nearly three Antrobian Years. He's a fierce ruler. If anyone is against his authority, they are not welcome here and, if arrested, are liable to imprisonment or deportation to a prison planet. That's why my tribe hides out here in the bush. Our way of life has gone since Enigma came. The minds of most of our swooth were somehow possessed by thoughts of bad will and racial discrimination to other different species of us. Before this, all of us, including the Antrogians, lived a happy and exciting multicultural co-existence.

"Once Zinkel-Mallkis went to investigate this alien light that arrived on that tall mountain on Antrogi, a possessive barrage of green lightning seared his mind. He developed a changed personality. It was horrible. See that little mount on the western limb of Antrogi up there."

There was a bright peak with a shimmering green aura around it.

"All of Antrogi has been subjugated—," Kloonket broke off. "See those three lights coming towards us, EVERYONE GET BELOW!" he shouted.

Wink immediately pressed the ship's alarm. Loud hoots of the scout ship's evacuation alarm shattered the peace. The top lid of the craft was slammed shut as everyone scrambled below and out into hiding in the woods. Wink quickly shut off the alarm, all the lights, closed the doors, and joined them in the woods. The distant incandescent apparitions had become three large Antrogians that flew overhead.

"There's the sound of the huge Antrogians in flight," said Kloonket.

The beat grew louder as they swished overhead. They slowed down and hovered around menacingly over the camp for nearly half an hour. Everyone was terrified of them after Kloonket's warnings. They retreated into the woods a little more.

"If they destroy our ship, we're done for," said Wink. "We've already all but lost the Splinkatrix in enemy action."

BOOM! There was a bright flash of green light that lit up all the inside of the forest. There was then another more distant flash and bang. The beating sounds of the Antrogians receded.

"That was probably our ship," said Yesl. "Just as well we hid in here."

Everyone emerged from the woods, coughing and sputtering amid the dense smoke of burning broccoli-tree sap and green bark. As the pungent smoke cleared, there was a blackened gash in one of the trees to the side, which was still smoldering. On the ground, there were some bits of twisted metal.

"Our ship!" exclaimed Mwaki.

"No. Look closely," said Kloonket. "It's our communications antenna, they got. Look over there. Your ship should be okay. Some of the camouflage you put on took most of the hit. There's a chip on the glass dome canopy, though."

"That should be fine for space flight," said Wink. "The laminated glass dome is designed to withstand meteoric impacts, though we will have to check it for damage."

"They must have intercepted our last communication when we took the ball train to Balkieston," said Kloonket. "We may need to hide better or move the ship without being discovered. I suggest that we all clear this campsite and get back on board to relocate to another hideout further away."

"We were so looking forward to going into Balkieston by train tomorrow," said Alison.

"Not a good idea," said Yesl. "The heat's now on after this."

After everyone had cleared the campsite onto the ship, including the remains of the broken antenna, they boarded and closed the doors. Wink turned on the controls and carried out additional pre-flight checks for critical damage. The ship gently ascended into the air as the light of Antrogi faded to a thin crescent just before dawn.

"We now fly with all lights out under cover of darkness," said Kloonket.

The ship skimmed low over the trees to avoid being spotted by any more Antrogian police patrols.

"There's another clearing where we could land," said Kloonket. "Maybe we could hide this ship better than at the previous site."

It was possible to land the craft into a large enough cavity in the tree cover for it to remain well hidden. As the door opened, the ramp extended. Kloonket flew ahead of everyone and greeted the secret community there.

"We're here," said Kloonket in Antrobian, "after abandoning our previous base when our radio was blown up by green lightning ejected by a patrol unit last night. It's a wonder they hadn't targeted this ship. They must have detected signals from our radio equipment and came to attack us. Unfortunately, a shard from the exploding antenna hit this ship's upper glass dome and chipped it. We have checked the damage close-up and have decided that it is severe enough to render the ship unspaceworthy. We cannot leave Antrobi in it without risk of a blow out in space. Meet our fellow Balkiens of the freedom movement. I introduce these six Tombalkiens, Matt,

Kara, Sean, Kaz, Alison, and Judith and our much-traveled Balkiens, Wink, Mwaki, Yesl, and Winxl with Dr. Baingae."

Little Quinket started to fly in crazy circles around everyone present.

"Now Quinket," said Kloonket sternly. "Stop this buzzing around this instant, especially here. We don't want to be discovered again. We've already had to abandon another camp."

Quinket obediently landed next to Matt and Yesl. Through the densely packed dark green trunks of broccoli-trees, one could see the rails of the main Balkieston line to the hinterland of the continent of Beekeo. A distant rumble was heard, which became louder by the second. The rail tracks started to screech to the growing sound. The noise reached its crescendo as many large silver balls sped past for about three minutes.

"This hideout is much closer to the ball train line where freight trains run to or from Balkieston City," said Kloonket. "These carry goods between Balkieston and communities in the Yastagliath."

The dawn grew brighter before Vega rise. Everyone was waiting at the side of the railway switchback where its city-bound trains had to stop on the siding to await the passage of outbound trains. Again, the rails emitted that shimmering sound.

"Here's our train," said Kloonket. "Hide amongst the trees until it stops."

The balls glided slowly along the sidetrack until they ground to a screeching halt, clanking into one another. Kloonket flew up to the round door of one of the ball cars and waved over it. The door slid open.

"All aboard!" announced Kloonket, who hovered by the doorway, like the Balkien equivalent of a train conductor. Everyone walked, clambered, or flew into the carriage, with small porthole windows.

"Tickets please," said Kaz jokingly.

"Doors closing," announced Sean as everyone got seated on the Balkien style cup seats. The trees started to move past the windows with the deep rumble of the wheels on the track with clanks while they passed from the siding onto the mainline. As they picked up speed, there was that somewhat familiar clickety-clack sound. Half an hour later the forests gave way to the many rounded mooties on Balkieston's outskirts.

As the train slowed down and rumbled into the city proper, everyone looked out of the porthole windows up at the city sights. The tallest tower that looked like the golf ball on its tee was majestic. The image of Zinkel-Mallkis was shimmering and rotated slowly around the spherical structure. There were also many other images of the Emperor appearing on many of the buildings.

"Everywhere you look, it seems," said Matt, "this Zinkle-Mallkis is everywhere. Every time a king or ruler starts this sort of display of narcissistic self-importance on Earth, there's trouble, often leading to war. Why can we never escape this sort of thing?"

The humans managed to jump off the ball car as it was pulling into the station and ran while the Balkiens hovered into the bushes away from the raised railway tracks. They emerged into the same meadow they were previously near the dilapidated temple of the Great One. They hovered or walked further towards a large gleaming dome. Before entering from the street, everyone gazed up at the rounded buildings. There were deep hovering sounds, of the Antrogians, similar to the beat of the patrol the night before. Therefore, many of the buildings had big enough doors for the Tombalkiens to get through. There were booming messages in a deep Balkien voice of warbles of propaganda all around them. Only a few small Yesl sized Balkiens flew past occasionally. It was surprising to the Tombalkiens that none of them paid much attention to them, let alone the Winkets, Kloonket, and the others.

They approached a dome that looked like a museum. As they approached the round entrance, two burly Balkiens, about two meters in diameter and of dark-colored swooth came up to them. They called in Antrobian, "Who or what are these creatures? Are they some robotic creations of yours?"

"They are of us," said Yesl. "We have permission to be here."

"We don't understand you," said one of the janitor Balkiens. Kloonket repeated Yesl's authority in a different Antrobian dialect.

"Okay, you may pass."

"They now speak a different dialect here," said Kloonket. "Our language has evolved a lot since all this happened; a mixture of Antrobian and Antrogian."

They passed from the rounded arched entrance, dwarfed by the dome-shaped glass-covered atrium filled with Vega light. The hum of Balkiens of all sizes hovered as specks against the bright purple sky just below the triangular arrangement of struts holding glass panels in place.

"Let's go over to that passageway and look at the exhibits there about the history of Antrobi," said Kloonket.

The entrance led into a long tunnel with many round display windows inset into the rock walls. In one display, Yesl could see old mootie furnishings that reminded her of life before leaving Antrobi. Wink discovered an exhibition about their departure. There were photo images, stained with age and rusty exhibits familiar to Yesl. One was a corroded data sphere. A circular placard with Antrobian script told the story of the *Balkieston*'s departure followed by that of the Splinkatrix, both of which had never returned after some 15 Antrobian Years (AY).

"Wink," began Yesl with consternation. "We've been gone far longer than we realize. I thought that we'd been away for only about two Antrobian years."

"How could this be?" asked Baingae. "The ship's log has logged us as having spent 1.5 AYs on the Splinkatrix since starting on our mission to look for the *Balkieston* and Baingae here.

"What about Einstein's theory of relativity?" asked Matt, remembering the aged look of the temple. "Can we ask what year this is?"

"It's the Antrobian Year 572 of the Second Age, established when the Union of Antrobi and Antrogi took place," said Kloonket. "That is when we discovered that there were giant Balkiens living on our other planet."

"But we left in 557," said Wink. "Our ship's log last reported late 558."

"It's 572," said Kloonket. "I remember seeing you off at Balkieston Spaceport in 557. We listed you as missing in 561 and in 563 this Zinkel-Mallkis took over."

"Look," said Yesl. "Come over here."

Everyone went over to where Yesl was in front of a display case almost hidden in a far corner of the museum. There behind the circular glass window set in a rocky alcove was an actual image of the *Balkieston*'s launch. The colossal craft had twelve spheres with short struts arranged in a polyhedron, like a soccer ball, plus one other more massive spherical structure on three struts pointing forward.

"So that's the *Balkieston*," said Matt.

"The Splinkatrix is much smaller, being the size of only the front part," said Wink.

"There's the many small craft hoisting her up using their gyro engines," said Mwaki.

"Just like the tugboats pulling mighty ocean liners out of port on Earth in olden times," said Kaz.

There were other images on the display. Some were once in bright colors now tarnished.

"Yesl. See this," said Kloonket.

"A photo of the crew on pre-flight to Splogita," said Baingae.

"There you are, Yesl," said Alison. "There are Baingae and Boongoo, I think.

"There's a plaque beneath," said Judith. "Can you translate for me?"

"Yes," said Baingae. "It means:

IN LOVING MEMORY OF OUR FELLOW SPACEFARERS, WHO GAVE THEIR LIVES FOR THE CAUSE OF EXPLORATION AND FOR FURTHERING OUR KNOWLEDGE ON OUR STELLAR-NEIGHBOURHOOD AND DEDICATION TO ONGOING SCIENTIFIC RESEARCH

"These astronauts were given up for lost."

Everyone emerged from the rocky alcove into the main hall with the glass dome and hexagonal paneled walls. The floor had large colored hexagonal tiles. In the center, a globe of the planet stood that slowly rotated. They wandered closer. In Antrobian script, with its rounded characters, were the names of Antrobi's principal cities and regions.

"There's where I was last with Baingae in Balkiesville before my accident in the North Beekalo Ocean," said Winxl.

"And there is Balkieston," said Mwaki.

"A lot of new towns to the north and east, I've not seen before," remarked Wink.

"Where's Ambunti?" asked Winxl. "It's not marked on this globe at all."

"What about Ambunti?" asked Wink.

"Ambunti is the town where my ancestors live and where I was born and bred before I moved to Balkiesville," said Winxl.

"Better move on quickly," said Kloonket.

"What have I said?" asked Winxl.

"You uttered a place name that must never be mentioned around here," said Kloonket in a hushed voice, "even in English, let alone in Antrobian."

"But why?" asked Kaz in innocence. "It's Winxl's hometown."

"Something terrible happened there," said Kloonket. "I cannot say any more in this place."

"Come to think of it," said Matt. "There's a village by that name on the Sepik River in Papua New Guinea on Earth."

"Yes, there is a connection," said Kloonket. "But, please, say no more now."

Just then there was a loud deep-pitched warble from three burly Balkiens about twice the size as Yesl.

"I see that you all have had a good time in our museum," said one in perfect English. "Who are you anyhow? And you have brought these guests from Tombalki."

"They have arrived here after a long space voyage," said Kloonket. "They came on the Splinkatrix, which has recently returned from searching for the *Balkieston*. We were looking at the displays over there about these ships lost in space."

"I'm Zinklus. We have heard about the Splinkatrix," said the museum guardian Balkien with swooth colors ranging from brown, through orange to yellow. "We observed it in orbit around this planet, but then it went off into space again. I wonder why?"

The other two official Balkiens of similar size and colors flew in close and telekinetically grabbed them and held them onto their course stringy swooth.

"Why the hold on us," asked Kloonket. "You speak the Tombalkien language perfectly."

YESL – The Balkien from Antrobi

"Never mind that; we have orders from the Emperor Zinkel-Mallkis to bring you before him to explain yourselves as to why you had not returned for so long and for sending away your mother ship so quickly. As returning astronauts who left before the establishment of the Empire, you all must swear allegiance to his Sphericity, Zinkel-Mallkis to remain citizens of Antrobi. You Tombalkiens must do likewise, as your planet will also soon be subject to the rulership of the Empire. Zinkle-Mallkis is referred to as *He who must be obeyed*. I assume that the blue prolate one here was with you. I don't remember him on the ship's original crew."

On departing from the museum, they were accosted by three other Antrogian guards and ordered to walk or fly to the Emperor's supreme court mootie via the wide thoroughfare towards a huge green glass dome in front of them.

"You must obey his Sphericity," said the brown-colored Balkien. "If you don't, you will be brought before the court of the TriMallkaetium on a charge of non-compliance with the edicts of the Emperor, who rules supreme.

"We will do no such thing," said Kloonket in defiance. "Run or fly away!"

As soon as anyone tried to get away, they were held by the telekinetic gravitational grip of the guard Balkiens with extreme force.

"Argh," groaned Matt. "This gravity is crushing. I can't do anything."

There was a scuffle between Balkiens, Tombalkiens, and a series of loud high-pitched flying warbles. The three guards could not hold all of them. They got away except for Matt, Kaz, Yesl, Baingae, Kloonket, and both the Winkets. Quinket was first to get away by immediately flying upwards. Quinket could see the expanse of Balkieston familiar to her for she had made many a mischievous flight over the city against the wishes of her father, Kloonket.

Now Kloonket was the one in trouble, as he and the others were escorted into the grand green mootie.

"You are all to appear before Zinkel-Mallkis and TriMallkaetium," said Zinklus.

"Who are the TriMallkaetium," asked Matt in a whisper.

"The TriMallkaetium are the Judge, Jury, and Executioner," said Kloonket, very softly, "ah - usually in that order. One is the judge; one agrees with the judge's decision of 'guilty' or 'not guilty' and the third decides the penalty if found guilty."

"Are they a panel of Balkiens?" asked Matt.

"They're not beings quite like us," said Kloonket. "They're smaller spherical beings of a different species called Mallkets. They carry out a lot of duties for the whole Balkien civilization and most have been deceived or enslaved by the Empire."

They were escorted through the main iris doors of the magnificent green glass mootie palace, passing through a long foreboding semi-lit passage along, which were positioned large Balkiens with metallic shielding on guard duty. There were ever-present whispers of "Zinkel-Mallkis - Zinkel-Mallkis - Zinkel-Mallkis" all around them as they advanced towards the grand entrance. The golden iris doors at the end of the passage automatically whirred open for them to pass through and then whirred shut again. In front of them in another great glass hall, similar to the museum, was yet another high image of Zinkel-Mallkis as large as the Antrobi globe they were studying. Zinklus them through another golden iris-door into the great throne room of Zinkel-Mallkis whose name continued to be whispered repeatedly in the background by the many voices of the emperor's court. The cavernous round hall had many small triangular panels. The edges of these panels, made out of single exotic crystals, were studded with little jewels that looked like ruby, sapphire, topaz, and emerald. The emperor sat on a sizeable pentagonal velvet throne studded with gems of every color around the golden frame. He was priding himself on how near perfectly round his colorful swooth was in his resplendent Sphericity.

There was a booming announcement by Zinkel-Mallkis, himself, first in modern Antrobian, then in English, "Welcome to all of you from Tombalki and to those who have returned on the Splinkatrix. It is indeed a great pity that some of my guests did not accept my invitation to be here. All will be well with you but on one condition. Since I became ruler of this great Antrobian-Antrogian Empire, there is a requirement that all residents, both Balkien and alien alike must swear an oath of allegiance to the Emperor above all else and all that we stand for."

"That is not possible for me or the others here," said Kloonket defiantly. "I'd like to see changes to your ways first. What about all those poor slave Mallkets? And the ones you have subjugated into abject slavery in the mines to bring you all the panels for this palace? We know the truth behind this finery."

"Don't ever speak of the Emperor like that again," boomed Zinkel-Mallkis. "Is that the view of all of you?"

Yesl spoke for everyone. "I'm afraid it is. Look. You're a beautiful Antrogian. I learned from history and the ship's logs that you had everything going for you. You were a great charismatic leader. You did great things for your subjects on Antrogi in establishing an egalitarian society for Balkiens, both Antrobians and Antrogians alike and all the species of Mallkets."

"Now you have fallen for the Enigma," added Matt sternly. "The evil Enigma has tricked you into a delusion that his vain ways are best—."

"STOP SAYING THESE TERRIBLE THINGS AND LIES," boomed Zinkel-Mallkis. He let out a series of simmering green flashes of micro lightning all around his swooth. With a loud beating, he hovered menacingly all around the cavernous throne room, flying close to the gathered party. It was like being right under an out of control helicopter with the downdraft going everywhere. The wind was so intense that Baingae got blown away towards the open door and out into the passage beyond. He did not return, using the opportunity to escape, hoping that his absence would not be discovered.

Zinkel-Mallkis settled back down on his throne.

"GUARDS, he called with a quietening and firm tone. "Take these rebellious enemies of the Empire away and put them in the prison cells. Have them all brought before the TriMallkaetium on a charge of rebellion and treason before the Mighty Emperor!" Zinkel-Mallkis thundered, "YOU MUST OBEY! YOU MUST OBEY THE EMPEROR IN THE ORDER OF SPALMINKATRIX." The whole palace throne room shook, hurting Matt and Kaz's ears by the deafening roar of Zinkel-Mallkis' pronouncement.

The three guards were soon joined by other large blue and red Balkiens of the palace guard, along with several blue-poled police Mallkets and Hellacks, who were brown colored spherical guards, generally a bit larger than the average Balkien with a leathery texture. These guards were partially covered by bronze-colored hexagonal and pentagonal metal platelets, forming a shield around their skin with several small eyes peering out from between them. Some of these platelets had small protrusions. One of these let out some sparks of green lightning as a warning.

"We're sure in a fix now," whispered Matt as they were led away out of the Emperor's presence and along several long narrow descending passages to a row of dungeon cells. They were all placed in one cell and locked in for the night. The sound of the round iris-valve door clanging shut was loud. The cell had a small hexagonal window with crisscrossing metal bars forming tiny triangular spaces so that not even little Mallkets could escape. The light of Antrogi at night was the only reassuring thing left.

"This is the first time I've been in a lockup," said Matt. "Here, we are on an alien planet, in a hostile regime where many beings are in the chains of slavery and have no rights at all. We've tried to persuade the planet's ruler of the error of his ways. Not a good move."

"Matt," said Yesl. "You did right. We can't go and sell our souls to this evil regime and betray our consciences to the enemy of those poor Mallkets and our fellow Balkiens."

"And what about the plight of the Molktrons on Splogita," said Wink. "It's the Enigma that's got a stronghold on Zinkel-Mallkis, who was a budding great ruler and was moving up through the ranks of government when we departed on the Splinkatrix.

"I guess we're in a mess now," said Mwaki. "Our mother ship's badly damaged. The scout ship has got a bust window."

"And now some of us are in the clink," said Kaz.

"At least only some of us are in here," said Matt. "Have you ever heard of the expression; *a glass is half full or half empty?*"

"Wasn't it odd and intriguing that Zinkel-Mallkis was already speaking to us in English," said Wink. "We did not teach it to him in any way, and we thought that no Earthly languages were spoken here until we got back."

"I can only think of one thing," said Kaz. "Zinkel-Mallkis must already have had contact with Earth."

Matt looked up. "What about the disappearance of Cammins and Holzapfel?"

There was a faint but familiar high-pitched warbling sound above the general hum of Balkiens, flying to and fro in the night air under Antrogi light. The sound grew louder. Looking out of the cell window, Matt recognized Quinket flying around as if she was searching for something. Kloonket called out to her in a loud whisper in Antrobian. Quinket hovered about aimlessly and started to fly away.

Psst," called Matt, "Over here." Then three guard-Balkiens flew past on patrol around the prison mootie. Everyone hid away from the window. When the guards had passed by, Quinket was nowhere to be seen. Everyone's hearts sank.

"If only Quinket had seen or heard us," gasped Yesl.

● ○ ●

14 ~ THE OUTBACK OF THE YASTAGLIATH

Baingae had attached himself to the palace ceilings and slowly rolled himself along the multi-colored jeweled hexagonal panels to which his swooth was well camouflaged. He rolled out to a small window in the atrium of the Palace grand lobby. Before he escaped, he saw the others being led out of the Emperor's throne room and down a side passage. He ascended high into the sky. The lights of Balkieston stretched out from horizon to horizon. The sky was a deep purple lit up by the light reflecting from Antrogi, illuminating the streets and glass domed-shaped buildings. Baingae kept up his relentless ascent into the heavens to make good his escape from the Palace before being pursued by any of the Emperor's guard Hellacks. Reaching a high altitude, he continued to fly east across the purple-colored broccoli-like forests stretched out below into the hazy dawn horizon. He was getting cold and decided to descend to avoid freezing up like his suffering fiancée years earlier. As he dropped down, dawn broke, and soon it was Vega-rise with the bluish-white oblate or flattened sun casting her intense rays across the deep dark green forests. He could see on the horizon a myriad of sharp needle-shaped peaks that were dark by contrast against the bright Vega light.

Baingae thought to himself, *'Where am I? There's nothing but trees. The landmarks I've known before are all but gone. I'm flying east. Maybe I should turn north.'*

Baingae banked around to a northerly direction, all the while warbling away to keep airborne. His energy began to wane as he lost altitude. *'Maybe I'll have to land and rest for a bit.'*

Then he could make out in the distance a long thin necklace of silver spheres snaking through the dense forest. He continued his descent and flew towards the train's rearmost ball car. You could call it the *guard's ball.* He hoped not to be seen by any guards, loyal to the Emperor. Baingae, beginning to tire of flying, kept his altitude above the rumbling ball train. He thought of stowing on it for a while hoping it would take him past their stop at camp where they'd traveled from the previous day. Alas, it was a freight train with the older style ball cars that rolled along the rails like marbles on a marble runner. These ball carriages did not have the small bogey wheels that modern Antrobian trains had. The freight in these cars turned around inside them like clothes in a washing machine. Baingae flew up over the train to the locomotive ball, hoping to find a stationary ball to stow away in. However, he realized that he was a long way past his stop for the train was now rumbling onward toward a less forested area. The thick forest had given way to regions of isolated trees, which grew out of the arid flat desert lands.

"This is way past our stop," thought Baingae aloud. "This is the Yastagliath, a vast arid region, northeast of Balkieston."

The humble little earthen colored Balkien decided to slow down and let this train go on. He flew up into the branches of a tall broccoli-tree and landed on its lush purple polyp-like flowers to have a rest from his flight from the clutches of the Emperor. Just before nodding off to sleep, he noticed some other brightly colored Balkiens dotted about on separate branches, all seemingly asleep. The rumble of the train grew fainter as it rolled away along the endless steel rails to an infinite horizon. When the noise faded away, there was silence, except for little wisps of wind. Baingae nodded off and had dreamlike visions, of the city of Balkieston as he remembered it before his departure to Splogita. He felt that he was *home* again and that this was the reality and that all that had happened was a nightmare. It was heavenly, to be with his Balkien friends in his beloved city, with gentler geodesic mooties and domes. Behind the cityscape were the majestic dark green jagged peaks reaching into the light purple sky with the thin crescent of Antrogi. He felt carefree as he hovered around with Yesl, Boongoo, and Winxl out on the town together. Then there appeared bright green flashes in the sky as if stars were flashing and exploding. Suddenly there was a terrific blinding green flash, and a thunderous roar as a fiery green ball came down from the sky like a meteor and landed inside the King of Antrobi's Palace Mootie. The strange thing was that the apparent impact did not destroy the Palace. There were another flash and bang, which sent Baingae wugging off his perch and down into the larger branches of the tree, waking him.

"I take it that you're the well-known Dr. Baingae," said an oversized Balkien who had many beautiful iridescent colors. "I'm Zoonxl. I'm not long back from a flight to meet with Kloonket, who told me all about your arrival from Tombalki. It took me ages to locate Kloonket's new camp."

"I'm indeed Dr. Baingae of the *BSS Balkieston*." BSS stands for 'Balkien Scout Service.'

"Welcome to our little treetop abode. We heard about you from Boongoo and how the Emperor had arrested some of you, including Kloonket, for not swearing allegiance to his Sphericity and worshipfulness. We're thrilled that you have returned and brought those Tombalkiens with you. I think we'll need them. They may not be able to fly unaided like us, but they're so much more familiar with the sort of thing that has befallen our beloved planet. Most of our race was duped by this evil monster, whatever it is."

"I've just awoken from a dream that began so wonderfully. But it turned hideous."

"That, my dear ponkety, was my relating to you how the Enigma influenced and took over the mind of Zinkel-Mallkis. Boongoo told me that you, Baingae, had been arrested. How did you escape? Where are the others?"

"Only I managed to escape. When we were before the Emperor, he flew up around the throne room in a rage over our disloyalty, and his downdraft blew me out into the corridor of the Palace. I made good use of that escape opportunity to warn you of what happened in there. I saw the guards, large Antrogians in battle gear, take the others down a passage into the basement of the Palace Mootie, presumably to prison."

"Where's Quinket?" asked Zoonxl.

"I thought she evaded capture and went with the others," said Baingae. "I could not find my way back to Kloonket's camp as I had to fly too high to avoid being hunted down by Zinkel-Mallkis' minions. I followed a train along this line but could not land on the older rolling type ball cars. I slowed down and landed on this tree out of sheer exhaustion and went to sleep."

"Quinket was not with the others," said Zoonxl. "She flew off independently amid all of the confusion during the arrests. So, she'll be very lost in a huge unfamiliar city. The little so-and-so! We knew that mischievous little Quinket would do this someday. She always gets into some sort of trouble. Now we'll not only have to search for Matt, Yesl, and the others but Quinket as well. We'd better have some fruit from the tree for breakfast and get you back to Kloonket. As you dozed off, six of us formed a ponkadliath around you and gave you the telepathic *dream* to show how our world had got this way."

"Do you suppose that this Enigma may have got hold of info about Antrobi from our wrecked scout-ship that crashed on Splogita," asked Baingae.

"That's possible but not proven. Let's go and guide you back to Kloonket."

Zoonxl took off with Baingae riding piggyback on his swooth, as he was still so tired. They flew alongside the ball train line towards Balkieston, occasionally flying under the forest canopy to avoid being followed by any patrols. They finally emerged into the clearing, meeting up with Kloonket.

"Baingae!" exclaimed Alison as everyone gasped. "You've escaped. Where are Matt, Yesl, and the others?"

"Only I managed to escape."

"We lost Quinket as well," said Kara. "I know that she was not arrested. She zoomed off in her inimical way over some nearby mooties, and we could not find her before we had to race off towards the forest to avoid capture. We hoped that she would see us."

"See you in a myriad of Balkiens?" asked Kloonket.

"It'd be like trying to find a kid in a crowd on Cup Final Day," said Sean. "There're millions of them flying around.

"But wait," said Alison. "Did you say that you shouldn't have gone to Splogita? What about the Molktrons? I'm sure that it was your destiny to go and see what had happened to them and maybe in the future, redeem them from their oppression. The Enigma would have found you sooner or later, I'm sure."

"I remember that the Molktrons were desperate for redemption," said Baingae.

"What about the ship?" asked Kloonket. "How are we going to catch up with the ball train, hurtling away from us?"

"Are you a rated pilot for that craft?" asked Baingae. "All of our qualified pilots have been captured. And we can't ever risk being shot down. It's the only craft we have. All the other scout-ships are way out near Roonkle, on the disabled Splinkatrix. I do hope that the crew onboard her has enough supplies to last out a long siege."

"There should be enough," said Boongoo. "Though this mission was overdue, the extra supplies loaded on from Tombalki should last for at least two more Angapooka months."

"Could we send out a distress signal?" asked Sean.

"Possibly," said Kloonket, "but not from this campsite. Its source would be traced, and we'd be fried alive with the surrounding forest reduced to ashes in the attack, perishing in flames. It's that bad! If any of that green lightning ever struck here, all this would go up in smoke. We've had an Angapooka-month drought, and these trees are getting too dry."

"Does it rain here like on Tombalki?" asked Sean.

"Yes. It does," said Baingae, being familiar with Tombalkien rain.

"Look. Some trees are losing their beautiful greenness as you have observed," continued Kloonket. "I think that our planet is beginning to respond to these evils and is making our environment harsh."

"Like a kind of curse," said Alison, "or the planet's response to this evil."

"Clickety-clack, clickety-clack, clickety-clack," went the ball train as the desert of the Yastagliath rushed by. Matt and Kaz sat on the floor of the freight ball car they were in, looking out of the small window. Kloonket, Yesl, and the Winkets were locked in a rounded mesh cage to one side, in what looked like a makeshift, confinement cell, for the train was a freight train, not designed for prison transport. The desert landscape was now devoid of trees. The metal walls of the ball car were almost too hot to touch with beads of sweat pouring off Matt and Kaz.

"Yesl," said Matt gasping. "Can you tell the guards that we need water to drink or we'll die of thirst and ask how far we have to go?"

"I'll try," said Yesl. There were exchanges of conversations with the two burly Hellacks.

"We'll have to stay onboard until our destination," said Matt with a slur as he was severely dehydrated. "Even if we could escape, we'd never survive in that desert. It's searing out here, and I bet it freezes at night too."

"The guards don't understand your need for much water," said Yesl.

The Winkets started shrieking loudly at the guards who loudly boomed back at them in a heated argument hurting Matt's and Kaz's ears. There were flashes of green lightning with cracks like those of a whip. One of the windows was smashed out by a strike. Another flash struck close to Kaz's tied hands not only burning his skin a little but also singeing his bounds. Kaz started to force his wrist against the blackened fibers, seeing his opportunity to unbind himself. The commotion continued. Kaz broke free and quickly but stealthily untied his legs and loosed Matt's binding. Yesl joined the Winkets in the altercation. They hovered back and forth, banging against the cage to try to break it loose. One side of it came away. The two Hellack guards immediately flew over to hold it down. Matt and Kaz jumped up, and Matt ripped off a metal strip from the doorway into the next car. He started beating on the metal shields and leathery skin of the two guards, who in turn flew around wildly, hitting them back. Matt smashed out all the windows to let fresh air in and broke the windows in the round doors into each of the adjacent cars. Matt continued to beat up the two guards until he dented some of their shield panels. Kaz pulled away from the loosened cage assembly, releasing all the imprisoned Balkiens. Matt hurled his weight at the end door. It did not budge.

"Matt," said Wink. "Let me open it." Wink waved himself over a hexagonal-shaped control panel to the side of the door, and it whirred open leading into the next car. The Balkiens flew through quickly, but Matt and Kaz had to clamber through the opening. It was less like an earthly train and more like going through the sections of a submarine on rails.

"Quick, the guard Hellacks are stirring," said Kaz. "Close the door."

Wink hovered over the control panel, and the round metal door slammed shut on the guards. "Let's get along through as many cars as possible," said Kaz. Wink hovered over the next control panel. The door slid open. Once again, everyone scrambled or flew into the next ball car, full of sizeable cylindrical metal cases, which had rounded Antrobian characters printed on them in blue and red, forming words, on white circular tags attached to the containers.

"Yesl you close the doors behind you and all of you push some of these cases against the door."

Matt kept the bar as a weapon if needed and knocked over a case so that it jammed the door. They clambered their way through to Ball 45 with Wink hovering over each door control panel. As they looked through the window to Ball 44, they saw the whole sphere rolling rapidly with a loud rumble.

"These are the older type of ball rail cars," said Kloonket

"We'll have to hide before they get us," said Matt.

"Smash out the windows," said Kaz.

Matt broke every window. "That's turned on the air conditioning. Wink, open the door to Ball 44."

Wink waved over the control, and the door with the broken porthole window whirred open. Yesl hovered over some cool blue spherical containers packed to one side of the carriage.

"Water!" exclaimed Matt. "Break one of them."

Wink hovered over a dark blue circular panel on top of one of the spherical containers. Wink unscrewed and lifted the lid, who now looked as if he was surfing the air on the circular cover. Everyone took turns to drink out of the opened container, all the while splashing about as the ball car lurched from side to side.

The door from Ball 46 opened suddenly. It was one of the guards. Green lightning flashed from him and electrocuted Kaz, throwing him across onto the water containers, which began rolling about on the floor. Matt immediately struck the guard's shields with his metal weapon with a loud clang, stunning him.

"You strike my buddy again!" he shouted in a fit of raw rage. "And I'll pulverize you to mulch!"

The Winkets screamed at the guard, translating Matt's threats into Antrobian. Matt struck the dark cobalt blue round leathery creature with his weapon again while Kaz kicked him back into the next car. The door was shut once more. Then he smashed the door's control panel with the metal bar, hoping to stop the re-entry of the guards. Water spilled out of the containers after being knocked around in the fight. Matt and Kaz held one each as upright as possible as the train continued to lurch. They submerged their faces in the water and drank until their thirst was satisfied.

Lying exhausted on the floor, Matt and Kaz shook hands in victory.

"We may have won this small battle," said Matt. "We've still a long war ahead of us."

"You're right," said Wink, his voice rising. "It's War! IT's ALL OUT WAR! This horrible thing MUST BE STOPPED AT ALL COSTS!"

Mwaki joined first hollering in Antrobian then in English "He who must be obeyed, MUST BE CONQUERED."

Thus, the battle cry went up from Ball 45, amid the loud rumbling of Ball 44 through the open door, as the train began to thunder faster on a long downgrade, traveling through mountainous country, with jagged tall spires scraping the sky.

"You know Yesl," said Matt. "I feel awful now having to beat up that guard so much."

"Matt," said Yesl. "You both were nearly unconscious, back there. There was no ventilation until you broke the windows. It's them or us. It's now war.

Fight for the freedom of the Balkiens. I now understand what it means to have to fight after helping you with your school history on Tombalki about world wars under your tyrannical dictators. We have one now. He's called Zinkel-Mallkis, influenced by the Enigma. He's allowed himself to be corrupted and possessed by it. None of our country Balkiens can understand what evil is. They don't know what's hit them. They're all confused. We're the only few that have learned how to confront this menace. Even Kloonket here doesn't fully understand what the issue is."

The train rolled on while the high rocks marched past. The updraft from the rolling Ball 44 was considerable. The rail line began to curve in and out of the deep valleys. There was a battering on the door from Ball 46. It was the two guards that had recovered their composure. One was emitting green lightning to try to fuse the lock open. Matt took his bar and bashed on the lock to jam it, but only worked for a while. Soon the door started to rattle loose as the Hellack guards pounded against it. Matt could now see five of them.

"They've come with reinforcements," hollered Matt.

"Matt," shouted Yesl, "We're oblated if they all get through. They'll use their combined telekinetic or gravitational energy to crush us into submission. We've got to get off this train."

"Then what'll we do for water and sustenance out there," said Matt.

Just then the door snapped ajar still held on by a piece of metal from the catch. Matt and Kaz clambered out of the open door in front, trying not to touch the fast-rolling Ball 44. It was tricky, but they managed to gain footholds on the outside of Ball 45, helped by the Winkets and Yesl. Matt and Kaz could hardly hold on as the train continued to accelerate. Above the mighty roar of the wind, Matt could hear the beating sound of large Antrogians. He looked up and there they were six of them flying in a 'V' formation above the train.

"Not more trouble," shouted Matt.

These six, resembling giant versions of the Winkets, in similar colors descended lower towards the train and lined themselves up with the rolling ball cars. Just then, the two guards emerged spewing out green lightning. Suddenly Matt slipped off the roof and was swept backward away from the flashes. Rather than hit his head on one of the following ball-cars, he shot up skywards, until he could see the train from above snaking its way down the curved track. Kaz was already airborne as well. Matt felt the soft contact with the giant swooth of one of the Antrogians.

Checkmate, he thought. He looked, and there were his fellow Tombalkiens, each riding atop each of the four other Antrogians along with Kloonket, Yesl, and the Winkets. Matt felt himself, being slid up the side of his Antrogian and onto his upper surface. There to greet him was Baingae. Kloonket had flown up from Ball 45 to join them.

"Matt," said Baingae. "These Antrogians are with us on this quest. You're atop, Boolboonkle. He's your trusted friend from now on. Kaz was also thrown up onto his assigned Antrogian, Poolpoogleponk."

"Baingae," said Matt. "There's plenty of water on the train in blue containers."

Matt looked down from the comfort of his new friend. The wind was almost absent as Boolboonkle held the air around him like a cocoon. Lightning flashes were emanating from Ball 45. Many other warriors joined the Winkets against the five guards, who were pulled from the train and then hurled away towards one of the tall mounts. Bluewater balls emerged from the train and were pulled up through the air into orbit around one or other of the Antrogians, who continued to follow the train towards its destination which now visible, as the deep gorge opened out on to a desert plain. The rail line headed straight towards a small settlement of dome-shaped buildings with triangular facets in shades of grey and brown.

"Matt," said Kloonket. "Up ahead is the prison camp. Those tall metal pylons stand over deep mine shafts. We're on a delivery train for equipment and supplies for the prison and the mining operations where you would have been slaves. We're planning a jailbreak."

About four larger diameter Balkiens flew along the tops of the front ball cars. One wielded a long stick with a hook on it. He caught up with the locomotive ball and dangled the hook down between it and the first ball car. With a clank, he raised the stick. The loco ball suddenly pulled away at high speed as its engine no longer had to tow the seventy or so ball-cars. It was too fast for the next curve in the track and left the rails bouncing along the ground, hitting boulders and knocking down some wizened broccoli-trees and into a dip before smashing into some rocks. There was a bang as the battered ball exploded with bits of metal and wheels flying in all directions. Even from Matt's vantage point, this was frightening as some of the debris rushed past a bit too close to Boolboonkle's swooth for comfort.

"We're not done, yet," said Kloonket. "That was the locomotive's tightly wound spring suddenly unleashing it's pent up energy. It was still wound up at the engine spring winding station in Balkieston for a further six-hundred kilometer. Watch the ball cars."

The now-driverless train with no brakes continued towards the prison camp at full speed. Just as the train was about to roar through the camp station, the raised rails collapsed.

"A group of us came down through the northern valley last night," said Baingae, "and loosened the rail supports after the last train had passed through to derail this one, which we knew had a lot of heavy goods and a larger number of the rolling type ball cars to create a bigger impact."

From Matt's view, the silvery necklace tumbled off the tracks as the balls became disconnected rolling in all directions, demolishing many of the spherical buildings, which split open like eggshells. Not long after, there was a cloud of buzzing black things emanating from the damaged buildings with more ball-cars rolling into the pylons, knocking them over like tenpins.

Fearing any encounters with prison patrols, all six of the Antrogians began a quick ascent and retreated into the tall peaks. Yesl and the Winkets had now joined Matt, Baingae, and Kloonket on Boolboonkle. As they flew away, Matt pulled out his binoculars and looked to see a scene of chaos over the camp. Smoke billowed up from the main complex.

"I sure hope that all of our prisoners and much-valued freedom fighters will make it out okay," said Kloonket. "No doubt, there'll be some oblations; a job for you, Dr. Baingae?"

Soon, the Antrogians were flying through deep narrow, darkened gorges away from the glare of Vega. The other Balkiens were straggling along in groups around them. They took a roundabout way through deep canyons with towering pinnacles of bare rock above them. The lower slopes had dark green vegetation. Dr. Baingae was tending Yesl, the Winkets, and Kloonket for heat exhaustion, dehydration, and some degree of oblateness.

"Yesl," said Matt. "You need to absorb some water into your swooth."

"He's right," said Baingae who said something in Antrogian to Boolboonkle. A small purple plastic-looking ball about the size of a large grapefruit rolled up to Baingae on Boolboonkle's tough-looking but silky dark blue swooth. It had a pattern of hexagons and pentagons like a small soccer ball. One of the pentagons was opened out. A soft wick was pulled out onto Yesl's lower swooth for her to absorb the water. Matt opened another water ball and drank.

"Ah," he gasped. "This water's so refreshing. It even has a rich, fruity taste."

Boolboonkle led the other five Antrogians deeper into the jungle of tall rocks. The gorges had small grassy banks beside glistening streams. There were clumps of dark broccoli-like trees.

"Nearly there," said Kloonket, "at our secret hideaway."

Vega was no longer visible in the valleys, but its light reflected off the brightly lit tips of the pinnacles. They glided around another bend in the valley and toward a small village with a few round wooden geodesic dwellings or mooties of different sizes for housing the Antrogians. The Antrogians with their beating flying sound slowed down to a soft landing on a vibrant dark green meadow between the mooties. After landing their flying sounds stopped. A peaceful silence descended on this place, except for the distant bubbling of the nearby stream and the voices of the local Balkiens gathered to welcome the party.

Matt stood beside Boolboonkle and stroked his swooth and leaned his head on him. "Thank you, Boolboonkle and all of you Antrogians for saving us from the train. I thought that I was going to die there and then."

Boolboonkle said something in his Antrogian dialect.

"Boolboonkle says that he was relieved to pull you all off the train. Welcome to Antrobi," said Kloonket. "The real Antrobi as it should be. May I introduce to you all the Antrogians here. Here is Boolboonkle, ridden by Matt, Polpodwink, ridden by Kara, Spalkius, ridden by Sean, Poolpoogleponk, ridden by Kaz, Zonkollus ridden by Alison and Woozbokle, ridden by Judith. This village is Moostica. The Emperor does not yet know this place and we have to keep it that way.

"Moostica is where Winxl lived after her birth in Ambunti far to the north of here," said Baingae. Winxl hovered among the mooties, pleased to be home again. Baingae flew after her and joined in ponkadliath with her as they flew around in contact with one another.

"It's so good to see Baingae and Winxl so happy together," said Matt.

"Matt," said Yesl, suspecting his thoughts. "It's Erin, isn't it?"

"Yes. I've missed Erin all along. I suppose it's a bit like when you, Baingae, setting off for Splogita leaving Winxl behind."

"Look how the Winkets brought Winxl to Baingae," said Wink. "You wait and see."

Wink and Mwaki had by now soaked up a little more water into their swooth from more spherical bottles and by hovering on the nearby ponds, to which Matt, Sean, Kaz, Alison, Kara, and Judith went over to drink.

"Our first swim here on Antrobi!" said Matt as everyone stripped off and donned their swimsuits from their luggage brought by the Antrogians from their scout ship along with their supplies."

"Aaah," said Kaz, as everyone splashed in the lake. The Balkiens flew around and skimmed over the water, rolling over it to give themselves a wash on their swooth.

It was a balmy evening as Vega set behind the distant peaks. Antrogi hanging like an oversized Moon was now lower than in Balkieston as they were farther into the northeast of the continent. The sky was a deep purple, where only the brightest stars were visible.

"I'm now seeing three other smaller moons," said Alison in her Scottish island accent, "two to the west and a tiny one up there." She pointed to an almost full miniature moon, only about a quarter of the size of Earth's Moon.

"Those two larger ones to the west are Angapooka, and the smaller one is Balkle, where Baingae comes from," said Wink. Everyone stood up waist-deep in the water with their swimwear or board shorts looking up to Balkle and then glancing at Baingae, who hovered up onto Judith's dripping wet shoulders.

"So that's your home-world," she said. "It looks idyllic."

"I'd love to go there when all of this is over," said Matt optimistically.

"Boodibah," was Baingae's way of expressing this happy thought.

After coming out of the water, drying off and dressing, they went to their accommodation mooties. The Balkiens, Tombalkiens, and Antrogians settled around in a circular group in the central meadow, which was bottle green in the light from Antrogi.

Through his binoculars, Matt looked up at Balkle and could make out parallel belts of oceans and continents with matching lines of clouds, which made this moon look like a Balkien. The other moon, Angapooka was more than twice Balkle's size, being the closest orbiting body other than Antrogi, being dark green. There were blue areas studded with small wispy cotton wool-like clouds."

Yesl hovered up and alighted on his shoulder. "Angapooka has forests and several large separate seas that do not join up as they do on this planet. That's where our Queen Mozl is from, wife of our deposed King Zozl, both of whom now live in exile in a secret part of this planet. I'll leave it to Kloonket to explain more."

"And your smallest moon?" asked Sean as he took his turn to use the binoculars.

"That is our outermost airless moon, Boonkpolm," said Mwaki, "very similar to your Tomkil, except that it's half its diameter and three times as far away. Boonkpolm takes one hundred and sixty-four of our days to orbit once, Balkle, eighty-two and Angapooka, forty-one."

"Now that we've cleaned up, eaten off the trees, and settled down, we convene a meeting," said Kloonket. "We must remind everyone here that this place is not yet known to the Emperor or his forces. We must keep it that way. If we are discovered, this planet and the whole Vegan System may be doomed! As we have seen, the Balkland Express was successfully sabotaged and derailed. For those of you not in the know, the plan was to cause all of the ball-cars to roll in and crash into various parts of that prison complex and make a way of escape for those of us interned there for offenses against the TriMallkaetium, our judicial system taken over by the Emperor. Things were already in motion to crash that train when we discovered that you Balkiens and Tombalkiens were on board. Our mischievous little Quinket, who was tossed out the window as the train past, managed to find us, only just. It was then that we had to pursue the train to rescue you. We had to quickly assign our loyal Antrogians here, one for each Tombalkien so that we could follow at a distance, looking just like an Antrogian patrol of the Emperor.

"Boolboonkle, here, has related how the Enigma suddenly appeared on Antrogi from Splogita. We wondered what it was. It was then that many of our fellow Antrogians started acting strangely toward one another. Many started to think of themselves as being more beautiful and spherical than their fellow beings. There was competition never before seen. If any were even only a little oblate or dull of color, they looked down on them. Ssh, be quiet."

There was a faint warble in the night air that sounded feeble and erratic. A small black disk appeared, silhouetted in front of Antrogi. The warble stopped, and the apparition dropped out of the sky with a dull thump onto the edge of the meadow not far from them.

"Better come with me, Baingae," whispered Kloonket. They flew over to where they heard the thud. There, in the silvery light of Antrogi, was a distressing, sorrowful sight. Lying *wugged* on the mosses was an emaciated oblate Balkien, whose swooth was dirty and straggly with colors challenging to make out.

"Yesl, Winkets," called Kloonket. "Over here."

Yesl and the Winkets hovered over to assist. Kloonket began to speak softly to the victim in Antrobian. The Balkien spoke very softly back.

"Quick," said Baingae. "The poor thing's covered in caked-on dirt and is having difficulty absorbing oxygen. Fly him over to the pond to wash him. I'll then do a diagnosis on him."

The Winkets, using their gentle telekinesis, lifted the emaciated being and flew over to the crystal-clear waters of the lake and laid on the mossy bank.

Alison and Judith walked over to the lake. Alison lifted and held this Balkien in her bare arms. She had on a blue tunic and denim shorts. She stroked his poor dilapidated swooth. "Dr. Baingae. Let's wash him. This poor thing needs it."

She laid him in the crystal-clear water. The dust and grime of years of slavery dissolved out of his swooth in clouds settling on the small stones on the bottom. She squeezed the water out like a sponge as gently as possible. After more rinsing, his blue and yellow swooth brightened up with radiance. Once out of the water, he began to speak in Antrobian. Judith took him and laid him on the table. Alison brought out her towel to dry him out. His swooth was now fluffier and healthy-looking, although his oblateness was still significant.

He was taken to one of the mooties to be laid on a Balkien seat, being a round stool with velvet-like upholstery. Everyone left him alone except for Dr. Baingae. He moved his swooth about examining him carefully and thoroughly. The round geodesic wooden mootie room was small, about the size of an average bedroom on Earth. There was a soft glow from a torch-like light on a hexagonal sideboard made of a wood-like material, which had a dark green natural color for this type of Antrobian timber.

After a while, Baingae emerged from the mootie.

"When a Balkien becomes oblate or a flattened spheroid, it is a sign of poor health. But, it's not as bad as it looks. He'll need a lot of tender loving care, and we can give that here. He'll recover from that oblateness in a few Balklian months, measuring our months by the orbit of our moon, Balkle, where I was born and bred. His name is Boonkliat."

"What mystifies me is; how did he get here?" asked Kloonket. "He's not a minion of Zinkel-Mallkis."

"Maybe he has escaped from the prison after the train wreck," suggested Kaz.

"Good point," said Kloonket.

"We saw hundreds of Balkiens swarming up into the air from the prison complex after the train crashed," said Wink.

Everyone went back to their meeting area outside, leaving, Baingae, and Winxl to watch over their patient.

"Like I was saying," continued Kloonket. "Antrogi was invaded by agents from the Enigma from Splogita who controlled the Molktrons and were possessed or influenced by this thing to subjugate the Antrogians. The agents appeared as ghostly apparitions in the sky one night."

"I guess the closest resemblance on Tombalki were what you called UFOs," Yesl added.

"They appeared beautiful and colorful. Something was not right. After this, the strange behavior among the Antrogians was manifest. Our Antrogian King, Zinkel-Mallkis, started having great rallies and gatherings of the affected Antrogians to stir them to invade Antrobi and take over the planet from our former ruler King Zozl who was dethroned by Zinkel-Mallkis while on a planned state visit."

"In a coup d'état," added Matt.

"The apparitions came to Antrobi and also influenced many Balkiens to an attitude of selfishness, hubris, and vanity.

"One of the astronomers who first detected the spectral signature on Splogita observed that the colors of many of the invaders were almost identical."

Kloonket left it there as everyone felt sleepy. They retired to their mooties and fell comfortably asleep on round beds. The Antrogians slept in a large mootie with hexagonal doors that had been a scout ship hangar. Baingae and Winxl slept close to their patient now less oblate, mumbling a few words in Antrobian, which Baingae found challenging to understand.

● ◯ ●

15 ~ THE RUINS OF AMBUNTI

Matt was in a ponkadliath with the Winkets and Yesl on his round mattress in his mootie. He awoke. "What a strange and odd dream I'm having. I was floating in space close to an enormous planet."

"Why don't you take your binoculars and go out and look at the planets in our system," said Yesl. Matt went out of the door into the pale light of Antrogi, now a thin crescent before dawn.

"There's Spalminkatrix up there," said Yesl.

Matt looked up with the binoculars. He could see a planet that appeared more massive than Jupiter and had about seven small points of light, which were some of its moons.

"Something's odd," he said to Yesl.

"What, Matt? Let's have a look."

Matt held the binoculars up towards Yesl's visual sensory areas as her myriad of eyes. "Matt, did you see what I'm seeing?"

"Yes. Something's distinctly familiar and very disturbing."

"Have another look."

Matt put the lenses to his eyes once more. "Zinkel-Mallkis?"

"Yes. Zinkel-Mallkis! Larger than life by many leagues! No wonder that planet seems a lot brighter than I can remember. Better go back inside. I feel that there's a presence spying on us." Matt retreated inside their mootie and closed the hexagonal door softly. "Seems like a huge image of himself projected onto a PLANET! I've seen everything now. What hubris. It gives me the creeps."

"Me too, we thought we'd left all of this behind when we boarded the Splinkatrix to come home. What home is this now? Being thrown in jail, then on a hot ball-train bound for a prison labor camp on some trumped-up charges of alleged treason by this pompous, overgrown poonkety who only thinks of himself and his absolute Sphericity to the exclusion of all others."

"Welcome to the Tombalkien way of life. You've seen a lot of it and read my history homework from high school. I only wish that we could do something to help you. Only what can we do? We're the aliens out here now."

"We have to find out from Kloonket and the resistance Balkiens what exactly is going on now," said Wink as everyone retired to bed.

YESL – The Balkien from Antrobi

There was a dull *thump, thump* on the hexagonal door. Matt stretched out on the bed. "Oh, I'm still sleepy." Vega shone through the pentagonal window. There were more thumps on the door. In her tiredness, Yesl arose and flew to the door and opened it. Kloonket hovered in and settled on the table. "You'd better have breakfast in haste. We have a long way to go to visit with important contacts farther north. We've confirmed that something terrible has happened, but we're not sure what. It has got to do with Ambunti."

"Everyone's out there eating a breakfast of broccoli-tree fruit," said Kloonket.

"That and a good cup of Antrobian tea will do me good," said Matt. The Balkiens used dried leaves of a particular herbaceous plant that grew in the Yastagliath to form a kind of tea, brewed in cold water as iced tea. Matt walked out of the mootie to join the others at the hexagonal table. "Kloonket, I looked at Spalminkatrix through my binoculars. There's an image of Zinkel-Mallkis."

"Most of us know about plans for an image of himself on that planet," replied Kloonket. He oscillated back and forth as the morning breeze ruffled his blue swooth. "So Zinkel-Mallkis has done it. Now all can see his image and pay homage to his absolute Sphericity. After all, a planet is a near-perfect sphere. He certainly has vanity and power."

Kaz had been finishing a bite of broccoli fruit. "It must be the strong influence of that evil Enigma."

"Certainly is an enigma," said Sean.

There was a flurry of activity as Balkiens flew to and fro between the mooties and the six Antrogians. Round plastic bottles were filled up from the lake and flown onto round cup holders harnessed to the Antrogians, like panniers. Other Balkiens were flying out into the woods to bring back broken tree branches to tie to the mooties and lay all over the camp clearing for camouflage. Matt saw a dark patch in the sky low down over the valley; they had flown down the day before. It looked grey against the purple sky above the jagged peaks. It moved to and fro changing shape more rapidly than typical clouds. "What's that over yonder? It looks like smoke. Maybe it's a bush fire."

"I'm not sure about that," said Kloonket as his swooth undulated over his body while looking up. "No way is that smoke!" COVER the Antrogians and mooties with branches at once! Clear the tables and put them away. Those are many thousands of Balkiens, and most of them will be loyal to Zinkel-Mallkis." Everyone rushed to clear the tables of the round, earthen dishes with some falling and breaking.

"Hurry," said Yesl. "Get back into your mooties and shut all doors and windows." The grey cloud was now much closer. There were thousands of black dots moving in unison.

"Get inside, everyone," called Wink. As the last door slammed shut, they could hear a low hum - the collective sound of thousands of individual Balkien warbles - growing louder. The sky became dark as the vast armada flew overhead.

Matt, Kaz, and Alison were nervous as they huddled by the small pentagonal window with the Winkets. Antrogians flanked the edges of the cloud. Not one slowed down. Soon, the sky brightened up again, like the passing of dark rain clouds as the density of the thousands of dots thinned out. It was awe-inspiring to think that each one of these specks represented a complex being, filled with a lifetime of thoughts and memories. The swarm of Balkiens passed on towards the hazy spires of rock against the pale violet sky in the distance. Then all was quiet and peaceful.

"I thought we were going to be behind bars again," gasped Kaz.

"I think it is all clear now," said Wink. Matt opened the mootie door out on to the courtyard, strewn with the broken branches. Baingae, Winxl, and Yesl hovered over from another mootie with their blue and yellow oblate patient. He was placed on the table out in the Vega shine.

"Boonkliat has told me some of his woes," said Baingae. "He was worked very hard down in the mines as a prisoner of conscience. About seven Angapookan months ago, he in some way insulted Zinkel-Mallkis' Sphericity and was arrested, found guilty by the Court of the TriMallkaetium, and deported to hard labor. He had lost all his strength hauling rock ore out of the mineshafts. He was coming to the surface with a heavy rock under his very oblate and dirty swooth, when one of the ball-cars from the train rolled straight into him, knocking the rock away from him. The power of his flying, such as it was, shot him up well into the sky. He became weaker during his flight here and *wugged* down towards a tree, hitting it hard, causing significant injury, hence the severe oblateness. It's a wonder Boonkliat made it at all. I've known him before. We'd love to have him with us."

"Are you sure about that?" asked Kloonket. "We don't want any spies into our camp."

"I know of your concerns," said Baingae. "He did, fly here all by himself, and knew the way."

"Yes," replied Kloonket thoughtfully. "Yes. He did know how to get here through all those twisting valleys. I guess that's as good as a password any day."

Baingae continued to speak to Boonkliat in Antrobian, explaining about their ill-fated mission to Splogita and introduced the six Tombalkiens.

Boonkliat spoke while Baingae translated. "Boonkliat is telling us that he remembered well the departure of the *Balkieston* and the tragic circumstances of Winxl's fall. Boonkliat was an acquaintance of mine when we were at the space academy. He was nearly chosen to join the *Balkieston's* crew, but his wife, Monketty, was expecting the birth of their first set of little poonketies and could not come. He sorely misses his family, since his arrest. He says that they would leave Balkieston if caught for fear of being arrested themselves. Where they would have gone, he knows not. There were twelve poonketies when he was deported, and he believes that she was expecting four more."

Kloonket flew over to join them. "It's a bit late in the day to set off for the North now. In any case, I'd let that armada get on ahead."

Boonkliat spoke again in Antrobian, while Baingae translated. "Boonkliat suspects that all those poor Balkien prisoners are being transferred under Antrogian Guard to the deep caves in the North of the Western Continent, over the Eastern Ocean. I did see flanks of large Antrogian guards on either side."

Matt arose rubbing the sleep away from his eyes from his circular bed with Yesl huddled up beside him. Balkiens hovered around amid the sounds of clanking of metal cases and rounded water flasks being loaded into the panniers on the Antrogians.

"You'd better dress up warmly, Matt," said Yesl. "Where we're going it's going to be cold, as we have to cross over a high range of snowy mountains. Matt dressed in his jeans, thick socks, and climbing boots. He wore his woolen patterned Fair Isle jersey, which Auntie Wendy had given as a birthday present while studying in Arizona. He had around his neck, the chain that Erin had given him before they left Tombalki on the Splinkatrix. Dangling from it was the small gold half heart with a serrated edge as if it was the one half broken away from the other.

"Yesl," he said. "As I wear this, I think longingly of Erin on Tombalki. She wears the other half heart. It's a symbol of our separation from each other." Baingae flew upon his shoulders to ponkadliath with him.

Matt went outside with his luggage towards Boolboonkle. He gently stroked his course swooth, which was bright and glistening from the morning dew in the brilliant Vega-shine.

"I hope my load is not too heavy for me," said Boolboonkle in his deep voice.

"I hope so, too," replied Matt. "But we'll need all of this water for such a long trip.

"Better eat in haste," said Kloonket. "We have a long flight to the North Lands, and we need to arrive before dark with little light from Antrogi to guide us, being so far north, and we don't want to land in the wild at night. There may be hackels out there. They've been known to severely *wug* and oblate Balkiens or even kill them outright and eat them. They are a kind of nocturnal creature that sometimes preys on Balkiens. They seem only to have become carnivorous since this evil befell our once heavenly world. It's time to depart before there are any more Antrogian convoys."

All Tombalkiens were swung up onto their respective Antrogians. As Matt settled onto Boolboonkle's course swooth, the loud, deep warbling started. The village of camouflaged mooties slipped far below them. They proceeded up the deep darkened valleys, following the winding fast-flowing river in the gorges below for many hours. The vegetation on the steep sides was a dark almost, iridescent green with small flowers in many colors. The summits of these mountains were mostly bare rock with bits of snow. Boolboonkle was the lead Antrogian with Matt, Kloonket, and Boonkliat seated on him. Boonkliat was now a more resplendent colored Balkien with royal blue and yellow bands of swooth.

"So much like deep Scottish glens," said Kaz as they flew past mountain vegetation that looked like heather with its tiny purple flowers. They had to fly much higher to go through the Pass of Ambunti, leading Antrobi's great city in the Far North. Towering up was a range of rocky crags wholly covered in ice and snow. The Antrogians were beginning to struggle with the thinner air as they ascended the near-vertical cliff face. Every human wore sunglasses for the glare from the snow. Behind them spread out below was an expanse of many mountains. The tall peaks in the distance looked like the serrated and irregular saw teeth against a darker purple sky. On the southern horizon below Vega, there was the thin crescent of Antrogi.

The hovering of the Antrogians was getting louder as they mustered up more power but progress up the mountainous rock face was painfully slow. Boolboonkle began to falter.

"Kloonket," shouted Matt. "Hadn't we better land somewhere and rest."

"I thought that the pass was near here," said Kloonket. "Hate to say it, but I think we've made a wrong turn back there."

"I thought you knew the way," boomed a low voice below them. "I've got to land. I'm about to *wug*."

"There's a thin ledge over there," shouted Kaz.

"Let's land there," said Matt. All the Antrogians managed to land on a narrow, snow-covered ledge on the cliff face, except heavily laden Boolboonkle. He flew close to the ridge but could not ascend enough to reach it. He began to drop lower down the cliff face and had to let himself go. He, with Matt, Kloonket and Boonkliat slowly plunged into a deep ravine. The rocks below them were now above them as the light grew dimmer.

"I'm sorry," boomed Boolboonkle. "I'm *wugging*." His deep warbling, which had been going non-stop for about four hours, died away with exhaustion. There was a thud and splash as they *wugged* onto the ravine floor. It was quite a jolt for Matt, who felt it in his neck, which would have been undoubtedly whip-lashed, had he not adopted a brace position. All was still, except for a slight trickle of water coming down from the ice above. Matt looked up and could see the deep purple sky, outlined by rocks around it.

"I sure hope that the others can find us down here," said Matt.

"Oh, I'm so sorry about this *wug*," said Boolboonkle in his deep Antrogian voice.

"Look," replied Matt. "Don't blame yourself. We loaded you up too much. We seem to have more than our share of water containers."

"I think we may have misloaded our supplies in our hurry to depart," said Kloonket. "Matt, Vega is now setting. I'll fly up to tell the others up on that ledge before it gets dark. We're not going to make it tonight. Wait here with Boonkliat."

Kloonket hovered up, leaving Matt with Boonkliat who could only speak a few words of English. Boolboonkle groaned saying, "I'm on the water and my lower swooth is getting cold and wet. Can you unload the water bottles so that I can hover to the drier ground? I'll help you."

Matt was swung down to the ground off Boolboonkle's top swooth. He landed in the water. "My feet are wet," he hollered in surprise.

He stepped onto the bank. Boolboonkle passed down the water bottles for him to place in a regular stack of spheres on the bank. Boolboonkle started warbling over to a dry stony bank. Matt put his hands to his ears for his noise was so great in that enclosed space. After a moment, all was quiet. He looked around to see where Boonkliat was.

No sign of Boonkliat, he thought.

He heard the sounds of Kloonket and the Winkets descending into the cave-like ravine. Baingae was also with him to assess and diagnose Boolboonkle for any health issues that may have led to his weakness.

"Kloonket," said Matt. "Boonkliat's not here. He must have moved down the gully a little when Boolboonkle hovered away from the river he'd landed in to dry off."

Dr. Baingae hovered all around Boolboonkle's thick swooth to sense his general metabolism. "I think he's just exhausted from the long flight. What are all these?" he asked, looking at the five water containers on the bank.

"Our water supplies were unevenly distributed before we departed," said Kloonket.

"Kloonket!" exclaimed Baingae in a loud shrill. "You should have checked our loading. And you too, Matt! The poor Antrogian is overworked. He'll have to rest for a day before we can continue. Especially up here."

"Look," said Matt firmly. "How was I to know who was loaded with what. We left in such a hurry."

"What hurry?" demanded Kloonket.

"That's just it," argued Baingae. "In case it's escaped your notice, I'm still the chief medical officer since the Splinkatrix left Earth and proper safety procedures had not been followed. First, we get arrested in Balkieston. Then find out that our mother ship is badly damaged out on the outermost planet, Roonkle. Our scout ship now has a broken cockpit - and now this!"

"I'm sorry that it's all gone pear-shaped," said Matt.

"Being sorry isn't going to get us out of this dark hole," said Baingae. "What are we going to do about it?"

"Well, let's stop this stupid and worthless bickering," said Matt. "I never thought that you Balkiens could squabble."

"I agree," said Wink softly. "It's happened, and we've got to help Boolboonkle get up to the ledge tonight to join the others."

"You'll do nothing of the sort," said Baingae firmly. "Doctor's orders override all other orders on the Balkien Scout Service regulations. And that includes any royal decrees of King Zozl himself. If Boolboonkle settles on that icy ledge in the cold of the night, his lower soaked swooth will freeze on him, and he'll stick to the ice. We'd never get him off, and he'd likely perish from exposure. There is enough room for all of us down here. It may be creepy, but it's a lot warmer."

Matt had turned on his torch. He looked up through the opening above him and could see a star-studded sky. He could see the black circular outline of Wink as he hovered up to the ledge to ask the others to come down.

"Where's Boonkliat?" asked Kloonket.

"Like I said," said Matt. "He vanished while we were arguing over Boolboonkle's *wug*."

"Oh, let's not start all this again," said Mwaki. "We've got to look for him, and I'd better fly up and get the others to come down here for the night."

"Matt and Baingae," said Kloonket. "You go that way down the gully to look for him, but don't stray too far. Mwaki and I will go this way."

Matt, with his feet still soaked through and chilled, proceeded to clamber over torch-lit rocks with an ever-faithful Baingae hovering beside him, occasionally alighting on his shoulder.

"Look, Matt," he said. "Sorry, I was so frustrated back there."

"Don't worry. You are the safety officer. We've all made mistakes I should never have been too inquisitive about the things in the square in front of that museum."

"Matt. Neither should I have."

"It was well that you escaped out of Zinkel-Mallkis' court to tell the others about us, Baingae."

"Ssh!" hissed Matt. "I hear something."

Matt could hear his heartbeat loudly. He could even hear the very tiny little clicking and singing noises that a Balkien's metabolism makes from Baingae on his shoulder. The air was damp and still. He could smell that beautiful fragrance of the Antrobian vegetation all around them. Matt turned off his torch. He moved into a cleft of rock he had noticed in the light. After his eyes had become dark-adapted, he could see the outlines of conifer-like trees and the distant black peaks against the sky full of stars. There were no recognizable constellations; no Orion and his belt, no Ursa-Major, no

Cassiopeia. He did recognize the Pleiades, a group of stars so close together and yet so far away. The Milky Way was bright.

There was a rustle in the grasses ahead of them. Baingae stayed close to Matt on his left shoulder. There was a distant warble of a flying Balkien.

"Who could that be?" asked Matt. "Boonkliat?"

"Not sure," said Baingae softly. "We don't want to give ourselves away."

"Who else, but Boonkliat could be out this way, anyhow?" whispered Matt. "Turn on the torch."

"Wait," said Baingae. "I've got to recognize Boonkliat's flying noise signature. I don't yet know him well."

The warble grew louder.

"I think it's him, but we'd risk disaster if it's an agent of the Empire," said Baingae.

That Balkien was getting closer.

"It sounds a lot like Boonkliat," said Matt. "Yes, it is. It still sounds a bit weak as if he's still recovering from his ordeal in prison."

"You're right," confirmed Baingae.

Matt switched on his torch. There to his astonishment lying in the heathery undergrowth of this sheltered oasis of woodland in the frozen mountainous wastes of the Great Northern Yastagliath was a ponkadliath of three small, bedraggled Balkiens who were dirty and oblate. Baingae hovered down to look them over and carry out an immediate diagnosis on each of them. They did not stir at all. Just then, the blue and yellow swooth of Boonkliat appeared from the forest and alighted beside Baingae and his new patients.

"Boonkliat," said Baingae in Antrobian. "Why did you go wandering off like that? We must stick close together way out here where there's danger all around. Never mind now. We'd never have found these otherwise. Let's take them back with us."

"I know these," said Boonkliat. "They're three of my fellow workers down in the mines."

"Then how did they get way out here in this state?" asked Matt.

Matt picked them up and tucked them into his warm zipper jacket with Baingae to comfort them. They went back up the creek to their makeshift camp. Before they arrived, they heard the loud sounds of the other Antrogians descending from the upper ledge. They greeted Matt and Boonkliat with warm hugs. They sat down amidst a few torches.

"It's so much warmer down here," said Judith still shivering with the cold.

"Maybe just as well that Boolboonkle *wugged* down into here," said Kaz. "A night out, there would have been awful. There's a bitter wind up there now."

"And just as well for these two," said Matt as he unzipped his jacket to reveal Baingae and his three new Balkien patients. "Good on you,

Boolboonkle." Matt stroked Boolboonkle's course, swooth. There were a few pleasant, deep pulses from him.

Everyone looked at the little beings laid out in the light of the torches. In Antrobian, Boonkliat said that he knew these three. One of them spoke very softly out of his weakness, explaining how the three got there.

Mwaki translated, "We three were slaves down in the mines for Zinkel-Mallkis. We're known well by Boonkliat. After the disaster with the ball train, many of us took the opportunity to escape. Unfortunately, this was not available to all of us. Boonkliat was one of the lucky ones. Many flew off in all directions after the accident. We were rounded up by the strong Antrogian guards of the Empire and deported to the great deep underground mines in the northern part of the continent of Beekio, far to the North-East of here. We were in convoy flying in formation under the heavy guard of the Mallkisians; a term adopted for those loyal to the Emperor."

"That must have been the cloud of Balkiens flying over us that delayed our departure," said Matt.

Mwaki continued, "These grew so tired that they couldn't stop themselves from *wugging* out of formation. Some of the Mallkisians hovered around for a while searching for them but gave up and continued over that icy ridge. The next thing they saw was Matt with his torch and Baingae."

"Just as well we waited until next day to depart," said Wink.

"All very well," said Kloonket. "But our base where we're going is not too far from their likely route. It's a worry."

"We're all tired," said Yesl. "Let's bed down for the rest of the night."

The humans slept close together, covered by as many Balkiens as possible to keep warm.

Alison was first to stir in the morning Vega, sending slivers of light through the dense conifer like trees, with tiny bulbous dark green smooth polyps, casting their shadows on the upper rock face of the deep ravine. There were strange musical noises in the forest like a cross between a hum and a buzz. She also noticed clouds of what looked like tiny spherical creatures hovering around over the Antrogians. One landed close to Baingae who was still asleep. It was a sphere about the size of a pea. On its shiny purple body, there were tiny little white spots around it just north of its equator. Below the body, there were many short legs, like those on a rounded centipede. Judith was next to stretch her slender body from under the Winkets and others in their company. Mwaki hovered around everyone to wake them up.

"Look at those little things," said Judith. "What are they?"

"They're our equivalent of the insects you have on Tombalki," said Yesl. "Strange. I've not seen any until now since we came back. Antrobi was full of them in the olden days."

Breakfast consisted of fruit and bits of thick leaves cut from the broccoli-trees before they left their last camp. Water was drunk from the stream, and the containers refilled.

"We'll have to wait here today until Boolboonkle is fit enough to tackle the remaining four hours of our journey. We've got him tipped over on his side to allow his south polar swooth to dry out," said Baingae. "He'll go out for a short flight this afternoon to dry off more."

The three escaped prisoners washed in the stream. Their swooth brightened up into beautiful colors. Dr. Baingae examined them. "They've got the oblate disease to varying degrees."

"Poor things," said Kara, as tears welled up in her eyes. Matt laid a hand on his sister to comfort her. The Winkets flew up onto her shoulders. "It's so sad to see what terrible things are happening here."

"Tomorrow," began Kloonket. "We continue over the ridge and onward to our destination. There we will meet with many of our comrades in arms. We have to devise some way of winning and recruiting many more of our population to our way of thinking, and we must tell them that the cause they're following is an evil one. Many of us are now regretting sending the Balkieston on that ill-fated mission to Splogita, which has brought to us ruin to our way of life."

"That's one way of looking at it," said Yesl. "We did meet the Molktrons, enslaved there. Someday, they'll need redemption from their oppression."

"That's a noble thought, Yesl," said Kloonket. "But first we'll have to save ourselves from this gloom before such a quest is ever attempted. For, tomorrow, we head out for the palace of Little Balkieston, where King Zozl and Queen Mozl live in exile, which is not far from Ambunti."

"Ambunti," said Matt. "Remember the village of that name on Earth - coincidence?"

"I think more than that," said Yesl. "The inhabitants of the Earthly Ambunti may have memories and legends of the ancient visit by Balkiens to Tombalki who arrived at what you call the Devil's Marbles in Australia, where we dug up that large sphere from around one of the round boulders. We've yet to analyze it. It's still on the Splinkatrix."

After their breakfast, they loaded up onto the Antrogians. After the crescendo of taking flight, the Antrogians left the lowly creek one by one and proceeded slowly up the icy cliff, made bright with the early morning Vega. Boolboonkle with Matt, Yesl and the Winkets on him, was first to make the ascent over the ridge. As Matt watched with some anxiety, the cliff face moved past them ever so slowly. With the thin air at this altitude, there were times when the cliff face would stop moving downward. The Winkets, Yesl, and Kloonket flew off and under Boolboonkle to push him up. The bare cliff bathed in the bluish-green morning light of Vega-rise slipped by more rapidly.

The icy ridge that was way above them soon moved below to reveal a great dark green carpet of forest that stretched towards the turquoise horizon. In the foreground were the foothills of the mountains they were passing over. Matt looked over to see each of his five relatives on their respective Antrogian mounts, which seemed to hang above the sharp ridge below them. They passed over and began to speed up for the long descent. Yesl, Kloonket, and the Winkets rolled up around Boolboonkle to join Matt before they picked up speed. It felt like riding downhill on a bicycle after a long pedal uphill. The Antrogians provided telekinetic protection for their riders by holding the air around them to form a protective bubble. The forested plains raced by below them. Matt looked back to see the crags they had passed over only about half an hour ago. They were now a distant black silhouette against the rays of the rising Vega behind the mountains, which cast long shadows across the forested plains north of the hot desert areas in the Northern Yastagliath. For about another three hours, they flew over what became a monotonous scene of trees and more trees. On the distant horizon, Matt saw purple peaks, like an island in a dark green ocean.

"That's our destination," said Kloonket. "We'll be able to get proper treatment for our poor oblate patients, whom Dr. Baingae is caring for over on Alison's Antrogian, Zonkollus."

As they approached the rocky island, Matt noticed there was one central, taller, mount amongst the other smaller ones that surrounded it. On the lower slopes, the forest gave way to light green meadows.

"There's the palace," said Kloonket as the Antrogians began to circle the mount.

"Why are we going around and not coming straight in?" asked Matt.

"I'll go and tell the King, that we are arriving," said Kloonket. "His guards might attack the Antrogians, thinking that they're enemies."

Bright objects rushed up towards them. Kloonket immediately flew off in the direction of the palace, with four golden geodesic domes or mooties. Suddenly they were surrounded by flying spheres that looked like the bronze, pea-sized creatures they'd seen only these were about the size of the Winkets. They menacingly hovered around the Antrogians. It was an anxious moment. Kloonket who had flown down to the palace perched on the side of the mountain returned with an entourage of colorful Balkiens, about twice the size of Yesl. There were twelve of them coming with a lot of shrills and warbles. The bronze balls immediately fell into an organized formation around the colored Balkiens.

Kloonket re-joined Boolboonkle. "I have just made myself known to the palace guard, who is escorting us in. I should have gone ahead sooner. Sorry about the reception committee, but we're all safe now."

They flew in towards the golden mooties and came to a circular landing apron that had a velvet carpet all over it, designed explicitly for Antrogians to alight. They landed softly on the apron. On one of the windows of the golden mootie was a regal Balkien coming out to welcome them, who had a distinct iridescence and was about twice the diameter of Yesl or the Winkets. He had bands of vibrant colors, starting with a bright blue equator. His other zones of swooth had shades of green, red, and maroon with white poles like Yesl. Another Balkien appeared on the balcony who was a little smaller and had bands of dark grey, emerald green, and white poles as well, also with a distinct shimmering effect on her swooth in the noonday Vega.

"On behalf of Antrobian Airlines, we welcome you to Little Balkieston, ladies and gentlemen," announced Yesl. "We hope you had a pleasant flight."

"There's King Zozl himself and his wife, Mozl, the rightful rulers of Antrobi before the Enigma arrived," said Kloonket. "They and their entourage of Balkiens of the palace court are flying out to greet us."

Everyone disembarked from their Antrogians and bowed, curtsied, or nodded before the Royal Couple in their splendor. The Balkiens hovered around the King and Queen forming a ponkadliath around them, before moving away to sit around in a circle.

"Baingae, Wink, Mwaki and Yesl," exclaimed King Zozl in English. "Welcome home! We'd given up on you all by this time. Kloonket sent emissaries to tell me of your coming. What kept you from arriving two days ago?"

"We were held up with some problems finding the Pass of Ambunti," said Matt, looking at Boolboonkle, and the three now somewhat refreshed escaped prisoners.

"These four poor Balkiens were found *wugged* and in poor health," said Baingae. "Boolboonkle here was too heavily loaded and lost the strength to get over the high cliffs over there."

Everyone looked in the direction they'd come from seeing the icy ridge in the far distance just visible to the naked eye against the light purple sky on the horizon.

"We were stranded for two nights on the other side of that ridge, while Boolboonkle recovered his strength to fly up over it," continued Baingae. "Although we missed the Pass, we found these three poor things in a terrible state. The fourth, Boonkliat, fell into our midst at our previous camp. They'd *wugged* out of a huge group of Balkiens who were on a forced flight from a prison mining camp on the far side of those mountains after the sabotaged ball-train crashed into it."

"So that explains the massive black cloud we saw passing by over there three days ago," said King Zozl. "We put our palace guard on alert and began to chop down vegetation to cover our mooties for camouflage in case they came this way. Though this is a beautiful location for our temporary residence, it is too visible to the enemy. We had to make a labyrinth of underground passages in the caves beneath these mountains to hide in case of discovery or attack."

"These Balkiens have had a terrible experience while being enslaved in the mines," said Mwaki.

Dr. Baingae continued to hover over the weak beings, carrying out his diagnostics and assessments on their severe oblateness.

"Boonkliat is on the mend," he said, "but the other three are in a bad way and may have to go into hibernation."

Queen Mozl quivered. "Our subjects are being brutally treated. We do have deep caves where they could go if needed."

"They'll need it all right," said Baingae.

One of them began to mumble feebly in Antrobian.

"Wink," said Yesl. "Start recording this on your imaging sphere."

Wink and Matt pointed their camera devices at them, while everyone remained silent, except for Kloonket who asked random questions. As the three oblate Balkiens continued to mumble in soft tones, cotton-wool-like material began to grow over them, forming the recovery cocoon for a lengthy recovery hibernation.

"They've had a terrible time," said Alison as she softly stroked their swooth as the cocoon formed.

"Guards," said King Zozl. "Prepare sepulchers for them. We'll arrange for a committal ceremony tomorrow - poor things."

Two largish Balkiens flew off towards the Palace Mootie to arrange for their internment.

"These Balkiens overheard one of their fellow prisoners saying that something terrible has happened to the city of Ambunti," said Kloonket.

"What about Ambunti?" asked Matt in a concerned tone. "We've heard from Yesl, Baingae, and the Winkets that Ambunti is a great and dazzling city to the north of here. We'd love to fly there tomorrow, to see this great city, the place of Winxl's nativity."

"Then you'd better take all of your provisions including the water bottles," exclaimed Kloonket. "And leave early in the morning so that we can return here the same day."

"Why?" said Kaz. "We'd love to stay there for a few days and see the sights."

"We're so sorry," said Zozl, his voice trailing off in a doleful tone. "All of those rumors you've heard are sadly true. The palatial mooties are no more, with the population taken into captivity. The whole city was savagely attacked and sacked by Zinkel-Mallkis' army of Hellacks."

"After what Boonkliat and the three oblated slaves were saying, there may be not much left," said Kloonket. "They have been very shocked by what has happened there. Their talk of some battle and rumors of destruction are entirely true, I'm afraid."

YESL – The Balkien from Antrobi

Winxl quivered uncontrollably. Baingae, the Winkets, and Yesl formed a ponkadliath around their suffering friend in great grief at this ghastly news. All humans along with the Royal Couple, Zozl and Mozl, joined in. Winxl let out a groaning wail, "Oh Ambunti!"

Matt put his binoculars to his eyes to get a closer look at the distant mountains ahead of him while riding atop Boolboonkle. It was a bright purple day. Only Kaz and Sean were accompanying him on their Antrogians to Ambunti, flying over yet more dark green trees. As they approached the mountains, the thick forest gave way to clearings of grasslands with scattered trees, which were knurled and ancient-looking. Some were looking withered with a sickly brown color. The air was getting colder as they continued northward towards Antrobi's Arctic Circle. King Zozl was with the Winkets and Yesl traveling with Matt. Baingae and Winxl were with Kaz. Kloonket and Boonkliat accompanied Sean.

"I can see some dark rounded shapes on the horizon," hollered Matt. "It must be Ambunti."

King Zozl held his telescopic visual device around his visual sensory swooth as they flew closer.

"Was Ambunti," said Zozl with alarm. "These shapes are not gleaming and looking smooth."

Matt again looked through the binoculars and saw distorted sub-spherical outlines of mootie like buildings, which were dark brown. Soon they were passing over withered grass and grotesque tree stumps that had been burnt out and blackened.

"Zozl," cried Matt, putting his binoculars away. "This is like some of the worst bush fires I've seen on Tombalki."

Zozl and the Winkets stared out from the top of Boolboonkle's swooth at an ugly scene of devastation. They passed over many ruined rounded outlines of charred remains of hundreds of mooties with burnt broccoli trees with blackened trunks and burnt foliage. They came to the once-great golden citadel mootie that was said to have been the jewel of the Great Northern Yastagliath. There were only rusting stumps of metal around the circular foundation also blackened by the firestorm that had devastated this place. There were twisted and partially melted metal panels distorted from their former triangular shapes and solidified rivulets of molten glass that had once formed the glass dome.

"Oh, Ambunti!" cried Wink. "Our home from home! Oh, what has happened here?" Wink and Mwaki started to oscillate while emitting moans, sounding like the Antrobian form of weeping. Matt picked up the Winkets and cuddled them. He began to weep. "This whole universe seems to be filled with horrors, not just Earth."

The three of them found an area of greener grass on which to land. When the Antrogian's deep flying warbles had stopped, there was an eerie silence. The area where they were, had flat hexagonal slabs carved from rock that looked like black granite. Many were chipped and cracked, with rubbery, dark green weeds growing. They grew long tendrils that spread to the bases of the ruins and twisted up and around the rusty girders and broken support struts. The Antrogians lifted Matt, Kaz, and Sean and deposited them onto the pavement. King Zozl and the Balkiens flew down and joined in ponkadliath around the Tombalkiens.

"I would like to know how this happened," said Zozl.

"I'd like to too," said Kloonket.

"This," said Zozl, followed by a long pause, "is the worst, I've ever seen; our once beautiful planet!"

"And now this!" exclaimed Matt as he eyed up his surroundings. "Where is the population?"

"Probably wugged and very oblated and may now be dead," said Baingae. "We'll have to look around, though it looks as if Ambunti's been like this for some time."

"We, the Winkets, had a great visit here just before we took off for Splogita and Tombalki to look for the *Balkieston*," said Wink.

"We'd better keep together," said Zozl. "We'll remount our Antrogians and take a quick look around."

"Boodibah!" said Baingae in his way of expressing joy though it was hardly a place of happiness. "This is where Winxl and I met. You Tombalkiens would call it our first date when we flew together all around this once beautiful city". Baingae's voice soon became more somber as the reality of what was once was no more.

"Didn't we, Winxl?" Winxl cuddled him. Matt held both Baingae and Winxl to his chest. Dangling around Matt's neck was the golden chain with the gold broken heart amulet.

"This must be terrible for you both," said Zozl as he looked at Matt in ponkadliath with Baingae and Winxl. "Matt. What's with that necklace?" asked Zozl.

"Oh! That symbolizes the separation between my lady-friend on Tombalki. Her name is Erin. We are male and female and marry, just like you Balkiens, like Baingae and Winxl. I'm missing her terribly." A tear or two welled up in Matt's eyes as he looked heavenward. Baingae comforted him in empathy. "Oh, I do wonder what Erin's doing now, working at JPL in Pasadena."

"This place is creepy," said Sean. "I'm seeing things moving over there."

"Where?" asked Kloonket.

"Over there!" said Kaz. "Let's get out of here!" Suddenly ugly round sponge-like things with leering mouths bearing sharp shark-like teeth started rolling out of the desolate and twisted ruins. Matt, Kaz, and Sean were whisked up in the air and tossed onto their respective Antrogians and telekinetically held there.

"Hackels!" shouted Wink, "take-off!"

Almost at once, they were about one hundred meters off the ground. The pale brown spongy things were jumping up and down and coming perilously close to them. Hackels were terrible swooth eating carnivorous creatures. Though they could not fly, they were bouncy enough to reach up to around two hundred meters and could cover some distance by bouncing along the grasslands.

"Go faster," said Boolboonkle in his deep voice swooth. "Wuuug! I'm being bitten."

Matt noticed that a hackel had attached itself to Boolboonkle. He took the only weapon he had, his binoculars, and swung them towards the hackel, knocking it off Boolboonkle. It fell to the ground below as Boolboonkle flew much higher. Matt retrieved his binoculars and tried to look through them towards their base, Little Balkieston.

"I think I've damaged them," said Matt realizing that his only means of advance sightings was lost. "I can't focus them now."

"Well, that hackel could have bitten you and poisoned you by now. That place is dangerous," said Kloonket. "Hackels were once harmless herbivores. It seems that the very nature of our fauna has changed since the Enigma came."

"We're heading back towards our base," said Zozl. "Sorry about the binoculars, Matt. We still have our viewing devices, so don't worry."

As they flew the long flight back to the mountain fortress of King Zozl, Matt's thoughts turned back towards his beloved Erin. It was dusk after Vegaset when they saw the tall mount of Little Balkieston silhouetted against the green twilight. The left half of the crescent form of Antrogi was still visible in this remote north-eastern location. The dark apron rose to meet the Antrogians as they finally landed as darkness set in.

"There's Balkle," said Baingae, "appearing in its last quarter phase."

Zozl and Mozl came out to join them from the palace mootie. Behind them, the Winkets and Kloonket hovered, carrying a small stubby golden cylinder. A Balkien of the King's Court called Bwinkle flew over with a stand, having five legs. Each leg was made up of adjoined golden spheres which could be moved in a snake-like fashion to steady the instrument on uneven ground. Bwinkle was about twice the size of the Winkets and only slightly smaller than the King. He had shades of golden brown and orange colors in his swooth.

"Guess what we've got," said Mwaki, "our version of a telescope."

"This so reminds me of Erin's back yard during our student days in Arizona," said Matt. "We so remember allowing Baingae to look through it towards his beloved Winxl."

The golden scope was pointed towards the sun or Sol, now a faint distant star, in the Antrobian constellation of Binkle-Malltrix. King Zozl introduced the Tombalkiens to the sky at night on Antrobi, showing the constellations that the Balkiens had conceived and drawn through the stars, just as humankind had done on the Earth.

Matt looked through the telescope and could see the faint yellow pinpoint of light in a dense star-field. It was the sun. Close by was the much brighter star, Sirius. He thought of Earth and Erin. He could feel the warm contact of some swooth on his shoulder. It was Baingae. Matt's view through the telescope became blurred. As he moved away from the instrument and sat down on the green, mossy textured meadow, he wiped away the tears from his eyes. He held Baingae in his cupped hands and wept.

"I'm beginning to feel the huge weight of the vast distance between us," he sobbed. "If only Erin could have come with us."

Alison was the first human to lay a hand on his shoulder. The others huddled around, both human and Balkien. Winxl landed on his head. "Matt. You will see her again. We all know in our deepest innermost swooth that we'll have victory over Zinkel-Mallkis and his empire. Remember how I felt after losing the presence of Baingae on the *Balkieston* and how we met up in the Barringer Meteorite Crater.

"I guess, I'll have to go back on the Splinkatrix someday when all of this is over," said Matt still sobbing. "I'm sorry that I'm going to pieces. Erin's the love of my life."

"Remember that she needed to stay on Tombalki for her work with NASA and the other Balkiens to oversee the rebuilding of the *Balkieston*," said Wink.

"That's all very well," said Matt. "I only wish that there was another way."

"Matt," began Zozl. "You've fought valiantly so far in our campaign to rid our world of this tyranny. You all have. We need your commitment to this cause. That is Matt, Kara, Sean, Kaz, Alison and Judith here, and Erin, too, in her role on Tombalki."

• ○ •

16 ~ CROSSING THE GREAT SEA

That night, the Milky Way dominated the sky. In the large dome at the Mount Wilson Observatory, Erin was writing notes by the dull red light on the desk set against the old white-painted wooden panels of the historic building. As she leaned over her laptop computer to check data, the necklace with her half-heart pendant dropped out of her coat and dangled in front of her. Her Balkien companion, Monku, who had volunteered to stay behind to keep her company, was with her. She climbed the ladder up to the telescope and reoriented the ten-inch instrument towards Vega. Monku hovered up to perch on her shoulder.

Erin softly stroked Monku's soft fluffy swooth. "Monku, I do so miss being with my beloved. I miss his loving tenderness and his iridescent multi-colored companion. Oh, the tears that well up in my dry eyes, that beautiful morning with the brilliant sunrise as I hugged and kissed him good-bye. I now understand what we as women went through when our sweethearts departed for far-flung shores in their zest for adventure to the battlefields in two world wars here on Earth. It seems that I said farewell Matt, his family, Yesl, and her crewmates as they departed to a similar conflict on Yesl's beloved Antrobi. To stand back and watch that scout ship lift-off from the bushland near Balladonia was so uncanny. It was just like any other departure to fly over to the Meteor Crater or the Grand Canyon, only knowing he and the others were going on such a long journey into the depths of the cosmos. Then I was all alone. Except that I had you, Monku, on my sagging shoulder. I wept as I saw the ship grow smaller and then become a tiny white speck before disappearing into that steel-blue sky while holding the keys to Kaz's 4WD SUV."

"Erin," said Monku. "I have a feeling through the Balkien medium that they are okay. Let's look at distant Vega."

Erin looked through the eyepiece at the sharp bluish pinpoint of light, which shimmered in the warm night air. The image in her eye blurred momentarily as a tear welled up thinking of Matt. *Had he already arrived?*

"Maybe he's looking back at the sun right now from the Purple Planet," said Monku. "Who knows?"

"Monku," said Erin as she laid a soft hand on his swooth, reflecting the red light. "What a romantic thought!"

"Remember. It was like that with Baingae and Winxl," said Monku.

"I wish they were here with us too."

"This is KSUR, Beverley Hill Golden Oldies. Good morning to y'all. We have great hits to have you rising and shining…"

Erin turned over in her half-awakened state and pushed the snooze button on her clock radio, half oblating Monku who always kept his swooth snuggled close to her hair in bed. She stretched and yawned while cuddling Monku.

"….Dow Jones was down 11.6 points in early trade on Wall Street" intoned the radio, "and finally, we have just had the news come in that divers in a mini-sub have just discovered the remains of the wreck of an alleged alien spaceship on the sea-bed in the North Atlantic. We have reported, many years ago that an alien craft ditched in the ocean off the West Coast of Scotland following an accident somewhere in the Solar System. Experts now believe that they have found a spherical section of the ship."

"That's the bridge of the *Balkieston*," exclaimed Monku as he awoke himself.

"We now go over live to the salvage ship, the Sea Scout."

"This is Amanda Hennessey reporting to you live from the Sea Scout. And Captain Gerhardt, what have you found?"

"What we saw is nothing like a wreck of an ocean liner," said Captain Gerhardt. "All we can say is that the find is large and spherical. It has a distinct geodesic design, though it is hard to get a full view in the darkness at a depth of about a kilometer."

"And can you tell us how this object was discovered?"

"We were led to it after we discovered a debris field during our grid search pattern. Samples of this debris retrieved from the seabed were made of the same unidentifiable metal alloy as that discovered on a Scottish island about six years ago."

Erin listened to the end of the news article and clicked off the radio. Before going to work at JPL, Erin turned on her computer in the study of her Pasadena apartment to check out the story on the internet. There, on the Altaness Courier website was the report on the discovery by the Sea Scout with more information. It read:

> There are reports that significant wreckage of the alien spacecraft that crashed into the North Atlantic seven years ago has just been discovered about fifty kilometers west of the Islands of Sgeir Mor, off the coast of Scotland. They say that they have found what appears to be a silvery geodesic structure lying on the seabed, looking like a soccer ball sitting on the pitch.

There was an image on the screen showing a dark outline of the structure with the lights of the camera reflecting off one of the ship's polygonal panels. The lights lit up only the central part of the structure. Otherwise, there was total darkness, peppered by tiny flecks of dust suspended in the murky water reflecting the light from the searchlights.

Monku pulsated and buzzed around the room in excitement. "It looks a lot more intact than I'd imagined."

Erin gasped in wonder.

"I only wish Matt and Yesl were here, Monku. I wonder if any of the crew is still on board, maybe in hibernation."

"It's possible," said Monku. "No lights on in the bridge anymore. It looks so dark."

"I've got to go to work now, Monku," said Erin. "If only I could have the day off. Can you go and tell Mwakus and Bwinkus with Dan and Nick, about the discovery?

"Certainly," said Monku.

Erin, dressed in her dark blue business suit, with her straight long golden hair flowing behind her with Monku sitting on her right shoulder, like a large scarf pom-pom, descended the stairs with the clicking of her shiny black high heeled shoes to the front door of the apartment complex. Monku flew off from Erin's shoulder in the direction of Altadena towards the dark purple crags of the San Gabriel Mountains still silhouetted against the yellowish sun, rising above the city haze. Erin stepped into her Dodge. Her broken heart pendant on her necklace glistened in the sunlight. She drove out of the apartment grounds towards JPL, thinking more consciously about the beloved man in her life.

Matt, now dressed in his leather bomber jacket, continued to gaze at the yellow pinpoint in the eyepiece.

He felt the warm touch of Yesl's swooth on his cheek. "May I have a look, Matt. You've hogged that telescope for the last twenty minutes. Zozl and the Winkets are using all the other telescopes of the Palace."

"Oh, I'm so sorry, Yesl," said Matt as he stepped aside on the purple ground, softly lit by the light of Antrogi.

"You must be still fixated on Erin like I was with Winxl," said Baingae, who gave Matt a ponkadliath cuddle along with Yesl.

Breakfast in the rising strong Vega-light was a great feast of the fruits of the Northern Yastagliath. The Palace was not gleaming in all its former glory as most of it had been painted with camouflage colors to match the surrounding rocks behind it. Many of the Balkiens of the Palace court were feverishly flying around laying more tree branches around to hide it from the enemy. In hexagonal bowls on a hexagonal table gilded by golden edging around a purple cloth textured surface, were fruits of many colors.

"Would everyone like to try some of this fruit?" asked Mozl.

"I'd like to have one of those orange-colored apples," said Judith. "They're smaller than the apples we have on Earth."

Kaz picked up a small bright orange fruit. "Antrobian apples?"

Alison and Kara picked up one each and began to bite on them.

"That resembles a grapefruit," said Sean. "I'll try it even though it's blue."

Matt gave thanks to all who were present for this otherworldly nourishment.

"I only wish that all of Antrobi was like this," said Alison.

"Indeed, once was," said King Zozl, while Sean was eating the blue grapefruit.

"Taste's a bit bitter," he said. "It seems that if it's blue, it has a bitter taste. I prefer the orange and green ones."

"The blue fruit has stronger vitamins to put it in Earthly terms," said Baingae.

"Zozl, Your Majesty or Sphericity," said Judith. "I see three black dots over there above the horizon."

Everyone turned around and looked beyond the parapet stonewall. The three dots were increasing in size and slowly changing to a triangular formation from a linear one.

"I hope that they're not agents of Zinkel-Mallkis," said Sean. "Better; take cover."

"Don't worry," said Queen Mozl calmly. "These are three of our agents from Antrogi returning from a fact-finding trip to Old Balkieston. They have displayed the secret formation on arrival. First, they appear in a straight line to us, then form into a triangle and back again, three times. Zozl shot off towards the incomers in a loud warble to greet them. They had remarkable color bandings on their swooth. Their deep, warbling noise became loud as they hovered into land. Like helicopters, their downdraught stirred up gusts of wind in everyone's faces. Breakfast fruits were blown off onto the ground. The trio touched down on the apron. All was silent again except for a distant buzz emanating from the forest.

"Greetings to you all," said Zozl in English. "Welcome back. May we introduce you to our newcomers from Tombalki. These two-legged beings are Matt, Kaz, Sean, Alison, Kara, and Judith. Of our kind are Yesl, Baingae, and Boongoo from the ill-fated *Balkieston* mission to Splogita, and their rescuers on the Splinkatrix, the Winkets, and Winxl. We welcome Zoozonkle, Bankeetl, and Ozonkle originally from the Xonkliat region of Antrogi. What news from Balkieston?"

Zoozonkle was first to speak in his deep, loud voice swooth. "It is not good. Zinkle-Mallkis is now completely obsessed with his Supreme Sphericity. He's paranoid about beginning to suffer any slight degree of oblateness. He's so vain. His swooth is beautiful to behold, but he certainly has lost his once benevolent personality and kindness he once had as ruler of Antrogi."

Judith gave a look of shock and incredulity. "How will we ever win back your planet?"

"We might if there are enough of us to resist the will of Zinkel-Mallkis or better still, the Enigma," said Zozl.

"We can help," said Zoozonkle. "We have been dissident toward the Emperor, and we relate how our kind was subjugated on Antrogi and enslaved in our minds to serve the Enigma having sent out the *spectral signal* to lure you and your technology to Splogita to be discovered and copied via the Molktron slaves. Remember how your scout ship crashed when the Enigma's lightning bolts struck it and downed two of your navigation satellites left in orbit around Splogita. It was from that wreckage that the Enigma found out where you came from."

"In our great quest to explore for life outside our planets," said Zozl falteringly. His swooth sagged, and momentarily, he became a bit oblate. "We've brought calamity on ourselves. Woe to us!"

"Oh Zozl," said Mozl in a consoling tone. "We'll learn from this."

"Oh, sure we will if we survive as a species," said Zozl in frustration.

One of the new arrivals took off in a loud crescendo, sending downdraft towards everyone. The strong wind blew over the breakfast tables, and what fruits were left were scattered all over the purple apron.

"Bankeetl's suddenly zoomed off," said Mwaki. "We'd better start finally loading up our supplies onto our Antrogians."

"Why?" asked Matt.

"I have a telepathic suspicion about Bankeetl," said Mwaki. "I've encountered this kind before."

"What do you mean, Mwaki?" asked Zozl.

"That Bankeetl may well be in league with Zinkel-Mallkis," said Wink.

"Oh, don't be so paranoid," said Yesl.

"But, look at his rash action," said Kaz as he picked himself up off the ground. "We should nonetheless prepare for a quick departure."

"Better load up our supplies onto the Antrogians," said Wink. "Just in case; it's a vast distance to cover with no food or water in case we have to flee."

Matt had loaded the last water spherical bottle into Boolboonkle's pannier. He looked around, and his heart was suddenly filled with fear and dread. The sky was darkening like the approach of a thunderstorm. There was a dense dark cloud with hazy edges. Slowly, the day almost turned to night as the cloud covered Vega.

Matt's heart was racing.

"Get out of here," shouted Wink. "It's going to be a wild storm."

Flashes of lightning could be seen emanating from the storm. There were straight streaks as well as natural forked lightning.

"That no ordinary storm!" cried Zozl. "Get out of here! Get them up!"

Before he could think what was happening, Matt was held tightly onto Boolboonkle's swooth like being on a wild roller coaster. Up became down as the ground raced away far below. Meanwhile, back on the ground, Zozl and Mozl were clinging onto Zoozonkle with what food and water supplies they could collect. A bolt of lightning streaked into the Palace mootie and blew off the roof with a very bright flash and a deafening bang. Zoozonkle took off quickly with a louder warble. More streaks of lightning came in zapping the Palace grounds.

"We're under attack!" exclaimed Zozl as Zoozonkle sped away. "That cloud is full of billions of Zinkle-Mallkis' army of Hellacks."

These were not ordinary Balkiens that had been influenced to fight for the Enigma. These were metallic, leathery-looking Hellacks from Splogita. They discharged lightning and spat out bolts of laser fire. These weapons were being controlled by Zinkle-Mallkis' army, mainly from Balkieston. The onslaught was relentless. As they all sped away in the direction of Ambunti, presumably destroyed by such weapons of war, more laser bolts streaked towards them. The enemy was hotly pursuing Boolboonkle. The wind in Matt's ears was deafening, as the forest raced by below. More flashes came past them. Suddenly, Matt noticed that two of the Antrogians speeding alongside him and the rest had been hit and were losing altitude and speed quickly. They were wugging into a thinning forest.

"Boolboonkle," cried Matt. "Alison's and Judith's Antrogians, Zonkollus and Woozbokle, have been hit."

Boolboonkle immediately went down with Zoozonkle, who had Zozl and Mozl, and Poolpoogleponk who had Kaz, to the forest floor to assist. As they did so, the mighty army of Hellacks buzzed over them, onward toward Ambunti. But a group of these things followed them down to finish them off, firing laser darts at them, all of which missed except for one that grazed Boolboonkle's swooth. Boolboonkle and Poolpoogleponk deposited Matt and Kaz beside Alison and Judith. There were lots of small pebbles everywhere. The forest had given way to the wilderness with scattered trees. More laser bolts sparked onto the stones around them. With their telekinesis, the able Antrogians picked up piles of the rocks and spun them around their swooth in rapidly spinning rings. Boolboonkle bravely ascended towards the menacing metallic balls, which fired bolts into the rotating circles of stones. As Boolboonkle zoomed towards the spheres, he spun the rocks very fast and let them go shooting them into the metallic objects. There were loud crackling, fizzing, and sparks of fire and a cacophony of bangs as the stones hit the spheres. There were splinters of metal and rocks flying everywhere.

While the battle raged, Matt and his companions hid in a thicket of broccoli-trees. The other Antrogians also picked up piles of smaller stones. Boolboonkle, Zoozonkle, and Ozonkle swooped low over the rocks picking them up and rose to meet their attackers, spinning them around their swooth, piling them barrage after barrage into Zinkel-Mallkis' hellish metallic army, though this had only a limited effect on their numbers, but threw the rest of them into confusion. Pieces of metal and stones were raining down on the broccoli-tree. Matt noticed one of the spheres humming towards him in their refuge. Without a moment's thought, he picked up a medium-sized stone and hurled it at the Hellack. The rock hit it, but it was only stunned. It came towards them firing off lightning, setting some of the trees on fire rapidly becoming a bushfire. Smoke was filling the air. The metallic sphere hovered up to Matt and came face to face with him and Kaz. It had bands of flashing lights.

"You must obey!" it said in an angry metallic voice. "You must obey the will of the Emperor. You tried to kill me with that stone. No one attacks Zinkle-Mallkis. That is treason. You all must die! You, strange-looking legged creatures from Tombalki are alien invaders!"

Matt had enough, "You have committed treason! You have brought evil and ruin to this planet. Why have you taken over the minds of those poor hapless Balkiens? We were brought here to help the Balkiens reclaim their world and freedom that you have robbed from them. We come as liberators of the Balkiens."

Lightning flashed, and Matt got a sudden shock and throwing him against the trunk of the tree. Kaz picked up more stones and started stoning the monstrous thing. Kaz was also struck and thrown into some bushes after being electrocuted. Just as the little beast was about to finish off both of them, there was a volley of pebbles thrown at the sphere by both the Winkets, who had the pebbles rapidly spinning around them. The Hellack fell to the ground and fizzed out. The Winkets, Yesl, and Baingae hovered up to tend to Matt and Kaz.

"Matt, Kaz. Are you okay?" asked Yesl. Matt and Kaz lay on the ground not far from Judith and Alison, who had been badly bruised in their fall when their Antrogians had wugged. Alison went over to Matt to feel for a pulse. Baingae rolled over his chest to check his heartbeat.

"He's still breathing," said Baingae. "But his heartbeat is erratic." Baingae lay on his chest after partially removing his clothing. Baingae applied a telekinetic massage through Matt's body tissue. The Winkets held a ponkadliath around his head.

"Oooh," Matt groaned.

"Matt, just hold still," said Baingae. "I'm regulating your heart. You've had a terrible shock. It's Baingae and the Winkets. We've killed the Hellack."

"Oh, I'm sore in my elbow," said Matt.

Baingae continued to massage his bare chest.

Matt slowly sat up. "Oh, Baingae, your swooth's so soothing and healing. I'm feeling so much better. You're a great doctor. I can see why you became the ship's medical officer.

The crackle of burning trees was replacing the grinding noises of stones hitting the army of metallic spheres.

"We've got to move out of here," said Sean. "This whole wood is going up."

The flames and rising temperatures generated strong winds.

Littered about were the remains of the limited number of Hellacks they were able to subdue. Those that remained alive or active were now in retreat as they were taken by surprise at the Antrogians, whom they had assumed to be loyal supporters to the Emperor.

"Oh, look at poor Zonkollus," cried Alison. "He is wugged, and the flames are getting near him. He can't take off!"

"Boolboonkle," said Matt. "Can you push Zonkollus? Roll him away from the flames."

Boolboonkle took off and forced Zonkollus' heavy ball of course swooth to roll over the sandy dirt away from the nearby burning bushes, into a clearing. In so doing Boolboonkle discovered that his strong downdraught had blown some of the spot fires out. He, along with Zoozonkle and Ozonkle, started hovering around the flames, blowing them out. They also picked up dirt and small gravel, and orbiting it around their swooth, hurled it onto the hot spots, and the base of the fires to snuff them out.

All the humans were coughing and spluttering from smoke inhalation. Sean wandered slowly about kicking some pieces of their fallen attackers. He saw that the parts, though metallic in appearance, were rubberier and more looked like dead tissue than inorganic bits of metal.

"Never seen anything like this before," said Yesl.

Kloonket hovered over. "I've heard something about these things or creatures. I think that they're the mutations, developed by Zinkel-Mallkis. I've heard that he's been working on some cloning operations either here or originally on Splogita; building his army."

"We've lost our hold on Little Balkieston," said King Zozl. "It may be a smoldering ruin now and probably overrun by the forces of Zinkel-Mallkis at the very least. I hope that those three in hibernation will be Okay. We'd better move away from here as soon as possible."

"Oh, what about Zonkollus," said Alison. "We can't leave him here. He's visibly oblated now after his awful *wug*. He landed hard to protect me from many injuries. Oh, bless him."

"Dr. Baingae is diagnosing him now," said Kloonket. There was a deep warble that started slowly at first and then got louder. It was Judith's Antrogian friend, Woozbokle, who hovered over to the group. He had also been *wugged* at the start of the battle but not so severely. "I can fly but can't carry any load."

"Don't worry," said Kloonket, taking charge of the situation. "We have our additions, Zoozonkle and Ozonkle to carry you both, Alison and Judith.

We have to move from here soon, but we shouldn't have to go far to find a hiding place tonight.

Both the Tombalkiens and the Balkiens looked around the area of battle amongst the dead remains of their attackers, burnt trees, finding their fallen luggage and supplies, repacked onto the Antrogians. Some of the water containers were smashed, which was a severe blow to attempting any long journey across this desiccated part of the Northern Yastagliath.

"Come on the Vega's getting low," said Zozl.

"Zonkollus is beginning to recover a bit," said Baingae. "It's hard to massage an Antrogian's huge swooth. I'm only a lowly Balklian from Balkle."

"Oh Baingae," said Queen Mozl. "You're a great and very clever doctor. You did a great job on Matt's heart. Your instructions to Zoozonkle to massage Zonkollus' swooth have paid off. See he's flying slowly off over there assisted by Ozonkle's lifting him."

Once the injured and oblated Antrogians were underway, the rest took off from that blasted heath. As Matt looked back from Boolboonkle's top swooth with Baingae, Winxl, the Winkets, and Yesl, he could see that the bush fire was spreading rapidly away to the south, sending a dark grey pall of smoke, which looked ugly against the beautiful Vegaset.

Baingae held himself onto Matt's chest to monitor his heart. "The smoke may look ghastly, but I reckon it'll hide us, and our route, from another attack by the Hellacks."

"Speaking of which," began Matt. "How is it that they all seem to speak English? What's happened to Zinkel-Mallkis' need for interpreters?"

"I'd never thought of that," said Yesl. "I can only surmise that they learned it from Tombalki."

"But how?" asked Matt. "I'm sure that no ship of any sort could have beaten us back to Antrobi from the Earth. Or could they?"

The whole group of Antrogians was now skimming across the trees at a very low altitude. As the air whisked past them on top of Boolboonkle, Yesl rested on his coarse green colored polar swooth in a contemplative mood.

"Matt," she began. "Remember how Dad gave you back that sphere after our graduation dance in Arizona, which was very useful. Only he had it for all of that time. I wonder if Captain Cammins got a hold of it for a while and managed to decode it or had it decoded at the Goddard Space Flight Centre."

"There's another possibility," said Yesl.

"Go on."

"I'm not ruling out the possibility that either the *Balkieston* or the Splinkatrix was followed at a great distance by some agent or entity of the Enigma from Splogita to Tombalki. I'm suggesting that this entity may have colluded with some people on Tombalki with criminal intent or innocently let this or these entities gather up knowledge and pick up the language of the Tombalkiens and then come to Antrobi faster than us to disseminate this knowledge. Perhaps Zinkel-Mallkis knew we were coming. Why do you think the Splinkatrix was attacked around Spalminkatrix?"

"There's one other awful possibility," Baingae said butting in. "You realize that there may have been some time dilation while we were in transit through space. Oh, don't worry too much, but I remember that Captain Wink on the Splinkatrix was a little concerned about the anti-time dilation device on our ship. The monitoring readings were a little over tolerance."

"So, it is possible, that we were not the first to arrive from Tombalki," said Yesl.

"Can't be ruled out," said Baingae.

"There is also the disappearance of Captain Cammins from the Black Forest," commented Matt.

As they flew across the cold wasteland of the Northern Yastagliath, Vega turned a light green color while setting.

"We've got to find a landing site for the night," said Wink to Boolboonkle.

Matt spotted two glistening straight lines going through the dark green tundra. "Rails," he said.

Maybe we could catch a ball train," said Yesl.

"What with guards and all to arrest us," said Matt. "My last ride on a ball train was not exactly Pullman Class."

"Boolboonkle and the others are getting tired, and we should keep going if possible, rather than be sitting ducks for another visitation of Zinkel-Mallkis' minions."

"Look," cried Wink. "Some balls are rolling along on the line."

Many silver balls were moving along the raised railway track looking like a long-outstretched necklace. Ball-cars and hexagonal platforms were running on the rail track behind the front line of ball-cars, and there were more silver ball-cars behind them.

"Looks like a robotic driverless freight train, on its way back from the mines of the Yastagliath," said Wink.

"We could land and sit on those hexagonal flat-bed cars," suggested Matt.

"It'd be cold for you," said Wink, "but great for the Antrogians."

"Let's do it," said Yesl.

The Antrogians, led by Boolboonkle hovered over the available flat-bed wagons as they trundled along and slowly landed. The sounds of Balkien flight gave way to the clickety-clack of the train, rolling through the semi-dark countryside.

"This train's now got passengers," said Kloonket. "I'm sure that we all could get into the two ball-cars in front of the first flatbed car. I used to be a railway engineer and know that most trains on this route are sent back from the mines, empty and driverless. Kloonket flew up to the hexagonal door in the end ball-car, which had a small hexagonal window in it. He maneuvered his blue swooth over the door catch, and it sprung open to the top.

"All aboard," said Kloonket.

Everyone was so relieved to clamber into the spacious ball-car. There were enough round padded cup seats for everyone to sit in, designed for medium-sized Balkiens. There were small hexagonal windows around the spherical cabin.

"At last, Pullman Class," said Matt.

Soon everyone was asleep in these comfortable 'Pullman' Balkien seats.

It was now almost dark. When one was half asleep, one couldn't help but dream of a sleeper train from Scotland to London, King's Cross, or on an Amtrak train to Tucson. The door at the back of the ball-car was left open for ventilation. During waking moments, Matt, while in ponkadliath with the Winkets and Yesl, looked up at the night sky. They were now so far north around towards the other side of the planet, that the brightness of Antrogi was almost below the horizon, obscured by a range of high mountains. He dozed off with fatigue from the day's trials and battles.

Vega had risen over a flat light green plain with distant tall pinnacles on the horizon with a violet color.

"There's something dark on the horizon," said Zozl.

Kaz looked out of the window. "There are tall spires with spheres on top, way in the distance."

Yesl hovered to look out, "It looks like a small town, and we're heading there."

"Better get off the train," said Kloonket with urgency. "We're coming to a wind-up station where the springs on the front three locomotives will be wound up for the return journey."

On the flatbed wagon, Boolboonkle waved back and forth as the train lurched and slowed down. Railway engines on Antrobi were dark bluish-colored metallic balls. They worked like clockwork driven motors in which large springs were wound up tight to give the power needed to cover the long distances between winding stations, similar to water towers for filling up the old steam locomotives on Earth. This method of propulsion was also used on early interplanetary spacecraft in their gyro motors in the pioneering days of planetary exploration in the Vegan system.

"The town's getting nearer," said Zozl. "We've got to get off!"

Everyone loaded their few belongings onto Boolboonkle. Matt jumped onto his swooth, and he quickly flew off the hexagonal platform. After a short flight, all Antrogians landed on a small mossy meadow perched high up on a nearby hill. With six on them grouped around in a circle, they watched as the rest of the Balkiens flew up to join them. The train that they had been on overnight had halted at the town's central station.

"Welcome to Balkisay," said Kloonket playing the role of the train's conductor. "I guess that when they've rewound the locomotive springs, the train will set off on its merry way and we can re-join it further up the track," said Kaz.

"I guess so," said Wink as he looked up. The green horizon, beyond the town full of an assortment of domes and mooties of varying sizes, seemed rather low down for their eyes. Matt fished out his bent binoculars, which were now barely functional after makeshift repairs back at the Palace of Little Balkieston. Wink had his vision band on around his swooth to view the city close-up.

"That's not deep purple sky beyond the green horizon," said Matt. It looks like a sea. A glassy calm one at that."

"Your right," said Yesl. "The train will go no further." As everyone looked down, they could see that the necklace of balls was now divided up into groups of five or six ball-cars shunted into sidings for loading up or maintenance. The ocean ahead of them did not seem broad. They could see an opposite shore lined with high cliffs surmounted by a few rock pinnacles, looking like a greyish violet slab of rock sitting on the flat calm purple-colored sea.

"So, where to from here?" asked Zozl. "We'd have to fly on up north closer to the frozen wastes of what you would call the Arctic Circle. We call it the Mollkullis Circle. Further north from here, our swooth would certainly freeze up if we got wet, and we'd be badly oblated, and I don't think that you Tombalkiens would fare much better."

"Then there's only one alternative," said Kloonket. "We have to cross over to Beekica, the continent on the other side. We'll camp here tonight and leave early next morning by the back of these hills up that valley to avoid being seen. Zinkel-Mallkis' forces will catch up with us sooner or later if we tarry too long."

Matt could feel the soft touch of a Balkien. Droplets of water chilled the rest of his body. Yesl was sitting next to his head. He lay on the soft moss, which was wet with morning dew. Vega had risen above the far distant cliffs to the East across the alien turquoise ocean. His companions were up and talking over a breakfast of light green pieces of fruits from their supplies and drinks of water.

"Oh, Matt, wakey, wakey, rise and shine!" hollered Sean. Matt stirred slowly and arose to join them.

"We've to get airborne," said Kloonket.

Soon everyone was atop the Antrogians and airborne, heading up the steep valley between two massive tall peaks of grey rocks and patches of light green mosses. With their loud warbling echoing off the sides of the mountain spires, they inched their way up the gorge and down the other side. They flew low over the shoreline and out across the dark purple glassy sea. Soon the shore of the continent they'd traveled across for more than a week was just a distant line of hills on the horizon behind them. The tall rock spires they'd labored over were now small needles sticking up out of the distant sea horizon. They looked ahead only to perceive that the far shore seemed to be no nearer than when they'd started. Boolboonkle and the other Antrogians battered on across what now seemed a never-ending stretch of water. The cliffs on the other side seemed to grow higher but never lost their distant violet haze. Everyone grew anxious about the Antrogians tiring out with nowhere to land and rest.

"This stretch of sea is never-ending," said Matt. "We should have landed by now."

"Those cliffs seem ever to be so far away," said Alison with concern in her voice."

"Don't worry," said King Zozl reassuringly.

However, they flew on until the Vega was getting low in the western sky. The cliffs looked a lot higher and were much brighter and showed a greenish color, reflecting the evening Vega.

"Zonkollus is tiring out," said Kloonket. "We're not all going to make it to land. Boolboonkle, go over and hold onto Zonkollus."

Boolboonkle flew towards Zonkollus and held onto him. Judith clambered over onto Boolboonkle to relieve him of his load, but he still faltered.

"I need to rest," he said in his deep Antrogian voice. The cliffs still seemed far away.

"This is becoming a nightmare," said Kaz in desperation. "I've climbed Mt Tetraval and experienced seemingly endless false summits, but this is uncanny."

Vega had set, and it was turning to dusk.

"Zonkollus," said Kloonket. "The water's still calm. Can you land on the water and float on it using a little kinetic force to repel the water from your swooth? I suggest we all do this and cling to one another in ponkadliath, floating on the surface for the night."

The group of Antrogians lost speed and hovered lower towards the dark purple water, reflecting the stars that were now popping out. Suddenly the deep warbling stopped. Everyone could sense singing in their ears after a much longer than expected journey. There was almost no breath of wind and silence, except for the whispering lapping of water around the large floating Antrogians on which everyone was seated. Sean lay on his stomach on Spalkius and looked over his swooth into the deep calm water. It was not at all black. Not only could he see the reflected stars, but he could make out strange glowing shapes in the water. On looking closer, he could make out iridescent globular things floating in the depths. He was both fearful and in wonderment at the sight.

"There seem to be glowing apparitions in the water," said Sean to Wink.

"Oh those," said Wink. "Like your oceans on Earth, ours teem with life. You'll see all sorts. We have strange fish in these seas a bit like your jellyfish. Only they're often a lot larger and can live in great depths. Most creatures in our seas glow in the dark as some of yours do."

Matt looked up into the starry sky with the splash of the Milky Way Galaxy.

The bright reflection of Antrogi was no longer above the horizon for they had traveled to the side of the planet away from its double companion.

"Boodibah!" exclaimed Baingae in excitement. "There's Balkle, my home moon, now after the first quarter."

"I'd love to come and visit your world, Baingae," said Judith as she held Baingae in her hands.

As everyone lay down across the warm, comfortable swooth of their Antrogians, Matt noticed that the water was brightening to a shimmering pink color. He looked up, expecting to see the light in the sky. There was none. The water began to stir noticeably. Everyone felt movement. The Antrogians began to drift apart and quickly held each other more tightly. The pink iridescence became stronger. Suddenly the water washed away, and all six of them found themselves sitting on a smooth rubbery surface, slightly curved like a floating island, glowing with its pink iridescence. The water, which lapped upon its sides, began to flow past at a quick rate.

"This is one of Antrobi's great sea creatures," said King Zozl. "This one's immense. Look. It's started swimming toward our destination. He'll not even notice all of us sitting on him."

"He must be far larger than our whales," said Matt.

"And much more like a giant jellyfish," said Yesl.

"See. We're making some progress towards the cliffs," said Wink. The cliffs were illuminated in Balkle-light, like Moonlight. "I think the Great Spirit of Antrobi must be looking out for us," continued Wink. He's sent the jellyfish to assist us in our quest to rid Antrobi of this evil. Sleep quickly fell on everyone, brought on by the gentle movements of their great rescuer. It swam in a manner that was a cross between an octopus and a dolphin.

The cliffs were at last close by mid-morning. Vega was well behind the wall of rock that confronted them.

"These cliffs are extremely high," said Matt. "They look to be almost as tall as Everest."

"These are the greatest cliffs on all of Antrobi," said Zozl. "They are called the Cliffs of Yazzalathia. In your measurement, I'd say they were about five or six kilometers high."

At the base of the cliffs, there was a narrow stony beach. They could hear the dull sound of the small swell washing up over the stones while still sitting on the bright pink rubbery surface a little way out.

"I don't think that our host can take us in any further," said Kloonket. The quiet scene was soon filled with the crescendo of the Antrogians lifting off from the magnificent sea creature and flying the short distance to the shore. The warbles reverberated from off the cliffs all around them. As Boolboonkle hovered away, Matt looked behind to see the gigantic globular bright pink shape in the water. Behind it, there were long flipper-like fins. To its front, there were a few dark blue spots like eyes. Soon they had alighted on the large rounded pebbles and rounded boulders. They were composed of sandstones of various shades of cream to brown, reflecting the colors of the rocks in the cliffs.

"On dry land at last," gasped Matt.

"That was much further than we thought," sighed Kara.

"When the air is so clear, distances can be so deceptive," said Sean. Everyone fell asleep knowing that they were safe on solid ground. As Alison dozed off, she could see the pink jellyfish-like creature heave around in the water and then swim out and disappear. She was so thankful that this creature had come to save them thinking, *'Maybe there are good spiritual influences on this planet helping us in our struggle.'*

Dr. Baingae was busy hovering all over Zoozonkle's swooth carrying out a thorough diagnosis on him who showed the beginning signs of oblateness. The earthlings all sat on the shingle cross-legged leaning against the soft swooth of Boolboonkle facing out to the sea. A sea breeze started to come in, making the waters rough looking with small waves lapping on the beach. The rest of the Balkiens were sitting around in a circle for an impromptu meeting.

"There's one thing for sure," said Kaz. "It'll take a lot for Zinkel-Mallkis' forces to cross such a huge moat."

"Don't be too sure," said Kloonket. "They're all over the planet."

"Just how are we to bring an end to this evil regime and to overpower Zinkel-Mallkis?" asked Matt. "Didn't we come here to do just that?"

"Not so simple," said Kloonket. "King Zozl and Queen Mozl will now fill you on the rest."

"For a start," began Zozl, "we have lost our base of operations, that being Little Balkieston, which was sacked by the Hellacks a few days ago. They're going to be a fearful and menacing army that we'll have to fight. What army have we got?"

Everyone looked around at one another. Matt cast his eyes on Kaz, first, then to the others, and cuddled Yesl.

"Seems that there's only us," said Kara.

"So how about we go in and march on Balkieston with about twenty of us throwing rocks against a mighty force of about three million Hellacks all spraying us with flashes of green lightning?" asked Zozl. "It would be a lot easier for Boolboonkle, here, to fly through that crevice over there." Everyone turned to look at a small crack in the cliff face.

"That's the size of it," said Kloonket. "There has to be another way. We'll need to raise a great army."

"From where?" asked Sean.

"Balkiens, of course," replied Kloonket. "We need to educate all the population who has been duped into believing that Zinkel-Mallkis is a demi-god who had to be obeyed and I have to say WORSHIPPED! Right now, he's re-educating all of the masses with his version of Antrobian history. They are erasing all knowledge of you Zozl and Mozl as the heirs to the throne from the thinking swooth of all of us. The mooties that held all our knowledge and treasures in Balkieston and elsewhere have been systematically blown up or burned down. We had one night of pillaging and destruction by the Hellacks who came in force, spraying the Main Library, as you call it, with green lightning, setting it alight. It contained all the annals of Antrobian history. Alas, the fire raged for about a day, destroying all archives within. The Temple to the Great Spirit of the Balkiens, which you all saw in Balkieston, was badly looted of its treasured archives. Being a former Temple Custodian after my time on the railways, I saw this coming after the disaster at the Main Library. So, I copied all the digital records onto several data spheres, making four copies in all. Two of these sets were in Little Balkieston."

"So those may now be gone too," sighed Matt.

"Not so," said Zozl. "Remember we were all but packed up and ready to fly off, just as the attack came. Mozl; bring those blue pouches, I told you to get as we left."

Mozl hovered up to Zoozonkle's panniers, slung over his swooth. She returned with two blue cloth bags. Wink and Mwaki hovered over the bags and to each of them, gravitated five silver data spheres about the size of tennis balls.

"In these," continued Zozl, "maybe the only two remaining copies of all of Antrobi's true history. Where the other two copies are, I don't know. Zinkel-Mallkis is systematically rewriting Antrobi's history, one full of LIES and deception." His voice became raised and agitated. "If this situation continues for much longer, Antrobi as we once knew it would be beyond redemption and, at best, we will become refugees wandering endlessly through the universe in the Splinkatrix until her fuel runs out. And maybe you Tombalkiens will be joining us if Tombalki succumbs to the evil menace too. We have to DO SOMETHING NOW! Our last remaining bastion of hope in Little Balkieston may now have gone up in smoke or worse still is being plundered by the Hellacks with all of our secrets being hacked into and handed over to Zinkel-Mallkis on a golden platter."

"Somehow, we have to tell the Balkien population that this evil leader has brainwashed them," said Alison.

"Brainwashed; did you say?" asked Matt. "If you Balkiens have minds that are in any way similar to ours as Tombalkiens, it'll be tough to convince the masses that they've been conned."

"Listen," said Mwaki. "This issue is far greater than the works of Zinkel-Mallkis. Our planets, Antrobi and Antrogi, have been invaded by the Enigma coming either directly or via Tombalki from Splogita. Remember that most of Splogita was destroyed in a terrible cataclysm or warfare, and something similar is now happening to us."

Kloonket's blue swooth nodded towards each of the six Tombalkiens. "And when the Enigma's finished with us Balkiens, it'll be you next."

"We already have suffered thousands of years of evil on our planet," said Judith.

"But were your cities totally destroyed?" asked Zozl.

The Tombalkiens looked around at one another.

"A few," said Sean.

"But not the whole planet," said Kloonket. "You in your history have a good taste of what is to come."

"Oh, it'd be terrible if this beautiful world with such lovely beings and our friendly giant jellyfish were to end up like Splogita," wept Judith. Alison placed arms around Judith and Kaz. Matt, Kara, and Sean joined in, forming a human ponkadliath. All the Balkiens joined them in a warm fuzzy ponkadliath on that lonely stony beach. The small waves gently lapped on the shingle. The Vega was getting low in the western sky.

"Looks like we're stopping here for the night," said Zozl, "time for a good hearty meal of broccoli fruit and those gorgeous purple fruits full of that delicious juice. Those are called 'sesles' from 'sesle' trees. Some of us picked them from the forest after we got off the ball-train before we flew over here."

"Tomorrow we'll have to tackle those five-kilometer-high cliffs," said Kloonket.

It was a chilly morning under subdued light, for the Vega was well behind the austere cliffs, which towered vertically above them, covering the eastern half of the sky with their dark overbearing countenance.

"I can still just see Spalminkatrix to the west," said Wink.

Everyone looked up to see the brightest object pointed out as the Vegan System's most giant planet. The Tombalkiens enjoyed a refreshing swim, before their ascent up the cliffs. Matt and Kaz swam around in the pleasantly fresh crystal-clear water catching their breath every minute or so.

"Kaz," called Matt as he stood up in the water in his bathers. "I could swear that I could see iridescent colorful things deep in the water far offshore."

"Maybe it's more of those jellyfish," said Kaz.

Kloonket, Wink, and Mwaki hovered above the frolicking youths, who were having the most fabulous fun since arriving on the Purple Planet.

"I'd be careful not to stay in too long," said Mwaki, "there are lots of strange creatures in the ocean. They may have been friendly in earlier times like our jellyfish savior last night, but I'm not too sure now."

Just then the waters began to get agitated.

"Everyone out," called Sean. "I don't like the look of these bubbles."

Everyone waded out, except for Alison who had swum too far out beyond the far side of the bubbling waters.

"They're sea hackels," called Kloonket. "Alison's out of her depth. She'll be bitten badly."

Alison started screaming, "Boolboonkle!"

There was a sudden loud warbling and downdraft as Boolboonkle took off and swooped down over Alison and wrenched her out of the water to his under swooth and flew her to shore. Several things that looked like pear-shaped yellow fish dropped off his swooth and Alison's foot back into the water. She was laid down gently on the beach.

"Alison. Are you all right?" asked Matt.

"Not really," she said. "Oh, my foot. It's so sore and throbbing." There was some blood around a deep bite on her ankle. Kloonket flew to look. Dr. Baingae immediately joined him.

"I've got to make a diagnosis on your foot," he said, being true to his form.

Baingae looked her over. "Alison had just been penetrated by the hackel's teeth, as she was wrenched out by Boolboonkle."

Matt took a bandage from the medical kit.

"Just as well you brought your bandages," said Baingae. "Our medical kits are only suitable for us, Balkiens."

Everyone quickly dried off and got dressed. All their belongings and supplies were loaded, being careful not to leave anything behind in case their trail should be detected. Excess fresh water had to be jettisoned from the bottles to lighten the load for the ascent up the cliffs.

"All aboard," announced Kloonket as everyone looked around.

"Okay," said Matt.

"Affirmative," called Zozl.

"Then up we go," called Kloonket.

The Antrogians started to warble at once. Their downdraft sent rough ripples across the otherwise calm waters. Soon the beach was far below. The cliff face drifted down past them. After climbing nearly four kilometers, the going started getting slower. They flew a little out from the cliff face and continued the ascent in a circular motion as if flying around and up to an imaginary spiral staircase. From farther out, they could see the cliffs sloping back covered by creeping vegetation growing down from the top in long light green tendrils. Boolboonkle and Zoozonkle continued their ascent, but the rest reached maximum altitude not that far from the summit. The ocean below was now a purple haze with a soft misty horizon.

"This ascent is almost as bad as our ocean crossing," said Matt."

"We're so near," said Zozl. "Let those Antrogians that make it, land, drop off their passengers, loads, and fly down to assist the others."

Boolboonkle finally rose above the top of the cliff. Vega was shining on a vast plain of green grasses and dark green mosses. In the far eastern horizon, there were ranges of light purple mountains. White cloud tops were above some of the taller peaks. There were isolated bulbous tree-like succulent plants. Each branch looked like a bright green toadstool. Boolboonkle and Zoozonkle landed on a clearing far enough from the cliff edge for safety. Matt, Kaz, and the Winkets quickly removed the equipment and food. Boolboonkle and Zoozonkle took off and dropped down over the cliff edge to assist the others. After an anxious fifteen minutes, all six of them hovered in over the precipice and landed. All became silent once again.

"That cliff would be great for base jumping," said Matt.

"Base jumping," said Kara. "It's a wonderful idea but not worth doing the ascent again. The Antrogians must be exhausted. The air's thin up here."

Everyone noticed their shortness of breath.

"We'll have to load up again and fly on as best we can, hoping to reach the lower ground to the east," said Kloonket. "It's a long way over this plain, but it does get lower."

"Oh, I'm still so dizzy!" groaned Alison.

"Oh, Alison," said Judith. "Are you okay?"

"No." Alison just managed to hobble over to lie down next to Zoozonkle.

Baingae flew up to her and did a further assessment on her bitten foot. "I fear that it must be venom in the bite from the hackel. We've never known these creatures to bite like this. What would they do to our swooth? She'll need to get an antidote for the venom and soon."

● ○ ●

17 ~ ENTRANCE TO THE UNDERWORLD

Matt applied antiseptic cream onto Alison's injury while replacing her bandage. She looked very pale and was losing her strength. Everyone was worried about her, especially in the thin air. The sky was noticeably darker. It was possible to see the odd star in broad daylight.

"What can we do for our sister?" asked Judith. "I wish we'd know about the hackels before we went into the water. It was so invigorating, and we desperately needed to wash."

"There's no use in having a litany of regrets," said Kaz. "We've got to get that antidote to Alison quickly."

"But, there's no hospital or drug store way out here," cried Kara.

"That may be the case," said Baingae. "Boodibah. Let me think. Yes. I think I know where to go. Where to go? Ah yes. Not too far to the east of here, there's a great entrance to an underground cave system. Yes. There's where we can find the special plant that has the antidote to the hackel's poison. I know for sure that this will work on us Balkiens, but on you, Tombalkiens, it's a new experiment."

"Then let's pack up and head over right away, experiment or not," said Kaz. "Alison's almost passed out now. She's still breathing, but her pulse is weak. We've no alternative but to try this treatment."

"So off we go to the caves for Alison we have to care. C'mon little Winkets," said Wink.

"We're heading to a huge cavern entrance, the largest on Antrobi," said Mwaki. "It's sometimes known as the Entrance to the Underworld. There's been many a tale and legend of Balkiens exploring in there and never being seen or heard of again. We've heard of one such unfortunate legend of a great one called Boonkihara who entered these caves many years ago. Boonkihara was a great colorful large Balkien who loved his subjects and was a wise old sage. Alas, he was never seen again. The whole community went into great mourning for about ten Antrobian years, for he was one of those who went on that first-ever mission to Tombalki."

As Wink continued relating this sad saga, everyone was soon airborne. Alison was stretched out on Zoozonkle. After flying away from the cliffs inland the exotic vegetation all but disappeared. There was nothing but desert, resembling that on Mars more than anywhere else on Antrobi. There was a sense of slowly descending across the featureless dirt-colored stony terrain.

"Kloonket," said Matt. "Look over to your left. I can see something dark over there."

After flying for another half an hour, Zoozonkle began to get exhausted again and began to waver while struggling with poor Alison still on top of him. They came to another cliff edge and there before them, was a deep canyon that stretched far into a bright green horizon.

"If we go down in there," said Kara, "it'll get warmer, and the air will be thicker for us."

"We'll have to land here just back from the edge to relieve Zoozonkle of Alison, and see how she is doing," said Kloonket.

After landing, a light but chilly wind was whistling in everyone's ears. On the far side of the canyon, there were layers of sandstone in a variety of earthen colors.

"This is so uncanny," said Matt. "I honestly wish that I could walk behind that ridge and find my car in the car park and drive back to Tucson to see Erin. It's so like the Grand Canyon. But wait a minute. The sky's purple and the sun, err Vega, is bluer, smaller and oblate. Let's see to Alison."

Alison groaned, as Zoozonkle gently lowered her to the ground.

Dr. Baingae hovered over to assess her. "Boodibah; she's still breathing and has a pulse, but we've got to get her to those caves."

"I vote that we descend into the canyon and out of this ghastly desert," said Matt. "Look, there's vegetation and a small river down there where we'll get food and replace out jettisoned water."

"The Antrogians are tired," said Wink, "but we'll convince them to go down to yonder green clearing down there."

Alison was telekinetically pulled up onto Boolboonkle. They slowly managed to hover just far enough off the ground to fly over the cliff edge. The sides of the gorge dropped away suddenly. It was much easier for the Antrogians to make a rapid but controlled descent. The humans had to swallow often for their ears. The air became warmer. Breathing became less of an effort. Vega became less hot and burning. Everyone noticed that they had got quite badly Vega burnt while being at high altitude.

"Our SP30 sun cream supply is now low," commented Kaz as he rubbed more into his Vega burnt hands and face. The light green, inviting meadow rushed up to meet them looking like an oversized golf putting green. The tall thin tree in the center looked like the flagpole, which had large dark green leaves dangling from near its tip flapping in the light breeze.

Everyone got off their Antrogians and flopped onto its abundant vegetation. The cliffs towered up into the now lighter purple sky. Alison had more color in her cheeks but was still barely conscious.

"This is where we'll have to pitch for the night," said Kloonket. "Our Antrogian friends have had enough today. Baingae assures me that she'll be okay until tomorrow, but unless she gets these cave-dwelling plants to eat, she'll take a long time to recover. Those hackels seem to have got much more poisonous now."

The golden evening turned into a brilliantly star-studded night. They were no longer in sight of Antrogi, making this their darkest night since they arrived on Antrobi. Though it was great to look at the stars and the Milky Way, it was difficult to see where they were, except for the very faint moonlight from Antrobi's farthest moon, Boonkpolm, in the first quarter. Matt managed to use his damaged binoculars to look up at Sol (the Sun), so faint and distant. He thought of Erin and dreamed of being with her. Baingae was on his shoulder, remembering his longing to see Winxl while they were with Uncle Herbert and Auntie Wendy on Baraignsay. Matt felt the weight of the great distance separating him and his siblings from Earth.

When Matt awoke, Vega was rising above the far cliffs. Kaz and Sean were carrying back water refilled containers from the stream. Alison was sitting up and quite lucid. She still could not walk with her badly swollen ankle.

"Oh," she groaned. "I think, I'll throw up any good food I have eaten if I even climb up on to Zoozonkle, let alone fly. Don't worry Zoozonkle. It's not your flying. It's just me. Here is a lovely place. I so wish I wasn't so sick."

"Alison may seem a bit better," said Dr. Baingae but the foot swelling's getting worse. We have to get to those caves for her antidote."

"I have an idea," said Kloonket. "Why don't some of us go to the caves and bring back the medicine to Alison? There are enough of us to do this. I suggest that Baingae stays with Alison and that Matt, Yesl, Boongoo, the Winkets, and I go on Boolboonkle to the cave entrance, which I reckon is not too far from here."

"Don't worry Alison," said Matt. "We'll be back a lot quicker if only some of us go and we don't have to pack up all of this kit and caboodle. In case anything should happen, I think that Zonkollus should come too."

Matt climbed onto Boolboonkle along with Yesl and the Winkets. Kloonket and Boongoo went with Zonkollus. They started warbling, and quickly rose off the golden-green meadow and headed down the valley, carefully noting where the campsite was in relation to the cliffs around it. The gorge got narrower and darker as they progressed then opened out into a broad plain where there were areas of forest and isolated bushes surrounded by cliffs and rocky outcrops. There was a dark opening near the center with a mistiness hanging over it.

"Kloonket," said Matt. "What's that dark opening?" Shivers began to run down Matt's spine. He cuddled Yesl, who was very reassuring. Something was foreboding about this place. The magic essence of the planet changed markedly. The sky grew darker. Vega became greener with the mist emanating from this shaded area. As they hovered closer, they came to the edge of a bottomless pit, about a kilometer wide.

"This is indeed the 'Entrance to the Underworld'," said Wink. "That name is our best translation of it into your language, Matt, for we don't exactly know what is down there. This may be more extensive than any cave system we learned about on Tombalki. It is west of Antrobi's main city on this continent of Beekica called Balkiesville in your tongue."

Boolboonkle and Zonkollus hovered just over the edge of the pit. The rocky sides descended into the inky darkness, their features getting fainter with depth and the failing light.

"So, is this the only place where we can find the antidote for Alison?" asked Matt.

"I'm afraid it is," replied Kloonket. "Looking into the darkness down there, it may be no wonder that poor old Boonkihara was never heard of again."

"I must say, that's very reassuring," said Matt.

"I'm sure we'll not have to go down that deep to find the mosses we're looking for," said Kloonket. "About half an Antrobian year ago, I had to go down there to get the antidote moss for Mozl, our beloved Queen, when she was attacked by one of these hackels not long after the arrival of the Enigma."

Before making the daunting descent, both Boolboonkle and Zonkollus landed on a rock ledge just below the rim of Antrobi's terrible secret. There was silence except for a mild upward draught blowing on Matt's ears. Looking down into the darkness was now ever more foreboding. Matt's heart began to beat a little faster.

"Let's roll!" exclaimed Matt.

Boolboonkle and Zonkollus began to warble and lifted off from the ledge over the hole and began to hover lower down into the abyss. As they dropped down, the circular entrance began to shrink and looked like a purple circle of light way above them continuously shrinking. The rocks on every side got dimmer. Matt turned on his torch.

"There's some of that fungus growth on those moist rocks over there," shouted Kloonket above the warbles of the Antrogians, which reverberated off the shaft walls and down into the total blackness below them. Boolboonkle hovered over to the rock face. "Matt, can you pull as much of it off as possible? Your hands can do it more easily than us Balkiens can."

As Boolboonkle hovered against the rock face, Matt wrenched off a mass of the fungus-like moss that was all over the rocks.

"Let's turn for home," said Kloonket.

With the slimy mass now on top of Boolboonkle, they began their ascent up to the light. It grew larger and lighter but ever so slowly. It took what seemed like an eternity to lift their heavy swooth towards the opening, way above them. Both Boolboonkle and Zonkollus noticed that their swooth was very damp, making them heavier.

"We're struggling to get up," boomed Boolboonkle. "That mist's soaking into our swooth."

"It's getting to me too," said Zonkollus. As they kept hovering with all of their strength, they noticed that the rocks were going past them ever so slowly, but in an upward direction. The purple circular aperture got smaller again.

"This is frightening and claustrophobic," said Kloonket. "Winkets! Take this antidote fungus for Alison by yourselves and fly back and tell the others what's happening. Hurry!"

Wink and Mwaki pulled the mosses towards their swooth and flew off up the cavern, though their swooth was also getting damp. Matt, Yesl, and Kloonket looked up to see the two black dots moving around the purple circular entrance until they disappeared out to one side, showing they had exited. For the Antrogians, their descent continued down. Soon the hole to the sky above them was tiny. Then they felt Boolboonkle nudge into the rock walls. The shaft curved a little, and their small purple window to the sanctuary above had vanished, closing them in. Except for Matt's torch and the spherical lighting devices that the Balkiens had, there was utter darkness. Suddenly the rock face lit up by the torchlight fell away.

"Maybe a ledge," said Kloonket. "Let's land.

Boolboonkle and Zonkollus flew into a side cave and landed. They stopped warbling immediately. Their sounds continued to echo down the shaft for several minutes. Even after about five minutes, Matt could still hear the very faint echoing of Boolboonkle. Or was it just Boolboonkle's echo from the far depths? Matt could sense that the distant warble sounded a little different in tone to Boolboonkle or Zonkollus. Though this was a dark world to human eyes, the Balkiens were able to see more into the infrared and ultraviolet ends of the spectrum.

After being in darkness for half an hour, Matt turned off his torch to save the batteries. He began to see a faint iridescence all over the cave walls. Matt looked over Boolboonkle's swooth, and over the edge of the ledge, they were on. He could see the sides of the shaft descending at a 45-degree angle. There were, what seemed like streamers colored iridescent blue and purple glowing faintly.

"I think that iridescence you see is from these creeper things that the Winkets have taken back to Alison," said Yesl.

"Looks like we're trapped in here," said Matt with a worried tone.

"I'm sure that the Winkets will be able to find us with the assistance of the others."

Then they could hear some more distant warbling that sounded more like Antrobians but far too deep a tone for it to come from either of the Winkets.

Kaz and Sean began to set up a rudimentary camp on the lush green moss-covered clearing, surrounded by an assortment of conifer-like trees with long broad dark leaves. Judith was sitting next to Alison. Baingae was monitoring her bodily signs by listening to her heart and breathing through her chest. Kara was assisting Kaz and Sean in cutting down leaves growing from the thick light green trunks. The edges of these large leaves were studded with small orange bulbs the size of peas. The ground beneath these trees was covered with those seeds. The leaves were tied together by fraying the edges into stringy strands that were tied through holes, punctured in the leaves to pitch rounded tents.

Kaz looked up as he heard a distant warbling sound. Judith turned around. "It's only the Winkets, I think. Maybe the Antrogians are not far behind."

The Winkets landed next to King Zozl. Wink and Mwaki were wet with the mosses on top of them. Baingae flew over to them.

"Boodibah," he said. "This should help Alison. Get some water. We'll mix this into a stew and give it to her."

The moss was mashed up and stirred into the water in a golden bowl, unpacked from their supplies brought from Little Balkieston. Alison could barely eat much of this medicinal stew at first.

"Where are the others?" asked Zozl.

"It's not too good," said Wink.

"How do you mean?"

"I'm afraid they're trapped in the cave system and couldn't fly out; neither Boolboonkle nor Zonkollus. Matt, Yesl, Kloonket, and Boongoo are with them. Kloonket sent us back with Alison's medicine."

"Winkets," said Zozl. "We'll get them out. We'll have to send out a search party. Let me think about what to do."

"We had to fly down much deeper than we thought to fetch this."

"The Entrance to the Underworld?" asked Zozl.

"Yes," said Wink. "It was very humid in there, and it seemed that the Antrogians' swooth got soaked very quickly and they became too heavy to rise out of there because of their much greater size. As we came out of the pit, we saw that their faint shapes disappeared around a bend deep down."

"Oh, there was also this extraordinary but beautiful aroma rising out of there," added Mwaki.

Baingae flew over from Alison and examined the smells and aromas around both the Winkets, who were also damp but drying out in the Vega shine.

"That smell's familiar. I've smelt it before," said Baingae. "Now, where and when was that? Wait a minute. Splogita! That aroma reminds me very much of the Molktrons. You reek of it, Winkets."

Wink tried to hover over to Alison but could not get up enough strength to get off the ground, though he'd managed to fly out of the cave system.

"Get some water and wash the Winkets down," said Baingae. "I'm convinced it's that strange essence that the Molktrons generated by rubbing the vegetation to cause us to be wugged away from being ensnared by the Enigma that is affecting them more. But how is it here; on Antrobi?"

Sean and Kaz dipped each of the Winkets in the golden bowl they had used earlier now filled with water from the nearby stream to wash out of them all the remnants of the mosses.

"Alison's foot is a lot less swollen," said Judith. "She's looking a lot better."

Baingae flew over to do another assessment on her by sensing her pulse, especially in her foot, and to the sound of her breathing on her chest.

"Boodibah, her vital signs look good. I think the antidote's working; never tried on Tombalkiens before. Boodibah. Great success! Oh yes. Her color's coming back."

Alison reached up to stroke the little earthen colored Balkien.

"Oh, I'm feeling the best since that awful bite. Thank you, Dr. Baingae." Wink, who was now cleaned up with his strength coming back, hovered over to Alison. "And you, too, Winkets, thank you."

"Alison," said Wink. "We now have another problem."

"What's that?"

"Boolboonkle, Zonkollus, Matt, Kloonket, Yesl, and Boongoo are lost down in the caverns. They were not able to get out. So, we had to come back ourselves with this antidote.

"Oh, dear; I'm so sorry that I've caused us so much trouble. What can we do?"

Blackness had given way to a vast dimly lit cavern. The tiny dark blue, glowing mosses that grew in these caverns generated the light. The air was humid yet had a distinctly rich scented aroma. The outlines of the cave walls could be made out by the fluorescence from the mosses. He looked along a narrow ledge leading to the right of the entrance they were resting in. He noticed a large group of tiny glowing spherical creatures. They were the size of large marbles and gently rolled along the rocky ground towards them.

"Yesl," he said. "Look over there. What are those creatures? Are they native to these caves?"

Yesl hovered to have a look. "Matt. If I'm not mistaken, these look strikingly familiar, yet out of place. Molktrons! We've never had them on Antrobi before as far as I know. Not even here."

Kloonket hovered over to have a closer look. There were several lines of these glowing spheroids rolling along in the mosses. They quickly moved up from the ledge and further down into the side cave where they had landed. Yesl and Boongoo followed them down into a narrow and winding passage that Matt could just climb down into, watching where he put his hands and knees so as not to tread on the Molktrons. Kloonket, Yesl, and Boongoo hovered down with him. The sloping passage was glowing with the blue creepers on its walls and the cave floor. Some parts were very narrow, where Matt could only just squeeze through.

"This is true spelunking," said Matt as he got his hands and knees covered in the mosses on the cave floor as Kloonket, Yesl, and Boongoo hovered down the passage alongside him, all the while passing over lines of Molktrons moving up and down the passage. The narrow and twisted passage opened out into a large cave that glowed much more brightly. This light was not so much from the glowing creepers, but rather from two central orbs, which gave off light in many colors gently moving across their surfaces. One of these orbs was glowing white with darker grey circular spots moving around her surface while the other was an effervescent turquoise with similar purple spots. Yesl immediately recognized their high-pitched buzzing language from their meeting with them on Splogita. To be able to better explain to Matt, Yesl, and Boongoo translated their buzzing into English.

"Boongoo," said Yesl. They're greeting us warmly. They're so grateful to see us again. The Queen on the right knows of us who visited them on Splogita a very long time ago and to her seems to be far too long."

"Time, dilation, I suspect. Remember; the lightning strikes damaged the Balkieston's anti-time dilation device on our departure."

The buzzing continued to emanate from both the Molktron Queens.

"They're saying that, not long after we had departed," said Yesl, translating, "some dreadful metallic spheres hovered around through the woods on Splogita striking lightning all-around burning a lot of their beautiful forests. These evil things hovered around our wrecked ship as we watched from a safe distance in the vegetation. Using robotic-like grabbers that protruded from their undersides, they reached into the wreckage, rummaged around, and took away about three of your silver spheres."

"Yesl; we left our calling card," said Boongoo in disbelief. "Those things are the same as the Hellacks we encountered at Little Balkieston that attacked us."

"They're saying that the Molktrons rolled into and around the wreckage to find and retrieve any remaining data spheres before the Hellacks returned for them. While the Molktrons were inside the wreck, a giant flying machine hovered over the hulk and sucked it up into its cargo hold with them trapped inside. They were brought before the Enigma, who they describe as some form of dazzling but ugly jarring energy force, which spoke in a deep thunderous buzzing voice in their language.

"To cut a long story short, three hives with many thousands of Molktrons were raided and forcibly brought to Antrobi in several spacecraft built by the Enigma's forces consisting mainly of these Hellacks. They were then brought into these deep caverns and enslaved into the service of the Enigma. The ones in here escaped from their prison hive chambers after a small antrobiquake (earthquake) in which cracks wide enough to allow then and the two Queens here to roll out. It took them a long time to roll up to this present cave. I reckon about half an Antrobian year. They fed on these creepers by absorption.

"Also, they're saying that the plant species that emitted that strange gas that caused our drowsiness on our first arrival on Splogita has been inadvertently spread to this cave system by the invasion of the Enigma."

"That'll be why Boolboonkle and Zonkollus lost their strength and couldn't fly out of the Entrance to the Underworld," said Boongoo.

"These Molktrons say that they stirred up the gas to stop us from flying down into a possible trap," said Yesl. "Terrible things are going on down there where, they say, there are millions of us Balkiens enslaved. The gas should by now have dispersed. They're telling us to go back to our Antrogian companions and fly up out of here immediately lest we're caught."

"Now, I've finally seen the Molktrons," said Matt. "I never thought that I would."

Matt looked at Yesl in disbelief, while cuddling her. The sight of the two Molktron Queens was so amazing yet reassuringly familiar, for this is close to how Matt imagined them to appear though he had seen images on the data spheres brought from the wreckage on Tetraval.

"Boolboonkle, Zonkollus, Kloonket, Boongoo," said Yesl. "We'd better fly back up the shaft and join the others to talk to them about these developments."

"We've made arrangements to meet the Molktrons back here in a day or so on our way down to investigate," said Yesl. "Maybe this is our opening move to deal with this terrible thing."

"I suggest that you, Matt, sit on Boolboonkle," said Kloonket, "and after lift-off, Zonkollus comes up to push Boolboonkle up from underneath to assist with the ascent."

Matt felt a bit of vertigo as Boolboonkle started warbling loudly and eased out of the side cave over the main shaft. Zonkollus followed and came up underneath Boolboonkle.

The other Balkiens flew alongside them as escorts. Yesl and Boongoo's flight back up the passage to the others, dimly lit by the ever-present blue effervescent creepers was tedious. With the warbling sounds echoing all around them, they eased their way up until they could see daylight as they approached the mouth of the cave. It was twilight. Slowly they emerged from the nightmarish pit and leveled out on their way back to camp.

"Boy," said Matt. "I'm sure glad to get out of there, but I miss those delectable Molktrons."

"You may see them again, Matt," said Kloonket, "when we go for further exploration."

With the wind going through their swooth, Boolboonkle and Zonkollus became drier and lighter in weight. There was a bright green twilight above the silhouettes of the distant mountains. Zonkollus separated from Boolboonkle and landed. Alison leaped up and almost ran to greet Matt.

"Alison!" Matt exclaimed. "You're so well. Mission accomplished?"

"Oh yes," said Alison. "The antidote mosses worked well. I can't thank you enough for going down there."

"No worries," said Matt, "We just had a thrilling, terrifying at first, hazardous and adventurous spelunk and met some interesting new friends, whom you've all heard about."

"Friends, we've heard about?" asked Judith. "Who?"

"Guess," said Matt.

"Give us a clue," asked Sean.

"Think back to all of the stories about Splogita," answered Matt.

"Let me think," said Kara. "Ah, Molktrons!"

"You got it," exclaimed Matt.

The Molktrons!" said Judith. "How did they get to Antrobi?"

"And Alison," chuckled Baingae, "don't go getting stung by hackels again. Some of us were nearly wugged!"

Polpodwink and Spalkius, Judith's and Alison's Antrogians respectively, hovered over to have a warming ponkadliath with the veterans of the Entrance to The Underworld adventure, and they needed it in the cold night air.

Yesl related their adventures to everyone, while seated around a glowing campfire, which Kaz had managed to light with some dead leaf-like debris, which he and Sean had collected during the day. Though there were some flames and warmth, it smoldered and smoked a lot due to the dampness of the fuel.

"Oh, that smell so reminds me of the smoke from Auntie Wendy's stove in those days of cuddling your swooth at Uncle Herbert's, Yesl," said Matt. "Here we are on Antrobi, reminiscing about it."

"It's great to be able to reminisce," said Kloonket in a more serious tone. "We soon won't have any more reminiscing to do if Zinkel-Mallkis gets his way. Think of those poor slaves deep down beneath, who are our country Balkiens. There's a war on, and we've got to fight this evil menace. The Molktrons have revealed a lot to us. Alison, if that hackel hadn't bitten you, we might never have met those Molktrons and found all this out. We've got to go down there and do something, even if it's only to investigate."

As the embers died down, Kaz glanced over towards the Antrogians and noticed something. "Matt," he said. "Look over there."

"Molktrons!" exclaimed Matt. Yesl, Boongoo, and Baingae hovered over to the lower part of Boolboonkle's swooth to see. A few of the little Molktrons had penetrated just inside Boolboonkle's swooth without being felt by him, while he was sitting in the side cave. They started buzzing in their language. Everyone gathered around. "So those are the Molktrons," said Judith.

"Yes," said Matt.

"Ssh," hissed Yesl. "They're speaking. They say that they didn't realize that Boolboonkle was not part of the caves and that they're cold and getting too dry out here. Matt. Go and get some water and warm it up on the fire for them to keep warm during the night."

Everyone was beginning to shiver. It was time to wrap up in blankets and be in ponkadliaths.

Matt awoke from pleasant dreams or memories transmitted to him by Yesl of beautiful idyllic scenes where the colors of Antrobi seemed to make those in their immediate environment look distinctly dull and unimpressive. Such was the influence of the presence of the Enigma.

"Oh Yesl," sighed Matt as he stretched out his arms on awakening. "What a beautiful place this was."

"And so, it will be again," said Yesl. "We didn't fly the Splinkatrix twenty-five light-years from Tombalki just to sit here and lament the passing of our once beautiful planet and true world. We're going to try and transmit these memories to the slaves down below and lead them to an understanding of what has happened to them and to remember their past and win it back. Baingae thinks that they were brainwashed or worse still had their life memories tampered with."

The Vega was bright. The others awoke talking about the days ahead. Kloonket and King Zozl called a briefing. Everyone from Tombalki sat cross-legged around the remnants of the campfire. The Balkiens deposited themselves with the Tombalkiens.

"Antrobians, Antrogians, Tombalkiens," began Kloonket. "We have reached a pivotal point in our quest to rid our once-great civilization of this tyranny that has befallen us. Beneath our swooth or our feet down in deep caverns, something unthinkable has happened. A great portion of our race was enraptured by promises of the betterment of this life with a promise of a great future under a bright shining being, known to our Tombalkien guests as the Enigma. Firstly, the Enigma brought these sayings to those on our sister planet, Antrogi, and appeared friendly to Antrogi's King, Zinkle-Mallkis. After a while, Zinkel-Mallkis was led to a twisted way of thinking and desired to conquer Antrobi. The result was that King Zozl is among us here in exile instead of being in his Palace in Balkieston, now illegally occupied by Zinkel-Mallkis."

The distant warbles of two Balkiens became audible. Kloonket paused in his speech, and everyone listened. Out of the bright violet sky, two greenish disks appeared. As they flew closer, they displayed zones of swooth in varying shades of green. Each of them was about the same size, twice that of Yesl.

"Quick," said Zozl. "We must hide."

"Too late," said Kloonket. "Prepare to fight if necessary."

The Antrogians immediately started to hover, and telekinetically grabbed the humans onto their swooth and took flight.

"Stop!" shouted Zozl. "These are our long-lost cousins, Mowika and Ponku."

Everyone landed and returned to their original positions.

Mowika and Ponku approached King Zozl and spoke in Antrobian.

"These two have just found their way out of these terrible caverns," said Zozl, translating. "They have been lost down there for about two Antrobian years. They went down there looking for me after I fled into exile. They got hopelessly lost and have lived on the creepers and the dampness since. They found their way out when they heard our flying down into the Entrance to The Underworld."

"That must have been the distant warbles we heard when we were stuck down there," said Matt.

"Tell them of our quest," said Kaz, "and our need to go back down into the caves."

Kloonket explained in Antrobian to Mowika and Ponku about the slaves in the caves. Mowika and Ponku talked back to them for a while.

"Mowika and Ponku," said Kloonket, "have a distant recollection of things going on down there, but for the most part have just been flying through an endless maze of catacombs to get out. It was frightening. But now that they are here, they're willing to obey their King and Master, Zozl."

"We're going down into the Entrance to The Underworld once more," said Kloonket. "It'll not be good for all of us to go, lest we get captured or something bad happens. We need volunteers."

Matt put up his hand. Slowly, Kara and Sean raised theirs. Yesl, the Winkets, and Kloonket nodded their swooth. Mowika and Ponku reluctantly volunteered to join them. Zozl, after careful consideration, was elected to join this mission.

"Good for you," said Kloonket. "We'll head off on Boolboonkle, Zonkollus, and Poolpoogleponk. I wish that Baingae could come with us, but he needs to oversee Alison's recovery."

Later that day, with the Molktrons, the chosen party flew back to that daunting pit into oblivion. As before, they began their descent into the dark mouth opening up, like the jaws of darkness in the otherwise pleasant light green Antrobian countryside. This time, the Antrogians' strength was unaffected by the Molktrons' stirring of the gases. Mowika and Ponku led the way down into the abyss while the skylight of the entrance grew more distant above them. Boolboonkle landed on the side cave they'd been on before to drop off the Molktron stowaways. As they rolled away to their respective Molktron Queens, they met with the other Molktrons, as arranged. The Queens gave directions in their learned Antrobian language.

All three Antrogians took off, and all continued down the angled shaft for about twenty minutes. The glowing blue creepers became brighter as they descended. Matt, Kara, and Sean had to keep swallowing as the air pressure increased. The warbling of the Antrogians echoed all around them off the cavern walls. The angle of the shaft became shallower and then widened out into a cavern. The fear of their surroundings soon gave way to glowing effervescent vegetation, now in many different colors. They could see crisscrossing tendrils of faintly glowing streamers all around. As the floor was now almost horizontal, all of them landed and stopped warbling. The echoes of their flying took about seven minutes to die away. The scene was like a bright starry night; only the glowing vegetation seemed to come up from a distance below them as well as above. Though the air was warmer, there was a draft coming in from the cavern.

"I think I can hear water ripples from over there," said Matt.

"Yes," said Yesl. "You're right."

A couple of minutes later, their words came back as distant echoes.

"Better speak in whispers," said Kloonket in a faint Balkien version of a whisper. From a distance, several low toned warbles were heard with echoing.

"Ssh!" hissed Sean. "Hellacks, I think."

Everyone looked up and saw a patrol of about twenty of them flying through the cavern, emitting sparks of lightning. These momentarily lit the roof of the massive cave, making it look about five-hundred meters high. Everyone noticed the flashes reflecting off the smooth surface of an underground lake. The Hellacks flew three or four circuits sparking more lightning before flying on to the far horizon of the lake.

"I think they've only been using their lightning as a torch to see their way down here," said Kloonket. "We could levitate across the water without warbling, using our telekinesis to float on it to make our way across."

The Balkiens and Antrogians started levitating across the shallow beach and over the calm water. There was no noise apart from rippling in the water. As they floated across the lake, they could see the roof of the cavern far above them, looking like the night sky painted in fluorescent blue acrylics on a black canvas. They floated for some way until there was a light breeze. They passed over small breaking waves and came to rest on a small beach close to rocks sticking up from the sand.

"We will rest here for what will pass for the night and then continue," said Kloonket softly.

Matt, Sean, and Kara made for themselves hollows in the soft dimly lit sand. They laid down, looked up at the glowing ceiling far above him looking like the night sky through strange thin cloud formations. Yesl cuddled up to him as Matt stroked her warm fuzzy swooth, which shimmered more. Perhaps it was because his eyes had dark-adapted to the faint glow of the creepers. The small waves from the lake lapped gently on the shore. There was a breeze blowing in off the water. As he nodded off, there was the occasional patrol of Hellacks, sparking lightning occasionally.

Matt awoke after a good sleep. Apart from his watch, reprogrammed to the slightly longer Antrobian day, it was hard to believe that it was morning for his other companions, Kaz, Alison, and Judith up on the surface. Thoughts of Erin entered his mind.

Zozl was talking with Mowika and Ponku in Antrobian. "Mowika and Ponku, you must know these caves very well."

"We do now," said Ponku. "We must have flown through this cavern many times. We tried all sorts of small passages up in the ceiling of this cavern, but they all led nowhere. We even tried to go up the giant cave to the other end of here but did not venture far enough up to see the daylight exit. We only knew to try it once more, when we heard all that deep warbling echoing down from there. Suspecting that these Antrogians maybe agents of Zinkel-Mallkis, we waited until it was quiet before we flew up to the surface, and there you all were."

"We're all crossbreeds between Antrobians and Antrogians," said Mowika.

"Yesl," said Matt. "Ask them about that ancient sage Boonki – ah, can't quite remember his name."

"Oh Boonkihara," said Zozl. Reverting to Antrobian, he asked Ponku.

"Boonkihara," said Ponku with a lower, slower sad sounding voice. "We met him down here not long after we got lost. We asked him to come with us, but his swooth was rather weak and noticeably oblate. You know he told us a lot of ancient legends. Many sayings were not yet recorded in Antrobian written history. He spoke of an ancient space mission to Tombalki, where they had a terrible experience with something dark and evil. That's all he could remember."

"Wait a minute," said Yesl. "We were on Tombalki after our return voyage from Splogita foundered. We went to see what they called the Devil's Marbles in Australia, a continent on that planet a bit smaller than Balkalay in our southern hemisphere. We found something buried there, which we dug up. It was a large data sphere that was brought back for examination. Only we had to leave in on our mother ship, far out past the orbit of Spalminkatrix."

"Where's Boonkihara now?" asked Zozl. "We've got to find and see if we can rescue him."

"Boonkihara was living in a small cave down that passage over yonder where the Hellacks were," said Mowika. "We left him, saying we'd go and find our way out and come back for him. That was over an Antrobian year ago. We never could go down that way again when the Hellacks appeared and started using the passage all the time. We've not seen him since. He also mentioned prophetic sayings of the Great Spirit. He was predicting that something terrible was going to come to our planet and bring pain and suffering to all Balkiens, on both planets. He even mentioned that bizarre alien beings would visit this world and assist us in some way. He also knew of these sayings long before the *Balkieston* was built let alone fly to Splogita. That was our last conversation before we were separated by the Hellacks in the only route we know to reach Boonkihara."

"Can't we just climb down there and sneak past the Hellacks?" asked Kara.

"Not a chance," said Zozl. "There's a narrow constrictive passage. If a Hellack were to come by, it'd be a better fate to crash into Vega and burn up."

"Likely, all of the slaves we've heard about are down beyond that opening," said Zozl.

"So, what'll we do?" said Matt. "It seems that all of this solid rock blocks our way."

"That warm air that has kept us sweating some of the night," said Sean. "It seems a lot warmer here than elsewhere in this cavern. There's a warm draft coming from over there. Let's take a look."

Mowika and Ponku levitated over towards the source of the warmth. Matt and Sean walked over behind them. They came to a gaping hole in the rock wall at the back of the dimly lit beach. A gentle draft blew on their faces. Sean and Matt walked in a little way. It was almost dark as the warm, dry air did not permit the growth of the illuminating creepers. There was a slightly pungent odor. As they wandered further in, Kara joined them with Yesl, Kloonket, the Winkets, and Zozl.

"Ssh!" hissed Matt. "Listen. I can hear something."

There was a faint regular rumble echoing from the darkness, not like the sound of thunder or an Antrobiquake. Further in still, there was a steady deep drone and the fading noise of metallic parts clattering together like industrial machinery.

"This may be our alternate route," said Kloonket. "We'll have to attempt it."

"What'll we do for light," said Matt. "My torch batteries are low. What about your light spheres, Kloonket?"

"Forget about the torches," said Yesl. "Any bright torches shone in here will be seen by the Hellacks. Why don't we grab some of the brightest glowing weed and wrap it around us?"

"Get some of the rope we brought from Earth out of Boolboonkle's pannier," said Matt. With his Swiss Army knife, Matt cleanly cut down some glowing creepers to wrap around everyone's body or swooth. Zozl stayed behind with the Antrogians who were too big to enter the dark, narrow, and foreboding orifice. Everyone ventured forth as the effervescently glowing Winkets levitating above the sand. For about half a mile the cave floor was reasonably level, but then it got uneven and slippery. Kara slipped and got her feet wet in a pool of water and nearly sprained her ankle. The disturbed pool suddenly effervesced, giving some more light as she climbed out.

"Got to be careful," said Wink. "Dr. Baingae is not with us to treat any injuries. We're on our own."

They found other pools of water. Stamping in them caused the glowing life forms to shimmer, giving more light. They could see long tendrils wafting in the clear waters of the pools. These were growing out from rounded anchorage points like limpet shells on rocks, similar to sea anemones. After about an hour of spelunking through the tunnel, the air got still warmer. All three humans began to sweat. They stopped for a moment to drink from the small round water flasks they had tied to their belts. The regular deep throbbing and thrashing sounds were louder. As soon as they resumed passage, they saw a faint red glow reflecting off the rocks ahead of them. On proceeding further, it got brighter. The passage widened out. The red light became bright enough to see clearly without the need for the glowing creeper branches.

"Could be a cavern with hot lava flowing," suggested Kara.

"It is a throbbing mechanical noise," said Kloonket.

They came to a ledge over which there was a steep rocky descent to the cave floor below.

"Looks like it is just as well we were in the Rock-Climbing Club at Arizona State," said Matt, "and that we all went to that rock climbing camp in Yellowstone National Park, the summer before we left Earth."

Matt tied the rope to solid rock at the edge of the cave. The first stages of the descent were not too hard for the three of them. After hooking up their abseiling tackle, all three of them, one at a time abseiled down the rock face to the next rock ledge. The Winkets retrieved the rope to retie it further down for the next abseil.

It was easy for the Balkiens who gravitated onto the rock and slowly rolled down, though the noise of flight would have been hardly audible above the industrial cacophony. Matt found hand and footholds on the hard, gritty rock with about ten meters to go when the rope ran out. Kara lost her grip with her left hand and was dangling only with her right hand.

"Ooh," she said. "I'm going to fall."

Mowika and Ponku rolled up to hold her from below. The Winkets positioned themselves under each of her arms. Without warbling, all four Balkiens lowered her to the ground with only a short warble to break their light fall. Sean made it down okay, as did Matt. Yesl untied the rope dropped it down and rolled down to join them. They walked a short distance further and emerged from the cave tunnel. The sight they saw was as grotesque as awe-inspiring. There was another colossal cavern in bright orange light. The throbbing and clattering noise of machinery was deafening. Throughout the chamber, there were mechanical installations that stood tall, like square or rounded gantries. Metallic arms were swinging to and fro like cranes lifting heavy metallic objects. Some of these looked like long girders. Some were metal panels that were triangular, pentagonal, or hexagonal and looked fantastic and energetic until one looked onto the shop floor of this factory. There were myriads of weakened hapless and oblated Balkiens. Some were so severely oblated that they looked like flattened round loaves of rye bread. Over in the far wall of this ghastly chamber of horrors, was a projection of Zinkel-Mallkis. They could hear what sounded like high-pitched music with a rapid beating sound with undulating high notes and was playing at a volume just above the noise of the machines.

"I can also hear propaganda lyrics in Antrobian in that music," said Kloonket loudly above the din. "These caves are now inhabited by zombie-like mind-possessed Balkiens who are in total enslavement to the Enigma and his evil ambitions! I'm appalled at their emaciated and severely oblate and disheveled swooth. The poor things look so unhappy but seem to swear absolute allegiance to their tyrannical ruler with what the lyrics of that music are saying. The chorus is singing, "He who must be obeyed, Zinkel-Mallkis, Zinkel-Mallkis, Zinkel-Mallkis.""

"They've all been brought down here to work endlessly in hiding from any who might observe these things from the surface," said Kloonket.

"I had heard of something like this from Boonkihara," said Ponku in Antrobian with Kloonket translating, "but I never realized that things are as ghastly as this."

"Any idea what they are making?" asked Matt.

"Not sure," said Wink. "They look like panels for buildings or maybe spacecraft?"

"Whatever it is," said Kloonket. "I'm sensing that they're all of one mind and one resolution. I can hear it in their lyrics as I hear them singing as they work. I don't think that they're aware of how oblate they are. Dr. Baingae would be horrified."

They could see the slaves levitating and flying to and fro, lifting heavy parts for assembly on the machines. There was grinding going on. Some of the smaller ones were being used to polish the metal panels. Their swooth was now severely worn and dirty just, like the swooth of the slaves in the Yastagliath mines.

"This is where we've got to work on their minds," said Wink loudly above the din.

"Some of you said that we needed an army to defeat Zinkel-Mallkis," said Kloonket. "Hey. Listen up. Here is our army! These poor Balkiens have likely been born recently and have known no other life, except working down in this underworld. The only vision of the future has been promised by Zinkel-Mallkis, who is in complete control of their welfare if you can call it that. They believe that they will be rewarded for their work."

They stayed hidden in the side of the cave exit watching. Yesl appeared to be sobbing as her swooth shook a little and whines were coming from her inner being. Matt cradled her in his arms as he looked on with tears welling up in his own eyes. Matt reminisced in his mind the visions that Yesl had implanted in him about Baingae's romance with Winxl in the beautiful meadows, high in the mountains of Yesl's home planet during his childhood when he first met *Yesl - the Balkien from Antrobi*. He hugged Kara and Sean, as they all formed a ponkadliath, amid the throb and din of industry, grinding endlessly on day and night in what, presumably, had once been as beautiful a cave, like the others.

They saw a large number of smaller spherical beings that were about the size of apples. They were whirring around above and between the machines. The name 'Entrance to Hell' would have been more appropriate for this restless slave pit.

"We better head back into the cave," hollered Matt above the screeching din.

Everyone took a few steps back. They crouched down into a crevice to try to escape the noise.

"How could these poor Balkiens, be so duped into this slavery?" asked Kara.

"You've got to understand that we Balkiens have never known evil like you," said Yesl. "Hello. Who have we here?"

Everyone looked down into the dingy corner of the crevice. There cuddled up in a tight ponkadliath were about seven very oblate Balkiens. Yesl went over to them. She talked to them in Antrobian. Two of them responded.

"These poor things have been down here for three years waiting for the promised rewards of Zinkel-Mallkis' wonderful release after their service down here. They are so sick with oblateness that they've sneaked away from their jobs on the shop floor and hidden in here. They were scared of us at first, thinking we were the TriMallkaetium police looking for them. I've explained that I am Yesl back from space on the *Balkieston*."

The Winkets hovered up to them to join in the ponkadliath. Matt started to see visions of beautiful scenes of Antrobi before his eyes. "Kloonket, I see visions of Zozl and Mozl on their Royal Throne in the Palace Mootie!"

"I see it too," said Kara.

"Me too," said Sean.

"It's Yesl," said Mwaki. "We're trying something. These seven have become disillusioned with Zinkel-Mallkis and were losing all hope of their promised reward. It looks like they're too greedy to let these slaves earn their rest and are keeping them down here in chains for far too long. What we see here may be just the beginning of a rebellion."

"So, this could be Zinkel-Mallkis' Achilles heel," said Matt. "It's an expression we have that means any weakness in an otherwise strong defense."

"I'm projecting these visions into the minds of all of us, including these slaves," said Yesl. "See they're already beginning to show a little recovery."

The bedraggled swooth on all seven of them began to grow out perceptibly as everyone watched. Yesl and the Winkets continued to converse with them in Antrobian in loud shrill voices above the background battering of the machines.

"Yesl translated what one of the seven was saying, called Spoonkthl. "They were told by Zinkel-Mallkis that King Zozl was greedy in living in his opulent palace while we were poor in our surroundings. Zinkel-Mallkis came in with an army of Antrogians and took over the Palace and drove Zozl and Mozl away into exile in the Yastagliath. We were shocked at first but told that the King and Queen were not good for us. Zinkel-Mallkis was going to lead us to a grand, new society with marvelous technology and that we'd all be going to the stars in spaceships, which we've been building down here. All of us have been in worship to the Emperor Zinkel-Mallkis since his grand orations in Balkieston's main amphitheater after deposing Zozl and Mozl."

Yesl continued. "Zinkel-Mallkis has been possessed by an evil spiritual force of darkness that has invaded our planets. He is the ONE that is no good for you. He's told you all a bunch of LIES about the malevolence of Zozl. I use the Tombalkien word 'lies' here, as it is not in the Antrobian vocabulary. We learned all about lies and evil on Tombalki, from where these three strange-legged-aliens come. They came back with us to help us understand this evil. You and all of the slaves have been led to WORSHIP this evil Emperor, especially Zinkel-Mallkis' vain Sphericity. He doesn't care at all about your misery. We've got to end this madness!"

Matt extended his hand and gently stroked poor Spoonkthl, who backed away at first. Yesl guided him to Matt's hand. Almost immediately, Matt began to see visions of Spoonkthl, and his family being rounded up by Hellacks marauding around Balkieston. He saw visions of Zinkel-Mallkis giving long speeches from the Palace balcony where, in Yesl's dream, he saw Zozl and Mozl. It was a startling contrast. Even the skies seemed darker. Matt warmly stroked Spoonkthl's swooth and cuddled him. Sean and Kara stroked the other six in turn.

"Yesl and Winkets," said Matt. "We could try and broadcast our thoughts across to the nearby slaves down there and begin to instill in their minds and memories of what Antrobi was really like under King Zozl."

"We'll try that," said Yesl.

"We'll join you," said Wink.

"But be careful you're not caught by the Hellack slave drivers and guards who are patrolling around this place," said Kloonket. "Try to be discreet. Hide in the clefts in the ceiling."

Yesl, Mowika, Ponku, and the Winkets flew boldly out across the factory floor. The loud machine noise concealed their flying warbles well. Once again, the humans began to see visions of Zozl and Mozl on the Palace balcony and other scenes of beautiful gardens around grand mooties, presumably in Balkieston. There were other scenes of Balkiens freely flying over oceans and high rock pinnacles, soaring like eagles. These images appeared to the humans to be projected onto an invisible movie screen superimposed over the ugly scenes of oblate Balkiens in the noisy factory. For moments the noise grew fainter to be replaced by the soothing wash of the waves on the beautiful pristine Antrobian beaches. Everyone stood in awe of what benevolent mind control could emanate from such small, unimposing beings. Aside from the visions, Matt began to perceive some chaos starting around the factory. The visions stopped suddenly as Yesl, and the Winkets flew in.

"Quick hide in the cleft," said Mwaki. "Hellacks are coming to see what the fuss is about."

Peeping from the cleft, they saw about fifty Hellacks hovering around striking lightning towards the slaves who dared to move from their positions. The image of Zinkel-Mallkis on the far wall got brighter. The shrill propaganda music also grew in volume.

"I think we affected them," said Kloonket. "But I think we need to do more."

"We may have to show ourselves and speak to them from here," said Matt.

"Don't be a fool," said Kloonket firmly. "Bravery alone will not win this war. Stealth has a better chance."

"Matt," said Yesl. "How many games of chess have you won against Uncle Herbert after losing your queen?"

"Very few," said Matt sheepishly.

"If we get arrested or injured by lightning here, we 'lose our queen' and the game," said Yesl. "Those Hellacks will burn and crush us all to a pulp."

"Let's emit thoughts again, but from right here," said Kloonket.

The pleasant visions started again. The seven escaped slaves in their midst were becoming less oblate, recovering well. After about fifteen minutes of pleasant dreams, the Winkets stopped their telepathic broadcast to see what would happen. There were more sounds of chaos on the shop floor. Everyone arose to their feet or quietly levitated. To their amazement just about every slave Balkien was flying around bashing into some of the cranes and causing general mayhem. Hellack guards were zooming all around striking lightning in all directions. Some bolts missed their intended targets and struck a few of the throbbing machines. One exploded in a huge bang and a bright blue flash. Another towering machine toppled over and hit another, causing gnashing of fast-moving metal. There was a cacophony of fast-flying slave Balkiens all around the ceiling of the cavern. The only thing that seemed to be steady was the bright projected image of his Sphericity, Zinkel-Mallkis. Rocks and automated tools were thrown at the Hellacks, hitting many of them. A few fell to the ground, and the falling machines crushed more, but many of them continued to attack the slaves with lightning, knocking them to the floor. Some of the slave Balkiens hurled spanner like tools at the projector. The tools struck the lens, and with a small explosion and a fizz, the projector fell from its stand momentarily throwing the image of the Emperor all around the cavern before its light exploded, extinguishing it. Mowika and Ponku flew out of hiding and flew around the cave exit and screamed in Antrobian many shrill words.

"Ponku is proclaiming the prophecies of Boonkihara to them," said Kloonket. "Mowika's telling them all to fly for it out through the other passage and THIS one!"

Suddenly a group of Hellacks surrounded them and blocked the entrance emitting lightning all the time. Matt and the others grabbed rocks and pelted them. The Winkets emitted green gaseous flashes of their own. A few of the guards fell from the entrance. The rest continued to defend their position. A spark of lightning stunned Matt, throwing him back onto Mowika who was *wugged* into the rock face. The menacing guard hovered all around Matt and Mowika trying to electrocute them. His lightning kept being deflected by Mowika's intense telekinetic energy. Matt ducked out of the way. The Hellack guard and Mowika were locked in mortal combat with bright forked lightning and gaseous green lightning flashing all around them. A flash sparked out and struck Yesl who was stunned and wugged to the floor. Sean battered more rocks at the Hellack, knocking it to the ground. Sean then kicked the guard out into chaos like kicking a long goal at a football match. It hit another machine causing it to wobble.

Sean went over to Yesl. "Oh Yesl, are you okay?"

"I'm stunned," she said. "But I think I'll be okay."

Everyone hid in the cleft again. There was a rush of thousands of slaves as they flew to their freedom.

"Spoonkthl," said Kloonket in Antrobian. "Go after them and tell them all we've told you and try to enlist them to be in our army for a great battle to win back our planets."

The seven led by Spoonkthl now had strength and energy to fly up after them.

"We've got to get back up that passage," said Kloonket. "I think we'll have to get Yesl to Dr. Baingae as soon as we can. She's hurt. The part where she was struck is showing a dimple. She needs therapy."

Matt cuddled Yesl fondly.

"Yesl will be okay, I'm sure," said Wink. "She may get a bit oblate, but she'll recover. We'll carry her as you climb up through the passage or maybe you should carry her in your jersey, Matt, as we may have to fight off the guards that will pursue us rather than you."

As they prepared to make the ascent, they noticed many small smooth round beings that were somehow different and smaller than the Balkiens. They had colorful zigzag patterns on their soft and textured bodies. They flew with a higher note of warble up the passage.

"Those are the Mallkets," said Mowika. "I'm told that they have been long inhabitants of these caverns but have often ventured out onto the surface.

"Mowika and Ponku," said Kara. "Can you take an end of this rope and secure it up in the passage for us to climb up?"

The duo held onto the end and flew up onto the ledge above, drawing the rope out of Kara's knapsack. Soon Mowika and Ponku returned, still holding the end of the rope along with Kloonket who had flown up to assist the other two in securing the rope around a rock outcrop further into the passage above.

"We will hold or bailey you all one by one with the rope," said Kloonket.

"I'll go first," said Kara, who was the most agile of the entire group. She deftly found footholds in the cliff face and before long she was over the ledge safely. Matt and Sean just managed the rock climb with the assistance of the rope tied to a rock outcrop by Kara and the telekinetic support of the burly Balkiens, Mowika, and Ponku. For Matt, it was a little harder as he had Yesl inside his jumper on his chest. She was now beginning to feel worse. After walking along the smoother passage for a while, a deep low warble was heard behind them in the dimly lit passage illuminated only by the fading glow of the creepers they had cut for their descent. Out of the darkness another large faintly glowing Balkien flew to join them. This being was about twice the size of one of the Winkets.

"Who is that?" asked Sean. The shimmering sphere hovered between them with an enchanting pleasant warbling sound. The large Balkien then stopped warbling and levitated just off the floor, who spoke in Antrobian to Mowika and Ponku who exchanged quite a few words, translated as follows:

"It has come to pass at last," said the newcomer.

"What?" asked Ponku.

"These tall legged creatures here with you," said the beautiful shimmering one.

"Why it's Boonkihara!" cried Mowika. "You've changed a great deal. You're much larger and much more colorful. What happened to you down there?"

"It's a long story," said Boonkihara.

"We'll first walk and levitate back to the great cavern," said Kloonket

"That's Boonkihara!" announced Kloonket to everyone present.

They emerged back out into the cavern where the Antrogians and Zozl were seated anxiously awaiting their return. It was like coming back out into the open fresh air. The glowing creepers on the cavern walls looked exceptionally bright after the darkness of the rock passage. The cavern was quite noisy with the echoes of many of the slave Balkiens flying out of the other cave in a frenzied bid to escape. There were still a few Hellacks flying around striking lightning at some of the escapees, leading to some wugging into the lake with splashes.

"I know we're tired and Yesl's wounded, but we've got to join this fight," said Kloonket.

Like a shot, all able-bodied Balkiens took off towards the fighting hoards above. Wink spotted a Hellack chasing a group of slaves upward towards the cavern ceiling emitting lightning. Wink closed in and shot bolts of green lightning at the Hellack. Two struck home, causing it to shriek and fall into the water far below. There were Balkien dogfights. The Antrogians managed to knock out a large percentage of the enemy with emissions of bluish-green ionized flares. Many fell into the water. To join Wink, Mwaki was flying as fast as she could while being chased by three aggressive Hellacks close to her swooth. Bolts of lightning streaked past her all of the time.

"You must obey!" shouted one of them in Antrobian in his menacing voice. Mwaki flew faster, emitting green lightning of her own. She led them up into the ceiling. Brightly glowing creepers covering spires of rock along with many limestone stalactites were hanging down from the rock ceiling. Wink deftly flew in between them with the Hellacks in pursuit, striking bolts of lightning occasionally knocking off stalactites, which dropped into the lake. Soon there were about eight of them after his swooth letting out blood-curdling shrieks saying, "You must obey the Emperor!"

Wink flew dangerously close to the rock stalactites. There was method in the madness. One by one the Hellacks hit the stalactites and *wugged* down into oblivion until there were only two left chasing Wink. One of them started to strike Wink and was beginning to penetrate through his outer protective swooth. He brushed into a stalactite, which caused him to start spinning out of control. Suddenly there was a very bright green flash with a loud crack. Several stalactites broke away. The two remaining Hellacks fell with them. Mwaki, catching up closer to Wink, had fired the fatal shots and raced after Wink who was still spinning down towards the water. Mwaki caught up close enough to Wink and locked onto him by her telekinesis from above and flew her back down to their resting place to join the others. Though they couldn't fly, Matt, Kara, and Sean managed to knock out some of the last few Hellacks by trying to hit them with rocks as they approached. They consistently missed, with the stones splashing in the water. One Hellack tried to fly straight at Kara, flashing lightning at her. She ducked out of the way, leaving it to fly straight down the entrance of the passage. It hit the far rocks in darkness with a big bump. King Zozl could still be heard hovering across the water towards them on the shore. The last remaining Hellack was chasing him. Boolboonkle dived down from above and bumped it down into the water. Boolboonkle landed on the sandy beach in a state of relief. Suddenly the water stirred, and flashes of lightning streaked out of the water towards them. The Hellack suddenly rose and flew directly at Zozl. One lightning flash hit Zozl, who was thrown back against the cave wall. More flashes streaked out towards Matt and Sean, who just avoided being hit by running to and fro. In a deafening crescendo, Boolboonkle took off again to pursue the Hellack and draw away its lightning. They could be heard hovering around the cavern with flashes sparking from his assailant. Boolboonkle's deep beating warble reverberated all around the cavern.

Boongoo and Yesl immediately flew to Zozl's aid. Zozl was groaning. The strike visibly blackened a small part of his equatorial swooth.

'We'll need to get him to Dr. Baingae as soon as possible," said Matt.

Yesl looked at him more closely. 'I don't think that this is as serious as it seems. Zozl's large enough that he'll recover soon. His ability to fly on his own could be compromised.

Boolboonkle led the Hellack on a chase through the stalactites in the cavern's roof hoping to lead his pursuer into a trap. Boolboonkle would occasionally knock into the stalactites managing to break some of them as he hit them with his muscular body. Rather than let them fall into the water below, he telekinetically held the long slender stalactites onto his equator. Boolboonkle suddenly turned left and dived down towards the lake. The Hellack fell behind in the chase. Boolboonkle rose quickly towards the ceiling. The pieces of stalactite started to orbit fast around his equator, keeping them aligned with his surface. As the Hellack raced towards him, flashing more lightning, Boolboonkle aimed his rocky arrows towards the Hellack. Many of them scored a direct hit causing a flurry of sparks and agonizing shrieks and fell into the water, with an echoing splash. Boolboonkle hovered around for about ten minutes, looking for the rest of the party.

"Boolboonkle's hit the Hellack," said Sean, "but he seems lost."

Kloonket switched on his light sphere and waved it. Matt turned on his torch, albeit the batteries were weak. As soon as Boolboonkle came towards them, he landed on the shoreline; the torches were immediately extinguished to avoid revealing their location to any more Hellacks.

Slowly, a myriad of the former slaves began to hover weakly towards them or levitate above the water, occasionally dipping themselves in it to clean off the grime, after years of toil. Like Yesl, Wink was nursing his lightning wound. Peace returned to the battlefield.

Matt gave Kara and Sean the big five and shook hands and stroked the swooth of most of the Balkiens involved in the fight in congratulations of victory.

Alex M Shepherd

"Well done to all of you," said Kloonket. "Everyone contributed! Even Yesl in her injured state managed to wield fast-moving gravel from the beach and felled about three of the menacing things just before they struck at Boonkihara. You're a heroine, Yesl, especially doing this in your wounded state. We'll get you, Zozl, and Wink to Dr. Baingae as soon as we can."

"Maybe this is our finest hour," said Matt.

"We may have won this battle," said Zozl, "but we've yet to win this war. But it's a start. We now have many of our subjects gathered around us here. They need guidance after gaining their freedom. Here to speak to them is Boonkihara."

All the released Balkiens formed a circular ponkadliath around the Antrogians, the Tombalkiens, and the missionary Balkiens from the surface. The effervescent Boonkihara began to speak in Antrobian.

"I am Boonkihara, an ancient old Balkien, who has been living for a very long time before any of you were born. I have been lost down in these caves for a great many years. Today, you are free from a terrible force of evil. Zinkel-Mallkis had only his agenda. For many of you, this will be a total shock, realizing that for many years you have been dreaming of a great future in the service of the Emperor, Zinkel-Mallkis while gazing at his projected image down in that torrid hellhole of a factory slaving away with your poor bodies, only to serve his utterly vain Sphericity.

"For a lot of you, like these seven here, you had begun realizing that Zinkel-Mallkis' wonderful future never seemed to be coming and all you had to look forward to was grinding away in that awful factory and oblating yourselves to a shadow of your former selves. Many sages, like me, had foretold this evil a long time ago. Before the evil one invaded our planets and deposed our King and Queen from their throne in Balkieston, most of you seemed to have no idea or concept of anything other than an idyllic, blissful, clean existence. There are ancient legends of a few brave Balkiens who traveled into the sky in a sky-ship to a far distant world. They called it Tombalki. There were extraordinary legged creatures that inhabited that strange world, where the sky was bright blue. Here we meet three of them. As foretold, in our prophecies, the hour has come for our release from the oppression of slavery and deprivation."

All the Balkiens listen intently. There was silence apart from the water lapping on the shore and the faint distant dying echoes of Boonkihara's speech. "I was hit by lightning by many of the Emperor's evil soldiers you call Hellacks, just as that factory was constructed. That's when I lost contact with Mowika and Ponku. I managed to fly through many caves and tunnels until I found a small alcove to hide. I dropped in there with my wounds and fell into the deep hibernating sleep to recover. When I awoke and emerged from my very thick cocoon, I could hear the terrible throbbing of machinery that you must have heard. I flew towards it and hid in many places around it for nearly half a year looking for you, Mowika and Ponku. Then there began all the commotion with machines blowing up and fighting. When it died down, I flew up the passage and met you all."

Everyone melted into a great ponkadliath. Matt, Kara, and Sean found it very soothing. There seemed to be a unique radiance from Boonkihara. Even the wounds of Wink and Yesl began to be less painful. Everything was quiet. There were now no waves on the lake reflecting the glory of the glowing ceiling of the cavern. Gaps in the iridescent cave ceiling were evident where some of the stalactites had been knocked down during the earlier battle. Then there was a very faint warbling sound from across the lake. It sounded distant and rather lonely.

"Perhaps it's another released slave trying to find us," said Kara.

Against the faint blue, glowing creepers, there was a distinct round silhouette, tiny at first.

"Sounds a lot like Baingae," suggested Matt. The silhouette came into their midst.

"It IS Baingae," said Kloonket. "What are you doing here, Baingae? We have a lot to tell you, and we were thinking about making our ascent to the surface.

"Boodibah," said Baingae announcing himself in his unique way. "Who are all these Balkiens?"

"We've just released them all from slavery," said King Zozl as the shock of his electrocution began to subside. "We'd better head back to meet you all up at camp. Maybe you've been sent to look for us."

"Oh, King Zozl," said Baingae in a doleful voice. "Something has happened to us." He began to narrate what had happened:

It was late afternoon with the tree shadows getting longer.

"I hope that everything's okay with Matt, Kara, Sean, Yesl, and everyone down in the Underworld," said Alison with a worried voice. "They've been gone a long time."

"I'm sure they're okay," reassured Kaz.

"I'm not so sure," said Baingae. "What if any of them are hurt and need me to diagnose and treat them."

"We should be getting some food on the go," said Judith. "Boongoo, what's there to eat on these trees?"

Just then, the peaceful silence was punctuated by a faint hum that sounded like the engines of a scout craft. Kaz looked up. "Look. See those golden egg-shaped aircraft high up in the sky."

Thinking no more of the sighting as the noise died away, everyone began to pick the small pomegranate-like fruits off the trees. The humming returned but louder. Everyone looked up. Two golden egg-shaped craft whined in and hovered over the clearing and landed. Kaz was filming this with Matt's camera, left behind, thinking that the caverns would be too dark. As they touched down, doors suddenly slid open, and a squad of leathery Hellacks bailed out sparking lightning flashes. Long mechanical snake-like tendrils with grabber clamps on the ends shot out of the egg craft and started grabbing onto the humans.

"Run for your lives," shouted Kaz. The Antrogians who were sitting in an open clearing just out of reach tried to attract everyone to themselves telekinetically. They could not do so, as everyone, both human and Balkien, were virtually sucked up into the craft kicking and screaming. Both Alison and Judith let out the most ear-splitting screams they could muster. The egg craft took off suddenly and raced off in a southerly direction leaving the camp abandoned. The three Antrogians also took off in a crescendo of warbling; raising a great cloud of dust, to pursue them but soon gave up this hopeless chase and landed near the 'Entrance to the Underworld'.

Baingae finally said, "I alone managed to hide in the swooth of one of the Antrogians. They didn't want to risk flying down here to look for you. So, I had to come down here on my own. I see that Zozl, Yesl, and Wink need urgent diagnoses."

"So, everyone at camp is now taken prisoner, except you and the Antrogians," gasped Matt.

"I'm afraid so," said Baingae disparagingly.

Dr. Baingae immediately went to work on diagnosing the battle wounds of King Zozl, Yesl, and Wink."

"Baingae," began Matt. "We've had a terrible battle down here but with a great victory, releasing all those former slaves here with us. The lightning of Hellacks struck Yesl, Wink, and Zozl."

"Let's see," said Baingae, who looked closely and felt the wounded areas of Yesl Wink and Zozl."

"I think that both Zozl and Wink will regrow their burnt swooth in a few days," he said, "but for Yesl, I think it'll take a bit longer. I'll have to wait to see her in daylight."

"We have to leave here at once and find out what has happened to the others," said Kloonket. "We'll sleep here for a few hours before the long flight to the surface, where we have memorized the route by landmarks at the far end of the lake. It'll take about three hours." The euphoria of victory evaporated as the news of the capture of the others back at camp had unfolded.

The flight across the lake was uneventful but subdued with a much larger group including all the rescued slaves still with them. After another rest on the far shores of the lake, they began their arduous ascent. The echoing warbles of thousands of Balkiens were almost overwhelming as they flew up the vertical shaft. Matt, who was sitting on Boolboonkle, looked up and saw the small circle of purple light straight above growing larger until they were flying around in spirals around the rim. At last, they emerged into the Vega light in mid-afternoon.

"Oh, the terrible state of these poor little poonketies," lamented Dr. Baingae, as he now fully noticed, in broad daylight, how disheveled the slaves appeared. "I'm mortified to see such a dreadful state of health in these members of our civilization."

Close to the edge of the dark pit were the three other Antrogians in a triangular ponkadliath, looking sad. They finally landed beside them on an expanse of the patchy meadow where they were sitting. In the daylight, Boonkihara was a distinctly resplendent Balkien. His multi-colored radiance gave him distinctive, beautiful colored banding around his swooth. Boonkihara had to shelter under the Antrogians from the strong Vega-light.

Boolboonkle, Zonkollus, and Poolpoogleponk joined Polpodwink, Spalkius, and Woozbokle, forming a ponkadliath. The swarm of escaped slaves was flying all around the mouth of the pit, like honeybees in excitement.

"We've got to get away from here," said Kloonket, "before we're discovered and have another battle on our hands. Baingae's full-on with treating the wounds on Wink and Yesl and Zozl. Head back to our campsite?"

"Not advisable to stay there," said Zozl.

Three of the Antrogians headed back to salvage any remaining supplies and equipment left at the former campsite, with Matt, Sean, Kara, Kloonket, and Mwaki. The rest led all the joyful slaves away from the pit towards a cluster of rock pinnacles, called *Monkoothtril* or, in English, the *Ring of Spires*, to hide and scout out a new campsite.

● ○ ●

18 ~ THE BATTLE OF BINKUS-MALLKUS

Zinkel-Mallkis himself was hovering in front of his large mirror examining the Sphericity on his swooth before his big appearance in front of his admiring subjects amassed in Balkieston's town hexagon (town square). He flew out onto his grand balcony to speak to the excited crowd of mesmerized Balkiens. Zinkel-Mallkis boomed his words out over the arena in Antrobian and English.

"Balkiens of Antrobi and Antrogi, for ages we have awaited this moment. We have nearly completed our first stage in our spaceship-building program over in Balkiesville. Now we commence a truly momentous occasion with the great cruisers of our galaxy successfully built. We shall show you the new ship on the video screen. Look behind."

The big hexagonal screen showed scenes in the Underworld, which appeared to be devoid of any Balkien slaves. Camera images then switched first to reveal a catalog image of the new golden egg-shaped spacecraft. A messenger Balkien flew out to speak to Zinkel-Mallkis.

"Not now," he thundered. "Can't you see it! I'm busy with this presentation."

"It's crucial," said messenger Zinklus, the burly Balkien with shades of orange in his swooth. "Something terrible has happened at the factory."

"Tell me later. I'm busy!"

"But you don't understand."

"SHUT UP!"

"YOUR FACTORY'S BEEN BLOWN UP!"

"What do you mean blown up? I'M BUSY!"

Zinkel-Mallkis re-joined his subjects on the balcony. "Let's see the real spaceship."

Zinkel-Mallkis looked at the screen in anticipation of the image appearing. The screen remained grey. A few minutes passed.

"Well. Where's the spaceship image?" shouted Zinkel-Mallkis. "Don't tell me you've busted the computer. FIX IT!"

Zinkel-Mallkis hovered back and forth nervously in front of the teeming audience trying to figure what was wrong with the projection.

Zinklus, the arresting officer who handed over Matt and his party at the museum, flew out onto the balcony thought, "*I vaguely recalled the prophetic sayings of Boonkihara. I'm beginning to realize the connection of Boonkihara's wise old sayings with what I'm reporting to Zinkel-Mallkis."*

"There's no spaceship to display," he said aloud. "I've just had word that there was a battle in the factory and that all of your slave workers have escaped, and the factory is now completely wrecked."

"Confound it," shouted Zinkel-Mallkis. "Fix that screen."

"There's nothing wrong with our equipment here in Balkieston. It's the destruction of the underground factory."

"Destroyed," gasped Zinkel-Mallkis. What! Destroyed! No space armada. What! My Mallkien dreams! OH NO! I don't believe it!"

Zinkel-Mallkis flew around in circles in a seething rage and then flew inside away from the glare of the masses gathered in the hexagon. The hexagonal glass doors of the Palace Mootie balcony whirred and clanged shut. The crowd gasped and hovered nervously about in the hexagon.

"What has happened?" asked one Balkien.

"In these years we've never seen any of our leaders act in such a way," said another.

"Rumor has it that one of the spacecraft sent to - where was it again? Oh yes, Splogita, has returned recently," said yet another. "The crew brought back extraordinary aliens, who stand on two tall support appendages, have two other long things which can hold objects, and have a round part on top a bit like us and they even have some swooth on them. I've heard that they and the Balkien crew who brought them have caused a lot of trouble. They escaped from a ball train in which they were prisoners and caused it to crash into a mine site."

"Oh dear," said the first, called Poonzl. "And now this!"

All the Balkiens assembled on the hexagon began to fly up in the air slowly and dispersed to their home mooties in disillusionment. The great razzmatazz of celebrations started to fade, leaving forlorn decorations and flags flapping in the evening breeze over an empty hexagonal apron where a few Hellack guards hovered around.

The Balkiens who had emerged from the Entrance to the Underworld flew over to their former campsite. Round water containers remained scattered around the clearing with some cracked. Matt found Kaz's knapsack lying in the moss with some of the contents spilled out. His binoculars, which he had lent to Kaz before he went underground, had been smashed against a rock and bent out of shape with the left lens cracked. He put them up to his eyes and could see nothing through them.

"Kara began to cry, "Where have they taken Kaz, Alison, and Judith?"

"Look, Matt," said Sean. "There's your camera." The camera was lying on the ground close to a boulder as if it had been carefully placed there.

"Why do we worry about a camera, when our cousins have fallen into the clutches of the Enigma!" he exclaimed.

"I know not to be concerned over it, but it's what may be on it," said Sean. "Let's playback any footage."

Matt turned it on in play mode. Thumbnail images displayed on the screen. He selected the last icon to playback. The scene on the screen was chaotic with shaky filming. Balkiens were flying everywhere. Hellacks were flashing lightning. Hellack guards forced Alison and Judith into a golden-egg shaped craft.

Kaz appeared on the monitor screen, "If you find this camera and play this back. I'm saying that we're under arrest for trespassing on forbidden territory and we're on a serious charge in the court of the TriMallkaetium. They're taking us to the spire of Binkus-Mallkus, to the west of Balkalay to stand trial before Zinkel-Mallkis says, one Hellack guard. Hope you find us. Watch out for—." The footage ended.

Matt looked over onto the clearing and saw the tripod marks of the spacecraft. "We've got to get to Binkus-Mallkus."

"That's on the other side of the planet," said Kloonket. "If we flew there as we are, it would take about 40 days, and there's a vast southern-ocean to cross; much too far for the Antrogians here with us and our water bottles as we've seen already."

"I wish we had our scout ship and that the Splinkatrix was close by," said Kara.

Yesl was still not quite herself, still suffering from her battle wound. Wink was still not quite right either after his dogfight. Dr. Baingae was continuing to assess their health problems by rolling around the swooth of each of them.

"This place is not safe," said Zozl, who was shaken by the capture of his wife, Queen Mozl.

All their remaining belongings and debris were removed from the site and taken to their new camp so as not to leave clues of their whereabouts.

All six Antrogians formed a ponkadliath in the soft meadow inside the Ring of Spires. In the center, there was a glistening lake, where the escaped slaves were bathing their swooth of years of hard toil. Baingae was there with the others, carrying out diagnoses on some of the more oblate ones. Matt, Kara, and Sean were gently washing a few of the Balkiens of factory grime and bringing out their bright colors. Most washed. After washing, most of them began to de-oblate overnight. Sleep was not relaxed, with their comrades in prison on the other side of their world.

At dawn, when Matt stirred, he could hear a distant hum.

"Kloonket, Mwaki, Zozl," he said. "It's a spaceship!"

Kloonket flew around to wake everyone saying, "There's a ship hovering over us. LOOK!"

"Wait a minute," said Mwaki. "It's not one of those golden super-egg things. It's our scout ship from the Splinkatrix. Let it land."

The round craft extended its legs and landed. The circular door whirred open. A large Balkien with orange swooth emerged and flew over to Kloonket.

"Zinklus," he exclaimed in English. "Why, wasn't it you who arrested us?"

"Kloonket," said Zinklus. "Don't worry. I've defected having remembered the sayings of Boonkihara. No time to talk now. I've seen a terrible thing happen back in Balkieston. Zinkel-Mallkis has gone mad with fury. He has found out about the destruction in the caverns and the escaped slaves. Until then, I was loyal to Zinkel-Mallkis, but when I heard about this ghastly slavery, I was horrified. There was a big riot in Balkieston the next day, with much larger Balkiens flying around hurling rocks into many of Balkieston's public mooties smashing a lot of glass. I fled out towards the Yastagliath and discovered your resistance mates who were guarding your ship. They had no qualified pilot to fly the ship until I came. So here we are. We knew to come here after we saw this place on the display screen at Zinkel-Mallkis' presentation before he heard about the escape of the slaves."

"Zinklus," said Kloonket, "my great friend of the contrasting colors. I'm so glad that you have seen the light and listened to Boonkihara's warnings and messages."

Boonkihara hovered over to meet with Zinklus. "I never thought that Zinkel-Mallkis' ways would have so convinced you. It took a visit to Tombalki and for six of her inhabitants to come here on your ship to help us understand this evil."

Kloonket's blue swooth contrasted well with Zinklus' orange swooth. They were both about the same size, a little larger than Yesl, and prolate. Mwaki flew into the spacecraft to re-familiarize herself with the cockpit. "We'll have to try and contact the Splinkatrix for assistance to rescue our captured ones. Poor Baingae is, once again separated, from his beloved Winxl." Yesl, Zozl, and Wink were immediately placed in the craft's sickbay for further diagnosis and treatment under Dr. Baingae by the Balkien swooth scanners on board.

"We'll have to fly in the ship to the Mount of Binkus-Mallkus west of Antron on the western coast of Balkalay," said Kloonket. "We'll take a few of the weakest Balkiens from the factory." Without having to carry us, The Antrogians reckon that they can get to Balkalay in about ten days. They plan to gather some of their friends in the southern parts of this continent of Beekica on the way. The rest of the escapees will follow them and spread the word in the city of mooties or Mootieburgh in the southeast before they cross the South Beekalo Ocean. Kloonket wrote an encrypted message and transmitted it to the Splinkatrix:

This is Kloonket, known to the Winkets. We have fought a great battle in the Underworld and released many Balkien slaves. Forces of Zinkel-Mallkis have taken some of us prisoner, and taken them to the greatest tall mount, with Zinkel-Mallkis' flashing beacon.

After radio transmission, the ship departed. Everyone looked out from the lower round window to see the ground between the spires dropping away below them. As they rose over the mountain peaks, everyone could see the six Antrogians majestically rise to be followed by a magnificent swarm of the escaped Balkiens. King Zozl, now sufficiently recovered, had decided to remain with his subjects and traveled with or on Boolboonkle to visit with and lead his population on this final quest. Boonkihara also accompanied the Antrogians to spread his prophetic messages among all the communities, on their way south. Boonkihara was commissioned to spread the word that the Enigma corrupted their once egalitarian society. They would have to resist its influence and fight for their former freedom, or their planet was doomed to destruction by wars fought amongst them as had happened on Splogita, leaving most of that world in a desolate state of ashen ruins.

"There's our army on its way," said Kloonket. "It seems to be taking less convincing than we thought to tell the truth to our country Balkiens."

Kaz sat cross-legged leaning against the rock wall of their cell. Alison and Judith lay on the hard rock floor trying to sleep. There was a thin slit window in the rock that let in a sliver of purple light. Mozl, Winxl, Ponku, Mowika, Boonkliat, and Quinket were in a ponkadliath. They had tried Quinket for size to escape through the window, but it was too narrow even for her. There was a deep warble along the passage outside their cell in their rocky jail. The thick metal hexagonal door opened with a grinding noise. A large leathery Hellack flew in balancing a hexagonal food tray balanced on his north pole.

"Here is your food," he said. "YOU MUST OBEY! It is the will of Zinkel-Mallkis,"

Kaz stood up and lifted the tray onto a stone table in the corner. The jailor hovered out, and the door whirred and clanged shut. On the walls of the cell were round pictures of Zinkel-Mallkis with inscriptions under in Antrobian. Translated, they read:

IN HONOUR OF HIS EVERLASTING SPHERICITY AND DEDICATION, WE ALL SWEAR ALLEGIANCE TO OUR GREAT EMPEROR, ZINKEL-MALLKIS, THE SUPREME RULER OF ALL WORLDS EVER SINCE THEIR BEGINNING AND WILL BE FOREVER

Zinklus and Mwaki were at the controls of their scout ship looking out of the cockpit. Ahead was the purple expanse of the South Beekalo Ocean. It was featureless except for a few spikes of black rock piercing up out of the sea of shimmering waves. Clouds billowed up from the larger ones. The tall spires became higher and more frequent as they flew on. Then on the far distant horizon, they could see a very bright pinprick of light.

"That beacon is very bright," said Kara. "Oh, it's so bright!"

"As we get closer, the light is almost too bright to look at for any length of time," said Kaz, "brighter than the Vega. Maybe just as well that your binoculars were broken, as using them on this light could result in eye injury or blindness, just as looking directly at the sun on Earth can cause permanent blindness."

Even to their naked eyes or visual swooth, this light became too bright as they approached.

"That is the Spire of Binkus-Mallkus ahead," said Zinklus. "For everyone here, this is one of Antrobi's great wonders. I now know that this is where Zinkel-Mallkis sometimes comes to consult with the Enigma residing somewhere deep inside that rock.

As the ship lost altitude, the light grew less as they dropped out of its horizontal beams. They could now see more clearly the massive shape of the tall mountain ahead of them. First, it looked distant but massive. As they drew closer, the violet color of distance changed to a gigantic dark foreboding rock-scape. There were wisps of clouds covering parts of the mountain, whose summit reached above the planet's atmosphere into outer space itself.

"According to Kaz's video footage, this is where they were taken," said Matt. "How are we going to find them inside that mountain?"

"This reminds of the Mountain of Light on Splogita," said Yesl, who was by now showing a considerable improvement in her health. Wink was with Yesl in a ponkadliath as they helped each other recover as directed by Dr. Baingae. Zinklus piloted the ship up towards the clouds to hide from enemy observance. Flying around the side of the mount in an anticlockwise direction, they could see the sheer rock wall off to the port side. It had many near-vertical dark clefts and crevices that would have been an extreme challenge for any rock-climbing mountaineer. As they continued to go around, Matt noticed that there were some artificial features such as balconies, where Balkiens could land, and tall pillars and tall gothic arches facing onto the terrace. Below this, a rectangular part of the rock face began to slide downwards.

"Zinklus!" shouted Sean. "A door is opening in the rock."

"We've been spotted," said Kloonket. "Two golden egg-shaped ships are emerging from a hangar inside."

"Let's get out of here!" hollered Matt.

With a sudden lurch, the ship sped away from the cliff face.

"Those golden egg-shaped aircraft are chasing us," said Alison.

"Super-eggs," hollered Kaz

The ship picked up speed and rose higher.

"It's no good," said Kloonket. "They're still on our tail."

Bolts of fire came out of the guns mounted on the small delta-shaped wings of the super-eggs. They exploded around the ship. Zinklus headed for deeper clefts nearby to try hiding to shake off the two patrol-craft. As the scout-ship from the Splinkatrix was built before the invasion, it had no weapons to fire back. The bolts kept on coming though none hit. Zinklus put the ship into a steep climb heading for space hoping that with their ever-accelerating gyro motors they could outrun the super-eggs. More fiery bolts exploded around them. As they climbed above the cloud level, everyone could see the endless height of the tall rock extending out into space with the bright beacon at the summit. The highest cliff faces of the slender spire that was above Antrobi's atmosphere were more luminous than those lower down. The ship continued to climb faster and faster. The super-eggs began to fall further behind.

"Kloonket," said Baingae. "Watch out for the level of the blinding light."

"Zinklus!" shouted Wink.

"What?" he asked.

"Remember about the damaged cockpit canopy," said Wink. "We need to descend low——."

THUD! The inside of the craft went misty. There was a roar of rushing air.

"THAT CHIP ON THE CANOPY GLASS HAS CRACKED AND BLOWN OFF!" shouted Matt. "DOWN, DOWN!"

Zinklus pushed the craft into a steep nosedive causing a violent tailspin too close to the cliffs. As they descended straight towards the ocean, the cliffs spun all around them. Zinklus put the gyro engines into reverse thrust. The rush of escaping air got less during their descent, as they leveled out before reaching the ocean.

"Zinklus," said Kloonket. "You did a great job evading the super-eggs. Sorry, we forgot to warn you about that chip on the glass canopy. A Hellack struck it by a fiery bolt on the ground north of Balkieston, while under attack."

Zinklus continued on a sedate, descending course directly away from the Mount of Binkus-Mallkus. There was a sudden loud WOOSH. One of the super-eggs passed them and took up a position straight ahead of them. A leathery, round Hellack emerged from a circular door on its side and flew back towards the front cockpit directly in front of them. Then three somewhat pear-shaped beings of a similar leathery texture emerged from the super-egg. These pearoids flanked around the sides of their ship. The leading Hellack flew up from the front of the cockpit-shield and instantly flew inside the scout ship through the opening with jagged glass edges, where the broken canopy once covered it.

"You have trespassed on the exclusive airspace of Zinkel-Mallkis," it said. "You're all under arrest. You must follow our patrol craft. YOU MUST OBEY! It is the will of Zinkel-Mallkis. Our other craft is behind us. YOU MUST OBEY!"

Zinklus and Kloonket tried to excuse their presence.

"STOP talking and follow us," ordered the Hellack. "YOU MUST OBEY!"

It then let off a few small warning sparks of lightning. Grimly, Zinklus followed the super-egg back towards the Spire of Binkus-Mallkus and approached the open hangar door in the cliff that they had passed earlier. The super-egg drew level with the hangar entrance. Soon the scout-ship hovered into the hangar and landed next to the leading super-egg. The second super-egg touched down shortly afterward. The door of the scout-ship lowered down from the floor at the rear. The menacing looking pearoids escorted Matt, Sean, and Kara. These creatures hovered with a deep warbling sound like the Hellacks but had a much lighter, yellow-colored leathery texture. They were shaped like pears and were about a foot tall, which even had a stem sticking out. There were six of them hovering around them. A hexagonal door at the back of the hangar whirred open. They all passed through into a long corridor with a hexagonal cross-section. They were marched down some more rock-walled passages by their captors. In one of these passages were heavy metal hexagonal doors about man height. They stopped at one of them. It whirred and clanged open. The Hellack and the pearoids ordered them all to go inside. The door clanged shut. They looked around the dimly lit rock cell.

"Kaz!" exclaimed Matt. "Alison, Judith!"

"Winxl!" exclaimed Baingae.

"A great reunion this maybe," said Kloonket. "But now we're all guests of Zinkel-Mallkis. None of us are now free to assist with any escape. Except maybe for Zozl and Boonkihara. Just as well they went with the Antrogians."

"Ssh!" hissed Zinklus. "Walls have ears. Don't think that speaking English will keep our discussions secret. It's surprising how much of the Tombalkien language is known here. I learned it myself as a useful course so that I would be qualified to serve the court of Zinkel-Mallkis directly."

"I keep thinking how odd it is that there's a lot of English spoken on this planet when we arrived," said Judith quizzically.

"Hey," said Matt, "Where's Mowika and Ponku?"

"And there seem to be only two of the seven escapees we thought we had with us," said Mwaki."

"They must have been close to the canopy when it blew out," said Kloonket. "So, they may have been sucked out a way up there and will have wugged."

"At that high altitude and with the speed we were going at, they'd have been badly oblated at best," said Baingae. "Not to mention the broken glass."

"However, they may have a better chance than us, here in jail," said Yesl. "If they survive the great wug okay they may well come and look for us."

"Is there any descendant of Houdini among us?" asked Alison trying to make light of their situation.

Mowika and Ponku hurtled down past the whitened cliff face. The sky above was almost black, with many stars visible. The air was thin, depriving them of their ability to fly. There was therefore virtually no wind resistance to their fall, which was at increasing speed towards almost certain impalement on the jagged spires rushing up to meet them. As the air grew denser, they found that they could fly a little to control their path of falling like a human skydiver. Mowika and Ponku maneuvered deftly towards the other five escaped slaves that had dropped out of the scout ship with them when the glass canopy blew off. All seven of them just made ponkadliath as a group of rock spires almost stabbed them. They had to manoeuver around dodging several rock spires as they fell, managing to steer themselves sufficiently away from the mountain. The sky became purple again as the air thickened. Their falling speed decreased. Holding onto each other tightly, Mowika and Ponku let out a loud warble to break their descent until they were in level flight around the cliffs. Monku saw that their ship was being escorted towards the cliff by the two super-eggs and a swarm of black things.

"Ponku," said Mowika in Antrobian. "Our ship's been arrested by the Zinkel-Mallkis' forces. We'd better fly towards the cliff and hide. All seven of them stayed in ponkadliath until they reached a crevice where there was a flat area to land.

Passing the time in prison was mind-numbing. Quinket was restless and annoyed everyone with her constant high pitch warbling around the cell.

"Quinket!" shouted Wink. "Calm down! I know it's frustrating in here. Mwaki needs silence to try to work on the door. With one last attempt at squeezing through the crevice that gave them some light, Quinket flew in and settled down in there. Mwaki rolled around the cell door and attached herself to where she thought the locking mechanism would be. Wink hovered back to join the others for a moment. The door suddenly slid open with a clang.

Hellack guards entered. "You all have to come with us. YOU MUST OBEY! Get up all of you. It is the will of Zinkel-Mallkis. You are to appear before him in the Court of the TriMallkaetium to face trial for your offenses."

Everyone walked or hovered from the cell under the heavy escort of eight Hellack guards. They walked along several long dark rock-walled passages, dimly lit by light green LED-type lights. They came to a highly reflective steel round door with a small oval stained-glass window, about the diameter of

Yesl. The pattern in the glass was an image of Zinkel-Mallkis. The door swished open with a dull thud.

"Get in now!" ordered the chief guard, who was a dark grey Hellack with a leathery texture.

"YOU MUST OBEY and get in now," repeated the chief guard. They pushed everyone into a large hexagonal elevator car with a domed roof. The guards entered with them to keep order. The door swished shut. The levitating Balkiens fell to the floor, and the Earthlings nearly collapsed to the floor where they stood with the strong upward acceleration. The air rapidly grew thinner during the fast ascent. There were a few seconds of weightlessness as the elevator braked hard and stopped. Everyone fell to the floor or landed on their feet. The door swished open.

"Get out now!" ordered the chief guard. They came out into a wide corridor. Unlike the rock walls of their prison cell, these walls were ornately decorated with hexagon panels. Some displayed images of Zinkel-Mallkis. The guards forced them into a side entrance, which led up a short, inclined passage and through an opening into a cavernous hall like a throne room, built into a natural cavern. On an elevated round podium like throne sat Zinkel-Mallkis himself. Everyone shuddered. Three smooth spherical creatures who had regular striped patterns around their pleated swooth sat before his beautiful and ornately arranged Sphericity.

"Why?" asked Matt. "These look like Mallkets with poles colored in varying shades of green."

"Green poled Mallkets signify their status as those belonging to the legal profession," replied Wink.

Zinkel-Mallkis spoke up. "So, you appear before the court of the TriMallkaetium once again," he bellowed. "You are at this moment charged with several counts. One; for escaping from custody in Balkieston and from a prison ball-train, two; for you legged creatures for entering Antrobian realms without invitation or authorization from the Antrobian Immigration Service. Three; for causing derailment of the aforementioned ball-train leading to a major accident and destruction of a production and detention facility and allowing thousands of convicts to escape from their bonded duties. You are also indicted on charges of treason before this Court, for rebellion and combat against our forces and of wanton destruction of our industries down in the caves in the Underworld. What have you got to say for yourselves?"

Matt was first to speak boldly, "It is you, Zinkel-Mallkis that have a lot to answer for. It is YOU who have deposed the rightful ruler of this planet. It is YOU, who have made vain, promises to the poor hard worker Balkiens down in those dark pits that you never intended to fulfill."

"SHUT UP!" roared Zinkel-Mallkis as he started to hover a little erratically off his throne before settling down. "I'm the ruler of these planets now. Zozl and his cohorts were useless at leading this civilization onto progress and better things."

"But they were delighted in their existence until YOU came along!" shouted Matt.

"Don't you DARE say anything in their defense, you, insolent alien Tombalkien with no civic rights whatsoever!" thundered Zinkel-Mallkis.

"Order in the Court," declared Judge Mallket. He sat in the center of the panel of the three Mallkets of the judiciary.

"Don't you interfere in the proceedings, Judge Mallket. I'm the order in this Court," said Zinkel-Mallkis.

"What kind of a court IS this?" demanded Zinklus.

"Zinklus is a TRAITOR!" shouted Zinkel-Mallkis

"Zinklus is right," said Kaz. Are YOU not the actual traitor here! On our planet, it is the court judge who presides over a case. Not even our monarchy."

"You've NO RIGHT to utter an iota about how an Antrobian court of law should be run," shouted Zinkel-Mallkis. "I find you all guilty as charged."

"But we haven't even begun to examine all of the evidence in this case," protested Alison.

"Evidence," said Judge Mallket. "We don't have to discuss it. It's plain that you're all guilty."

"We also have evidence that signals are being transmitted from space," said Zinkel-Mallkis. "They seem to be reminiscent of the codes of the *Balkieston*. Answer me, Yesl."

"The *Balkieston* was completely wrecked on Tombalki," said Yesl.

"Then how do you explain this transmission from the ship's crew?" demanded Zinkel-Mallkis. The transmission was replayed to the court, as recorded in Antrobian.

"I translate this to say; 'This is Captain Woozl of the *Balkieston*. We're on our way back and request permission to land.'"

Yesl, taken aback, said, "We don't know anything about this."

"If true," said Zinkel-Mallkis. "We'll be waiting for them! I find you all guilty as charged! Guards take them back to their cell to await sentencing. And after you have locked them up, go and prepare the bomb for attacking Zigollomont."

The doors of the courtroom swished open to letting everyone out for escort back to their dark cell. There was a high-pitched shrill of a warble. Something streaked past them and started buzzing all around the courtroom. During slower moments, they recognized that it was Quinket. No one had noticed that Quinket wasn't among them. She flew around like a buzzing bluebottle fly.

"After that thing!" shouted Zinkel-Mallkis, who started to hover around with a loud warble after Quinket. Quinket was too fast for them all. The guards chased around after Quinket, sparking lightning strikes at her. She was too nimble for them. Most of the sparks hit the ceiling and wall panels, damaging them with some shattered into pieces. In the middle of the melee, everyone made a run for it down the passages using Quinket's diversion to escape. As they ran along the paneled corridor, guard Hellacks flew after them. Mwaki summoned the elevator by waving herself over the sensor. As everyone stood at the hexagonal door, the Winkets let out some bolts of green lightning at the guards, who responded with their own. One bolt nearly hit Yesl.

There was a loud, deep warble as well as a shrill one. It was Zinkel-Mallkis chasing Quinket.

"You MUST OBEY the will of Zinkel-Mallkis," shouted his Sphericity. One of the guards telekinetically grabbed Quinket. The elevator still hadn't arrived, and they were outnumbered and outgunned. All six of the Earthlings held up their hands in surrender, not realizing that the Antrobians would not understand this Earthly gesture. One guard fired a warning bolt at Kaz's right arm. Everyone stood to attention instead.

"Now that's another charge for which you'll all be found guilty," bellowed his great Sphericity. The elevator door swished and clunked open.

"Get in now," said his Sphericity, "back to your cell to await another court appearance for this offense and sentencing on the other charges."

While under guard escort, Quinket was resting on top of Yesl quivering with fear, but confident that they were not defeated, however. The elevator trip back to their cell was like being again in space in a state of weightlessness until the elevator car braked hard to stop on their floor. They were all back in their cell.

"Remember Zinkel-Mallkis' order to prepare some bomb for an attack on Zigollomont," said Yesl.

"And what Zinkel-Mallkis said about the possibility of the returning *Balkieston*," said Kloonket.

"That was the right signal of the *Balkieston* and the voice of Captain Woozl," said Yesl. "When we left Tombalki, we left instructions with other Balkiens in our mission to assist the Tombalkiens to rebuild our ship. We also left samples of the metal alloys for them to emulate.

"You were working on the door, Mwaki," said Matt, "Do you think we could open it with your telekinesis on the lock."

"The lock is strongly magnetic," replied Mwaki.

"I nearly managed to disconnect the magnetic lock," said Kloonket, "but it was too hard for the time we had."

"I have just discovered a way out of here," said Quinket in her high soprano voice. "See here." Quinket flew into the crevice window and disappeared up into the crack in the rock. "I can fly out into the open," she said in her faint echo back down the hole. "I'll fly around to the other side of the door and let you all out."

It was only a few minutes before Quinket could be heard flying on the other side of the door. There was a hum followed by a dull clank from the cell door's lock. The door slid open. Everyone walked or flew out of the cell and down the passage.

"What could we have done without you, Little Quinket," said Judith to everyone's relief.

"We need to get back to our spacecraft and out of here," said Kloonket. "Can anyone remember how to get back to that hangar? And even if we get back to our ship, we'll only be able to do a low-level flight with our bust cockpit canopy."

"The passage to the hangar leads off down here," said Zinklus. "I've been down here a few times in the service of Zinkel-Mallkis. Follow me."

They walked or hovered down the passages they were escorted up after their arrest.

"We've got to get our ship over to one of the other islands and send a warning message to the *Balkieston* to take evasive action," said Yesl, "and not to arrive at Antrobi triumphantly. I'm sure that Zinkel-Mallkis will attack her."

They came through an opening into the hangar. The great hangar entrance door in the cliff was in the lowered position. From there, they could see out into the sky and the purple ocean far below. Other rock spires looked almost as tall as the one where they were.

"It seems that there's no one around," whispered Kaz. "It all seems to be too easy. Let's get on board and take off."

There came a sudden dull, distant thud followed by some vibration in the rock and a deep, ominous rumble.

"Listen," said Zinklus. "It's an antrobiquake. Don't worry. These have occurred every time I've been here. I think that Zinkel-Mallkis may have made a big mistake setting up on this one. Oh, but of course. It's the tallest, and that appealed to His Sphericity's vanity. I personally strongly counseled him against using this mountain as his main HQ, but he wouldn't listen. He very nearly put me in jail over the issue as if I was over-ruling his greatness. This mountain is so tall and slender that it has become unstable."

There was another sudden shaking and a louder rumble. Some bits of loose rock fell off and crunched onto the hangar floor.

"That is a somewhat louder rumble," said Kloonket.

While they looked at the locked door on their ship, they realized that it was externally locked by a steel bar across the door."

"Those guards!" said Yesl angrily. "I thought it seemed too easy."

The echoes of deep warbling started coming down the passage.

"The guards," said Kloonket. "We'll be caught. "Run or fly out through the hangar entrance and see if you can hide on a ledge outside. Hurry!"

The humans ran out to the edge of the hangar. They walked around and onto a small ledge beyond the door and started to climb up the rocks. It was hard and inadvisable to look down from such a narrow pathway to the ocean below partly obscured by wispy clouds. Zinklus and the Winkets were able to fly into the scout ship through the broken cockpit. The other Balkiens followed the humans to assist them out on the rocks. The scout ship started to whine into action. Suddenly the hangar was full of angry Hellack guards sparking lightning at it. The ship lurched to and fro bumping into each of the parked super-eggs, which were being quickly boarded by their pilots. The scout ship raced out of the hangar and off over the ocean and took a downward path. Matt, looking around, could see the Winkets in the open cockpit nodding at them.

"The Winkets have seen us," said Yesl. "I'm sure they'll come back for us."

The two super-eggs whooshed out of the hangar after them.

"Not a repeat of what happened before," cried Judith.

"That ship must break free," said Yesl. "It's our only means of warning the *Balkieston* of the trap she's headed for."

Everyone perched themselves on the rocks and watched the dog fight between their scout ship and the two super-eggs, which were firing bolts at it.

The ship dodged these well, but luck could not last too long. Matt looked over the cliff a little more.

"Matt!" said Yesl, "careful of the edge."

"Look Yesl," he said.

Yesl hovered out over the cliff.

"That looks like our Antrogian friends have joined in the fight," she said.

Matt could recognize Boolboonkle and Zonkollus following the super-eggs. The other four, Poolpoogleponk, Polpodwink, Spalkius, and Woozbokle came into view also and grabbed onto the super-eggs giving the scout ship a good head start. The Antrogians were just powerful enough, with three on each super-egg to be able to throw them into wild tailspins. They let them go, and the two machines spun down and down. One of them crashed into the cliff, exploding in a ball of fire and golden wreckage, which fell into the mists below. The other continued to dive out of sight into the misty clouds, presumably to regain control and fight again.

Matt and the others began to climb up away from the hangar in case of discovery.

"It won't be long before the rest of the guards and pearoids come out looking for their super-egg fighters," warned Kaz.

On these white-washed looking rocks they continued to climb. Kara was deft at finding her hand and footholds on the cliff face Wink hovered and pushed her on her back to assist her.

There was another familiar warble from below. It was Ponku. "I've led your six Antrogian friends up here."

Boolboonkle was the first to emerge from the depth of the cliffs below. He hovered up alongside the clefts they were standing on. The other five Antrogians came alongside and perched themselves onto the cliffs.

"All jump onto us," said Boolboonkle, "and we'll take you all back to our camp."

With a leap of faith, everyone jumped off the cliffs, as they were telekinetically attracted to their respective Antrogians. The flight across the ocean below was such an exhilarating relief from the clutches of Zinkel-Mallkis. As they flew further away, the magnificence of the Spire of Zinkel-Mallkis became more apparent and looked like a huge rock, which extended way above them towering into the light purple sky. Its upper slopes appeared almost white as the Vega shone on it without any inhibition from the planet's atmosphere. As they descended and flew away from Binkus-Mallkus, they were soon flying over the shoreline of the neighboring island. This island also had a towering rock, similar to the Spire of Binkus-Mallkus. Though not as high, it still protruded out into space. Soon they landed on the dark grey pebbly beach, which had small green succulent plants growing. There was a brisk sea breeze blowing that blew on up the mount as Vega's rays heated it, causing convection currents, often resulting in wispy clouds forming as the air grew cooler with altitude that would caress the rocky slopes. As a result, these slopes were covered with dark green moss-likee vegetation and dangly creepers that grew straight from the rocks and hung down being ruffled by the moist drafts.

"By the way, where's Quinket?" asked a worried Kloonket, "and Mowika?"

Quinket hovered along the endless passageways, having become separated from the other escapees. Though she appeared lost, there was method in her madness. With the excitement of their escape and the return of the *Balkieston*, Quinket thought that she might be able to locate the secret weapon destined for Zigollomont. Though she had not heard that name before, she reckoned that it was a secret base of the resistance. Everyone else in their bid to escape had forgotten all about the bomb, but Quinket realized how important it might be to stop its use. The little orb hovered along another passage, dimly lit by small lights set like jewels into the rock walls, running off to the left just before the entrance to the hangar. It led to a small cavern. Standing in the center of this was a metal dome structure with flashing colored lights. Quinket hovered around it and started exerting her telekinetic energy on it.

Suddenly a small switch clicked, and red lights began flashing. A humming noise started. Quinket panicked and flew down the passage towards the hanger, hoping to catch up with the others only to see the whole hangar full of Hellacks flying in all directions. She continued up the central passage to look for another way out.

The Antrogians were not alone for they had led their vast army of escaped slaves all the way down the western continent of Beekica, recruiting many more Balkiens, convinced by the sayings of Boonkihara.

"You can hardly see the beach for all of these Balkiens," remarked Matt.

"Like those nature programs on TV with scenes of penguin colonies in Antarctica,' said Alison. "Only we now see a vast multi-colored carpet made up of thousands of rounded furry orbs."

Boonkihara emerged from this crowd and flew up onto a rounded boulder making an excellent natural dais.

"Today," he began in English having learned the language from King Zozl. "We're going to witness or be a part of the great and terrible event as foretold in our sayings and legends of long ago. We have just been able to access the recordings from an ancient data sphere brought back to us from Tombalki on the rescue ship, the Splinkatrix, sent out many years ago to look for our ill-fated lost sky-ship, the *Balkieston*. A colleague of Zinklus, Bloonkut, also a dissident of Zinkel-Mallkis' regime managed to commandeer one of these golden egg-shaped aircraft while under the rule of Zinkel-Mallkis and fly out to rendezvous with the badly damaged Splinkatrix, orbiting Roonkle. We have brought back some of her crew along with this relic dug up on a continent on Tombalki, called Australis or Australia.

"Ladies and Gentlemen, human and Balkien, we discovered something terrible on the data and images we viewed on that sphere. We now realize that though that mission returned to Antrobi millennia ago, only a third of her crew made it back. On Tombalki, they encountered something terrible and evil on another part of that planet. We know that it was not in Australia, where this data-sphere was buried, close to many large rounded stones that formed naturally in the hope that their spherical shapes might attract a future mission to find this object. This recorded event was a previous encounter with the Enigma.

"So, what Boonkihara had told us was true," said Baingae. "We were so naïve to think that the beacon emitting those spectra from Splogita were harmless and interesting to us for exploration."

"And it has come to this," lamented Zozl.

Boonkihara concluded, "We now prepare this day to do battle against the forces of darkness on this mount as foretold."

"Matt, Yesl, Wink, Baingae, Mowika, Ponku, and Winxl," exclaimed Zozl, "and my dearest darling, Mozl–looks like we're all here. Now it's time to get ready for battle. We could not attack with all of you up there as prisoners."

Matt looked around and recognized their scout ship. It was parked askew with the front landing leg bent and further damage to the lower bodywork.

"We took a hit from a super-egg bolt," said Zinklus. "We only just managed to slow down and made it onto this beach. It'll still be able to fly but only at a low level without its canopy. We transmitted a warning in the direction of Tombalki on a wide area signal. I suggest that this ship is flown out of the area of combat as she is not battle-worthy and is our only means of contacting the Splinkatrix or the *Balkieston* for that matter. I only wish that we still had that super-egg."

"Then two of you must fly the ship to our remote citadel built high up on the Mount of Zigollomont." Zigollomont was a city carved out of one of the spires with many caverns inside. The city population did not agree with Zinkel-Mallkis' government and managed to keep themselves to themselves and were able to hide many dissident Balkiens by modifying some of their chambers so that unused caves became secret hideouts."

"Bwinkle and I will take the ship away from here," said Queen Mozl. "We'll act as lookouts and protect our garrison at the high up outpost."

After Bwinkle and Queen Mozl boarded, the scout ship slowly rose and flew off over the purple waters in the direction of the tall mount of Zigollomont. King Zozl, Boonkihara, Kloonket, Zinklus, Mowika, and Ponku assembled in front of the vast crowd of Balkiens.

"A super-egg!" cried Zozl. "Take cover!"

The golden craft flew in menacingly close, but then its side window close to the cockpit slid open.

"Bloonkut!" shouted Kloonket, who immediately flew up to the open window as the super-egg hovered into a vertical landing. The main round door in the side slid open.

"I managed to 'borrow' this craft from his Sphericity," said Bloonkut, who was a larger prolate Balkien with a range of pink to crimson colors in his swooth. I've also got plenty of zapper guns to issue to everyone here. I don't think we'll win with just rocks and boulders, which we'll still have to use as these few guns are all I've managed to raid from Zinkel-Mallkis' armory without arousing suspicion."

"Today is our great day in your history and destiny," began Matt. "We're here to face off against your great oppressor, the self-styled Zinkel-Mallkis, who dares to call himself Emperor. He has deceived you into false hopes of a great future in his wonderful technically advanced civilization, he claimed. Instead, he has brought you nothing but MISERY and SLAVERY! Where are the great promises of the wonderful resplendent dream mooties for you? What happened to the awe-inspiring cities with beautiful gardens and vistas?

What happened to those promises of you all going to live on the other planets in comfort? This freedom was only available to the elite few. As for the rest of you; ABJECT HARD LABOUR!" Zozl translated into Antrobian.

There were many shrills and Balkien anger raised against their oppressive rulers.

"AND, TODAY," shouted Kloonket at the top of his swooth, "we're going to FIGHT for that freedom. We're going to FIGHT for the Antrobi that we once knew and will know again and with a greater understanding of ourselves than before so that we'll not so easily be gullible and be taken down like this again."

"I, Zinklus, once a fervent proponent of the New Antrobian Order under Zinkel-Mallkis, was HORRIFIED to learn of the ghastly slavery and oblateness that many of you mobilized here had endured and then rescued by our fellow Balkiens, here, along with our great friends from the planet, Tombalki. These Tombalkiens taught us all about their great understanding of the evil that has befallen us, not only from Zinkel-Mallkis but the mind-bending influence of the evil force–*the Enigma*–we encountered on Splogita with its enticing spectral signal that lured us into his trap. WE FIGHT FOR FREEDOM."

"This day, foretold by our ancestors in the sacred writings of the Great One, is that I have repeatedly told you about in times past," said Boonkihara. "This will be our greatest victory."

Matt stood up to speak for the races from Antrobi, Antrogi, and Tombalki. "Today, we'll rise and resist the terrible thoughts and ideologies of the Enigma who has so influenced Zinkel-Mallkis, the former King of Antrogi; King Zozl's counterpart."

There was a louder cry from the tens of thousands of Balkiens. All eyes and visual swooth focused onto the Spire of Binkus-Mallkus. There was a sense of foreboding in the air.

Zinkel-Mallkis, smug in his colorful countenance, occupied the exquisitely paneled geodesic throne room. "Ah, this is my strong fortress-palace, the tallest mount in all of Antrobi." He continued to gloat and preen his swooth, admiring himself as he looked narcissistically in any one of the five large hexagonal mirrors around the throne room.

There was a loud, dull bang from deep inside the rock as if a large meteorite had hit the Spire somewhere close by. The ceiling shook dislodging two of the triangular facets, which fell out and shattered onto the white, bejeweled floor.

"What was that," exclaimed Zinkel-Mallkis sounding a little concerned. "Go and see what has happened," he ordered Hellacks.

"Your Sphericity, I think that is an antrobiquake," said one of the guards.

"Get those panels replaced!"

For a few seconds, there was a faint rumbling.

"A thunderstorm coming," laughed Zinkel-Mallkis. "How convenient! All these pathetic rebels are going to get very wet. Their useless disheveled bodies will fall into the sea. Ha."

His leathery guards flew up to the small pentagonal windows to look out at the clear purple sky with not a cloud in sight. The rumble fell away.

Matt looked towards the Spire of Binkus-Mallkus. "Zozl, Winkets, Yesl; can you see what I see?" Four or five bright golden objects were leaving the cliffs of the Spire.

"Super-eggs!" cried Zozl. "They'll be here to attack us SOON! RUN and fly like the wind!"

"All of you," cried Kloonket. "Take up your guns and attack all the installations on the Mount and find that weak point and see if we can bring it down."

Immediately all six humans were whisked up onto their Antrogians armed with their lightning zapper guns.

"CHARGE!" shouted King Zozl. The Antrogians rose into the air surrounded by a vast cloud of Balkiens. Every Balkien had small stones spinning in orbit around themselves. There was a crescendo of thousands of aggressive warbles as the whole armada of Balkiens flew with one aim into the Battle of Binkus-Mallkus. Boolboonkle had hundreds of medium-sized pebbles racing around his equator while Matt rode astride him armed and ready with his zapper gun. Dozens of super-eggs flew out to close in on them.

"What is this?" said an agitated Zinkel-Mallkis from his perfectly round velvet throne.

"We seem to be under an assault," said a Hellack attendant.

"Then mobilize the rest of our super-eggs," said Zinkel-Mallkis menacingly. "We'll soon crush this feeble resistance." Zinkel-Mallkis started to heave up and down with deep guffaws of Antrogian laughter. "This will be my opportunity to eliminate this uprising once and for all. This weak and insufferable rebellion will be snuffed out just like that. Prepare the great guns!" These cannons stood on emplacements around the fortifications of Zinkel-Mallkis' palace headquarters. "These guns fire great zaps like energy missiles that can destroy any targets they hit. This is a great opportunity!" Zinkel-Mallkis began to cackle with amusement at his plan.

Suddenly, there was another shaking of the room with more deep rumblings. A few panels fell from the ceiling and landed on Zinkel-Mallkis' beautifully preened and ponkolated swooth.

"Another antrobiquake!" he shouted. "Get those damaged panels off my swooth and fix the ceiling! This place is an absolute mess. I'll go and oversee the defenses."

YESL – The Balkien from Antrobi

Zinkel-Mallkis flew from his throne room and emerged out onto the whitewashed balconies, several kilometers up the Spire from the deep ocean below. He could see that the sky was darkened by the incoming army of resistance Balkiens, led by his adversary, King Zozl, to do battle against his Sphericity. For the first time, Zinkel-Mallkis felt threatened by this growing resistance to his authority. A number of his Hellacks and his pearoid minions gathered around him on the balconies.

"All of you great guards and pearoids," ordered Zinkel-Mallkis. "Go out and use your mind control tactics to resist this threat coming into attack us! GO! GO!"

The Hellacks had used mind control before to subjugate the population; similar to the telepathic transmissions that Yesl did to Matt. The pearoid beings took off and flew over towards the approaching dark cloud.

"Guards, man the guns and zap em," shouted His Sphericity.

The Antrogians, mounted by the Tombalkiens were approaching the Spire with its stark white and light grey cliffs. Yesl was with Matt. The Winkets were with Kaz. King Zozl was leading just ahead of Judith, who had Kloonket and Boongoo. Zinklus was with Sean. Mowika and Ponku were with Kara, and Dr. Baingae was with Alison who insisted on being part of the battle though still was not quite recovered from her injury by the hackel.

Ahead of them, a super-egg roared past, nearly knocking them all off their Antrogians.

"Split up and keep flying in zigzag paths!" shouted Zozl. "Have your rocks and guns ready!" Looking around, Matt saw a super-egg coming straight for him, firing bright bolts. Boolboonkle spun his boulders faster and let some of them go at the super-egg. Most missed though some shattered into its cockpit, which splintered into smithereens. It fired back straight lightning bolts with one just missing Matt as he ducked away in time. He lifted his gun and aimed at the broken cockpit as the super-egg flew past and fired, missing the Hellack pilot. He fired another shot at the wing flaps and the rudder, which exploded. It then lost height, and far below it exploded. Other super-eggs were roaming around in amongst the army of Balkiens. The super-eggs struck many of them. There were many more Balkiens releasing volleys of rocks from their fast-spinning orbits while all of the humans on their Antrogians flew around firing their guns. These combined tactics were enough to shoot down many of the bolt firing super-eggs, which were, hitting many of them who were wugging towards the ocean.

The Antrogians, led by King Zozl got level with some of the structures on the Spire and let out most of their volley of rocks while Matt and Kaz took shots at many protruding spires, bringing them down onto Zinkle-Mallkis' palatial quarters. They hit home and shattered a lot of the structures. Several of the super-eggs exploded in a hangar just as they were about to take off, though many of them became airborne successfully.

"There's Zinkel-Mallkis up there," shouted King Zozl as they flew up as close as they could get safely. "Zinkel-Mallkis," shouted Zozl across the divide. "Your day of reckoning has come. We're fighting to free our world from your despotic and selfish tyranny."

"You think that you can thwart the will of Zinkel-Mallkis, do you?" retorted Zinkel-Mallkis. "YOU think that YOUR stupid silly poxy oblatoid little puchty of a past defunct little balkleiod can ever be King again? Do YOU?"

Zozl was incensed. Matt was filled with rage and fired off a few lightning bolts from his gun at some of the pearoids who rose to attack with their weapons. He scored three hits, with the pearoids which sent them falling to their doom in the ocean.

"I'm done negotiating with you!" shouted Zozl angrily. "You are now the utterly despicable evil one, who was once my friend and co-ruler! WE ARE FRIENDS NO MORE! Have it YOUR WAY, YOUR SPHERICITY! Antrogians! Let him have it!"

The rocks, which were still spinning around the Antrogians, began to turn faster. When they let go, the boulders all shattered onto some rock spires above Zinkel-Mallkis. These crumpled and fell onto his swooth.

More super-eggs, Hellacks, and pearoids began to emanate from holes in the cliff face, which opened without being noticed. Though some of the super-eggs were shot down by Matt and the others with the zapper guns from their Antrogian mounts, the rest started to zap the poor Balkiens who *wugged* in more significant numbers. The Hellacks started emitting sparks of lightning. Bolts of fire were also zapping from the guns on ramparts of the Spire. Zinkel-Mallkis was himself flying around in a somewhat agitated state. He let off the odd spark of pinkish lightning.

"What are we doing here?" asked Yesl. "Matt. Why are we here?"

"Yesl," said Matt." I wonder that myself."

The Balkiens flying around the cliffs began to fly in a disorganized manner. They had ceased to fight vigorously. During this moment of confusion, many pearoids zapped a lot of Balkiens and sent them *wugging* ocean-wards.

"What are you all doing?" exclaimed Zozl as he flew just ahead of the Antrogians. "Fight! You're all confused!"

"Watch out. Zinkel-Mallkis may be using mind control influences— RESIST IT!" shouted Matt above the noise of thousands of warbling Balkiens in combat. "They're trying to control our minds."

Kaz fired off a few more laser shots that struck home at more of Zinkel-Mallkis' Hellacks that were firing lightning strikes at them.

Suddenly Zinkel-Mallkis dived towards them; firing rocks picked up off the cliffs as he had not his other weaponry to hand. They all missed except for Boolboonkle.

"AARGH!" groaned Matt. "We've been walloped!"

Matt nearly fell off Boolboonkle, but just managed to hold on, assisted by Yesl.

"Boolboonkle," shouted Yesl. "Make for that rock ledge over there and stay hidden." Boolboonkle just managed to land safely on the ledge before a possible plunge into the sea. Matt slipped off, Boolboonkle.

"How is he?" asked Matt. "He's got a sharp rock embedded in his body through his thick swooth. Zinkel-Mallkis, himself, hit him."

"I wish Baingae were here," said Yesl.

"I'm glad you are," said Matt. "Do the inner parts of Balkiens or Antrogians bleed if we remove anything impaled in their swooth?"

"No."

"Then, I'd better pull these two rocks out."

Matt tugged on the rock sticking out of Boolboonkle, and it came out suddenly almost letting him fall off the cliff. With some warbling, Yesl managed to pull out the other smaller rock. On the ends of the rock was a light green jelly-like substance.

"That's a Balkien's equivalent of blood from our inner bodies that are well within our swooth," said Yesl. Boolboonkle's quite hurt, but I'm sure he'll recover. He won't have the strength to fly off here, though."

From their landing area, the cries of battle seemed to be growing more distant and quieter. Large silvery balls were now emerging from the cliffs. These had many small holes in them, looking like rounded shields allowing them to breathe.

"These look like pongballs, a term used to describe a Balkien's protective spherical space suit or suit of armor," said Yesl. "They have Hellacks in them and have zapper guns. The big ones may have evil Antrogians, loyal to the Enigma."

"These great steel things will have the strength of armor as we had on Earth in the Middle Ages," said Matt. The pongballs moved on out over the sea zapping at will.

"Yesl," cried Matt, "It's not going well. Many of our friends have wugged. Boolboonkle is hurt. We're on enemy territory. We fully expect to be prisoners again." He wept. "Oh Yesl, I'm sorry that it's come to this."

"Matt," be encouraged by the prophetic sayings of Boonkihara," said Yesl. "You and I have been through a lot together. We mustn't give up now."

"Will I ever see Erin again?" said Matt with tears in his eyes. "I've missed her so dearly."

"I'm sure that we will see Erin and we will get through this," said Yesl trying to reassure Matt, though she was beginning to see that the great battle was lost.

"Oh, what about my family and friends on the other Antrogians?" hollered Matt. "I hope that Zinkel-Mallkis isn't going for them too."

Through his tear-soaked eyes, Matt looked up, out over towards the other tall islands as if to have one last look at his surroundings before succumbing to an inevitable arrest. He cuddled his dear Yesl for comfort.

"I'm sure that they'll come for us and put us in that awful dungeon again," moaned Matt, "and this time we'll not escape Zinkel-Mallkis' wrath."

Matt looked up again over the top of Yesl. He saw something strange. The deep purple sky began to fill with another myriad of tiny black specks.

"Hey Yesl, look," said Matt. "They're coming back to attack again."

"Those look larger than our army," said Yesl.

The specks grew into an army of great Antrogians with various colored features and covered with armor-plated shields or pongballs. They raced in towards a final assault on the Emperor's lair, firing their zapper guns just like those of Zinkel-Mallkis. A lot of lightning emanated from the Spire, close to Zinkel-Mallkis' Palace directed at the new force. Flashes from zapper guns were fired in all directions. There was a deafening roar of boulders hitting the stronghold. Bits of the spires of rock broke off and fell and crashed close to where Matt, Yesl, and Boolboonkle were cowering. Matt waved his arms madly, wielding his jacket. Some of the invading Antrogians flew up close to the cliff. On one of them, he noticed a human figure.

"Yesl!" cried Matt, "Fly down to that Antrogian and tell him to come up here. That must be Alison or Kara."

Yesl flew down to join the human sitting on the Antrogian as he hovered back and forth, trying to avoid falling rocks and stray projectiles fired in the fighting. Matt looked below and saw Yesl landing on the Antrogian beside the human figure. They immediately flew up to land beside Boolboonkle hovering in with a typically loud, deep warble, ruffling Matt's hair by the downdraft from the Antrogian as he landed. He held himself steady holding onto Boolboonkle. The warbling stopped. Yesl flew down to Matt.

"Matt," said Yesl, "come up with me onto Spoonkoothtil, the great Antrogian leader of the garrison on Zigollomont."

The female human figure stood up atop Spoonkoothtil.

"Erin!" exclaimed Matt.

"Oh, Matt, my sweetheart!"

Spoonkoothtil guided Erin down onto the ledge. Matt and Erin embraced and kissed one another fondly. Baingae and Winxl also alighted from Spoonkoothtil.

"This is very reminiscent of the meteor crater in Arizona," said Baingae. "I was sent here to diagnose poor Boolboonkle by Zozl. We saw you being hit."

"Matt," said Erin after their tearful reunion. "We came on the *Balkieston*. It was dredged up from the Atlantic Ocean and rebuilt."

Another sudden deep rumble came from deep within the mountain. The ledge they were on shuddered and shook. Small rock spires, some of which had carvings of the empire's design crashed around them. The sculptures were mainly of giant stone spheres set atop the spires. They looked very round and emulated Zinkel-Mallkis' Sphericity. Some of the larger ones were painted in his colors. As they looked up, they saw that a large part of the Spire had begun to topple over slowly. There was another loud, throbbing rumble, far worse than they had ever heard before. The ground started shaking violently. Both the Antrogians wobbled profusely.

"Matt, Erin," shouted Yesl. "We've got to get off here! I think this mount's going to go down. Hurry!"

Matt and Erin were whisked up onto Spoonkoothtil, who took off, slowly at first. Spoonkoothtil slipped off the ledge and headed down to pick up flying velocity. Yesl flew down to the other Antrogians hovering nearby and told them to lift the disabled Boolboonkle off the rock ledge. More rocks started to descend towards Boolboonkle. The whole ledge on which he sat began to heave and move downwards. The floor of it began to crack apart.

Matt and Erin looked on with horror clinging to one another as they witnessed the whole Spire of Binkus-Mallkus beginning to bend over and start to slide down along the known angled geologic fault. The part of the Spire upward from the geologic fault began to grind slowly over the lower part. They could see Boolboonkle beginning to tumble down with pieces of falling rock. The other Antrogians were following him. Three of them managed to hold onto Boolboonkle and fly him away from the falling boulders and bits of the spire. They came over ever too slowly toward Spoonkoothtil. As they caught up along with Yesl, Baingae, and Winxl, they gradually flew over towards the far shore to find a landing place.

The magnificent edifice of Zinkel-Mallkis was slipping at a much quicker rate. The Spire was at a noticeable angle. Soon, there was a growing deep roar as it began to crash down. Tiny splinters of rock were breaking off amid clouds of dust and ash. The deep rumbling roar grew louder above the warbling of the Antrogians trying to hold onto Boolboonkle.

"I'm glad we removed the two rocks, embedded in Boolboonkle's swooth, without Dr. Baingae's permission," said Yesl.

"Look Yesl," said Matt, "everyone's flying off the beach below. They're all heading for what ledges they can find on the other spires high up. We'd better do the same. There'll be a fearsome tsunami when that rock mount hits the sea."

They landed on a large-enough ledge on the other nearby spire. Everyone watched. The roar of the fall of Binkus-Mallkus was not only coming through the air but through the rock, where they were sitting. The upper part of the

Spire was now sliding down towards the ocean. Clouds of dust were billowing outwards. Pieces of the magnificent rock spire were breaking off and tumbling down. About mid-way up an orange glow appeared that looked like hot magma with gaseous emissions bubbling out in clouds of steam, which exploded towards the east, thankfully, not towards them.

Finally, the lowest parts of the mass began to hit the ocean sending up a massive plume of water. The roar grew ever louder. BOOM! The shock wave of exploding gas from the magma hit them about five minutes later.

"What about all those wugged Balkiens in the ocean," said Yesl in her Balkien form of weeping. "They'll never survive the tsunami. Will they, Baingae?"

"I'm sure many of them will," he replied, "but those that do will be severely oblated after their initial wug, let alone the tsunami. Many may not survive at all."

They watch in awe and horror as the Spire of Binkus-Mallkus continued to rumble and slide down into the sea with white and grey billowing clouds expanded outwards and upwards. Very high up this erupting cloud began to form into a colossal anvil shape, blown on the stratospheric winds toward the east. The splintering rocks continued to splash into the water. The developing tsunami began to build up into a massive wave of about five hundred meters high, before spreading out in all directions, including towards them. The mount kept crashing down. The summit appeared out of the upper cirrus clouds before passing down into the ash cloud. The bright light, the Beacon of Zinkel-Mallkis, observed by everyone earlier on their initial approach to Binkus-Mallkus, continued to shine out. The beacon flickered from being so bright to be a lot dimmer then it flickered out altogether.

"That wave's coming towards us," said Yesl. Everyone looked and gasped. Thousands of little Balkiens occupied every nook, creek, and crevice. These Balkiens were of all shapes, colors, and sizes and were unable to fly or were caring for the injured. There was a sudden loud crack and rumble. Everyone looked around for the lightning, thinking for a moment that, more Hellacks were once again coming to attack.

"That crack may have been the sound of Zinkel-Mallkis' beacon blowing up," said Yesl.

The Balkiens were perched here and there in little ponkadliaths. The massive deep purple wave topped with foaming white flecks was now halfway towards them and was nearly at their height.

Those Balkiens that were able-bodied telekinetically or gravitationally held the injured ones between themselves and the rock crevices waiting for the wave they hoped would miss them.

"Matt, Erin," said Yesl. "Spoonkoothtil will hold you on to her. We've all got to stay here to hold onto Boolboonkle. If only we could fly!"

With the wave getting menacingly closer to them at their level, Baingae and Winxl hid inside Matt's buttoned-up jacket. Matt and Erin were held on tightly to Spoonkoothtil. The three Antrogians that had rescued Boolboonkle all surrounded him and held him down. The wave came upon the lower slopes of their mount. The vibrations from the rock became a distinct shudder. There was a roar of rushing water as the massive tsunami lashed their fortress rock, which was like being assaulted by far greater force than any Zinkel-Mallkis could muster. There was a dull thud followed by a slap of water as it raced up the slope towards them. Tongues of white frothing water blasted up past them and stopped rising just several meters above them in places. Torrents of water and spray washed down onto them. All the Balkiens, Matt and Erin were held on tightly as the remaining water gushed past them. Finally, a mass of water splashed down onto Spoonkoothtil, soaking him. As the waters started to rush away, half-drowned and oblated Balkiens began popping out of the ebbing wave and landed hard on the Antrogians, for the Antrogians had telekinetically plucked them out of the water. Antrogians flew out over the roiling sea to pluck up more of them. The wave washed down the slope and receded.

Matt and Erin just clung to each other in fright and relief that it was over and that Spoonkoothtil still held them. Erin, now beginning to shiver from being drenched, peaked into Matt's jacket to see that Baingae and Winxl were still there and okay if a little bedraggled and half soaked. Matt couldn't help but notice Erin's smiling face looking up at him as she tenderly fondled Baingae and Winxl with her left forefinger. Matt and Erin held a long gentle kiss. The drama of huge waves and falling mountains, for a moment, faded into a fuzzy backdrop, while they held each other in an embrace and rubbed one another's noses. Baingae and Winxl who were still on Matt's chest began to pulsate in excitement, not only at seeing a great couple united in romantic love but also that their world was being liberated from years of tyranny as foretold by that wise old sage, Boonkihara.

Several deep warbles became audible. It was Kara, Sean, Kaz, Alison, and Judith on their Antrogians coming into land close to them.

"Erin!" exclaimed everyone almost in unison. "How did you get here? Were you involved with sending in the Antrogian reinforcements?" asked Kaz.

"To cut a long story short," said Erin. "We came back on the *Balkieston*, which was lifted from the seabed and rebuilt in space using the services of the International Space Station, and the use of several scout ships retrieved from the sunken bridge section, raised from the Atlantic. These scout ships were found to be still operational. We got your transmission and diverted to the Planet, Roonkle. We came in the scout ships and joined in with the mobilizing of the Antrogian army."

The air was now clear again. The rocks they were standing on were now wet and slippery. Balkiens, who were too soaked and heavy with the water in them to be able to fly, rolled about in a daze. Baingae and Winxl emerged from between Matt and Erin. They flew over to oversee the state of the injured, the wugged, and the oblated. There were three hapless small ones about Baingae's size clinging onto Boolboonkle. They looked to be of one family as they had alternating bands of dark blue, green, and red swooth. One was groaning with a gash on her swooth consistent with a bolt of lightning or super-egg flash in the heat of battle. Dr. Baingae passed his diagnostics over all three and took a long look at Boolboonkle's wounds as well.

"Boolboonkle's in terrible shape," he said with an anguished tone. "We'll have to get him off here and into rehab on the citadel of Zigollomont. We've all got to fly to Zigollomont, under the control of great Antrogian, Spoonkoothtil, who is our royal Antrogian in exile."

After drying off in the Vega light, the Antrogians lifted off from the rocky perches and flew the half-hour trip to Zigollomont, south of where Binkus-Mallkus once stood. Matt and Erin, with Baingae and Winxl, sat atop Spoonkoothtil as they rounded some more white cliffs and saw the fantastic golden citadel of Zigollomont perched on the cliff supported by massive struts. It was a fabulous fortress city, built by a legion of Antrogians, who remained loyal to King Zozl and who had just fought with gallantry. On its leading platform, there were many tall cylindrical buildings topped by spheroid mooties.

"It's great to have this place built for Antrogians to bring poor Boolboonkle," said Zozl. Kloonket and Zinklus had finally joined them. Zinklus was unharmed, but Kloonket had a graze on his swooth by a Hellack, which Dr. Baingae needed to examine. Everyone landed to a hero's welcome on the main open landing area or balcony of Zigollomont. After a glorious green Vegaset in late twilight on the balcony, there was a faint high-pitched warbling from afar.

"Quinket!" exclaimed Kloonket. "Where have you been in all of your mischievousnesses?"

"I found a huge cavern in Binkus-Mallkus with a metallic machine inside," said Quinket rather sheepishly. "I moved a switch on it, and it started flashing red lights and humming. So, I flew out as fast as I could, and there was a thunderous bang which blew me out into the open, and all this fighting was going on, and the mount began to collapse."

"You WHAT!" scolded her father, Kloonket, who then pulsated and joined his errant daughter in ponkadliath. "Quinket! It was YOU who brought us victory!"

"I remember Zinkle-Mallkis talking about a bomb to be used against Zigollomont. I went to investigate," replied Quinket.

"That must have been the bomb you activated in there," said Kloonket. "So, it exploded on Binkus-Mallkus in the greatest backfire ever!"

Everyone, both Balkien, and Tombalkien, came around little Quinket and cheered. Matt held the little Balkien in his hands with awe that such a petite ball of swooth could greatly assist in bringing down an Empire.

In the Bay of Koolkooltic to the east on the mainland of Balkalay, Balkiens, loyal to Zinkel-Mallkis, looked up to the west to see that the far distant bright beacon of Binkus-Mallkus had gone out. Looking closely, they could not see the tall, dark Spire silhouetted against the bright green Vegaset sky. The ocean horizon was very rough. The waters on the beaches, in front of the industrial installations, receded far out exposing the seabed, where hackels, like the one that bit Alison, writhed on the wet sand. There was another bright beacon that shone from the summit of one of the tall mounts nearby. Many Hellacks patrolled in front of the round video screens around the installations. On these, were displayed the image of Zinkel-Mallkis projected onto Spalminkatrix from its geostationary satellites. The waters returned with a roar as the tsunami washed over the exposed shore to a menacing height. Alarm hooters sounded all over the industrial town of Antron. Thousands of disillusioned Balkien slave workers swarmed out and joined the skyward exodus. The mass of water knocked down many buildings. A second wave reared up over the first smashing into the metal tower emitting the green laser beam causing it to buckle. The great image of Zinkel-Mallkis began to wobble on the screens, while the green beacon went out, for it was a mirror that reflected the beam out to the geostationary satellites around Spalminkatrix.

King Zozl arranged for everyone to look through the telescope on Zigollomont set in an astronomical observatory mootie on an outer balcony. Erin was at the eyepiece.

"Look at Spalminkatrix," she said. "Matt, you won't believe this. Come and see."

Matt looked through the eyepiece, expecting to see Zinkel-Mallkis large as life. What he saw was that the image was wobbling and flickering on and off with fuzzy lines, like an old analog TV set going off the channel. Suddenly the image of Zinkel-Mallkis went out, leaving only the former natural color banding of the planet.

• ◯ •

19 ~ THE RESTORATION

The groans and wailings tempered the jubilation of victory from the Balkiens who were injured. Baingae was busy diagnosing them in the grand hall mootie on Zigollomont.

"Baingae's doing a lot for them," remarked Erin as she relaxed in Matt's arms. "Why, he and Winxl remind me of Florence Nightingale who tended the war wounded in her day. Matt, I'm so glad to have met you and been part of this adventure. For a long time after you departed Earth, I was so lonely, thinking I'd never see you again until NASA raised the *Balkieston*."

Monku flew over and landed on Erin's shoulder. "Matt. Here's Monku. He's been my faithful friend just like Yesl is to you, since the Splinkatrix left. I remember looking at it through the main Mt Wilson telescope every night thinking of you until the ship was too faint and red-shifted to see. Oh, I was so longing…" Erin cuddled up and lay in Matt's arms and relaxed. Monku and Yesl lay on their chests as they dozed off.

In the night air looking from outside the grand mootie, distant squeals were sounding like the defeated Hellacks, above the sea noise roiling around their shores in the aftermath of the collapse of Binkus-Mallkus. King Zozl rested on a large stone circular table overlooking the rough seas, full of debris. Queen Mozl sat with King Zozl. Something caught Zozl's vision swooth. There were moving lights that arose from out of the roiling ocean waters where the Spire of Binkus-Mallkus once stood. They streaked off upwards into the night sky. The waters continued to pour forth steam as they frothed, in a maelstrom, possibly caused by remaining volcanic activity after the mount collapsed.

Zozl flew inside the great hall. "Everyone. Wake up. You'd better come to the balcony and see this."

Baingae and Winxl flew over to the sleeping couple. "Matt, Erin, Yesl, Monku. Wake up. Boodibah."

Everyone arose and emerged onto the balcony. Kloonket and Zinklus sat on the stone table with Zozl, Mozl, and many other Balkiens to observe what was happening. The ocean continued to boil with steam clouds continuing to rise into the night air lit by the light of Antrogi. Boonkihara hovered over to be in front of the gathering. More strange little lights continued to shoot out of the maelstrom.

"Everyone gathered here," said Boonkihara in Antrobian and then in English. "What we can see here may be the defeated spirits of the Enigma. Be careful all of you. What is causing those waters to boil is not only hot lava or gasses coming up from the depths but also those disenchanted spirits. Focus your minds on what is good. Don't let evil thoughts influence you or divide you. You've all experienced the terrible results of war and evil conquest this day. I exhort you all to continue to resist any lasting vestiges of the evil influence. We may feel liberated now, but as foretold in our sacred writings, we'll now have to bury our dead, commit our seriously injured into long periods of hibernation in the many sepulchers on these rocks."

The waters lit up brighter and roiled fiercely. There was a white glow getting brighter coming from beneath the maelstrom. Suddenly bolts of lightning flashed out of the seething, white, frothing waves. A few minutes later, there were deafening claps of thunder reverberating around the surrounding cliffs. Everyone reeled back, fearing another great wave was going to rise and engulf the citadel.

"Everyone," ordered Zozl. "Back inside! There's going to be another great explosion!"

Before anyone turned to move indoors, there was a bright flash from behind the big rock almost between them and the roiling waters. The humans covered their eyes. The waters gushed some way up into the air, and an ugly bright apparition of flaming fire shot up into the sky. It moved heavenwards getting dimmer until it was like a moving star of average brightness.

"That was the Antrobian presence of the Great and Terrible Enigma!" exclaimed Boonkihara. "We've finally won this victory over our oppressor. It is thanks to all of you, resisting its mind control effects. If you look carefully, it is heading in the direction of Splogita, maybe to where it originated?"

"What about those Molktrons we left on that world?" asked Wink.

"And what has happened to Zinkel-Mallkis?" asked Kaz.

"As yet we don't know," said Zozl.

"I think that Boolboonkle and I may have been the last to see him before the mount collapsed," said Matt. "That was when Zinkel-Mallkis himself, pierced poor Boolboonkle with the two rock spears that nearly sent us both falling into the sea. After Boolboonkle landed on the ledge, I saw Zinkel-Mallkis flying erratically around as the mount was rumbling. Then my dearest Erin appeared on Spoonkoothtil and rescued us just before the great eruption."

With relief, everyone began to chatter and talked about their experiences and victory. The evening sky began to change color into a deeper purple. The ocean was no longer boiling, where the Spire had stood. The air seemed to get pleasantly warmer. Yesl, Baingae, and the Winkets began to fly around in a jubilant mood. Even Yesl and Wink's battle wounds began to heal up as a sense of wellbeing descended on the whole citadel.

The able Balkiens started flying around the cliffs in happiness and jubilation. Yesl looked at Matt and Erin, who were holding hands gazing out to an ocean that seemed to have more vibrant colors than those they had seen before.

"This is like the Antrobi I knew before we left on our mission to Splogita," she said. "I now feel that I'm indeed at home. Yesl quivered in Matt's arms.

"That's a Balkien's way of weeping for joy," said Dr. Baingae. "You two have a great time together on your great day of reunion. Come. We've got a lot of work to do tending the sick and injured."

"Wait a moment," said Matt as he pulled out his necklace pendant shaped like the one half of a broken heart and showed it to Erin. She reached down into her green and crimson mottled T-shirt and pulled out the other half. With arms around each other, they looked at one another smiling. Each held out their broken heart pendants and joined them together. They made a perfect fit forming the whole heart shape.

"Erin," said Matt with a laugh, "broken no more." Matt knelt on his right knee before Erin with Baingae and Winxl present. Baingae sat on Matt's shoulder and Winxl on Erin's. "I love you, Erin," he said softly to her, bathed in the beautiful Antrogi light. "I've missed you so much since having to leave you behind on Tombalki when we came on the Splinkatrix. I often looked up at the night sky to the sun as a faint low magnitude star with my old binoculars and thought of you and also using the telescopes at King Zozl's fortified palace at Little Balkieston. I wonder what state it's in now after the attack by the Hellacks when we had to run for it."

"Matt," said Erin softly with a beaming smile. "I did the same looking up at far distant Vega from the Mt Wilson Observatory thinking of you while doing my research work and while the *Balkieston* was being repaired and rebuilt."

"Erin. I now look forward to honoring my proposal?" said Matt softly.

"Oh, it's been such a long time and a great distance," replied Erin. "I fervently hoped to be able to join the mission on the *Balkieston* to be with you!"

"Then we'll have to announce our previous engagement on Tombalki before all of the Balkiens here in the citadel," said Matt. "And what about Baingae and Winxl, who went the scenic route via Splogita to be with you. Ha."

Winxl hovered over to Baingae. They flew off Erin's shoulder together and landed on the stone table, remaining in contact with one another. While Matt and Erin, arm in arm watched. Baingae flew around Winxl twenty times and settled on top of her briefly as was the Antrobian custom before finally landing beside her. "Winxl, I have traveled to the ends of the galaxy to be with you. Will you marry me?"

"Why, Yes! Of course," replied Winxl. Both of them started to pulsate in happy moods.

"Boodibah," said Baingae as he and Winxl flew off for several circuits around the balcony area swooth in swooth while Matt and Erin walked around several times following them holding hands.

"We'll have to plan a double wedding," suggested Erin.

"Great idea," said Winxl, "maybe in the Temple in Balkieston."

Baingae and Winxl flew off tending to the wounded. Baingae ran many diagnoses on them while Winxl comforted them, assisted by Monku and Yesl. A few of the Antrogians flew low over the waters in a search pattern pulling up the floating; injured Balkiens knocked down in battle or by the tsunami. They were brought to casualty areas on balconies on several levels. Three Antrogians flew low over the beach where they had assembled before for battle. Lying forlornly on the shore was Zinkel-Mallkis in a very wet state. He was disheveled and oblate, lying unconscious. Heavy with water, it took the power of about twenty large Antrogians to lift him with strong ropes and fly him up to a large cave in one of the high rock pinnacles nearby, prepared as a sepulcher for his long hibernation. After drying in the Vega light, cocoon-like material grew around his once beautiful swooth. He was placed into hibernation until a future time when Zinkel-Mallkis may be restored after this awful encounter with the Enigma.

"Is it possible for such dictators to be reformed?" asked Matt. "It seldom happens on Tombalki, though not unknown."

"We'll have to wait and see," said King Zozl. "Zinkel-Mallkis was such a great and charismatic ruler on Antrogi before the Enigma came. He then started introducing tight regulations and forming an elite group of Balkiens and legalistic Mallkets to enforce these policies. Then Antrobi was invaded, and I found myself in exile. We were so shocked and disillusioned when our fellow Balkiens turned on us, and so gullibly accepted all the changes in society. Life for us became miserable, vexed over the non-return of the *Balkieston* or the Splinkatrix, and what would happen if you did return."

In orbit around the outer great gas giant, Nentharsis, the planet beyond Spalminkatrix, the *Balkieston* floated in space in all her majestic glory above the billowing white clouds in that planet's emerald green atmosphere. From the front, the original *bridge* sphere, recovered almost intact from the North Atlantic and incorporated into the new ship still had most of its computers and navigation equipment working or repaired by Captain Woozl and his crew. The front geodesic sphere looked well travel stained. There were even still a few barnacles after being on the ocean bed for many years. It was the only part of the original ship that had been raised and carried back into space using its smaller gyro engines and re-attached to the rest of the enormous ship, rebuilt from the instructions left behind, with information extracted from the data sphere, given to NASA by Matt's father.

"All of this would not have been possible had it not been for knowledge of manufacturing of the metal alloy including the samples left with NASA," said Woozl.

The *Balkieston* diverted to Roonkle, where the badly damaged Splinkatrix orbited. Makeshift supports were made for the rear struts of the Splinkatrix damaged by the Enigma's lightning from the image of Zinkel-Mallkis on Spalminkatrix. These supports, like scaffolding, stopped her from disintegrating while being towed back to Antrobi.

"We've just received a transmission that the evil on our planet was defeated in a final battle," said Woozl, "and that we are cleared to bring this great ship finally home after her great odyssey."

The Splinkatrix was attached to the side of the *Balkieston* for the trip back.

"The rear part of this ship will almost need as much rebuilding as the *Balkieston* did," said Woozl.

The *Balkieston* was not entirely rebuilt to her original layout with five of the accommodation globes being remodeled to accommodate a human crew of thirty personnel, mainly of NASA astronauts and scientists from the Jet Propulsion Laboratory including Erin, Dan, and Nick.

"Time to take her in," said Captain Woozl. The gyro engines started to turn. There was a light hum and throb while gravity slowly returned to them on board from a state of weightlessness. Slowly the Planet, Roonkle began to slip away behind them.

Captain Andrew Gerhardt was the leader of the NASA crew. "I sure hope that Erin's okay down there. As Captain, I was very reluctant to let her go."

"Don't worry," replied Woozl. "I've just had another message. Erin has just sent out an announcement of her plans to marry Matt following her engagement back in Arizona. Also, in the same transmission, Baingae and Winxl have announced their engagement."

The astronauts cheered and gave a rousing clap of applause. The Balkien crew hovered around the bridge, pulsating in unison.

"Back on Tombalki, she kept saying that she might never see Matt again," said Woozl. "Just like Winxl pining for Baingae leading to the mission of the Splinkatrix."

It was bright after Vega-rise. The sky was a beautiful purple with wispy cumulus clouds over some of the more distant tall rock pinnacles rising out of the ocean, which had returned to its serenity, hiding the terrible events of the previous day. The Tombalkiens and Balkiens were seated in the grand mootie hall to listen to Boonkihara and for the Winkets to officiate in a commemorative ceremony for the dearly fallen.

YESL – The Balkien from Antrobi

First, to take to the dais was Kloonket. "Today, we have finally driven back the evil menace from our system. Our victory is, indeed, tempered by the loss to death of so many of our fallen and beloved Balkiens. We shall also mourn for those who because of their severe injuries, may have to go into recovery hibernation for many years. Dr. Baingae reports that many may not wake up for several decades of Antrobian years. I now introduce to you your restored loving King and Queen of Antrobi."

King Zozl and Queen Mozl warbled up from the front of the audience, to take the stand. "This has been a great victory to see your rightful King and Queen restored to office. We shall bring you peace and happiness to our once-troubled land. On this momentous occasion, we bring a great release from tyranny but tinged with sadness for the lost, who gave their lives for all of us. Now is the first time on our planets, Antrobi and Antrogi, have we had to fight valiantly against the forces of evil that we unwittingly attracted to our civilizations. We had an ideal society since the creation of these planets and us on them until we sighted a tantalizing signal from space. In our quest to explore, we unwittingly brought this trouble on ourselves. And by way of introduction, I now call upon Boonkihara, our wise old sage, whom many of you will never have heard of, for he was lost in the Underworld to the north for many decades since he went in there to explore and got himself lost in the endless catacombs and cave systems there. Please give a warm welcome to Boonkihara."

King Zozl hovered back to his royal bocklass or seat, and Boonkihara hovered up to the tall rounded dais, which had a velvet bocklass on it for a Balkien to sit. "I'm greatly honored to speak to you. I can only see four Balkiens in this room apart from the Royal couple, whom I've met before my unfortunate disappearance in the catacombs. I welcome Yesl, the Winkets, and Kloonket. I'm especially indebted to them and their cohorts for rescuing me and guiding me out of those dark lonely passages, where I wandered endlessly, which had also been occupied by the slaves of the Enigma, which befell us after I was lost. Balkiens, Antrobians, Antrogians, and Tombalkiens, we have seen the terrible results of following our selfish ways. We know what Zinkel-Mallkis became when influenced by the Enigma, who was attracted to our planet by our presence on Splogita. Those that have been there, namely Yesl and the Winkets have told me all about it.

"All of you have to realize that we were gullible and listened to the great promises of our former King of Antrogi, Zinkel-Mallkis. He was the first to be beguiled by the Enigma when it invaded our planets by influencing our minds. We learned to be selfish and not to be considerate of others. First, you Antrogians invaded Antrobi and telepathically lured all of us Balkiens into thinking that there was a greater glory for obeying the 'Will of Zinkel-Mallkis.' We all fell for it, believing that if we went down into factories and mines, we could work to earn our reward in his Empire.

"Many resisted this change of governance, but slowly but surely we all turned to believe in the edicts of Zinkel-Mallkis and to forget about our true past, heritage and knowledge of where we came from through the Great One who made us. Over time we forgot our past lives and only recognized the 'Will of Zinkel-Mallkis.' I roamed the passages of the Underworld, lost and lonely. I was foolish to go down there with an inquisitive mind and learned my lesson the hard way.

"I firmly believe that it was Providential, that Alison, one of our Tombalkien guests here, was bitten by a hackel in the sea, necessitating a descent into the abyss to find an antidote cure for her resulting sickness. That led you to see the evil slavery brought on by Zinkel-Mallkis and to lead me back to be with you all once again. Maybe we shall have to do something about those poor Molktrons on Splogita. I met some of them down in the deeper caverns, shortly before you came down. They had been brought here by the Enigma. We shall have to visit with them soon. So we must not lose sight of our heritage and of who we are when we once again go exploring the stars, which I'm sure we will someday, thank you all for listening and we wish you all well in overcoming this tragedy."

Boonkihara warbled and rose from the podium and flew back to his front-row bocklass. Matt stood up and walked onto the stage in front of the tall dais, "I may stand here and bask in all of the accolades for this great victory. I sincerely think that Yesl, here, who befriended me made all of this possible by her courage to get to know us Tombalkiens and learn our language and learn about the evil things that happen on our planet and bring that warning to us here. Were it not for my dear mother finding Yesl in that shop and giving her to me; we would not have come, though perhaps, things may have worked out in some other way and were it not for those Balkiens being bought by that family from America, I'd never have met my dearest, Erin. So, I thank you all for your support here on Antrobi." Matt bowed and sat down.

Many Balkiens pulsated in applause and let off some shrills. Kloonket rose to dismiss the meeting with a prayer of thanks to the Great One for their deliverance from their dark age of oppression.

There was a beep on a headset looking device that Monku was wearing. "We've just had a message that the *Balkieston* will be entering Antrobian orbit in two days."

"Then we all have to make our way to Balkieston to welcome her and her Balkien crewmates and her Tombalkien crew," said Zozl.

"How shall we get there in two days?" asked Yesl. "Our scout ship from the Splinkatrix is not airworthy, let alone space-worthy."

"Call the RAC," said Matt jokingly.

"That's a sensible idea," said Erin. "Let's see if we can get the *Balkieston* to send some large scout ships ahead of her arrival to transport us to Balkieston."

"And remember the Antrogians too," said Kloonket. "Many of them are too sick to fly on their own."

Everyone assembled on the balcony in broad daylight to gaze upon the calm seas and the beauty that is Antrobi as it was meant to be. Looking to the West, Matt was suddenly scared. "Zozl, there's a dreadful dark shadow racing towards us. Run for cover!"

No Balkien moved.

"Look!" continued Matt.

"Don't worry stupid!" said Yesl jokingly. "It's *the ponkul*. It's when Antrogi's shadow crosses Antrobi at this time of day."

Suddenly the shadow reached them. The ocean became a dark purple with bands of shadow racing across. It quickly grew darker until it was like night. Stars popped out along with the spread of the Milky Way Galaxy.

"It is now the season for these *ponkuls* to occur every day," said Yesl.

"You mean the daily eclipse by Antrogi," said Sean.

"Of course," said Kara. "Like the ones we get of the sun on Earth."

One could make out the edge of the night side of Antrogi facing towards Antrobi by a thin yellowish-green curved sliver of light framing that part of Antrogi's dark disk.

It was only a few minutes before the brightness of Vega re-emerged from behind Antrogi a little further over on its dark disk, like the diamond ring effect after a Solar Eclipse on Earth. The shadow passed by and daylight returned once more.

"As this is only the beginning of the ponkul season in the South Beekalo Ocean, it only lasts a few minutes and will get longer each day as this season progresses," said Yesl. "During the maximum equinox time, this ponkul can last a bit less than one of your Earth hours."

"I've contacted Woozl and Andrew Gerhardt on the *Balkieston*," said Erin. "They're going to send us about forty ships to transport us all, with about eight capable of accommodating the Antrogians. We may need to run a shuttle service to get you all over there."

Erin went to her bag in the corner of the great hall, where she had slept and brought a wrapped box to Matt. "Here's our reunion present, Matt."

"Oh, Erin! How wonderful you are to think of me."

Matt tore off the wrapping paper to reveal a box containing a brand-new pair of binoculars. Matt kissed Erin on the cheek. "Erin. How thoughtful of you. Just what I needed since my old pair got broken."

Matt and Erin sat in the front seats, belted up, on a newly built scout ship to transport them from the Citadel of Zigollomont. Matt noticed that there was English writing on the control dials of this craft piloted by Kloonket. This ship was built on Earth, to the Antrobian designs left with NASA to replace the ones destroyed when the original *Balkieston* foundered. In the back seats were Sean, Kara, Kaz, Alison, and Judith, along with many Balkiens, including Yesl, the Winkets, Baingae, and Winxl.

The great city of Balkieston was spread out before them. Their craft came into land at the main spaceport apron from where they had taken off, many years before to Splogita. The terminal mooties now looked forlorn and abandoned. Not long before they emerged from their craft, many Balkiens flew over to greet them, hollering messages of welcome in Antrobian. Woozl spoke with them in that language to explain Zinkel-Mallkis' defeat in the battle with King Zozl restored to the throne.

"We're so grateful to be home again," said Woozl in Antrobian. "Here's Yesl, Boongoo, Baingae, and Winxl and meet our Tombalkien friends, without, whom, we would not have won our victory." Many of the Balkiens flew around jubilantly. "Our great ship, the *Balkieston*, has been rebuilt on Tombalki and is now taking up orbit around Antrobi."

While on the apron, the ponkul came over once again hiding the brightness of Vega behind Antrogi revealing the stars. The whole of Antrogi dimly reflected the light from Antrobi. This Antrobi shine was brighter than Earthshine reflected off the Moon. There was one bright moving star that slowly passed from the east to the west during the hour-long totality of the ponkul, longer in the northern hemisphere. Matt put Erin's new binoculars to his eyes. There was the distinct shape of the *Balkieston*, moving over the city she was named after. Later that day, everyone flew in the scout ships to look at the temple to the Great One that they had seen, just before their arrest and imprisonment by Zinkel-Mallkis.

Matt eyed the structure up and down. "The Temple's looking a bit old and in need of some TLC; Tender Loving Care."

Wink hovered up closer to the circular entrance in the central sphere at ground level. "We'll soon restore this edifice to its former glory as a meaningful place of worship of the Great One."

The silver spheres and pillars were dull and dirty. Rumors from Zinklus had it that there were plans for the Temple's demolition. A service of rededication was held there, followed by a service of commemoration for the fallen in battle. In the central sphere, third from the base was a circular table draped in a purple velvet tablecloth. Standing on this were golden globes representing the planets, Antrobi and Antrogi, the satellites, Angapooka, Balkle, and Boonkpolm. The humans, both from the *Splinkatrix* and the *Balkieston,* were seated reclined in Balkien style cup seats or bocklasses. Many Balkiens sat in smaller bocklasses in tiers around the spherical chamber, which had many round windows letting the bright purple light.

The Winkets sat beside one another on bocklasses close to the edge of this altar-like table. They began to speak in Antrobian, then in English. "We are gathered here in this service of rededication of this temple to our beloved Great One and for our victory over this time of darkness. Many of you, older ones, will remember our great and wise one, Boonkihara before his disappearance long ago into the Underworld. Him we now introduce."

Boonkihara hovered up to a third bocklass near the altar. "I am so happy to have been rescued from that dreadful underworld."

Boonkihara related the events leading to the freeing of the Underworld slaves and the Battle of Binkus-Mallkus. After this, the Balkiens sang beautiful soft melodic Antrobian songs and anthems.

Over the following weeks, the damage and broken windows left by the tremendous Balkieston riots were repaired. Many of the mooties throughout the city kept many former slave Balkiens busy for weeks in repairs and rebuilding. There had been many changes and additional buildings constructed by Zinkel-Mallkis to fit the Antrogians of great size. Many of the former slaves felt like tearing a lot of these structures down.

"These new buildings are going to be a terrible reminder of Zinkle-Mallkis and our years of tyranny," said the one called Spoonkle-Millket.

"I realize your concerns," said Zozl. "But we can't afford to tear down all of these and rebuild the original. Many of these are now ready for use by our Antrogian neighbors, who helped to win our battle and, also, for the newcomers from Tombalki in need of suitable accommodation."

Balkieston once again became the vibrant and awe-inspiring city it once was. Several former Antrogian mooties in a few nearby streets were remodeled for human habitation for the NASA crew under Andrew Gerhardt on the *Balkieston* and Kaz, Alison, Judith, Sean, and Kara. Until their marriage, Matt stayed with his family in their mooties and Erin in one of the mooties in the NASA camp.

While Matt and Erin were taking in the sights of Balkieston, a group of banking and financial Mallkets conducted a tour of the building operations. They had yellow poles to signify that they were members of the finance industry and like those of the TriMallkaetium, were about two to three inches in diameter. These Mallkets were from the Balkarus Credit Union.

"Who's going to pay off the loan on these buildings?" asked Spinkelwitz, the team leader who was yellow with black zigzag patterned lines. "We require payment in full of all the sgegas lent to you for the reconstruction of the *Balkieston* and your terrible University fees. We were ordered to buy your debt by order of Zinkel-Mallkis." Spinkelwitz hovered around them, scanning each of them, looking for payment.

"Why that dirty double-crossing former Emperor," said Matt.

"What a scoundrel," sighed Erin. "Sorry Spinkelwitz, We've no money."

"I had fully forgotten about the loan financed on Earth," said Matt.

Matt pulled out his pockets, indicating his lack of wealth.

"Then you both will have to work hard until the debt is fully repaid," said Spinkelwitz.

King Zozl flew up to the Mallkets. "What's the *puchty*?"

"Zozl," said Matt. "These little Mallkets say that they're from the Balkarus Credit Union and want from us a great deal of money that involved unknown dealings by Zinkel-Mallkis. As we can't pay, they're going to make life difficult for us, and we may have to delay our wedding plans."

Zozl hovered up to Spinkelwitz. "Spinkelwitz, what is the total amount owed by everyone here?"

"Your Majesty, Andrew Gerhardt owes us 565 million sgegas for rebuilding the *Balkieston*. Matt and Erin owe us 27 thousand sgegas for their university fees on Tombalki as transferred to us by the Bank of America on their home planet."

"Spinkelwitz," said His Majesty, Zozl. "Come to my Palace Mootie, and I'll repay you all in full. The *Balkieston* is our spaceship belonging to the Government of Antrobi so that bill is my responsibility. Matt and Erin's debts will be paid in full as well since they were instrumental in the defeat of Zinkel-Mallkis' Empire who got you into this mess in the first place. Come, we'll settle this." Zozl and the finance Mallkets flew off together to settle the transaction.

Matt looked at Erin. "It looks like it's going to be business as usual here. We'll have to earn a living and borrow money for our mootie just like on Tombalki."

"I still don't fully understand how Zinkle-Mallkis had acquired that debt from Tombalki," said Yesl.

"Look over there," said Zinklus, who had just hovered up from the main terminal mootie of the spaceport. He wavered towards a silver egg-shaped craft standing in a giant hangar mootie with two of its hexagon doors open. The ship was four times the size of a normal Antrobian shuttlecraft.

Zinklus continued, "That egg-shaped craft was discovered amongst Zinkel-Mallkis' main fleet of super-eggs when we resumed control of this spaceport. All of the signs and notices within are in English. I was here when it landed one and a half Antrobian years ago or about seven of your Tombalkien years."

"You mean, it came from Tombalki," said Yesl.

"Precisely," said Zinklus.

"Who was on board?" asked Kaz.

"None other than Captain Cammins," said Boongoo. "I had recently learned from Zinklus that we had two Hellack stowaways onboard our shuttlecraft when we took off from Splogita the second time. That's the only reason that our departure was successful. They also brought the two Queen Molktrons as comatose prisoners. They were the ones we met up within the Underworld. There was an evil plan to enslave all of the Molktrons produced to emit Molktronic energy to power the fleet of spacecraft for Zinkel-Mallkis' armada. These were liberated."

"Oh, how ghastly," sighed Alison with a look of horror drifting across her face, reflected by everyone present.

"Who was with Captain Cammins?" asked Matt.

"Professor Holzapfel, the two Hellacks, and the Molktron Queens," said Zinklus.

"He must have figured out how to build that great super-egg over there," said Sean.

"I remember our Dad giving that sphere to Captain Cammins," said Matt. "I remember reading that article in the Evening News at Auntie Ethel's after you had departed, Yesl, and how funding was cut for Captain Cammins' project and how that Professor Holzapfel could not analyze the Antrobian metal alloys found on Tetraval."

"All smoke and mirrors," said Zinklus, curtly. "Your Dad, Matt, may have been given back the missing sphere but its data had been copied before he returned it at the meeting in that Tombalkien city of Linden, I think it was called."

"London," corrected Kara.

"From that information, Cammins and Holzapfel assisted by the Hellacks secretly raised one of the *Balkieston*'s engine pods from the Atlantic Ocean and fashioned it into the egg-shaped craft. Their journey to Antrobi took them only about three of your Tomkilian months and arrived here about four Tombalkien years before the Splinkatrix."

"You mean Lunar months," said Matt. "That certainly explains the mysteries we've observed since arriving here. Where are Cammins and Holzapfel?"

"Vanished," said Kloonket. "Maybe they were in the Great Spire of Binkus-Mallkus when it collapsed or just gone into hiding after the battle. We don't know."

All the guests gathered in the large central sphere of the Temple. For Matt, Kaz was the best man with Sean, Dan, and Nick as groomsmen. Andrew had the honor of giving Erin away on behalf of her parents. Alison, Kara, and Judith were Maids of Honor. Baingae's best Balkien was Boongoo with Yesl, Ponku, and Mwaki as the Antrobian equivalent of Maids of Honor who hovered around the resplendent bride. Winxl was bedecked in layers of delicate, golden chains forming a spiral pattern around her smooth furry body.

The Balkien Choir began to sing a beautiful song in Antrobian. It was the same tune played by Boongoo on the piano in Uncle Herbert's living room. Gracefully Erin walked in wearing her bright white wedding dress, next to Andrew in his NASA uniform, bearing the mission badge of the *Balkieston*.

Her wedding dress had dark blue hems. Her broken heart necklace hung around her neck behind her veil. Winxl hovered in gently touching King Zozl with her. At the dais, they stood before Wink who, in his priestly role, officiated at the ceremony. Everyone sang A few hymns in Antrobian in honor of the Great One. Wink then related the principles of married life. As this was a double wedding, he married both couples at the same time. Wink spoke in English and Antrobian.

"Do you, Matt and Baingae take these beings Erin and Winxl to be your lawful wedded wives unto each other for richer and poorer, in sickness and health as long as you both shall live as couples."

"We do," said Matt and Baingae in unison.

Hovering a little to Erin and Winxl, Wink continued, "Do you, Erin and Winxl take these beings Matt and Baingae to be your lawful wedded husbands unto each other for richer and poorer, in sickness and health as long as you both shall live as couples.

"We do," said Erin and Winxl in unison.

"Then by the grace and authority of the Great One and by the laws of the Kingdom of Antrobi under King Zozl and Queen Mozl, I pronounce you, Matt and Erin, Man and Wife and you Dr. Baingae and Winxl, Balkiens united in matrimony. Matt and Erin in her white wedding dress led the procession out into the open in front of the Temple to the strains of beautiful, scintillating Antrobian music. Baingae and Winxl hovered together in front of Matt and Erin, who were followed by Kaz, Matt's Best Man, and Alison, Matron of Honor. The Winkets then followed, hovering at about human head height as a pair. Everyone else, both human and Antrobian, followed in a long procession. The six Antrogians, along with a few others, were sitting outside to greet them. NASA photographers took wedding photographs.

The reception took place in the Great Palace Mootie with King Zozl and Queen Mozl looking on from their royal seats or bocklasses. Matt led Erin on a beautiful wedding waltz to the tune of Boongoo's song. Boongoo played the piano himself, which was a lightweight, specially built, and brought to Antrobi on the *Balkieston*. Woozl organized this, knowing that Boongoo had learned to be a prolific pianist at Uncle Herbert's house. Baingae and Winxl twirled around like a waltzing dumbbell swooth in swooth. Wink and Yesl also spent quite a few dances in one another's swooth during Boongoo's piano repertoire, which he played exquisitely by levitating back and forth over the keyboard and telekinetically pressing the notes. Mwaki and Kloonket had some waltzes too. As the beautiful evening advanced, Earthly music was fed into the sound system from Matt's digital music player, retrieved from the damaged scout ship that was flown to Balkieston for extensive repairs and made ready and decked out for the newlyweds to depart for their honeymoons. Antrobian music was played using Antrobian music players or by the Balkien band present. Music from the 60s to the 90s from Earth was played. Many Balkiens twirled around in loops and figures of eight, like at the barn dance in Arizona after Matt and Erin's graduation. Kaz, Sean, Judith, Alison, and Kara, enjoyed the company of the NASA crew and danced all night with them, which included Dan and Nick, Erin's brothers, who had joined NASA as university cadets before being assigned to the *Balkieston* mission to Antrobi. They looked forward to their Tombalkien presence on this world far distant from their own culture.

"It was a great occasion for you, Matt and Erin," said Yesl. "We've been through so much since we met on that Christmas morning."

"Yesl," said Matt, holding a glass "This is twenty-one-year-old Malt Whiskey, from a case brought to Antrobi, duty-free of course, though I'm sure Spinkelwitz would love to change that. I knew that you were going to be my favorite 'toy' as soon as I laid my hands on you. I'm sure that my Mom never thought how buying you in Mackay's souvenir shop was going to change our lives and the history of three planets and their moons."

"We'll have to wait and see," said Yesl. "There's still the matter of the Molktrons on Splogita, where the Enigma seemed to be headed when it left our world."

"Anyone for more Plugian Wine from west of Balkieston?" asked Nick as he came around with a spherical shaped bottle of red.

Parked on the apron, next morning at Balkieston Space Port, was the same scout ship they had left Earth in, fixed and serviced. A new canopy had been fitted to replace the broken one. Colored streamers were affixed in the true tradition of a departing wedding vehicle. Yesl was present at the door of the ship to welcome the two honeymooning couples aboard, playing the part of an air hostess well. Kaz, Sean, Kara, Judith, and Alison along with the NASA people and many Balkiens were standing there to see them off. Antrogi was a bright crescent in the southern sky. It was like the departure to Splogita, but thankfully this time they were only going to Baingae's home moon, Balkle. Everyone heard the approaching beating warbles of two Antrogians. Into view came Boolboonkle and Spoonkoothtil. Matt proudly rode on Boolboonkle and Erin on Spoonkoothtil. There was a rush of wind from their downdraft as they landed beside the ship. They lowered the happy couple onto the apron. Baingae and Winxl also descended from the Antrogians, after flying from where they had spent their wedding night in a mootie. Matt and Erin carrying a small suitcase each said their goodbyes to everyone and walked onto the ramp into the ship. Winxl and Baingae flew up behind them. Yesl and Wink, Kloonket, and Mwaki hovered on board and took up their positions at the ship's controls. The ramp door whirred shut.

"On behalf of 'Antrobian Space Ways,' we welcome you aboard this flight to Balkle," announced Yesl in a humorous tone. "We do hope that you will have a pleasant trip with us. Please observe the *fasten seat belt sign* and follow the safety instructions in the seat pocket in front of you."

The engines started whirring. The ground, seen from the round window below their seats slipped away into the distance. Matt and Erin waved at everyone on the airfield below. Soon the whole city of Balkieston was laid out like an aerial photograph below them.

Yesl flew over to join them, "This was exactly the scene from this ship when we left for Splogita. I'm sure glad not to be going on a journey of that length now, though you never know in the future?"

Baingae looked down with the same thoughts while Winxl remembered her departure to the Splinkatrix to look for her beloved, who was swooth in swooth with Baingae now. After several hours, the double planet was in view as they sped towards Balkle. Matt brought out his new binoculars and scanned over Antrobi. He and Erin could see the route taken by ball train out into the Yastagliath and over the ocean to the Great Cliffs. Their view of where the Spire of Binkus-Mallkus once stood was just visible on the edge of the planet between the sea and the inky blackness of space.

The ship turned around to begin its braking phase descending towards Balkle. Baingae was pulsating with excitement to be going home with his bride who needed a rest after treating the injured after the Battle of Binkus-Mallkus. It was not long before the whole viewing window filled with the much bluer ocean of Balkle than on Antrobi. There were wisps of clouds and landmasses that followed along the lines of latitude looking like a giant Balkien. The ship slowly descended towards a small group of mooties around a green meadow serving as a landing pad. It was close to some beautiful golden beaches with lush dark green and purple vegetation in the dunes. The oceans were as calm as a millpond right out towards the horizon. The ship landed, and the ramp opened downwards. Matt and Erin walked slowly and gracefully carrying their luggage, which was lighter due to Balkle's low gravity, out onto the meadow. Baingae and Winxl hovered behind them. There were many Balkiens, there to meet them and all shrilled and warbled with excitement in their Balklian dialect. Balkle had been relatively untouched directly by the troubles going on for so long on the mother planet, but there were many shortages of supplies as trade links and spaceship flights had all been severed. These smaller looking Balkiens, about the same size as Baingae, had to return to an agrarian form of living, abandoning all technological advances after King Zozl was deposed. Theirs was the third spacecraft to touch down on Balkle since the demise of Zinkel-Mallkis' Empire.

Matt and Erin walked or instead jumped in slow motion, like the NASA astronauts on the Moon, through green vegetation that had beautiful little purple, round flowers. The local Balkiens, all of whom were delighted to see their intrepid traveler, Baingae, return with his bride, Winxl, led them along the beach to a clump of rustic mooties built of some wood-like material. The Winkets, Kloonket, and Yesl assisted by flying alongside with their luggage. Matt and Erin settled into one of the mooties painted red, while Baingae and Winxl settled into a smaller mootie. Baingae reassured Matt and Erin that these waters had no awful stinging hackels or any other nasties. They went into the crystal-clear warm water for a nice relaxing swim and splash. The waves moved slowly in a strange sensation with Balkle's low gravity.

"Matt and Erin," said Yesl, "I wish you both a great holiday here and to you, Baingae and Winxl."

"We sure will," said Matt as he held and cuddled Yesl tightly. The Winkets and Kloonket cuddled them all in a ponkadliath on the beach in front of the red mootie.

"We'd better be flying back to Balkieston," said Kloonket. "We'll be back in a month to pick you up. Have a good well-earned rest."

"See you all soon," said the Winkets in unison.

"Bye for now," said Yesl. Matt chuckled as he saw Wink and Yesl flying off back to the scout ship together. Kloonket and Mwaki did the same. A short while later the scout ship revved up its engines and lifted off into the steel-blue sky until it was a tiny silver spec before it was too small to see.

Baingae and Winxl flew over to the nearby village to meet with Baingae's parents, who had been at the wedding, and all the members of his local tribe. Day turned into evening, as Matt and Erin ate a meal from all the Antrobian vegetables brought in on supply ships, which had resumed operations to all the Antrobian system satellites. The cargo included their favorite broccoli-like food from the trees north of Balkieston, which they had begun eating on their arrival from Earth.

As dusk turned to night, Matt, Erin, Baingae, and Winxl sat down on the beach looking up at the faint blue night sky, lit up by the two grand crescent shapes of Antrobi and Antrogi low down to their west. Matt and Erin sat on the side of the beach lit by the Antrobi shine and Antrogi shine with his arms around Erin. He took his new binoculars and both he and Erin looked up at Sol, the Sun, as a faint a star. From this part of the galaxy, Sol was close to Sirius and Canopus in the Antrobian constellation of Binkelmaultrix. Both he and Erin had thoughts of their families and friends back on Tombalki. They sat on the seashore for long into the warm balmy night.

"I wonder what our families are thinking now and if there's any way for them to know that the *Balkieston* has arrived okay on Antrobi," said Erin.

"I wonder that myself," replied Matt, "considering that it takes a standard radio signal over twenty-five Earth years to reach here.

"Oh, this is so wonderful, Matt," said Erin.

"Boodibah," said Baingae to Winxl, "It's a wonderful planetoid here."

"Oh, Baingae," replied Winxl. "We're all so glad that we traveled on the Splinkatrix to look for and successfully find you all."

Alex M Shepherd

APPENDIX

Antrogi is about 90% of the size of Antrobi. Antrobi and Antrogi form a double planet system, where each world orbits the common center of rotation about once every twenty-five Earth hours, such that there is a day-night cycle for each planet. The two bodies are tidily locked such that each world always has the same hemisphere facing the other as the Moon does to the Earth. Antrobi orbits Vega in just less than 5 Earth years.

This double planet also has three smaller moons orbiting further out. The two closer moons both sustain floral and faunal life, consisting of different races of Balkiens looking similar to those on Antrobi but with unique features. These moons are named Angapooka and Balkle. The farthest satellite is airless and lifeless like the Moon but is only half the Moon's diameter, known as Boonkpolm, meaning 'lifeless' in Antrobian.

An Angapookan month is equivalent to about 6 weeks, being the orbital period of Angapooka, Antrobi's first true moon after Antrogi. Balkle, the second moon orbits the double planet in approximately 12 weeks, while Boonkpolm takes around 24 weeks to complete one orbit.

Please note that all the planets that orbit the known star, Vega, in this novel and depicted on the diagrams on the following pages are purely fictitious and any actual orbiting bodies around Vega have yet to be discovered or confirmed by future more advanced ground and space telescopes.

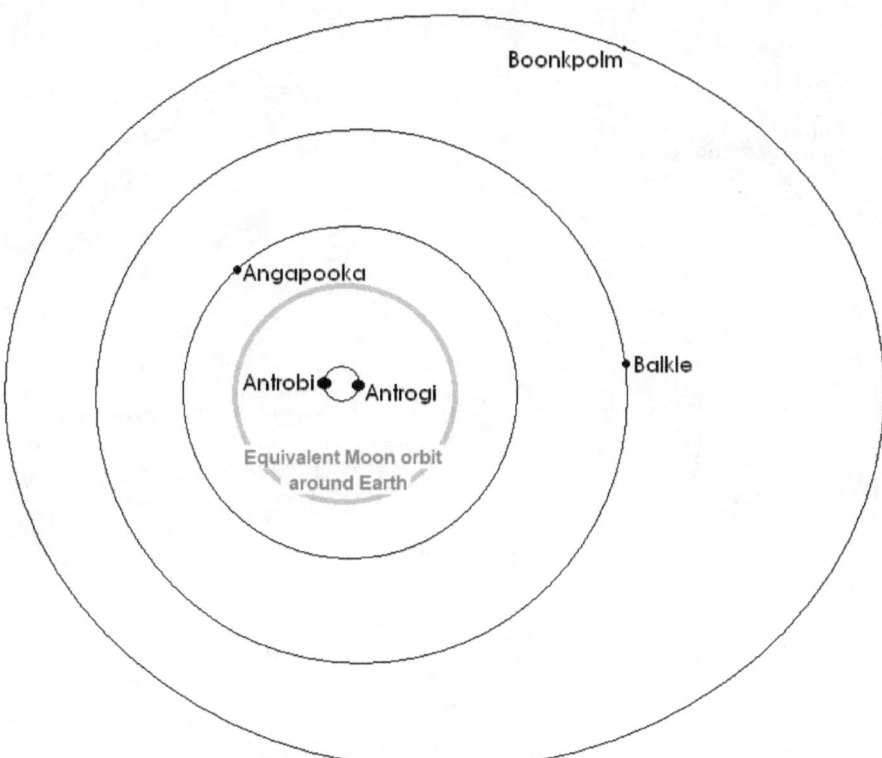

Distribution of the double planet; Antrobi and Antrogi and the other three moons of the Antrobian System

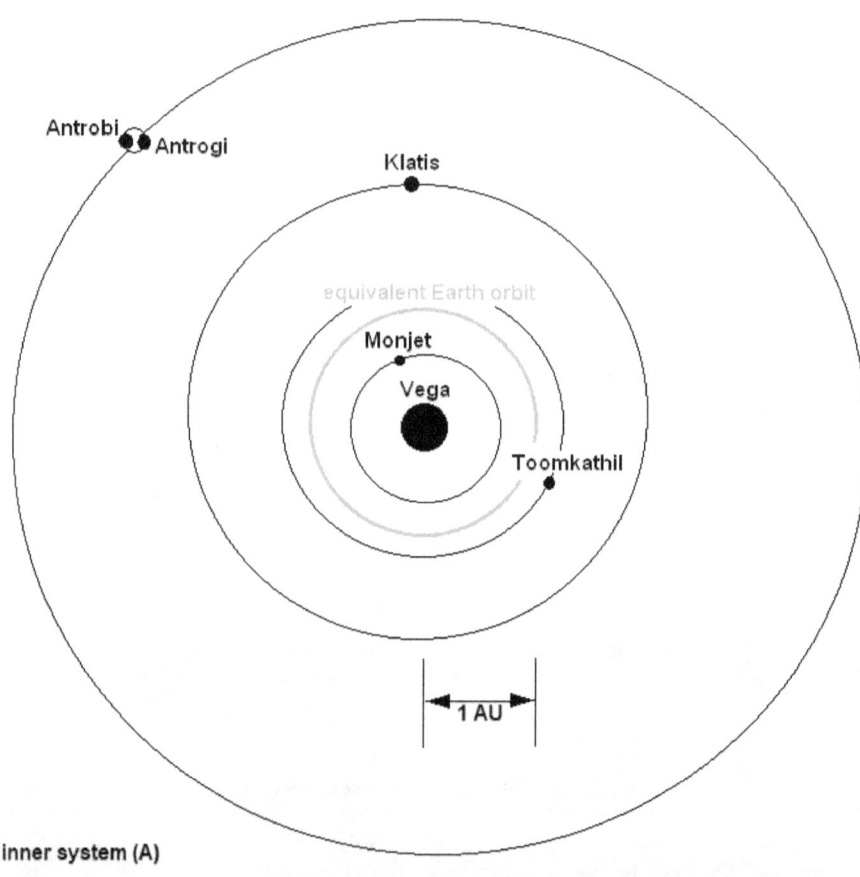

inner system (A)

Distribution of Inner planets of the Vegan System with the equivalent orbit of the Earth around the Sun (in grey);
1 Astronomical unit (AU) is the distance between the Earth and the Sun

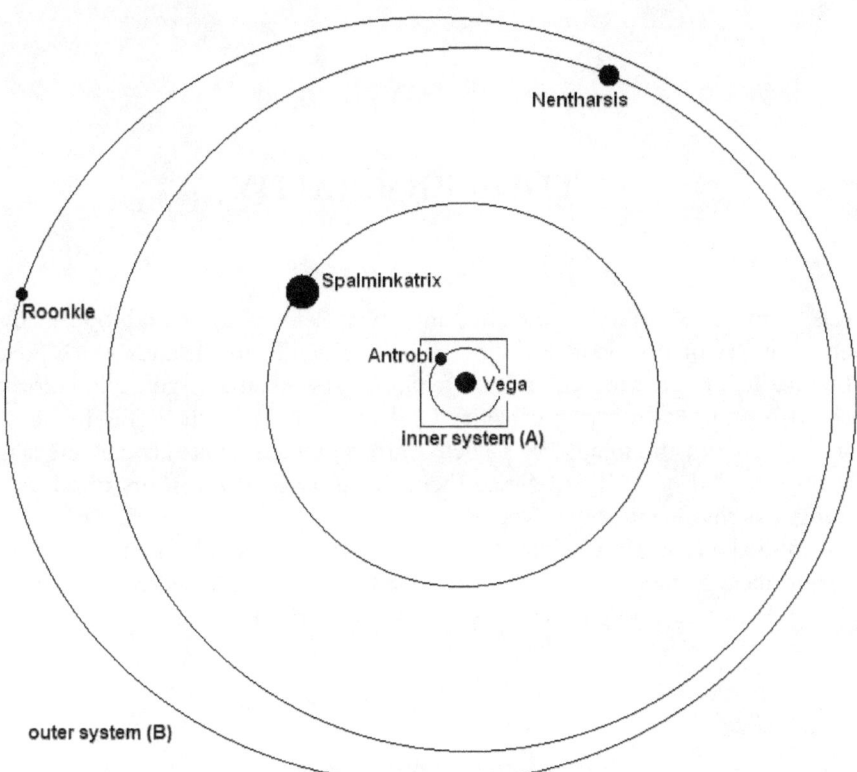

Distribution of outer planets of the Vegan System

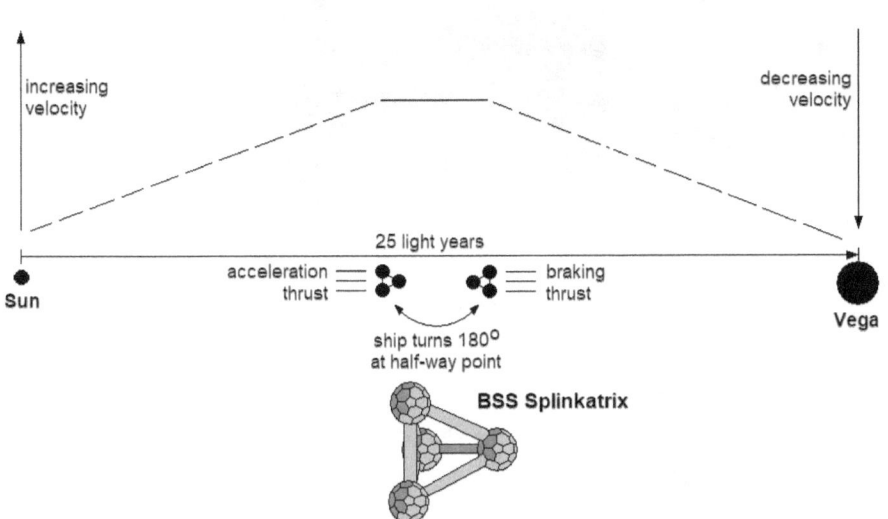

Trajectory of the Balkien Scout Service (BSS) Splinkatrix from the Earth to Planet Antrobi

AUTHOR BIOGRAPHY

I was born in Edinburgh, Scotland, and spent a lot of my childhood in the Hebridean Islands of Scotland. Life in the Highlands and Islands was a great influence in my growing years. As a child, I was given a large multi-colored woolen pom-pom by my mother at Christmas and imagined this to be an alien being from the imaginary planet, Antrobi, which orbits around the star, Vega and called her 'YESL'. Since then, the story evolved in my mind until writing it as my debut novel.

I studied Geology at Edinburgh University and was a member of the Astronomical Society of Edinburgh with a keen interest in recent discoveries of 'Exo-planets' orbiting other stars. I now live in Perth, Western Australia.